$\mathcal{M}$afia

Protection

Ali Lee

RADUPUL
Publishing

Mafia Protection
Copyright © 2018, Ali Lee
Kadupul Publishing 2018
ISBN: 978-1-7320901-8-7

Dedicated to every person who supported my dream.
To every reader who demanded I write.
Lots of Love

Chapter 1

Ramble. That was all his father did—on and on until Angelo neared the brink of insanity. One of his hands squeezed the dark strands of his hair; his other pounded the table, leaving a cracking sound to echo throughout the ritzy restaurant.

"I said enough," Angelo snapped, his deep voice silencing the aging man sitting across from him. Several diners shifted uncomfortably in their seats.

Angelo lowered his tone to a harsh whisper and leaned forward. "There's no way I will consider the daughter of that fool. Christ, we'd be on the radar of every fed in the state if I got involved with that man. We don't need that drama that he's brought to his ranks—to his own family."

"But the businesses, Son..." Antonio scowled at Angelo's disrespect. "You would gain his estate and his ranks in exchange for her protection. Gregorio would be out of the picture."

"Who cares what I gain," Angelo said. His deep brown eyes glared into Antonio's, causing the creases on the older man's forehead to widen. "I'm making a fortune with what I have."

"You know how it works," Antonio replied. "Money makes the rules...money that you don't have enough of right now."

Angelo inhaled as he closed his eyes. Lately, his father talked of nothing else but her. "And what of the girl? You want a strange woman that we've never met to fall in with our family. Do you really expect me to trust her as my wife considering the man that raised her?"

"Because you've chosen not to meet her. How do you know you won't like her if you never put forth the effort? You don't know. You might actually like her."

"Rafa..." Angelo glanced at the man with dark, wavy hair sitting next to him. "Talk some sense into my father." Angelo had hired Rafa specifically to take on problematic situations—like Antonio.

Though Rafa's input counted as much as Angelo's did, he huffed and straightened his tie, wishing he could ignore them both. "You already know how I feel about it. I have already pointed out the pros and cons of the marriage." Rafa paused and took a drink of his coffee. "Look, next time, could you wait until after we eat to start arguing? You might both be calmer after breakfast. Have you ever thought about that?"

Both men stared at Rafa in silence until Angelo tossed his napkin on the table and stood. "Thanks for the input, Rafa. This visit is over. We'll have to eat after we drive to Key Biscayne."

Antonio's brow narrowed in grievous fashion; his lips pursed together, making the wrinkles around his mouth to deepen. "Fine, Angelo. Ignore my wishes if that's the type of man I've raised you to be."

Angelo shook his head and let out a frustrated breath. "I'm not ignoring your wishes. I wouldn't mind meeting the woman if Gregorio weren't her father. I know you like him, but wherever he goes, trouble follows. You already know that. Find another woman for me to marry, or you leave me no choice but to choose my own wife. I'm not getting any younger."

Angelo walked away, jerking his chin for Rafa to follow. As the door shut to the restaurant, Angelo stopped for a moment to think. "How long has it been since my father and Gregorio started this shit with the daughter?" Talking about it made him mad all over again. He stormed down the ramp to the parking lot.

"Well, you could meet her if it will satisfy them."

"Right," Angelo groaned. "You know even if I did, they would still harass me about marrying her."

"How old are you turning this year, Angelo?"

"Twenty-nine," he said, blowing out an annoyed breath.

"Then marry her," Rafa said simply. "It isn't like you have another woman in mind."

"I had a woman in mind," Angelo said. "My mother hated Giana."

"What are you talking about? She wasn't wife material. Besides, you couldn't stand that woman." Rafa walked ahead of Angelo to open the door to the black Escalade. "She couldn't even make a cup of coffee much less raise a family like you want."

"Well—" Angelo rubbed the back of his neck. "Even if that's true, she was still loyal."

"Sure she was...for all the wrong reasons. Just marry Gregorio's daughter. The daughter of another boss will suit you. It's like you said, you're not getting any younger. Do you really want to turn forty by the time you have your first kid?"

Angelo's eyes narrowed as he slid into the backseat and slammed the door. "Well, this doesn't affect you. Why do you care who I marry and have kids with?"

Rafa sat in the backseat beside him. Angelo did not discuss the daughter anymore and slapped the driver's seat in front of him, catching the attention of the blond-haired man behind the wheel. "Brett, step on it—Key Biscayne. Get me out of here."

Brett looked back, silent as usual with a smirk on his lips. He started the car without question.

Chapter 2

Ella stepped onto the red brick patio of Santiago's, a beachside restaurant with a magnificent view of the ocean. If there was nothing else to look forward to on this day, Ella was grateful for the calming waves beyond.

Her heels boosted her petite frame as she scooted around a few early guests, her eyes on a table closest to the rail that surrounded the covered patio. The soft breeze soothed her mind as she sat down, carefully keeping her knee-length skirt free of wrinkles. Ella propped her hands under her chin, sulking as her dark blond hair scattered over her left shoulder. Why did Mr. Santiago have to retire? He could not sell the restaurant yet. So many memories throughout her life revolved around Santiago's.

Ella unsnapped her purse and took out an old, worn photo. She gazed at the image of her mother with sad reflection, remembering the days when they sat together, both of them laughing without care. She had felt lost without her mother in her life. Ella still could not believe it had been six years since somebody murdered her. Her father was never the same and seldom spoke to her anymore. Everything changed on that day.

"I guess you heard that somebody is interested in the place," her friend Lila said and sat down across from her. The short redhead had worked at Santiago's since Ella moved to Key Biscayne seven months earlier.

"Yes," Ella sighed and shook her head. She looked around, admiring the exotic plant life that the new owners would throw away. Why did they want to make the restaurant into a souvenir shop? There were so many of those already. To Ella, Santiago's was a historical building that she had visited every summer since she could remember.

"I'm sorry, Ella. I wish there was some way I could help."

"Well, if I could lease that hotel on the coast, then I would have enough money to buy this place myself. The people who are looking haven't put down any earnest money." Ella looked down at the photo again and then back at Lila. "That means it isn't sold yet."

"Has anyone called about the hotel?"

Ella shook her head. "No…not one." She slipped the picture back into her purse. "I have rented smaller homes but no one has asked about the hotel. My father's company might have to lower the price if somebody doesn't—"

"Whoa," Lila interrupted, forgetting the sensitive topic that she and Ella were discussing. "Check out the gorgeous men who walked inside. They must be lost or something." Lila pointed behind where Ella sat.

Ella turned around. Three men in high-end, dark suits sat down one table away from where Lila and Ella sat. Ella wondered if they were the people that wanted to buy Santiago's. She kept staring at them even as the breeze picked up and whipped her long hair in front.

Two of the men had brown hair and one had blond. One of the men with brown hair had it cut shorter than the other. It was combed so that both sides met the back of his neck. She watched a couple of strands fly out of place and noticed how his serious brown eyes scanned the place. Was he meeting someone? If not, he seemed strangely suspicious. They could not have wanted to buy the restaurant. Men like that were not interested in a souvenir shop.

"Too bad I have a boyfriend." Lila pouted and tucked her hair behind her ear.

Ella smiled but did not look at Lila. "Men like that are already taken."

As she spoke, the man she stared at looked in her eyes. His gaze almost seemed troubled, but his expression remained stoic, giving off no hint about what he thought. There was no smile; rather he simply returned her stare.

Ella smiled as a blush spread over her cheeks. She turned around fast, embarrassed that their eye contact had lingered. The two brown-haired men reminded her of the men who used to visit her father. They always wore serious faces and never smiled or showed any other emotion. Ella felt disappointed.

"I don't see a single ring on any of their fingers." Lila gave a devious grin and pointed at Ella. "I might have a boyfriend, but I haven't seen you go out with a single man since you've been here. Why don't I introduce you to the table? One of them is staring at the back of your head."

"What?" Ella peeked back to confirm that the man was still staring. "No, Lila. My father would chase him away like he did with the others."

Lila's smile grew. "You noticed him, too. Go introduce yourself, Ella."

"I'll pass," Ella said.

"Did your father ever give you a reason why he didn't want you to date?"

"No, he didn't. I tried to ask but he would change the subject."

"But you're a grown woman who takes care of herself now. I don't think those rules still apply."

Ella let out a frustrated breath. Her face felt hot. The men could probably hear everything Lila said with her loud voice. "Another time, Lila."

Ella stood to escape the discussion. There was no reason to introduce herself with her father's strict rules. Anytime that she had brought up the subject of dating, her father refused to listen. It was true that she lived on her own now, but his ways remained deep inside her head. It was as though he looked over her shoulder. Ella did not want to take a chance and get her hopes up again.

"I'm going to talk to Mr. Santiago while you serve those men. I want to know more about these buyers." Ella excused herself and stood but left Lila with a last thought. "I wouldn't keep them waiting long, Lila. They don't look very patient."

***

It was about time the server decided to get up and do what she was supposed to do. Angelo did not like to wait, and Rafa was even worse about a worker who talked on the job. Still, his time had not been entirely wasted. The blond woman had captured his attention. She was dressed nice for this type of restaurant. Everyone else wore casual clothing, but she wore a silky blouse and business skirt. Her smile was genuine, a rarity in his company. He also found her blushing cheeks refreshing and wondered how she answered her friend's questions. Her responses were too quiet for him to hear.

"Good morning. My name is Lila." The server smiled. "What brings you to Santiago's today?"

Angelo stared at the patio door long after the blond disappeared. He was lost in his thoughts. He had not realized the server stood at their table, waiting for him to acknowledge her. Rafa cleared his throat to catch Angelo's attention as Lila began to shift her weight from one foot to the other.

"Business," Angelo replied but did not elaborate. He hated when restaurant staff asked him personal questions. Did they really expect him to tell them anything?

"Okay." Lila took out her small notepad and pen. "Did you want me to bring you some freshly brewed coffee?"

Holding his finger on the menu, Rafa's eyes darted up. "Are you telling us that you serve coffee that isn't freshly brewed?"

"No," Lila answered right away.

"Yes," Angelo interrupted before Rafa could say another word. "Bring us all coffee. We're also ready to order."

Lila straightened her shoulders, regaining her composure. "Yes, go ahead."

All three gave their orders and Lila disappeared through the doors, returning shortly with their coffee. Coffee was exactly what Angelo needed.

"Rafa, give me the number to the agent," he said. "I want to set up a time."

"Do you want me to call?"

"No," Angelo shook his head, "I will this time."

Angelo took the number from Rafa and pulled out his phone. He found it odd that the number had an Orlando area code. That implied the agent did not work for a local realty company. He expected it to be local or at least closer to Key Biscayne.

"Hello," said the voice on the other end. It belonged to a woman—a young woman. She did not sound like anyone he had ever dealt with. Her sweet voice was not what he expected. He actually found it soothing.

"Ella Collins?"

"Yes."

"My name is Angelo Tomassi. I'm calling about a property listing with a beachside hotel. Is it still available?"

There was a pause before she answered. "Yes…did you have any questions about the listing?"

"No questions. I've seen the pictures and stopped by the building earlier. Since I'm in Key Biscayne today, I want to look inside the place. I don't have any other day available until next week."

"Of course. I'm available until one this afternoon. I could meet you at a restaurant called Santiago's. I'm there now. Are you familiar with the area?"

"Santiago's?" Angelo asked with surprise. "I'm familiar enough. I can meet you there in," Angelo looked at Rafa and smirked, holding up his phone, "thirty-five minutes."

"Great, I'll wait for you on the patio until you arrive."

"Perfect, I'll be there." Angelo clicked off the phone as Lila set down their plates. Rafa waited until Lila left to speak.

"What was that about?" he asked.

"It's interesting," said Angelo. "The agent wants to meet us here. She's here now and will wait for us on the patio."

Rafa gave him a look and turned toward the door of the main dining. "What are you up to?"

"Don't worry about it," Angelo said and took another drink. He thought about the patrons he passed in the restaurant. That blond woman was the only person dressed in anything remotely business related. She must be the agent.

As if reading his thoughts, the blond came back out and sat at a different table this time. She was closer to the restaurant's wall and faced the door. She opened a tablet and scrolled through her screen as she sipped something out of a cup. Angelo figured that she was preparing for her potential clients and admired her organization, but soon after, she gazed around the beach.

"She's a very young agent, Angelo." Rafa pointed out. "One minute she looks focused; the next, she looks lost. How do we know we can trust her? The listing never stated what real estate company she worked for."

"Child or not, we already agreed to see the property. This is the only property close to what I've been looking for."

"I say we get back inside the Escalade and drive back to Miami. Who recommended this place to you anyway? Look at her; she's playing with the hem of her blouse. She's nervous."

"Then we'll use those nerves to our advantage," Angelo said, unaffected by Rafa's sarcasm.

"If I was the realty company, I would've never placed such an expensive piece of property in her hands. It would serve them right if she sold it for any less than eight million. What kind of realty company is this?"

"She seems motivated. Notice how she's waiting for us even though I told her it would be over half an hour until we came."

"Yes, I can see her too, but I think it's because nobody else has looked at the place. She's probably eager to get rid of it and collect her commission."

"Rafa, I want this property—got it?"

"Perfectly." Rafa emptied the last drink of his coffee and stood. "Screw thirty-five minutes. Let's get this over with so we can eat and then go home and start looking for another one. I saw a good listing for something near Orlando."

"Too far north," Angelo said and scooted out his chair with a silent Brett following suit; then all three men walked toward the table where Ella sat.

***

Ella glanced up at the men coming her way. Confused with what they wanted, she closed her tablet to give them her attention. The man's outstretched hand did not register with her for a second as her mind tried to guess why they had come to her table.

"Ella Collins?" the man asked.

"Yes," she answered a little dazed. The three men looked much more fearsome while standing than when they sat.

"Angelo Tomassi," he replied. "I called about the property on the beach."

Did they know who she was. Had they been sizing her up and wanting the upper hand when it came to negotiations. They had resorted to intimidation. She should have shaken his hand right away. First impressions were lasting.

"Mr. Tomassi." Ella came to her senses and stood. "How did you know I would be here?" she asked, holding out her hand to him.

"We didn't," Angelo said, shaking her hand and noticing how timid she appeared. "We stopped in and called you from here. Your clothes gave away the rest."

"Right." She nodded. It could have been a coincidence. Very few restaurants in the area opened before noon.

Letting go of her hand, Angelo pointed at the two men beside him. "This is Rafa and that's Brett." Rafa gripped her hand firmly, a little too firm as if making a statement while Brett smiled, keeping his hands in his pockets. "Now that we've met, we want to see the hotel."

"Of course, please follow me." Ella put away her tablet. She could not believe they wanted to get right down to business. Most of her clients had at least a page worth of notes.

When they reached the parking lot, Angelo shook his head and stopped Ella before she could lead them to her car. "I'll need to go in mine." He started walking in the opposite direction, making Ella follow him instead.

"Mr. Tomassi, what's wrong with my car?" Ella hurried to keep up with him. "It's my responsibility to drive my clients."

"Yes, I know." Angelo stopped and regarded Ella. "What do you drive?"

"A beautiful dark gray Civic," she answered. "It barely has six thousand miles on it."

"Not safe enough." Angelo resumed walking toward Rafa and Brett who were standing next to the Escalade. "We're taking mine to be safe."

What did he mean that her car was not safe enough? Was he expecting her to have an accident? Why was he making this a difficult task for a place eight minutes away?

As Brett unlocked the Escalade, Angelo opened the passenger door and waited for Ella to enter. She froze. How did she know she could trust these men? They were strangers in suits who were supposedly interested in a property she was leasing.

"Would you rather go in separate vehicles?" Angelo asked. "I could have Brett follow behind you, but then I wouldn't be able to ask questions."

"No," she lied and slipped inside the backseat of the vehicle with Angelo beside her. Since the hotel was not that far away, she had to take that risk. They were the first people who were interested. If she did not go, she would lose Santiago's.

They rode in silence for several blocks. Ella stared through the window while Angelo stared at Ella.

"Comfortable?" he asked.

Ella finally looked over and sighed, speaking freely. "Why shouldn't I be, Mr. Tomassi?" she asked. It was obvious that they made her uneasy.

"I don't know." His words came out casual and relaxed as he crossed his leg, making her more stressed than before. Angelo knew he intimidated her.

"Well, if you don't want to see the property...let me out here. I can walk back to Santiago's," she said. Yet even as she spoke the words, Ella was uncertain about what she had said. She did not really want them to drop her off in the middle of the island and blow her one chance to lease the hotel. Why had she not kept her mouth shut?

Angelo leaned toward her and lifted her chin. His fingers were gentle; his expression was stern. "Do you talk to all of your clients like that? You told me that you'd show me inside the hotel, and I will get what I came for. I'm not here to waste your time, and you won't waste mine either. Is that clear, Ms. Collins?"

His voice was an eerie sort of calm, but Ella sensed the quiet warning behind his words. Angelo was close—too close for her to answer. She could feel his breath against her face. It made her flush as a slight chill ran down her neck. Was she afraid or attracted to the man? She could not tell the difference. Both would put her on edge.

"Show us the property, Ms. Collins. You aren't the sort of person who has anything to worry about with us." He gently lowered his hand and returned to his own seat for the rest of the ride.

Chapter 3

As Angelo looked at the magnificent beach property, the Escalade came to a stop. The waves roared with the stiff breeze, enhancing the smell of saltiness in the air. The tide glistened underneath the morning sun, pushing the water closer to the large rundown hotel. The peeling white paint made the hotel look much older than it probably was. Sand mounded across the street on one side with newer hotels and restaurants down the beach on the other. The spacious piece of land was located in a prime spot near the main road. It also had an oversized parking lot behind.

Angelo and Rafa followed Ella up the steps, past an outside porch area to the entrance. As they inspected the stairs, she unlocked the door and walked inside. Ella flipped on the lights, looking relieved when they lit up the room. The light showed what used to be the lobby, now covered in a layer of silt.

"Please take your time. I'll be right outside," she said.

Angelo walked around. He knocked on the wall; then he lightly kicked the trim against the base of the floor. The ceilings looked sturdy. There were no cracks, and the light fixtures were intact and not broken.

"What do you think?" he asked Rafa. "It'll be good for a nightclub. The foundation is solid."

"It looks worse than it is. It won't take that much to renovate. The building is five stories high, so we can knock out the second and fourth floor. Then you'll have high ceilings for the main lounge and the VIP room, plus a third floor for personal use."

Angelo nodded. "Renovation shouldn't take long at all, and that porch outside can seat overflow. Let's see what they're asking for this place."

"You don't want to check out the top floors?" asked Rafa.

"No." Angelo shook his head. "It's the property I want. The rest is cosmetic."

As they exited the building, Ella was standing against one of the pillars underneath the covered entrance. She looked at peace in her solitude, satisfied with watching seagulls circle above the shore.

Angelo wondered if she was sheltered as a child. She watched everything at the restaurant and now here with sheer fascination. Perhaps it was her perfect aura of innocence coercing him to feel an interest when he should not encourage his own thoughts. Even if she was a feasible interest, she was out of place with his group. She would never be able to handle the life.

"So," he said and closed the door behind him. "How much is this place going for? If we can come to an agreement, I'd like to sign the paperwork next week. I don't have much time left to discuss it."

"Seven hundred thousand," Ella replied and took out her key to lock the deadbolt.

"What?" Angelo whipped his eyes from the building to her. "Is that some sort of joke?"

"What do you mean by a joke? That's the standard price for this property in relation to the properties around it."

"Ms. Collins, I know you're new to this market, but even a new agent would know how much a piece of land like this is worth. I wouldn't expect to spend lower than seven million and that's with a trade. Give me a fair market price and we'll talk about my company buying the it."

"Oh," Ella frowned, a look of awareness spreading on her face, "seven hundred thousand covers the lease."

"Lease?" Rafa said as all three started down the steps.

"My company has placed this property for lease, not purchase."

"What?" Angelo paused mid-stride. "The listing said nothing about a lease. This property needs major renovation. Who's going to spend that kind of money to renovate when the property isn't theirs? I won't."

"I don't know what to say." Ella stepped off the last step and walked back to the Escalade. Inside, she pulled out a stack of paperwork with company letterhead and handed it to Angelo.

He looked through the sheets and then again. "What the hell do you mean it isn't for sale?" He pinched the bridge of his nose and practically threw the papers at Rafa. Ella flinched at his reaction and stared ahead, avoiding eye contact with either man. Her arms protectively moved around her chest. It made Angelo inhale slowly, filling his lungs full of ocean air. He turned his attention back to Ella, redirecting her focus as he gently grabbed her upper arm.

"Come." He led her to the back seat of the Escalade and opened the door, lifting her hand to help her inside. "I know you had nothing to do with this mishap. Stay here with Brett while I call your company and sort out this mess."

The closed doors on the vehicle did little to shield Ella from Angelo's growling voice as he shouted at the person on the other end of the phone. He paced one way and then the other. His hand flew up in the air and took the phone away from his ear as if he would throw it to the middle of the sea. Then he talked some more, finally saying little and letting the other end speak.

When he was through, Angelo clicked off his phone and dropped it to the inside pocket of his coat. His arms crossed as his temper raged in silence. Rafa did not say a word to him and waited. It took minutes. They finally exchanged some words and Angelo pointed at the Escalade, walking back to the opposite door of Ella. His glaring eyes earned no words from her. She had already given up on leasing out the property.

"The company you work for switched the details of this property with another a mile down. Tell me why I should trust your company when they fucked up like this? That's not good business."

"I don't know what to tell you. This hasn't happened before." Ella started to smooth her wind-blown hair, looking for something to divert her attention from him.

"Why aren't you looking at me when I talk? I'm the client. Don't you want to talk about the property?"

"What? You're still interested?" Ella was shocked. After all of that anger, she figured he would take her back to Santiago's and be done.

"Your company is selling the property for nine million. I'm going to need a week to crunch some numbers together, but I want to close on it next week."

"For sale," she mumbled. Now she would not have the twenty percent down payment for the restaurant. "Not for lease—now what?"

"What's the problem with the property being for sale instead of lease?" Angelo slid to the seat and shut the door as she looked away.

"There's no problem." She tried to make light of the subject but her voice sounded sad.

"Do you get a cut in the sale?" he asked. Ella shook her head and laid her hands in her lap. "Why not?" he questioned further.

"Because I'm the leasing agent. Somebody else handles sales," she answered.

"That makes sense," Rafa added as he stepped into the front seat.

"Rafa." Angelo pointed at him. "Don't," he warned and then looked at Ella again. "So now you're upset because you won't see a dime out of this?"

"Well, yes. I would've been promoting the other property instead of this one. It's not only my time today that I wasted. I guess mistakes happen, though." Ella felt out of sorts as she buckled her seatbelt. "You'll be negotiating the price with someone else, Mr. Tomassi."

"You seem pretty upset about this. What were you going to use your commission for? Vacations? Cars? Jewelry?"

Ella shook her head as her eyes lit up but then looked sad again. "No, nothing like that. I would've used the money to put a down payment on Santiago's, but I need twenty percent of the sale price and I don't have enough right now. You know that restaurant where you ate? Well, the old owner is selling it, and I've been going there since I was young. The buyers who are looking at it will turn it into a gift shop—another pointless gift shop."

Angelo gave her a peculiar look. He never expected her to want to invest the money. "Santiago's," he repeated.

"Yes." She smiled, reflecting on the restaurant. "I've always wanted to have it. It's perfect where it sets on the ocean. I have ideas for the menu and the interior, and the wine cellar is gorgeous—the attraction of the place. They take their customers inside and let them choose their own bottle if they'd like. When I found out Mr. Santiago was retiring, I knew it was mine. I could only hope that someone else wouldn't buy it before I leased that hotel."

Ella was animated in her goals, completely forgetting about her nerves as she talked of Santiago's. Her love of the restaurant was easy for Angelo to see—almost contagious. He could not resist what he was going to ask next.

"All right, you've convinced me. Why don't you give me a tour of Santiago's next week after I finish signing the paperwork on the hotel?"

Wondering what Angelo was up to and how much money it would cost, Rafa half-turned from the front seat and glared. Angelo did not usually act on impulse, but something about Ella caught his attention.

She knew he had money yet showed no care for his wealth. If nothing else, he was curious.

"Of course I'll show you around. Mr. Santiago won't mind. I'd like to look around a last time too."

"Good." Angelo pulled out his wallet and handed Ella his card. "My information is on there. Unless you hear something else..." Angelo looked at Rafa.

"He's free next Tuesday," Rafa said as the Escalade stopped outside of Santiago's again.

"Got that?"

"Okay," Ella agreed.

"Good." Angelo opened his door and stepped out, holding out his hand to her. With all of the talk, she took his hand without thinking, taking in a quiet breath when they touched. Angelo made no notice and spoke again unfazed. "We'll be back next week, Ms. Collins."

"What time do you plan to come?"

"I'll give you a call Tuesday morning to confirm. Unless something comes up, I'll see you around six," Angelo said and stepped back inside the Escalade, waiting to leave until she reached the front door.

Chapter 4

At the Royal Flush that night, Angelo sat at his desk and flipped over documents that Rafa laid in front of him. Some contained numbers; others showed charts and reflected the growth of his businesses. The last few were printouts that had nothing to do with work.

Angelo rested his head in his hand and thought about her. Where had a woman like Ella been hiding? Did she grow up in Orlando and what were her parents like? He assumed they were low profile with how proper she was and wondered if there was more meaning behind her attachment to Santiago's than childhood visits?

He did not know why he cared in the first place? He never bothered to look deeper than the surface for any woman? It must have been her pretty eyes or maybe her smile. Angelo looked at the ceiling. It was definitely her smile—pure and genuine, like her childlike excitement for the restaurant. Everything about her was real.

"Angelo," Rafa said and tapped on the desk. He was waiting for Angelo's approval on the numbers so he could leave for the night. "Tell me you aren't thinking about her."

"Thinking about who?" Angelo ignored the question and started signing.

"That girl."

"What girl?" Angelo nodded when he reached the end of the stack and slid the paperwork back to Rafa, tossing a brown envelope on top. "I want the information on Santiago's kept separate," he said and leaned back in his oversized chair, propping his feet on top of the desk.

"Angelo, what good is a tiny restaurant like that going to do for the group?"

"It's personal," Angelo said. "I wanted that information for myself—not the group."

Rafa shook his head and grabbed the entire stack. "Angelo, it can't happen. You know that. Your father won't approve of her. Even if he did, she's no match for your life. She couldn't handle someone like you. She's too innocent."

"For god's sake, Rafa, shut up. There isn't anything to happen. Let it go." Angelo scooted back and grabbed a glass and a bottle of bourbon out of the drawer. "Leave—go wherever it is you're going tonight. If I knew you were going to be this much of a pain in the ass, I wouldn't have taken you in."

"More like forced," Rafa huffed. "I should've explored my options since you always have a problem with my advice."

"Right...we both know you liked the money."

"Rafa looked thoughtful for a moment. "It helped but don't think that was the only reason I joined you."

"Then tell me what other reasons you had."

"Maybe another time." Rafa left the question unanswered. Angelo never asked Rafa about his life before he joined; Rafa never volunteered. Maybe Angelo would know more about him one day. The one thing he knew for sure was that Rafa was loyal.

"You have what you need. I'm going to the casino," said Angelo. "I need a break from all this paperwork."

"You're going to the casino—alone? You know there's always some sort of trouble that I have to fix the next morning every time you go alone."

"Jim is down there. Thomas and Sammy too—maybe Brett."

Rafa shook his head, looking worried about Angelo going alone. "Fine, I'm leaving. I have a life too...and a date—sort of. I'll be staying in my room tonight. Call me if you need me." Rafa said, walking out.

"Finally," Angelo sighed after Rafa left. The tight muscles in his neck were starting to loosen as he swallowed another shot and then two. He enjoyed the tingling sensation of the liquor as it trickled down his throat. He needed the numbing effects. After a morning with his father and an upcoming renovation, he did not want to think.

***

On the first floor of the Royal Flush, the elevator doors opened to the most prestigious casino in Miami. Angelo had opened the hotel for business almost five years earlier and added the casino a year after that. With rows of slot machines, oak poker tables and a full-sized circular bar in the middle, the casino was the highlight of the hotel.

Angelo walked in stride through the crowded room, being given respectful nods when passing guests. Down the hallway in back, he stepped into the VIP room where men in suits sat around several tables with stacked poker chips. While the private attendants served, women danced in the soft glow of the chandelier, exchanging glances with some of the men, possibly to entertain further after their shifts.

He found the dancers a common scene and walked past them to the bar, an instant understanding between him and his newest member, Thomas. Thomas was the working bartender tonight; he unlocked a private cabinet, popped a cork and handed Angelo a bottle. "Mr. Tomassi," he said.

Angelo nodded and looked around. There were games in session at every table, so he took a seat closest to the bar. As he waited, he poured himself a glass of wine. It seemed the more he drank, the more he could drink. It was funny how that worked.

He did not wait long. Angelo still inhaled the fragrant liquid when the card game ended. The dealer waited. After Angelo took a drink, Jim, the tallest of the group with straight black hair and brown eyes, sat down next to him.

"Hey Boss," said Jim. Jim was one of Angelo's highest-ranking members. It surprised Angelo when Jim nodded at the dealer and wanted to play.

"Since when do you gamble?" Angelo passed his bottle of wine to Jim.

"I'm feeling lucky."

"Lucky?" Angelo pressed. "Is that because your brother isn't around?"

"It's because I'm using his money. Ray bet me five hundred on that last boxing tournament. Can you believe that? He'll be here in a minute when he's done punching the wall."

Angelo looked amused. Jim and Ray were inseparable and had been since he found them on the steps of the hotel looking for work. He gave them an opportunity; their loyalty and fast thinking skills earned them a spot at the top. Angelo could count on them to drop whatever they were doing when he called.

"Where's Sammy?" asked Angelo.

"He's coming. I think he was grabbing more glasses for the bar."

Angelo picked up the cards in front of him—nothing but junk. It did not matter. He was not here to prove himself. "Fold," he said without exchanging for new cards; then he picked up his wine while three other players threw out theirs. Two players remained. It was Jim's bet.

"A hundred," Jim said and threw in his chips.

"Raise you three hundred," a man with light brown hair and blue eyes said from across the table.

Angelo looked at him from above the rim of his glass. He did not recognize the man. Had he come in before when Angelo was away? Somebody must have given him a pass to the VIP room but it was not Angelo who approved the pass.

"All right." Jim matched the raise and pointed. "Call."

Angelo lowered his glass in disbelief when the man showed his cards. Any veteran player could tell that the man did not know his game. Did he really believe he would win? "Hey," Angelo pointed, "you're going to have to bluff better than that if you expect to win with a pair of fours."

"I was warming up," the man mumbled as Jim pulled in the chips.

"Anti," said the dealer and passed out the next hand.

Angelo looked at his cards. Having four hearts was good enough to continue; it was his bet. "A hundred," he said.

The next two players matched the bet, followed by the brown-haired man across from him. "Here's mine…raise four hundred."

Jim threw in his cards. "Not this hand." He sat back to watch the rest of the game.

"I'll match you and raise you two," said Angelo. He looked in the man's eyes when the other two players folded.

"You're going to be sorry." The man threw in the extra chips

Angelo threw out the one club and received that fifth heart he needed—a flush. He felt good about the draw. "Here's my bet." He slid in the chip.

"Raise you five." The man tried to play off the large amount by casually tossing in the chips, but the beads of sweat on his forehead proved that he had nothing in his hand.

"I call." Angelo tossed in the chips. Looking humbled, the man turned over an ace and a jack. "You're kidding," Angelo scoffed and turned over five hearts. "You bet over a thousand dollars on two high cards. I was hoping that you were acting dumb, but you're sweating through your shirt. Get out. It takes more than money to play in this room. Come back when you can play."

The man hung his head and stood after Angelo called him out in front of the room. Angelo did not mind taking the cash, but he hated seeing men create an image of power by throwing it around. What was it about money that made people feel smart? They were as dumb with or without it.

Angelo looked down for a second. He felt the smallest twinge of guilt as he pulled in the chips, but then something sharp touched the back of his neck. His eyes shut with the chill. His breathing ceased. His fingers clenched tightly together as the rounded metal muzzle pressed further. After all he had been through in the mafia, would he lose his life over a poker match?

"I would think hard about what you're doing before you click that hammer," Angelo said between his teeth. Jim looked at him. His hand reached for the gun inside his coat when Angelo slightly shook his head.

"Lower your fucking gun," said another voice from behind. Angelo let out his breath. Rafa could not have come at a better time.

"I'm sorry," the man pleaded as Angelo turned around. "I wasn't going to shoot." Angelo's stomach had knotted in seconds, the heat of nausea reaching his throat.

"Of course you weren't," Angelo said. His voice became calm as though the matter were a simple squabble over a drink. "Come with me; we'll talk about it." Angelo looked around the table as he started to stand. "Jim, stay here. I'm out for the night." Then he walked to the bar, looking at another new member of his group. "Sammy, I'm going to need you back here."

The door to a room behind the poker players clicked shut. Rafa stood against the door with his arms folded while Sammy forced the man on a chair.

"So," Angelo said. "How did you think pulling a gun on me would work out for you?" The man stayed silent. "What? Now you can't talk. That's another reason you shouldn't have come to this room. Fucking coward. You have one more chance to answer me." The man squirmed. Fear reflected from his eyes, yet he would not speak.

"Nothing," Angelo huffed with disgust. "You can't even answer for yourself." Angelo reached out and grabbed his jaw, looking the man in the eyes. "Why did you pull a gun on me?" he demanded in a low but furious tone.

"I don't know why," the man finally spoke. Angelo slammed his fist into the man's gut, knocking the wind from his lungs.

"You didn't even think it through—the consequences? I hate fuckers who act on impulse. You shouldn't have brought a gun in this hotel. Playing with the big boys was your first mistake. Pulling a gun on me," he shook his head, "that was your last. Sammy—" Angelo pointed and walked to the door where Rafa stood. "Rafa—" Angelo slapped the top of his chest. "You couldn't have timed that better. I don't know how you always know when something's wrong."

Rafa's brows lifted as though it were some secret gift; then he moved out of the way so Angelo could leave.

Chapter 5

Six days passed. Ella looked down at the white tablecloth and then at the front door. She had done this repeatedly over the last half hour. Her sweaty palms were evidence of her anticipation for six o'clock. No matter how many times she rubbed her hands on her skirt, they remained clammy and uncomfortable. She did not know whether to expect Angelo early or if he would arrive on time. Ella gave many tours of homes and offices, but none made her this nervous. What was it about him that filled her with anxiety?

"Mr. Santiago," an older woman with speckled gray hair said. There were two women and they were following Mr. Santiago to his office. "Thank you for agreeing to meet us tomorrow morning. I'm happy that we found this place. It'll be perfect."

"Of course," replied Mr. Santiago. Ella noticed no joy in his eyes. His back slouched more than the years on his body usually allowed. His head hung toward the floor.

"Would you mind if we took one more look around? I'd like to see the wine cellar again. It'll be a great hidden cubicle for our saltwater taffy line."

Saltwater taffy! Ella thought. They wanted to replace the antique wooden wine cellar with lines of colored candy against the walls? Mr. Santiago should have forbidden such a mockery of the cellar's intended use. The women had no idea what they wanted to buy. Ella vowed never to eat taffy again.

Mr. Santiago took a breath and looked at Ella. Her face flushed as she swallowed back any tears that threatened to escape. This was it. Santiago's final days as a restaurant were numbered.

Ella would not watch as the women gloated over how they would remodel the place. She stood up. She could not stand to be around the women another minute and flung open the front door.

Ella covered her face with her hands as she sat on a wooden bench at the end of the entrance. She lost her composure. She used to travel with her parents to Key Biscayne every holiday. Many happy memories with her mother were here: how she talked about the months she spent away at school; how they shared a slice of chocolate cake because they were too full to have their own; how they watched the sunsets on the patio over a cup of tea. Her last smiles and laughter with her mother would fade away with another pointless boutique.

"Ms. Collins."

"Hm?" Ella muttered. Her vision blurred through her watery eyes. With the prospective buyers, she forgot all about Angelo. She looked up and around him, disoriented as she searched for the two other men.

"Did you forget we have a meeting?"

"Oh," she said and shook her head. She opened her mouth to continue but instead looked past Angelo where the two women buyers exited the restaurant. They were chatting, still giddy about transforming the place. Ella felt the inside of her stomach tighten.

"Ms. Collins," Angelo said again. This time his tone was dry and annoyed.

"I'm sorry, Mr. Tomassi." Ella blinked a couple of times and wiped the tears from the corners of her eyes. "There's no point in showing you the restaurant now. Those two women who left are the ones who are going to buy it. They start the paperwork tomorrow."

"And what do they have to do with me? You agreed to the tour."

"Yes, I did," Ella sighed and gripped the arm of the bench, pushing herself up. "If you still want to see the restaurant, I will show you around."

"I didn't come to waste my time."

Did he not hear her? Ella could not figure out why Angelo still wanted a tour, but she did agree and he was standing in front of her. She might as well have one last good look herself.

As Ella neared the front door again, Angelo opened it for her and waited. His gesture made her stare for a second. Angelo's eyes met hers. She found a certain beauty within the severe dark color. It made the pit of her stomach knot as she realized a handsome man hid underneath the intimidating business suit. The gaze she thought seemed troubled before was not troubled at all. It was either an interest in her or simple curiosity. She did not know.

"Thank you," she said, glancing at him even after walking through the door. He was stern yet polite at the same time. Angelo must have had other matters, more important matters to attend. Santiago's was on a much smaller scale in comparison to the hotel he had purchased. He could not have been interested in the restaurant.

"Well…" Ella smiled. "Here's the bar—twenty feet long with another three feet around both sides. Solid hickory." She knocked on the top and held out her arms. "And the strong glossy coating keeps the wood safe from sand and salt. It's so beautiful, especially with the way the light shines off the top. I almost always sit at the bar." She smiled with her words.

"I like the display behind the bar." Angelo pointed. "It looks like the owner keeps a well-rounded stock of liquors. There's plenty of choices for everyone."

Ella nodded and walked to the walls. "These are pictures that the customers donate. Mr. Santiago has them cleaned once a week. You won't find dust on these like you would in other restaurants. He takes really good care of the place."

Ella watched Angelo cross his arms and look at one. It was the shadow of a man looking out onto the ocean. Angelo's eyes almost had the same expression as the man, a yearning for something yet nobody knew what. Maybe both got lost in their thoughts.

"All right," said Angelo as he turned away. I see the dining room is filling up. It's a good sign for the chef. I've seen the patio, so why don't you show me that wine cellar you talked about?"

"Of course, Mr. Tomassi." Ella led him past several tables to the back where a restored antique piano sat beside a tinted door. "This used to belong to Mr. Santiago's grandmother. He's made some minor repairs but treats the piano like gold," Ella said.

"It's in pristine condition." Angelo moved his fingers over the polished keys as if hearing a silent tune. "It's a beautiful piece to have in the restaurant. Do any of the customers ever play?"

"Only a couple," said Ella as she opened the door to the side. Angelo took a breath, briefly glancing at the piano and then following her inside.

Ella walked around several dark oak pillars in the center of the cellar. An exquisite stairway led to the bottom, where bottles of wine were lined from the floor to the ceiling. "What do you think?" Ella asked and looked at Angelo before looking back at the stunning glass bottles. "The white wines and Rieslings are on the lower shelves," she pointed, "and in the cubbies on top are the merlots and cabernets."

"Impressive." Angelo nodded as she turned back around. He smiled at her, hinting an interest that reflected back a curious stare. He found her intriguing—naïve. Ella never realized that he was not complimenting the wine cellar, although he did find the room attractive.

"I like it too," she said. "Do you drink wine, Mr. Tomassi?"

"All the time," he said, a slight grin on his lips. He would not mind having a glass with her.

"Do you have a favorite?" she continued. Angelo looked around and then back at her. Nobody ever asked him what he liked without trying to make a buck, but that could not be the case for Ella. She would not profit from his choice.

"I have a few favorite years, but I doubt this restaurant carries them in stock."

"They might. I want to give you a bottle before they're all auctioned off. You might as well enjoy one."

Ella looked sad as she scanned the bottles from the top down. Angelo wondered where her attachment to wine came from. She seemed young yet also informed. It was a strange combination to him.

"I don't mind the Dominus Estate," he said to redirect her thoughts. It was a decent bottle but at a much lower price than what he drank. He was not about to disclose his favorite bottle, one that cost short of two grand.

"You don't mind it," she said, "but it's not preferred, is it?" Ella glanced back and then started to look through labels, taking out the exact bottle he said. "I would have expected you to ask for the Chateau Ausone."

Angelo chuckled. She was right; he would have preferred the other. "What do you know of wine, Ms. Collins?" he asked, growing more interested with every word she said. He wondered if she had a genuine knowledge or learned it in books.

"My father owned a wine cellar. He was so proud of it that it made me want to know more. I used to stand in front of the bottles and admire them. I loved the different shapes and the labels and colors. As I got older, he would let me taste them. I guess that makes me a wine connoisseur." Ella grinned, discrediting her knowledge with a smirk. "I'm not really an expert or anything, Mr. Tomassi, but I do know a lot about wine."

"I see that," he agreed.

Ella smiled. She had the most amazing smile with the way her eyes lit up. It was natural with no traces of deceit—real.

"Here," she said and handed him the Dominus Estate. "It's a gift. You can drink it here or after you leave." Ella started toward the stairs but then looked back again."

I'm hardly finished here. He thought as she paused at the light switch, waiting for him to speak. Chills had started to form on her arms. Angelo wanted to talk to her more but could not keep her in the cellar all night. It was far too cold with the thin-strapped dress she wore.

"Are you busy tonight?" he asked as they neared the exit of the cellar.

"No, not really. I was going to go home and try to figure out how to keep those women from buying the restaurant." Ella looked down and shook her head. "At least I can't say I didn't try."

"Why don't you share this wine with me? You have nothing better to do, and I have a full bottle of wine that I don't want to drink by myself."

"Mr. Tomassi," Ella sighed. "I said that I have to figure out how to keep this restaurant from being sold. That's very important to me."

"Yes, exactly, let's talk about the restaurant while we have a glass of wine."

Ella's mouth opened and then shut again. Angelo could see the flurry of thoughts run through her mind as she tried to reason what he wanted to talk to her about. Had Rafa been there, he would have advised Angelo against the entire idea. That was why Rafa was left behind.

Chapter 6

This time Angelo led as Ella followed. He chose a table away from the chatter of guests and opposite of the front door. His manners surprised her again. He pulled out her chair and waited for her to sit. Ella could not help but smile at him. She enjoyed talking to him and felt more comfortable tonight. Maybe his work contributed to his stern disposition, but somehow she saw kindness behind his eyes. Maybe they were a touch sad—kind of like the painting on the wall.

Ella quietly watched as he turned the bottle of wine over, inspecting it for imperfections. There was no dust. It had been stored properly and at the correct temperature. She knew he would find nothing wrong with it. All he needed now was an employee who would open it and give them some glasses.

Then Ella remembered that Lila worked tonight. Ella shook her head as Lila started for the table. She wanted another server. Angelo looked up at Ella as she waved at Lila not to come. He must have caught the silent conversation out of the corner of his eye. Ella gave a sheepish smile in return.

"Good evening," Lila greeted and set down two glasses. Angelo winced at the voice and Ella went quiet. She could instantly tell that Angelo had overheard Lila the previous week. Her cheeks grew pink all over again as she willed Lila to hold her tongue.

"I'll get that for you," Lila said and opened the bottle for Angelo. Maybe having wine here was not a good idea after all. Ella should have recommended the back office to talk. "Would you like to see a menu?" Lila asked and set the bottle on the table.

"No," Angelo answered immediately. "We won't need you any more either."

"All right," Lila said. Ella exchanged looks with her. It was a desperate plea for Lila not to say what was on her mind. Lila started to open her mouth but seemed to catch on, Ella exhaling a long, silent breath when she finally walked away.

"How long have you been friends with the server?" Angelo asked and poured them both some wine.

"Seven months," she said and took the glass he held. She was going to need the wine tonight, especially with Lila lurking about. "I met her here on the first day that I moved to Key Biscayne."

"Ah, so you aren't from around here."

"No," said Ella as she sipped a drink. "I'm from Orlando. My family used to travel here twice a year. After I got my bachelor's in business, I moved here permanently."

"And your parents don't mind you being so far away from home?"

Ella rested her chin on her hand as she looked to the side in thought. "I love Key Biscayne. I wanted to move here for this restaurant. My father did mind at first. I don't know what made him change his mind, but he did. He said I could live in the vacation home where we used to stay. It isn't a big house, but it has everything I need. I wasn't going to pass it up."

"I've never heard of anyone moving across state away from family for a restaurant. What's your reason?"

"Mr. Tomassi," Ella let out a breath. "Some things are too hard to talk about."

"It's okay. If you don't want to talk about it, I won't press it."

She went silent for a minute. Ella looked down at the table in sad recollection, but she would not cry about it—not again. Nothing would bring her mother back anyway. Yet even as she thought this, her mind resorted back to six years earlier to that dreadful day in October.

Ella was two months into her junior year at boarding school. It was well past curfew when she heard the ding of the elevator door. She never noticed how loud that ding actually was until it echoed in the dead of night. Ella ran out of the elevator and down the hallway without making a sound. She had not meant to be late. It took that long to complete her school project. Her studies were more important than following a curfew. Her grades would be her ticket out of her sheltered life.

The soft glow of the lights led her past the dean's room and many others that lined the walls. She wondered how she ended up in a dorm room at the end of the hallway. Ella was relieved that they did not catch her coming in late again. Maybe they chose simply to ignore that she was late. It was obvious by now that she was not getting into trouble.

They knew who her father was. They knew he was strict. It was not as if she could get into trouble if she wanted. Her father made sure of that. He always seemed to know what she was doing whenever she had tried. By now, Ella knew that she could get by with nothing without him knowing.

"Melissa?" Ella asked and shut the door behind her. "What's the matter?" Melissa was her roommate. Tears streamed down her cheeks, and she did not speak a word. Melissa pointed.

"Father?" asked Ella. He was sitting on the sofa beside the dean. Ella looked at the book and notebook in her hands and thought it was a little rash to expel her for studying hard. Then she noticed her father's eyes. They were red as if he had been crying. His flushed face sent an instant chill into Ella's chest. Something was not right.

"Come here, Ella," he said.

Ella did not move. She had seen that look before except without the tears. It was when he told her he was sending her away to school in seventh grade. This was worse, much worse. She did not want to know the news.

"Ella," he said again.

She shook her head. If he was here, hundreds of miles from Florida, the news was bad. There was no telling what he wanted to say.

"Ella." He started to stand. Ella had never heard her father's voice so emotional. He had always been kind but also made of stone. Nothing made him waver.

"It's your mother, dear. I don't know how to tell you that she...that she—" Her father wiped his eyes as if not believing it himself. "The doctors did everything they could. She didn't make it through the surgery. She's...gone."

"What?" Ella mumbled. "How?" She saw words come out of her father's mouth, yet she could not make out a single syllable. The room started to spin. A blur of her father, the dean, and Melissa merged with the small red sofa and the pale white walls. Her body pummeled to the floor. Even though her eyes had closed, Ella could see her mother's smile as she sat next to her at Santiago's. Her mother was real. Ella could hear her laugh. Her voice echoed in Ella's head. This was a bad dream. Her mother could not be dead.

"Ms. Collins," Angelo whispered her name and gently shook her arm. Ella looked at him but her expression still seemed dazed. "Ella." He tried her first name, hoping it would bring her from whatever nightmare memory had taken hold. It worked. Ella shook her head and then looked around.

"I'm sorry. I haven't been a good host. It's that...this restaurant holds the last memories of my mother, and now I won't even have that."

"I see." Angelo now understood its value.

"It's all right, Mr. Tomassi. It's been years since it happened. Maybe it's silly to hold onto the restaurant anyway. I know I should let it go."

"No, it's important to you. There's nothing wrong with that. Why haven't you asked your father for the money? Doesn't this restaurant mean something to him too?"

Ella shook her head again. "My father has pushed away anything that reminds him of my mother...including me. He made it clear that if I moved, I would be completely on my own."

"And you two don't talk?"

"No." Ella slouched in her chair. "I haven't talked to him since I moved. All I have is an emergency phone he gave me. I never use it. He doesn't want to talk to me anyway."

Angelo thought about her father. How could a father push away his daughter, especially one as sweet as Ella? She was the type of person who needed someone to watch out for her. She had a strong mind but still seemed naïve.

"All right," Angelo said and leaned forward. "Listen to me carefully. I have an idea that I want you to consider. Since the buyers want to sign paperwork tomorrow, that doesn't leave you much time. Are you with me so far?"

"Yes, I'm listening."

Ella looked at him with an unpretentious, serious expression. Her business-minded shift in demeanor almost made him smile. She must have known what he would propose, yet she did not jump to conclusions. She merely stared and waited to hear what he would say. If she felt that strongly about the restaurant, his money would go to a worthy investment.

"I'm willing to purchase this place and let you manage it. It has a steady flow of business. I enjoyed the breakfast I ate last week. I haven't tried anything off the dinner menu, but I see how the place is busy right now. That's a good sign to me. The owner has properly maintained it, so I won't need to remodel. It looks like an easy investment."

Ella said nothing. He could see her thinking about what he said as her eyes looked at him and back to the dining area. Did his proposal shock her silent?

"You want to buy the restaurant?" she asked.

"Yes, that's what I said," he answered.

"And have *me* manage it?" she mumbled, but her eyes started to shine at the idea.

"That's right, but I'm going to have to see the books every few weeks at first," he added.

"I can't believe you would do that, Mr. Tomassi. You just purchased a hotel on the beach. Can this restaurant mean anything to you?" Ella asked without looking at him. She was thinking hard.

"Well, it's not a big investment to me, but I'll still see a return on my money unless you want another gift shop. If you'd like to see it stay a restaurant, you'll need to manage it. I doubt there's anyone else who will care about it like you do, and I don't have enough staff with the hotel I bought. Do you agree with the terms or not?"

"The terms," Ella started to stand. "Well I—" Her words faltered. Angelo was not sure if she would pass out or shake his hand. He stood as well in case he needed to catch her unconscious body. Angelo thought the news may have been more than she could handle. Having thought the restaurant was gone to now managing it was bound to take a toll on her mind.

Ella did not move. She held onto the side of the table, looking at his face and scanning his clothes. If only he could put her thoughts into words. He considered how he might become more interested in her if he knew what she thought. The longer she stood there, the more his patience was running thin. He hoped she would not be so absentminded when she ran the place. She could not lose her focus as manager.

Angelo finally cleared his throat to snap her out of her latest thoughts, bringing her eyes immediately back to his. Then her smile convinced him that he did the right thing to offer to buy the place. Ella did not give him time to admire her expression. She flung her arms around his neck and squeezed.

"Thank you so much. Of course I agree to show whatever you want to see," she said.

Angelo hugged her back with a hint of humor in his eyes. He did not know why, but such excitement lured him to return her affection. He would not mind seeing her body at all but felt it best to let her naivety go. Ella did not realize that she thrust her body against him with no consideration to what she did. He smiled at the thought of her blushing cheeks if she had. A handshake would have sufficed.

Chapter 7

Four weeks' time had transformed the weathered hotel. Angelo ran his fingers along the twisted chrome railing; a double oak stairway had replaced the single set of stairs that led to the front entrance. Round marble tables now speckled the patio with cushioned swivel stools around. A clear awning above the porch replaced the dark panels from before. He did not know how Rafa pulled it off, but the hotel was turning into a nightclub perfectly. He crossed his arms and gazed around.

"I was wondering when you were going to get here," Rafa said as he pushed through the double doors of the entrance.

"You did good, Rafa." Angelo nodded.

"Of course I did...and look at that view. The overflow out here might as well be permanent seating. I think a lot of people will want to sit outside."

"You think...even with the dance floor and TV's inside? I guess we should add that rooftop balcony for people who want more privacy. I remember we talked about that."

"I think so. It'll be good for guests in the VIP room. They won't have to come all the way downstairs."

"All right, make it happen."

"Already done." Rafa handed over an envelope.

"Is this from Santiago's?" Angelo asked.

"Yes—I still can't believe you bought that place. But I really can't believe you're having that woman run it with no management experience."

Angelo shrugged and opened the envelope. "You can't believe a lot of things I do," he said. "She deserved a chance to prove she could run the place. I don't think anyone I found would have cared for it more."

"They wouldn't, because you wouldn't have bought something so insignificant. Why'd you do it anyway?"

"It's personal," Angelo replied. "It's my personal money and my business. If it's so insignificant, why do you care?"

Rafa let out an agitated breath. "I care because your father is going to care. He's going to ask you why, and then he's going to figure out that you bought it for a woman."

Angelo rubbed his head. Why did Rafa always have to point out the downside of everything? Why couldn't Rafa leave him alone for once? "I'm not marrying Gregorio's daughter, Rafa," he said.

"And you're interested in this woman?" Rafa asked.

"Rafa," Angelo warned.

"Angelo, she's not the type of woman that you can fuck one night and send away. She's from a different class of women than what you're used to."

Angelo's expression became sour. He opened his mouth; he could feel the insulting curses on the tip of his tongue, but a thought came to mind. Rafa had pointed out the obvious. Ella was not the same as the other women. That was where his interest stemmed.

"Rafa, you're absolutely right," he said as his mind considered Ella's favorable qualities. He considered her sincerity her greatest attribute.

"Which part am I right about?" Rafa asked.

Angelo ignored the question; instead, he shook his head at one sheet in particular. "This can't be right. What was she thinking with this salary? I don't have time to go to the restaurant and fix this today. She needs to come to me." He took out his phone to dial her number when it rang before he could. "Yes," he answered. "Yes, hold on," he said and looked at Rafa. "Call Ms. Collins and have her come down here right away." He gestured with his chin and started speaking into the receiver again.

***

Angelo thumped the end button and let his hand fall to the sofa, exasperated with the hour worth of calls. He looked around. Raw sheetrock and texture surrounded what would become the VIP room. The building had come a long way so far, but it still had a way to go.

He walked down the circular hallway to the dark glass door that allowed him to look out but no one to look in. He preferred the one-way mirror. It would help keep the VIP room free of unwanted guests.

As Angelo opened the door, he heard a loud, unwanted voice. *Lila had better not be here too.* He thought. He continued down the unfinished steps to the main part of the club and stopped. Ella was sitting on a chair at one of the tables with Lila and a man he did not recognize. He let out a breathy growl. Could Ella have not come alone?

Angelo snapped his fingers as soon as he saw Rafa within distance of where he stood. "What is Lila doing here, and who is that man with them? I wanted Ella to come alone. I'm not in the mood for this bullshit right now."

"Ella asked if I wanted her to bring us food. I told her that would be fine. She brought them along to help carry it inside."

"Well that's great." He pointed. "Now get rid of them and send Ella this way." Angelo walked off to the side; yet even as he stood back, he could see them. He watched closely as Ella smiled at the man. He did not want to see her look at the other man that way. It provoked something in him that he had never felt before. He walked to the table to get rid of them himself.

"Mr. Tomassi," Ella greeted and immediately stood. She must have noticed the annoyed look on his face. Her smile vanished as she stretched out her hand to shake—formalities. "I was finishing an interview. This is Seth. He will be a new bartender at Santiago's."

"I'm going to train him," added Lila as she stood to her feet with Seth doing the same.

"Yes," Ella said. "Seth will be joining Lila behind the bar; then I have one more bartender to hire after that."

"Seth," Angelo said, not bothering to shake his hand.

Seth's arm drew back to his side and he looked at Ella, avoiding Angelo's probing eyes. "So when can I start, Ms. Collins?"

"Be at Santiago's tomorrow at ten. Lila will meet you there and will show you everything you need to know. Plan for a long day. Normal shifts will be from six at night until after two in the morning when everything is cleaned and restocked. Does that work for you?" Ella asked.

"It sure does. I can't wait," Seth said. "I'll see you in the morning. Thank you, Ms. Collins."

"I'm glad you're on board." Ella smiled at him and shook his hand. The shake seemed too endearing for a new employee. Angelo cleared his throat, hinting that their time with Ella was done.

"I have business with Ms. Collins," Angelo said. "Did all of you come in the same car?"

"No," Ella answered for them. "We came in two." Then she turned to Lila. "I'll be back in a little while. See you then."

Lila stopped for a second. She looked at Ella and smiled, devising some remark in her mind until she glanced at Angelo. Her devious expression shifted with a raise of her brow, yet her smirk never left. "Business talk could be fun." Lila could not help herself and whirled around from his glare. "Come on, Seth," she said.

Angelo fumed at the mirth of her tone. She had better watch her mouth around him or she might not have a job. Employees like that were the first to go when business got tight.

After the doors closed, Ella looked back at him. His thoughts were still on Lila and Seth when he finally opened his mouth, Ella interrupting him before he had the chance to speak.

"Mr. Tomassi, I never meant to make you wait. It's that you were busy and Seth showed up when Rafa called. I brought him with me to help, but then I figured that I'd get the interview out of the way."

"That seemed friendlier than the ordinary interview. You're running the restaurant and that was too personal."

"Yes, I understand that, but I feel like I will get the best work if I know more about the employee. It's a method I used when leasing properties."

"No, that's not the method that you'll use when running the restaurant," he countered. "It's much different than persuading someone into spending their money. Restaurant managers need to keep it professional. Do you understand?"

"Yes, I do." Ella yielded with a frown.

"Good," he said and sat down in one of the vacant chairs. "Let's go over these numbers."

"What's wrong with the numbers?" she asked and sat down beside him. Angelo gave her a look that immediately stopped her from speaking more.

"I have a couple of questions. Is the restaurant any busier than it was last month?"

Ella shook her head. "A little but nothing significant."

"All right, then why is there a ten percent increase in profit?" Angelo turned the sheet around and slid it between her hands. Her fingers clenched a little tighter with the closer he neared. It was subtle. She probably did not know she was doing it.

"The new cameras caught one of the cooks on the night shift taking food from the cooler. Then two days later, I saw the bartender put money in his tip jar without entering the order in the computer."

"Did you fire them?" asked Angelo. If she let the employees stay, Ella would not be a suitable manager.

"I had to. I don't want the restaurant to fail. That money adds up."

"Very true...I'm glad you didn't feel sorry for them and let them stay. I would've had to fire you."

"Mr. Tomassi," she began. Another disappointed frown started to form on her lips. "I was saving up to buy the—"

"I wasn't through, Ms. Collins," he interrupted her. Her teeth grit back the words that she wanted to say as Angelo cracked a smile at her pout. "What did you base your salary off of, Ms. Collins?"

"Well, I took an average of what the highest employees were paid and added three percent."

"What time do you get there in the morning?" Angelo asked.

"Around six in the morning."

"And what time do you leave?"

"Sometimes I leave at closing, and sometimes I leave around ten. It depends."

"All right, Ms. Collins. Look, my point is this. You're there any time the restaurant needs you. Plus, your hours are the same as a double shift and you aren't being paid by the hour. Raise your wages by ten percent for now. We'll discuss more about it later."

Angelo reached for the pen stashed in his shirt pocket as he pulled the paperwork back in front of him, but Ella's eyes widened. "Are you sure that isn't too much?" she asked as he marked through a few numbers on the reports.

"Are you serious? I swear you're the only woman who would complain about earning more money. You have a degree. That's a fair amount—maybe even a little low, but I also want to leave room for you to grow and improve."

"Thank you, Mr. Tomassi. You don't know what this opportunity means to me." Ella's voice was sweet and soft. Angelo felt her eyes glued on him as he put down his pen. Her expression said it all—a mixture of awe and genuine appreciation. There was nothing false in her gaze. He could tell that she was trying to make sense of his reason for helping her. Her transparency made her an easy woman to read.

"Rafa," he said and raised his hand. Angelo knew that Rafa was close, keeping a lookout for him. He was probably still wondering what Angelo was doing with Ella. Angelo had to admit, his business with Ella was unusual behavior of him. Warming to her was completely against his nature.

"What?" Rafa asked and walked in front of them both.

"What day do I have open next week?"

Rafa nearly smiled as his brow rose. He looked at Ella and then back at Angelo. "You have Thursday open until one."

Angelo stretched his neck and stood. "Isn't Thursday the same day I'm supposed to meet with my—" Angelo did not finish and stood, brushing off any qualms about the day. "Fine, then so be it," he scoffed at Rafa's antagonistic tone. "Come on," he said to Ella. "I'll walk you to your car."

It was a quiet, short minutes' walk down the stairs. Ella did not speak. There were no words to inflate his ego, no hint that his gesture to walk her out could mean any more than a show of decency—at least to her.

Angelo half-smiled as she unlocked the door to her car. He opened it and waited for her to step in; then he held the door fast, not attempting to shut it back. Angelo hesitated for a moment before he said anything more, Ella looking up at him with the most sincere smile, questioning his reason for staring at her.

"I have Thursday morning open next week. I was thinking about taking a day cruise off the coast of Miami. Would you like to go with me?"

Her smile widened. Angelo thought that such a woman as Ella would be less threatening than the others he knew, but in that instant, her simple smile and earnest gaze proved otherwise. Ella would be his weakness.

"Thank you, Mr. Tomassi. I would like that," she replied.

Chapter 8

Ella ended a call and gazed at the rolling waves out of her office window. They were bold and beautiful under the setting sun, giving her a sense of independence. She had made the decision to go out with Angelo without asking her father's permission. For once, she felt in charge of her life.

Angelo was thinking about taking a day cruise, Ella recalled. *By himself?* She smiled. Was that his way of asking her on a date? Ella looked at the screen to her phone. Angelo had called to confirm their outing for eight the next morning. She wondered if he had ever asked a woman to go out with him. Her eyes looked to the ceiling. Whom was she kidding? Angelo was a gorgeous and intelligent man. He must have gone out with many women. It was logical.

Ella sighed and turned the screen back on to her phone when a prompt for a passcode appeared. It confused her. She turned the phone around and inspected as though she accidentally pressed a button on the back. She never had needed a passcode before. She clicked it off and on again; when that did not work, Ella restarted the phone. Still, the passcode screen showed up.

Ella took a breath and picked up the office phone. The real estate company stayed open until seven. She would have to get the passcode from the company. They must have added it for security on all employees' phones.

"Hello," she said. "Yes, I need to speak to Jacob Sullivan... Okay, is Robert Collins in his office?" Ella slouched. Nobody was there. "All right, this is Ella Collins. I need to talk to someone who can tell me how to get into my phone. There's a passcode and I don't know it."

As the receptionist talked on the other end, Ella's face became warm and then hot. She could not believe what she heard. "What do you mean I'm no longer employed? My father owns the business." Ella tried to stay calm but her frustration began to rise. "Nobody told me they were downsizing. Why would he get rid of his own daughter as an employee? Yes, I understand. I will definitely be calling him, thank you." Ella hung up the phone and mumbled, "Yes, thank you for nothing."

She laid her head on the desk with disbelief. Now her father was cutting all ties with her. He could not stand her so much that he fired her and did not bother to tell her himself. She had worked hard for him. He did not hand anything over to her for free. She earned every penny, working for it much more than his other employees. How could he do that to her?

"Ella." A knock came at her office door.

"Come in," she groaned.

"My shift is over, and I wanted to kn—" Lila stopped mid-word. "What's the matter?" she asked.

"My father fired me," Ella said. "And he didn't even tell me. He cut off my phone and I had to call them."

Lila gave her a sympathetic smile. "Why don't you go out with me? I was about to ask you anyway, and it'll take your mind off your father. I'm headed to Miami to meet my friend Brandi. I think you'll like her."

"I don't know. I have to meet someone at my house in the morning, and I don't want to be out late. I might miss him."

"Him?" asked Lila with a grin. "Are you going on a date?"

"No," Ella tried to lie. Why did she have to open her mouth? "It's a business thing—nothing big."

Lila let out a laugh. "Business…right." She smiled but did not say another word about it. "We won't stay out late, I promise. Are you in?"

Ella looked around. She hardly ever went anywhere. Where was the harm in taking up Lila's offer? "Sure, I'll go, but I'm driving. I have to have my car with me."

"Good, then I'll ride with you."

"All right, but you have to promise that we won't stay too late."

"I promise," said Lila; but by the grin on her lips, Ella was not convinced.

***

Colorful lights flickered against the walls in the darkened room. Chairs filled with people cluttered the aisles as Lila dragged Ella by the hand. She caught a glimpse of a woman in red panties and tassels that covered her nipples. Ella had been intrigued by the bright red sign on the outside. Now she considered how appropriate the name, The Flaming Torch, was for the club.

"Lila," she shouted. "I thought we were going to have a good time."

"Oh, we are." Lila looked back.

"This isn't what I had in mind," Ella said as her eyes lingered on the dancer for a second. "I don't exactly fit in." Ella thought about the pinstriped skirt that she wore. Some of the other women they passed wore short dresses with most of their legs exposed. Even Lila wore a thin-strapped tank and short shorts with heels.

"Relax, after a couple of drinks you won't even notice." Lila stopped moving as a cocktail waitress held out a tray of shots in front of her. "Just what we needed." Lila threw some bills on the tray. "I'm taking four." She turned around, gave Ella two, and then took two off the tray for herself. "Drink up. You need it."

Ella did not know what were in the shots, but she did need something if she was going to stay. "You said you were meeting your friend Brandi, didn't you?"

"Yeah, but she gets off at nine. We passed her on the way in, but she was in the middle of a dance."

"You mean the girl with the tassels?" Ella looked back.

"Yeah, that was her. Let's wait for her at the bar."

For a moment, Ella pondered where she was. Her father would have thrown a fit if he knew. He was always on guard when it came to crowds. It made Ella do the same. She looked around and scanned the crowd as her father used to do. It seemed everyone was enthralled with the dancers and their cocktails. There would probably be little to worry about other than moving out of the way for a fight.

Ella turned back around as the bartender approached where they stood. "How're you doing, sweetheart?" he asked Lila. "And who's your friend?"

"Robby, this is Ella. Ella, this is my boyfriend, Robby."

"Hello," greeted Ella.

"Hey," Robby said. "I know what Lila wants, but she'll have to wait 'til my shift ends. How about you?"

Ella stared at his spiked brown hair and the devious smirk on his face. He was more open than she would have liked. If she were Lila,

Ella might take offense, but Lila did not care and was all smiles as she leaned over and flashed her breasts for his gawking eyes.

"I'll have a glass of merlot. What do you have in your private stock?" she asked.

Both Robby and Lila's heads turned sideways and stared at her. Did she ask for something unusual? Ella could not figure out where their confusion stemmed. "Honey, we carry liquor and beer—no wine," said Robby. Ella frowned at his statement. Was it so odd to ask for wine? Why did they not carry wine anyway? "Mixed drinks," he added. "You know what they are, don't you? You take your favorite liquor or liquors and mix it with tonic or soda or something like that."

If Ella did not know better, she would think he was making fun of her by the humored tone in his voice. Should she play dumb or return his subtle insult? Ella looked him in the eyes and gave him her sweetest smile. "Then I'll have an embassy cocktail. It's a complicated drink. I hope you know how to make it. If you don't, I'll gladly show you how."

Robby chuckled and grabbed a glass from the bar. "Your sarcasm is noted." He smiled. "And I think I can manage, thanks."

"My boss is something else, isn't she?" Lila pointed out. "You think she's nice until you say something that gets under her skin."

"This drink is on me," Robby said. "I think you'll fit right in here."

No, probably not. Ella thought but smiled when she took the drink. There was absolutely no way she would ever fit in with this crowd if she wanted. She was surprised that one of her father's assistants had not barged in yet to carry her off. That was what happened when she was in college, and it was still a mystery to Ella about how they knew where she was.

"Hey, Lila." Brandi approached. A sleek short dress replaced her red tassels. A hair tie now pulled up her long brown hair that showed off her bleached blond tips. "Hey Robby, give me a shot of tequila. After that last table, I need it," she said.

"Well, what'd you expect with your new outfit? Even I had to fan myself." Robby opened his mouth and waved his hand in front.

"Yeah, but I know that you won't try to touch. Lila will keep you in line."

"Yep." Lila glared at Robby in jest. "But you did look hot out there. You can't be all that surprised."

"The new outfit was a hit, and"—Brandi felt Ella's eyes on her and pointed—"what are you staring at?"

Was she staring? Ella thought she was listening to their conversation. Ella found it interesting that Lila did not seem to care if her boyfriend was looking at the dancers. Ella would not like it at all.

"Ella," she said and held out her hand to Brandi. "I came with Lila."

Brandi shook hands and looked at Ella, scanned her white buttoned blouse and then looked back at Lila. "I can't believe you brought her in those clothes. She looks like a virgin preschool teacher."

Ella's brows rose as she smoothed down nonexistent wrinkles on her skirt. Was that how she came across to people—a virgin? Even if she was, they did not have to know it was true. She acted as though the comment did not faze her at all.

"It'll get me free drinks then." She held out her glass and took another sip.

Brandi's face darted back to Ella. Her eyes lit up with the wide smirk forming on her lips. "You and I should hang out more. My favorite word is free."

Ella smiled. She would have laughed except Brandi's expression showed that she was serious. Ella was not sure what to make of Brandi yet. She typically did not like people who did not intend to pay for themselves.

"Well, I'm finished with my shift tonight, Lila. Why don't you and Ella come back to my place? I have a couple of bottles at home and I need a shower."

"I'm in," said Lila. "Are you, Ella?"

"I'd better not. I have to be up early," Ella said.

"Oh..." Lila smiled. "That's right. Ella has a date in the morning."

"You have a date in the morning?" Brandi exclaimed. "What kind of loser takes you out in the morning? Where's the fun in that?"

Ella shook her head. "Thanks, Lila."

"Sorry, Ella." Lila's bottom lip stuck out.

"And you're going to leave me here alone?" Robby said, making the women look back over at him.

"I forgot that you were even there," Brandi laughed. "You always see Lila. It's my turn."

"Sorry, babe." Lila gave him a quick kiss on the lips. "You don't get out until closing anyway."

"Fine, but don't have too much fun without me."

"Never, babe." Lila blew him a kiss as he moved to help another customer.

***

When the women exited the club, there was not an empty space in the parking lot. Ella had already parked away from the building, but with the spaces filled beyond where she parked, she was glad that she remembered the aisle number.

"I parked on number eight," she said as Brandi and Lila followed her to her car, a bouncer behind them making sure they were safe.

Ella stopped in front of her Civic and stared. Her car leaned slightly to the left. With something not right in the lean, Ella took a few steps to get a closer look.

"Ella, you have a flat." Lila pointed.

Ella gazed at the left front tire. It was not only flat, but the rim touched the pavement. Ella wondered how the tire could have lost air that fast. Then she saw the left rear tire.

"Did you piss someone off?" Lila added to her aggravation.

Ella reflected on who would have done such a thing. Her father might not approve of where she was, but he would have made her leave—not kept her from going.

"I don't know what to think," Ella replied. Having one flat tire would be bad luck...but two. It appeared intentional. "I'll have to come back in the morning when the tire shops open. I'll have to call someone for a ride tonight."

"No need," Brandi said. "How far away do you live?"

"About twenty minutes in Key Biscayne."

"I'll give you a ride then. Come on."

Ella nodded while looking back. It made no sense. She never made anyone mad—not mad enough to follow her to a club and flatten her tires. Who would have sabotaged her car?

Chapter 9

Angelo pulled onto a narrow paved street and drove for about a mile from the main road. Ella's beach house was in a private, secluded area. Her family must have liked their privacy when they vacationed in Key Biscayne. There was not another house in sight.

The street ended with a small parking space that reached a couple of palm trees. The tiny house must have had one bedroom—maybe two. Wooden piers held the house up high. A concrete walkway led to the house and parted; on one end, it stretched across a short bridge to the empty beach. The other reached a long white stairway that led to Ella's front door.

Angelo turned off the ignition and got out of his car. He gazed at the sand dunes surrounding her house as he climbed up the sturdy white steps. It really was a private place, almost dangerous for a single woman to live. If she had to leave in a hurry, it would take a couple of minutes to get to her car. Angelo stopped and looked around. Where was her car?

Angelo knocked on the front door and waited. The door was average size, and there were no chips in the paint. It pleased him that she kept the house up to date. The porch was small, yet there was enough room for a swing. He pictured Ella outside and swinging, relaxing with the sound of the waves. At the same time, if someone were mad at her, she would be an easy target to track. It was part of his nature to think ahead for dangerous situations. Ella was probably in no danger at all.

"Hello, Mr. Tomassi," she said and opened the door. "Would you like to come inside?"

Angelo glanced at the small sofa that was big enough for two people. If he went in, he would likely be a threat to her in the secluded space. "No." He took a step back. "Are you ready to leave?"

"I'm ready." Ella ducked behind the door and grabbed the strap to her purse.

Angelo turned to the ocean and waited for the door to click shut before he spoke again. "I noticed you're car is gone. Is it being worked on?"

"Well—" Ella started walking and reached the steps before glancing back. "I went out with Lila last night. We couldn't have been inside for more than an hour. When I came back out, both of my left tires were flat."

"Both of them?" asked Angelo. "Where did you go?"

Ella hesitated on her way down. She did not want to tell him the truth. He already did not like Lila and would not like where they went.

"Well?" he repeated.

"A club in Miami." She tried to avoid the name.

"Which club?" he persisted.

Ella blew out a puff of air. "The Flaming Torch," she mumbled.

Yes, he knew of the place. He should. His father used to own it, and it was in no way a suitable place for Ella. "You didn't know what kind of a club it was, did you?" Angelo looked at her and opened the passenger door of his black Mercedes.

"No," she answered. "It wasn't that bad, though. I met a couple of Lila's friends."

"Not that bad," Angelo scoffed and shut her door, moving around the car to the driver's side and opening his. "That club is on one of the most dangerous streets in Miami. It's risky to walk through the parking lot much less going inside? Lila wouldn't have been able to protect you. You should have gotten right back inside your car when you realized what kind of club it was."

"I couldn't leave her there."

"Why not? She'd gone there before. You said she had friends."

"Mr. Tomassi," Ella protested.

Not letting her finish, Angelo held up his finger to her and took out his phone. "Brett, where are you?" He nodded. "Good, you and Sammy meet me at The Flaming Torch. I'm about twenty minutes out."

"What are you doing?" Ella asked.

"You think I'm going to let you go back there by yourself?"

"It's my problem. It was probably kids. I'm not a target."

Angelo looked over at her as he entered the causeway. Was she really that naïve? Did she not understand the dangers of Miami? "Oh, you mean because a woman in a pretty dress who stands outside of a strip club won't attract attention."

Ella glanced at him with her lips pressed together. "Now you're making me feel bad. I was with Lila. It would've been rude to leave her by herself."

Angelo knew how coldhearted he could be, but he could not help it. He did not want Ella to get hurt, so he was taking responsibility for fixing her car to make sure she was safe. He hated to think of the potential danger she would be in by herself.

When he pulled into the club, a few cars speckled the lot. He noticed they did not have flat tires, so the offense likely belonged to Ella alone. Brett and Sammy were already waiting for him to arrive. As soon as he stopped in front of Ella's car, they pulled to a stop next to him.

"You wait in here." He pointed at Ella. "I don't want you to get your white dress dirty."

He stepped out and motioned for Brett to do the same. Brett followed him to the driver's side of her car. "Go look at the rear tire, Brett. I'll look at this one." He squatted down and strummed his fingers against the outside. The tread looked brand new. There were no reflections from nails or screws, and no damage to the valve, yet the tire's rims touched the ground.

"Brett, did you find anything on that one?"

He watched Brett get low on the pavement and start feeling the back of the tire. Brett was a faithful member. He did everything that Angelo said—no questions asked. It had been two years since Brett saw Angelo shoot a guy outside a local gas station. Instead of running scared, he banged on Angelo's car window and asked for a job. The gun Angelo pointed at his head did not shake him. Nothing did. No matter what slew of curses Angelo shouted, Brett gave a determined grin. Angelo either had to shoot him or hire him, so he let Brett in the car.

"Boss," Brett said. "Somebody stabbed the back of the tire." Brett got up and went to the front of the car. It took him a few seconds before he spoke again. "They stabbed this one too. It's a clean cut. They knew what they were doing."

"All right, call Regg. Tell him to have one of his men come fix it." Angelo walked back to his car and opened Ella's door. "Someone slashed your tires. Do you know who it could be?"

Ella slowly shook her head back and forth. "I thought about that last night, but I couldn't come up with anyone. It didn't make sense to me."

"Well, somebody's mad at you—probably hoping to catch you alone when you left. Since you parked so far away from the front door, I doubt the cameras picked up anything. You need to start being more careful from now on. Go ahead and give me your key."

"But I can't let you fix my car. It's my problem."

"Brett's already on the phone with the shop I use. No point in arguing with me. When they're finished, they'll drive the car to the restaurant."

"No wait time." Ella reflected. "You must be well known."

"You could say that," said Angelo. "It's all a given in my work."

Chapter 10

Ella observed Angelo's demeanor as he pulled next to a dock and parked in front of several small cruise ships. The veins in his arms were not as defined. His stern expression and the creases around his mouth seemed to relax. His breathing was steady—calm. A small part of her hoped that being around her put him at ease. It must have been hard for him to let down his guard with anyone at all. Maybe the company he worked for kept him on edge.

"Have you ever been on a day cruise?" he asked and looked over at her.

"I've never been on any kind of a ship," she admitted. "I haven't done a lot in my life." She glanced out of the front window as the scent of his cologne awakened her senses, reminding her that she was alone with him on a date.

"Then you should enjoy this." He stepped out and opened her door. "This boat normally fits thirty, but it's only us this morning. It'll take about an hour to finish, so make sure you have everything you need." Ella showed him her purse and slipped it around her head, letting it fall diagonally to her side. "All right then." Angelo's hand touched her shoulder and guided her as though protecting her from the unknown. She briefly thought about her flat tires when the warmth of his body kept brushing against her as they walked. His closeness distracted her; it made her forget about everything else.

Angelo stepped over the water from the dock to the boat and held out his hand to help her across. With her hand still in his, Angelo led her to the back of the ship. There was a long, gray cushioned bench where Angelo sat, waiting as the ship started to move. Instead of sitting, Ella walked to the metal rail, gazing at the wake the ship left behind.

"I'll bet this ride is beautiful when the sun sets too." Ella glanced back at him, noticing he paid little attention to the passing scenery. Even though he seemed relaxed, Angelo showed no hint of pleasure for the sea. His hands rested nimbly on his lap; his facial features appeared clouded—almost sad. Ella stared at him closer, analyzing him and trying to read his thoughts. He knew so many people, yet the vibe she received from the blank look was almost the same as what she felt most of the time—loneliness.

Ella felt sorry for him. In a spontaneous move, she sat down next to him and looped her arm through his, waiting for his reaction. Angelo's arm flinched but then relaxed with her touch. She was glad that he did not push her away.

"They should have drinks here. Do you want a cup of coffee?" she asked. If nothing else, the hand-to-mouth motions with the cup would help distract his mind.

Angelo nodded. "I'll take some coffee and cream—no sugar."

"I'll be right back," she said with a smile.

Angelo stared at her as she walked away. How could one little woman cause him so much distress? Ella probably thought he was having a bad time or thinking about work. Little did she know, he was thinking of her. A smile flashed across his lips. If she made him a good cup of coffee, he could tell Rafa that Ella would be the perfect wife. That was Rafa's biggest complaint with Angelo's former interest. According to Rafa, the coffee predicted the future.

Angelo crossed his arms and leaned back. Why was he thinking about Ella for a wife? She deserved better than the life he would offer. From losing her mother to being on her own without the help of family, Ella was finally getting a taste of freedom. Who was he to take that away? Yet he could not let go of the idea either.

A few minutes later, Ella handed him a tall cup of coffee. "Maybe that will make you feel better." She smiled and walked back to the rail. Angelo cautiously took a sip; then another.

Perfect. He smiled in thought. Ella made his coffee exactly the way he liked. Maybe Rafa's ridiculous reasoning meant something after all.

"Mr. Tomassi, you don't seem to be enjoying the view at all," Ella said, glancing back at him. "Why come on a day cruise if you're going to sit?"

"I'm enjoying the view fine," he countered with a smirk. If she had not turned back to the water, she would have seen the satisfied look in his eyes. He felt an overwhelming urge to walk behind her and wrap his arms around her waist. Angelo wondered how she would react to that so soon.

The thought humored him. Unlike anyone else he had met, Ella had a way of making him smile and she did not even know it. He could not resist the tranquil grin on her face as she gazed at whatever attractions they passed.

"Look." He pointed and stood up to join her. "There's Santiago's."

"Hm," she hummed. "It looks even more glamorous in the morning sun than it does from the parking lot. Do you think you'll ever sell it?"

"I have someone in mind. It depends on when she's ready to take over. I'll wait until that happens."

"Really?" Ella turned her entire body to look at him. She had no idea that he was standing directly behind her and bumped him with her breasts. She blushed and tried to gain her composure, standing up as Angelo tried not to laugh. He could not help smiling with the horrified shock on her face. His smile made her face flush more; Ella's red cheeks caused him to chuckle.

"I'm sorry," Ella apologized and stepped away. Her voice betrayed her embarrassment.

"It's fine." Angelo wrapped his arm around her shoulder and pulled her to his side. "I'm not hurt," he emphasized. Such a simple bump caused Ella to go silent. It was not that big of a deal. Angelo wondered if she had ever been on a date before. "So," he cleared his throat to redirect her thoughts, "have you talked to your father since you started managing Santiago's?" he asked.

"No. My work phone stopped working yesterday. I called the company I was leasing for, and they told me they didn't need me anymore. My father fired me and couldn't even tell me himself."

"Wait a minute. You worked for your father?"

"Yes," Ella mumbled. "It wasn't a free paycheck, though. I worked hard for what I got. Everything we did as a family was for show. At home, my father was always having some private meeting in his office. We rarely saw him in the house."

Angelo ran his fingers through his hair and pulled the strands back in place. If she were not running the restaurant, Ella would have no way to take care of herself. Her father was not earning any points with him.

"So...when will you be opening the hotel?" she asked, tired of talking about her father.

"Hotel?" He looked up and thought. "Oh...you mean the nightclub."

"Hm," said Ella. "That explains the remodeled awning and the tables at the entrance. It looks beautiful by the way. How long will it take to open?"

"Thank you. I guess I'm looking at another six to eight weeks. I'll know more in a few days after I get the last few estimates for the interior."

"Have you picked out a name yet?"

"Illusions," he said and held out his hand to her as the ship's speed started to slow. It seemed like a thoughtful gesture, but Angelo wanted an excuse to hold her hand.

"Illusions," she repeated. "Couldn't that have hidden meanings— things being different than how they seem. It sounds like my life." She smiled.

"It's all in perception, Ella," he said.

"Yes," she agreed. Her eyes lit up at hearing him call her by name. "It's always about perception, isn't it?"

Chapter 11

Back inside the Mercedes, Ella noticed that Angelo was not taking her to Santiago's. They had passed the causeway leading to the Keys and Angelo did not bother to enter. She glanced at the bridge and back at him, waiting for him to answer her unasked question. His eyes faced the road. His expression was so much more serious than it was on the cruise. It was almost a look of dread.

Ten minutes later, they pulled into a large parking lot near the beach. A long wooden ramp connected a restaurant that extended over the water. Angelo turned off the ignition. His slow movements alarmed Ella as he looked at her and stopped. What was he thinking? He was hesitant in his thoughts.

"We'll have lunch here. There's a man—" He paused and seemed to consider his words carefully. "I'm here to meet a man for business and decided to bring you along. I wouldn't have had enough time to bring you back to Santiago's and still be here on time."

"My flat tires caused that, didn't they? Won't I get in the way of your meeting?"

"No, it's fine if you're here, but only talk if we ask you a question. Can you do that?" he asked but tapped on the wheel. Angelo had obvious concerns about bringing her with him.

"I can handle that," she agreed.

"Good." Angelo nodded and stepped out. "I think you'll like it here anyway. I told them to give me a table on the back wall. You'll be able to see the water through the windows there."

After he opened her door, his hand stretched out, his eyes locked onto her face. Ella was unable to stop staring back. They were close when he helped her from her seat—close enough for her to feel the heat radiate off his skin as he stood a mere inch from her face. Her heart beat fast against her chest. She wanted his kiss.

"Come." He turned his face away and grabbed her hand instead. Ella let out a silent sigh and followed. He probably did not kiss her because she was shaking. He thought she was afraid. That was what she told herself. Any other reason would upset her.

Inside the restaurant, soft Italian music set the tone in the dimly lit dining room; round mahogany tables were arranged in neat rows throughout the room. The décor indicated genuine designs out of Italy. Everything about the restaurant hinted at its authenticity.

Angelo spoke a couple of foreign words to the hostess before they followed her to the back of the room. There were a few diners around but not many. The time showed after one so the lunch rush had ended shortly before.

A gruff-looking older man stood when Angelo approached. He stared at Ella, especially when Angelo pulled out a chair for her to sit. Then both men sat and said nothing to the other. Ella wondered what kind of business meeting this was, because it was like none she had ever seen.

"Would you like a glass of wine?" a server asked Angelo. The other man at the table already had a glass of red wine in front of him.

"What about you?" he turned to Ella. She wondered if she should drink wine this early in the day. "It'll be fine," he said, reading her thoughts.

"I have a wine menu," said the server.

"No, I won't need one, thank you. I'll have a glass of chardonnay…maybe one similar to Pierre Matrot."

"We have that on the menu…and you, Mr. Tomassi? Will you have the usual?" Ella thought about it. Angelo had been here before; maybe he was well known at every restaurant.

"Yes," he answered and waited for her to walk away. "Ella, this is Antonio," he introduced.

Antonio held out his hand which Ella graciously shook. "Ella," he said. Antonio stared in her eyes and watched her closely. "What kind of work do you do, Ella?"

"I," she started but paused. When did the meeting between Angelo and Antonio turn into a personal interrogation? Ella looked at Angelo who nodded for her to answer. "I run a restaurant on Key Biscayne," she said as the server set down their glasses of wine.

"Will you need a few minutes?"

"No," give us two of your chef's specials." Then Angelo looked at Ella. "Is lobster okay with you?"

"Sounds good," she said.

"That does sound good. Make it three," Antonio added, continuing with his thought as the server walked away. "So…now it makes sense. Santiago's? Right?"

"Yes." Ella wondered how Antonio knew the name.

"Do you live in the Keys or Miami or some other town close by?"

"Right now, I live in Key Biscayne," she answered.

Antonio nodded. "And how do you know Angelo?"

"Well...he called about a beach property in Key Biscayne and I showed it to him."

"Did you also show him Santiago's? I understand that he bought the restaurant."

Ella did not know what to say. Why did Antonio ask her all these questions? It caught her off guard after the relaxing morning she had with Angelo. Ella felt relieved when Angelo cut in and did not let her answer.

"That was my own doing. I asked for a tour and Ella knew the owner. It was a private sale without an agent."

"A restaurant, Angelo? You talked about the beach property."

Angelo took a drink of his wine and returned Antonio's serious expression. Ella did not want to be in the middle of a fight. The conversation looked like it could turn to an argument.

"It was a last-minute decision. I made an exception this time." An unspoken understanding passed between the two with the seconds that followed. Antonio's frown proved he was not pleased.

The food finally arrived to take some focus off the escalating tension. Other than a few glances at the men, Ella kept her eyes on her plate. It was not until Angelo pushed his plate to the side that anyone bothered to speak.

"Angelo," Antonio said and stood. "I need to talk to you—outside."

Flinging his napkin to his seat, he closed his eyes, gritting his teeth as he stood. He did not look at Ella and followed Antonio to the balcony outside. She watched both men walk to the rail with scowls on their faces, an immediate exchange of words to follow.

"Angelo," his father said. "Why would you buy a no-name restaurant for that woman when it will bring you nothing but pennies? This isn't like you."

"I used my own money. The restaurant has nothing to do with the group." Angelo defended his decision.

"Fine. Do whatever you want with your money. I can see that you like her, but I'm not sure why you brought her to meet me."

Angelo looked up at the passing clouds; his father knew very well why he brought Ella to meet him. "Your approval," he said.

Antonio leaned against the rail and shook his head. "Approval for what? To seduce her? To make her your mistress?"

"You know why. If you didn't, you wouldn't have talked to her like you did."

"I did that because she's with you. Can't be too careful. I like her though. She's polite. She knows her wine. She'll be a beautiful woman on your arm. Go ahead. Show her off, but she can't be your wife."

"She needs protection if she's with me. She doesn't get that unless we're married. I can't do that to her. She'll need protection from the group."

"Look, Son...you can't marry who you want. It's all about our name, about what's best for it. That's the way it works." Antonio took out a cigar. Angelo could feel the burn in his chest at his father's way of dismissing the discussion.

"I'm not marrying Gregorio's daughter," said Angelo. "I won't."

Antonio sighed, "The marriage has already been decided, Angelo. It'll be good for business and relations. Why do you make me repeat myself?" He paused and pointed inside. "She's beautiful. Her manners are perfect. Buy her a house. Give her half your nights. Keep her close and watch out for her yourself." Antonio stubbed his barely-touched cigar and tossed it in the metal can. "Either you do that or give her up. You won't get my blessing to marry her."

Angelo looked back inside as Ella looked out. They made eye contact. The innocent look she gave made him feel worse. She might not be able to handle the mafia much less to become his mistress.

"Son, if you can't follow the rules, maybe I should have chosen someone else to take my place. You made an oath and now you're trying to back out. You're showing signs of weakness. It won't be long before the group sees it too. If you want to keep that respect, then do what I say."

Antonio scooted past Angelo to the door and back into the restaurant, leaving Angelo alone on the patio. As his father drank the rest of his wine, he said something to Ella and grabbed his keys. Angelo waited for him to leave before returning to his seat.

"Are you finished with your food?" he asked as he handed over a card to the server.

"Yes, thank you," Ella replied, seeming confused about what had happened. His change of expression and the argument between him and his Antonio put her on edge. If she only knew the reason for the visit.

Angelo had a hard time looking at Ella while waiting for his card. Having her next to him would make it that much harder for him to give her up. He had to face reality. She would not be able to handle life as a mistress. It did not suit her at all.

All the way back to Santiago's, Angelo submersed himself in silence. He did not want to hear her voice. She would make him falter. He needed to put her out of his mind so he could cope with the rest of the day.

Once they made it to the restaurant, Angelo opened the car door and walked her to the entrance. He paused a second to look in Ella's eyes; her gaze questioned his next move.

"I will send Brett to collect the reports tomorrow. I will be too busy to come myself." He had thought of the quick excuse but took no pleasure in the words.

"All right, but would you like to go somewhere again sometime...when you're not busy with work?" she asked, but her tone showed that she already figured out the answer.

"I can't. There's too much going on right now for me to get away." Angelo could see the disappointment in her eyes as he swallowed, quickly turning away. He should have never asked Ella on a date in the first place. She was forming an attachment to him way too soon...or was he the one forming the attachment to her?

Chapter 12

Ella yawned as she picked her head up off her desk at work. Her hair scattered in disarray, making some loose papers fall to the floor as she sat up in the chair. She looked around, disoriented with where she was. This was the fourth day in a row that she had done this, yet it was the first time she did not wake up until morning.

Working was the only thing that seemed to keep her mind in check. Her father would not talk to her, and it had been several weeks since her date with Angelo. She was not sure what happened or why he suddenly lost interest. If it were not for the reports, she probably would not have seen him at all. It was not hard to understand why she worked so much. She found it difficult to stay in a completely silent house with no one to keep her company. She did not like being alone all the time.

The clock on the wall showed half past seven. Ella panicked. That meant the delivery truck had been outside for thirty minutes, waiting for her to unlock the door. She could now clearly hear the banging on the back wall. It was probably what jarred her awake.

She combed through her hair. Yesterday's business suit would have to do. There was no time for her to go back home now.

"I'm coming," she shouted and grabbed a full set of keys. She ran through the empty restaurant, through the kitchen and to the back door. "I'm so sorry," she said when she saw a man standing in front. "It has been a hectic week."

"Must have been." He smiled. He had nice blue eyes with wavy brown hair over his ears. The strands kept blowing onto his face. "Did you sleep here last night?" he asked.

Ella let out a breath and gave a sheepish grin. "Yes, is it that obvious?"

The man chuckled and reached for Ella's hair. "I don't think I would have been able to tell except for these three paperclips."

Ella laughed. "That's one way to give myself away, isn't it? You're new, aren't you? I'm Ella. Please come in."

"Caleb," he said and pulled a blue dolly through the door. "Where would you like these crates put?"

Ella took a breath and yawned again. "I'm sorry. I haven't been able to sleep lately. Set them by the piano in the dining room. Oh, and please don't block the door."

He smiled at her. Caleb had nice smile. Any smile that Ella could get was welcomed. "I would think that was common sense."

"You would think, but the last driver not only blocked the door, he set a crate on top of the antique piano."

Caleb laughed. "I guess that's one reason they hired me."

Ella nodded in agreement. "If you need me, I'll be picking the staples out of my clothes." She grinned and walked away. Caleb was a friendly man. She enjoyed their short chat, but for now, she had to go to her car. She had left a ream of copy paper in the back seat that she needed to print out Angelo's reports.

Ella exited through the back door. Her car should have been alone in the employee parking lot, but there was another car parked next to hers. She shrugged it off. It probably belonged to one of the employees who went out the night before. They did it all the time.

When Ella approached her car, she heard the window of the car next to her roll down. She spun around to see who was inside. A man sat behind the wheel with another in the passenger's seat.

"Good morning, Ella."

Ella stared at them a moment. She tried to match the faces and brown combed hair with anyone that used to visit her father. They looked familiar. She had seen them a couple of times when she passed by her father's office. No doubt, he knew about her strip club rendezvous, and they were here to deliver a message. Ella shook her head and waited. Her father had cut off ties. His words meant nothing to her after all this time.

"May I help you?" she asked. "I have a lot of work to do."

"Your father told us to find you here."

"Okay? I'm kind of surprised that he still keeps up with me."

"Robert said you were seen with a man a few weeks ago. He wants you to stay away from Tomassi."

"You mean my father who fired me a few weeks ago?"

"He didn't have a choice. He closed the doors on that location."

"I was told he downsized. Now you're saying he closed the business. How many realty companies does he own? A dozen? He could have transferred me to any one of them. Did the other employees get moved, or did they lose their jobs too?" The man behind the wheel hesitated to answer. "That's what I thought," Ella mumbled.

The man shrugged. "We had nothing to do with any of that."

"Why don't you tell me why he sent you?" Ella folded her arms across her chest, feeling uncomfortable with standing in front of them.

"He wants you to cut contact with Tomassi. He's a dangerous man."

"No." Ella frowned. "I wouldn't have a job if it weren't for him. Tell my father the next time he has a message for me; he can come himself. I'm not dealing with you anymore, whoever you are to him." Ella stopped and thought. She opened the door of her car and reached inside, grabbing a pen and napkin from the console. "Give my father my new number and thank him for cutting off my phone."

The men seemed surprised by her tone. The driver yanked the napkin from her hand and rolled up the window, turning the ignition back on as he did. There was no further exchange of words.

After they drove out of view, Ella put her hand over her heart. She could not believe she talked as she did. If her father showed up tomorrow, that would be the end of the Keys.

She grabbed the copy paper and slammed the back door to her car. As if there were not enough worries, Brett would be there any minute to pick up the reports. It would take her at least thirty minutes to prepare them and print them out.

"Ms. Collins."

Ella threw the copy paper to the ground and whirled around to see Angelo a few feet away. Her heart was beating hard already. Even a soft voice would have startled her, but Angelo's strong tone sent her into a panic. He must have parked in the front.

"I'm sorry. The reports aren't printed," she said and bent down to get the paper.

"Who were the men who sped out of here?" he asked.

"Nobody," she answered. What was she going to tell him—her father wanted her to cut off contact with him? How would that work?

"Nobody," he repeated. "Then why don't you have the reports ready? I thought I made myself clear about them."

"Yes, you did. I'm sorry. I've been working a lot lately and I meant to have them printed, but I fell asleep at my desk last night while I was getting them ready."

"You slept here?" he asked.

"I know. There's been a lot of work. I hired an assistant to help me, replaced another cook and found two new servers. The restaurant is busier than it used to be. I could bring the reports to you when they're ready."

Angelo shook his head. "You open in an hour. Do whatever you need to do today; I'll come back tonight."

"Thank you. I'll have them ready," she said, watching Angelo nod and walk off.

***

Fuck. Angelo thought as he pulled into Santiago's, the evening sky already beginning to darken. He could not keep Ella off his mind no matter how much he had avoided her. It was wrong of him to want her. Her freedom would be gone in his world. He doubted she could handle his life in the first place. It also went against his father's wishes. Even though he despised Gregorio, a part of him did respect what his father wanted for him. Everyone and everything kept reminding him that she was the wrong woman to pursue, but it did not seem to matter...he still wanted Ella.

Angelo walked through the front entrance and up to the bar. He looked through their wine menu and ordered a glass of cabernet, noting the updates to the list. Ella had expanded the menu. The classical music that played over the intercom created a relaxing environment. The restaurant now seemed more upscale than it had during his first visit.

He gazed around at the guests in the dining room. They wore formal dress, enjoying their wine and appetizers. Two women smiled happily as they indulged on a shrimp cocktail. Angelo saw that his money had gone to a good cause. He would not regret his splurge on the restaurant.

Where was Ella? It was unusual that she was not waiting for him as she did the first time he arrived. Angelo stepped away from the bar to hunt her down. He walked to her office and found the door locked;

then he went to the old piano and peeked inside the cellar—no Ella. He crossed his arms, careful to hold his glass of wine upright. He should have checked the patio first. Of course, she was there. That was where she waited for him before.

When he exited onto the patio, he noticed Ella not waiting for him at all. She was sitting with a man in a dark navy suit who held his own glass of wine. Angelo's temper flared. He moved to the rail at the other end, turning his back to the ocean as he watched their interaction.

He tapped the metal bars beside him, contemplating whether to leave her alone or sever the man's head. He waited instead, knowing that he was probably jumping to conclusions, which was...until the man slipped a kiss onto her hand.

His teeth clenched together at someone other than him touching her hand or any other part of her body; his eyes would not leave their spot. The man had nerve to kiss what he had already claimed even if it were in his thoughts. The gesture bothered Angelo more than it should. Every muscle in his body stiffened with every vein swelling. As much as he wanted to unload a clip in the man, he refrained; but he was not going to stick around and watch the man seduce her. Angelo simply walked out.

He had barely reached his Mercedes again when the sound of her heels resonated behind him. He turned around, angered that she would come after him. If Ella knew he was there, she should have acknowledged him inside.

"Mr. Tomassi." Her voice was soft and remorseful as she caught up to him. "I have the reports. Please, don't leave."

"I don't need them anymore."

"But I was trying to hurry with the new sommelier; the meeting ran over."

It was the wine sommelier. Angelo thought. Ella should reconsider her choice and choose someone who acted more professional. She should have recognized his seductive ways.

"It was not like it looked. He was being polite."

"You don't have to explain anything to me," Angelo said. "We aren't dating." His words came out as uncaring and matched the hardened expression that masked how he felt. He was too different from her. Being cold was what he did best. Ella would not be able to cope.

"No," she stopped short and shook her head, "we are not."

Angelo could not make up his mind. One minute, he justified seeing her; the next, he found a reason to leave. He unlocked his car door and fell to the seat, wasting no time in turning the key. In a last attempt to lighten the situation, he rolled down his window halfway and looked at her disappointed expression. "Good night, Ella."

"Good night, Mr. Tomassi," she whispered.

Chapter 13

Ella glanced at the invitation on the passenger seat of her car. Why would Angelo send her an invitation to the grand opening of Illusions when he barely spoke to her in weeks? Did he really want to see her? Was it guilt? Maybe it meant nothing at all. He probably sent one to every business in the area, and it had nothing to do with her.

She also would not pass up the opportunity to find out and pulled up to the night club. The building glowed with its lustrous lights and large sign, attracting a full crowd who were eager to take part in opening night.

After five minutes, she finally found a spot. Ella carefully gathered the material of her long red dress and stepped out of her car in a pair of clear-strapped heels. She had hoped there would be an occasion to wear her mother's dress. It was one of the only items she managed to snatch before her father got rid of her mother's belongings.

She handed her invitation to the attendant at the door. The place bragged of costly oak finishes, marbled pool tables, and exquisite lighting. There must have been substantial amounts of money behind the company that Angelo worked for; they spared no expense for massive room. The chandelier looked like genuine crystal.

"What can I get you tonight?" a bartender asked, ignoring the line of customers that were there before her.

"A margarita," she said, mesmerized by the gorgeous bottles placed perfectly in cubbies above him with sparkling wine glasses hanging within an arm's reach. The warm lighting cast a pleasant glow off the bottles, the shine reflecting off the bar-top veneer.

"Ice and salt?" he asked. Ella nodded. While she waited, she noticed the old stairway that used to lead to the upper floors of the hotel. She wondered what Angelo created at the top of those stairs for the club. If the main floor was any indication of its potential, she could imagine the grandeur that waited for her.

She took her margarita, walked past the restrooms and started up the stairs at the end. The higher she went, the more excited she grew. At halfway, she passed a large tinted door that must have been for invitations only—the VIP room. Even if she had a pass, she could not help but continue to the top.

At the end of the staircase, she pushed open a mahogany door, one of two that towered above her. She stood in the doorway a moment, her breath taken by the flickering lights that cast down on the beach below. She could see for miles and drifted onto one of the marble benches, pleased with the quiet escape. The rooftop view allowed her to see in every direction, making the view from her own front porch seem dull. The full moon shining down was a scene out of a movie.

"What are you doing here?"

Ella glanced at the door. Angelo looked more muscular and tan than she had noticed before, but he was not there to enjoy the romantic setting. By his distant expression and tone of his voice, he did not seem pleased to see her.

"I didn't send myself an invitation," she said, "and I didn't sneak into the club either."

"Rafa," he mumbled. Angelo seemed irritated as he turned around and looked at the door as though he needed to scold someone for the mishap.

"Is there something wrong with me being here?" she asked as he turned the knob but stopped. He looked at the sky and thought in silence before letting out an aggravated breath. "I want to know if you have a problem with me, Mr. Tomassi?"

Letting the door close again, he moved toward her and sat down on the opposite end of the bench. "That depends." He propped his foot over his left leg and leaned back, stretching his arm across the top.

"What depends? I don't know what I've done to get this cold—"

"It depends on how deeply you want to get involved?" He cut her off. "Your freedom, Ella. Do you like being able to do what you want? Running the restaurant?"

Frustrated with his cryptic meaning, Ella shifted sideways and matched his gaze. "How does my freedom or the restaurant have anything to do with—"

"Everything," he said. "And for your own happiness, it would be better for you to leave me alone."

Angelo stood and threw the ice from his glass over the rail. Conflicted with his thoughts, he gave Ella another look, his eyes lingering on her for seconds. Then he shook his head and left, leaving Ella disappointed and confused as the door slammed behind him.

***

Outside on the balcony, Angelo flipped open his cigarette case and glowered at Rafa across the table from him. He didn't know what Rafa was trying to pull but sending her an invitation was a bad move. "Who were you on the phone with?" he asked when Rafa ended his call.

"I'm still trying to get us a permit to open the damn gentleman's club. It would be easier to pick out a different spot than trying to change the rules for that area."

"It's about time they updated their rules. That street is prime, so make it happen."

Rafa dropped his phone on the table and swallowed a shot of scotch. "Nothing's going to happen at this time of night. I'll go down to the city in the morning and see what I can do."

Angelo blew out a puff of smoke and looked around the room, at the tables and then the bar. "It looks good."

"Of course it does," Rafa said.

"And it hides what's sitting on top of us perfectly."

Rafa nodded. "Being off the radar is the only good thing about this place."

"It's easy access too."

Rafa seemed to think about it and nodded again. "We can move stock here fast. It makes a good transfer spot."

"It's also a straight drive north and west."

"I still like Miami better." Rafa pointed.

Angelo pulled the cigarette from his lips and blew. "The Keys have other good points."

"You mean like the girl you bought a restaurant for?"

"Yeah, like her. Why'd you invite her anyway? You were the one telling me she couldn't handle me, and then you fucking bring her here."

"Because she's running a place that you own," said Rafa. "The more connections she makes, the more money that goes in your pocket."

"Oh please. You expect me to buy that shit of an excuse?" Angelo crossed his arms as Rafa stared through the glass doors at the dance floor in between sips of his drink. All he could really think about was the confused expression on Ella's face when he left her on the roof.

"What the hell do you keep looking at?" he asked as Rafa continued to glance behind where he sat.

"Oh, nothing," Rafa shook his head, "just a pretty little blond in a silky red dress...dancing with Sid."

Angelo gritted his teeth, releasing a slow breath to keep in control of his temper. Rafa was antagonizing him more than usual, his intentions deliberate. He did not know if Rafa was screwing with him but turned toward the dance floor to check.

That's it. Angelo dropped his cigarette in Rafa's drink. He had enough. He could not think straight when he saw it was true. Ella's arms rested around Sid's shoulders with Sid's hands settled far lower than what was casual. Angelo had to close his eyes and turn back around, though he would have dragged the man outside and shot him. "You set that up." He brushed it off as though it did not matter. "How much did you pay Sid to dance with her?"

"A thousand." Rafa shrugged.

"You wasted your money. I have no interest in her."

"No?"

"No." Angelo took another drink, being careful not to shatter the wine glass within his clenched fingers.

"Then I guess you won't care that he grabbed her ass. I only paid him to dance with her."

Angelo turned his head back to the dance floor to see if what Rafa said was true. If seeing Sid's brown curly hair did not annoy him enough, Sid's hand not only touched the bottom of her dress but also squeezed. "Well..." He stood. Angelo could feel every muscle in his face tighten with the angered heat that started to build. He reared his fist back and smashed the smirk off Rafa's face for paying the asshole to touch her.

"I guess the bastard shouldn't have taken your money," Angelo said as he slipped off his coat and dropped it to the back of the chair.

Rafa stretched his jaw. He knew Angelo would punch him. He had waited for it. "Just giving you a good reason to make a move," Rafa said. His smug tone made Angelo want to punch him again. "Sid should have known there were strings attached to my money."

"Fuck you, Rafa. I'll deal with you later." Angelo pointed at him and left.

***

Ella could not believe he grabbed her upper thigh. When she agreed to dance with him, this was not what she had in mind. Their casual conversation turned into a groping escapade when she did not want to dance in the first place.

"This dance is over," she said, forcing her hands between them and shoving his body away. "I already told you to move your hands." She took a giant step back and half turned but Sid closed the gap and wrapped her in his arms. Ella could smell the alcohol on his breath. Sid drank too much in the short amount of time the club had been open. The bartender should have cut him off.

"What the fuck are you doing?" Angelo marched up to them and grabbed Sid by the collar, throwing him against the wall beside them.

"Look...I'm trying to dance with my—" Sid stammered his words at seeing Angelo standing next to her. "Fucking Rafa," he groaned. "I didn't know she was your girl."

"You think that made it okay?" Angelo could not take any more of this night and punched Sid in the temple. His eyes rolled back and his body collapsed on the stage. "Sammy," Angelo looked around the room and stopped, gesturing with a tilt of his chin at a man with short, parted hair. "Throw him out," he said and looked at Ella. "I thought you were smarter than that, dancing with someone you don't know."

"I was taking care of it." Her voice trailed as Angelo grabbed her hand and dragged her out of the club. "I was having a good time in there," she said as he stopped on the balcony to look at her.

"With Sid?" he scoffed and started to walk again, leading her down the stairs. "I doubt it. It looked like you couldn't get him off you."

"I could have played pool or had another drink. I came here to have a good—"

Angelo held up his palm. "I didn't want you here. Rafa sent you the invitation, not me. He paid Sid to dance with you to make me jealous."

"What?" Ella looked down. "Why would he do something like that? I didn't need his help."

"Is that why you came? To pick up men?"

"What does it matter to you?" Ella jerked her hand away and stared at the beach in front of them.

"Tell me why you came," he said again.

"Why do you care?" Her voice lowered. "You've had a problem with me since our date. I never did anything to you."

"Then leave," he said and continued walking.

She found him infuriating and shook her head. What was it going to take to get answers from him? "I wanted to get your attention."

"And what would you do with my attention?" He stopped and turned around.

"You looked lonely. Maybe I wanted to spend more time with you. Is that so bad?"

"Nobody gives me their time, Ella. Not without a reason."

"Shame," she said and kicked off her heels that were digging in the sand. "No wonder you're always in a bad mood."

As she gathered the hem of her dress to keep it dry, she admired his muscular build underneath the moonlight. He defined sexy with his rolled shirtsleeves putting his forearms on display. She appreciated the way his shirt tucked in at the waist of his buckled slacks. The shadow of growth above his lips and chin made him more alluring still.

"I don't know," she added. "I don't have a reason. Maybe I'm interested." She shrugged in shy realization of what she had said. Ella could feel her cheeks gain heat as she admitted the truth. Angelo said nothing in return to her admission. He merely pulled a cigarette from a case in his shirt and lit it up.

"So why did you choose to be in real estate? You almost have to be a crook to be good at it. I can't see that it was your childhood dream."

"It wasn't. It started when I went with my father to look at the new houses he was selling. I fell in love with all the floor plans. I imagined what people could do with them. A new home is kind of like a new life. Maybe I wanted a different life. I don't know. How many children actually grow up doing what they wanted as kids?"

"Who knows? I never had a choice. I did what my father raised me to do. Every birthday put me one step closer."

Ella nodded, knowing exactly what he meant about a father's control. "When is your birthday?" she asked, changing the subject.

"Next week—on the ninth."

"Do you celebrate?"

Angelo looked at her before rearing his arm back and throwing a shell as far as he could throw. "Yeah, I celebrate...I celebrate every morning when I wake up alive."

"Oh," Ella whispered, not knowing how to respond when Angelo walked in front of her and took her hands with his.

"Why didn't you go home, Ella? Didn't you hear a word I said about your freedom? You're about to get yourself into something that you never dreamed or wanted. Your life will change. It's my only warning, sweetheart; leave and don't come near me again."

Ella breathed deep and shivered under his stature. Something about his expression bordered bewitching and fierce, as though his deep brown eyes could seduce and kill her in the same moment. Yet, she still paid no attention to his warning. "And what if I don't listen?" She glanced up at him; the tremble in her legs worsened with the serious gaze of his eyes.

"If you don't..." Angelo slipped his hands around her cheeks, gently stroking them with his fingers and bringing her within an inch of his chest. "If you don't, it will be too late to change your mind."

With that, he gently pressed her forehead with his lips and lifted, gazing at the spellbound look in her eyes. He knew what even his lightest kiss would do. With it, he sealed her fate.

Chapter 14

Ella clenched a card between her fingers, one that had taken her forty-five minutes to find and one with the perfect message. With her other arm, she cradled an expensive bottle of French cabernet like a newborn baby. Ella had a hard time finding the rarity. There were few of these bottles for sale anywhere in the country, and she thought it was the perfect gift for Angelo's birthday.

She tiptoed into Illusions. The club was dark and quiet, much too quiet with an hour until the doors opened. Ella expected the employees to prepare for a busy Friday night; however, she did not hear one employee step.

"Who are you to come in here and make demands like you're my boss? How did you think that would work?" Loud, continual thuds followed and hit every step until it stopped at the bottom of the stairs. Ella knew it was a person falling down. Then she heard the sound of heavy boots stomping close behind.

Ella froze and caught her breath. She had never heard Angelo talk like that. His fierce tone sent chills down the back of her neck, spreading to the tips of her fingers. Her hand immediately touched the wall, balancing her legs when a piercing click echoed throughout the silent room. Ella felt an instant moment of déjà vu when he pulled the trigger twice.

Ella huddled in a corner near her father's open office door. Vicious curses echoed throughout the house. She had never heard his voice rise to that level. He was shouting at a man whom she had just let inside through their front door.

"You have nerve coming to my fucking house and talking to me that way. If you had something to say, you should've waited until I got to the damn office. There isn't a good enough reason to come here where my daughter is. You should've known I wouldn't put up with that shit."

"Come with me," said Sullivan in a firm but gentle tone. Ella's caretaker grabbed her hand and led her from the empty den where her father's office set. "This is no place for you. Follow me."

He wrapped his arm around her head and tried to cover her ears so she heard nothing more, but even his strong biceps could not shield her from the metal clicking sound. Then something like a bomb exploded. Ella collapsed to the floor out of fear for her life, but Sullivan quickly scooped up her body and carried her off.

With the shock of the memory, Ella raised both hands to her mouth. The card flew from her fingers and the bottle tumbled. She jolted forward and tried to save the wine, but it was too late. The costly cabernet crashed to the floor and shattered.

"Who's there?" Angelo commanded as he stepped out into the dim light of the stairs and crossed his arms. Ella said nothing. Her body trembled with the unfolding scene; she could not answer him if she tried. "Answer me or you'll be next," he warned. Angelo had already fired a gun twice. She knew by the sound of his voice that he did not make threats. Ella wanted to avoid the confrontation and bolted through the door.

She ran across the patio, skidding down the stairs. She could see her car from the side of the club where she had parked in one of the closest spots. Ella was almost in the clear with a few more feet to go when a pair of hands jerked her up from the ground and dragged her through the back door.

"Nice try." Rafa set her on her feet. "It looks like I'm going to get to know you a lot better now."

Ella tried to catch her breath. She could not stop her hands from shaking as she followed Rafa's lead, knowing it was pointless to run. She had no idea what they would do with her now.

"Brett," Rafa said. Ella turned around to see Brett standing behind her and smiling as if they had caught a mouse, a creepy sort of enjoyment in his expression. It put her situation into perspective. "Go lock the front door and find someone to clean up the wine off the floor." Rafa kept a straight face as he spoke, his hand gripping Ella's arm as a reminder of her intrusion with Angelo's warning on the rooftop suddenly becoming clear.

"The VIP room is through this door," he said and placed his thumb over a small black plate. "There are two ways to get in and out. Either you have a card or your thumbprint is added to the security system."

Rafa looked back. "You don't have either one, so don't try to run. There's no point."

Ella shivered as the cool air hit her around a curved hallway. As the music grew louder, the soft glow of the hallway became brighter with every step they took. Finally, the hallway opened to another large room. They were in a casino. A baccarat table stood on one end with slot machines in between. There were several men playing roulette by the bar.

Rafa ignored everything and walked past two women who danced on stage in the middle of the room. Ella frowned as they showed off their stringed panties and bedazzled breasts. How was this different from the strip club? Angelo probably saw them every night and had the nerve to tell her that she did not belong at that club.

Rafa led her to the poker tables where men concentrated on their cards. As someone laid out three of a kind, he pulled out a chair, taking their attention from the cards onto her. "Join the game," he said.

Rafa spoke with an eerie amusement. Ella wondered if the game was with cards or something different. All the men at the table paused to look at her. She felt like they were toying with her and trying to make her break but Ella had grown accustomed to masking fear. She simply stared at the pile of chips in the middle and waited.

"There," Rafa said as an attendant set a couple of stacks of chips in front of her. "That's courtesy of the owner."

"The owner?" Ella's brow rose as she looked behind her. Angelo could not have been the owner. He kept talking about the company as if he were an important employee. It could have been the older man he took her to meet. Antonio. That could be why he asked her those imposing questions.

"He says you can keep anything you win. If you lose, he will find a way to get his money back."

Ella rested her hands on her lap and looked at the ceiling. In between the simple hanging lights, cameras looked down on them. She had no doubt that that the owner was watching her now.

"Okay," she said and tried to focus on the game. She did not want to think about what Antonio would do with her if she lost his money. "What's the high and low, and how much is the ante?" she asked.

The dealer gave a small smile as Rafa answered, "Five hundred high, fifty low—Twenty-five to ante."

Ella nodded and threw in her chips. The second the dealer passed out the cards, she picked them up and shifted them in order.

"Your bet," said Rafa.

"A hundred." Ella threw in two chips and thought back to when she was at home. Her mother and Sullivan used to play the game with her. Poker was not that difficult. It was all about paying attention to the other players. Sullivan taught her how to play it well.

Two players folded and Rafa and two others threw in the chips. Ella watched the man to the right of the dealer throw out his cards for exchange. When he pulled in the new cards, he also snagged several chips underneath. How sly. It was such a subtle gesture; she was surprised that she saw it at all. Ella was not going to win with a cheater at the table, but she slid in her chips anyway.

"Another hundred." Ella waited to see what the others would do.

"I'm out," said one of the men. Throwing in their chips, Rafa and the cheater remained.

"I call," Ella said.

Ella turned over three tens, Rafa turned over a full house, and the man who took chips showed a pair of fives.

"Ante," said the dealer as Rafa pulled in his winnings. All players did; then Ella noticed something off about the dealer. He passed out two cards to the player to his left. Ella's eyes narrowed as she glanced at her cards and threw them out.

"I fold."

"What?" Rafa asked. "You aren't even going to try?"

"I want to sit this one out," Ella replied.

"Suit yourself."

Now Ella watched every man at the table. One took chips. One took extra cards. The dealer misdealt. That left three other men, and Rafa kept whispering into an earpiece. Other than that, it played out as normal.

"Are you in this hand?" Rafa asked.

"I'm in." Ella pressed her lips together as she received her cards. She glanced at Rafa as though he would know what she had. Ella peeked at the cards without ever lifting them up. If someone told him what was in her hand before, the person would have never been able to see.

She threw out two cards and received two more. Rafa placed a bet and she followed suit, but all of the other players folded. What a coincidence since there was no way they would beat her straight flush.

"I call," said Rafa. Ella looked at the table where they played. The dark tinted glass made it difficult to see her cards from underneath, yet it was still made of glass. All of the men were deliberately manipulating the game. Why?

Ella turned over her cards, and Rafa had a straight. She pulled in her winnings, merely replacing the chips that she lost. Now her chips matched what she had started with, neither gaining nor losing. She was finished and crossed her arms. Ella was not going to let them make a fool out of her.

"Sitting this one out?" Rafa asked.

"I'm not playing anymore," she declared. "All of you are mocking me."

The dealer halted his shuffling, and all of the men's eyes focused on her, waiting for her to continue. Not a smile formed on any of their mouths. Somehow, they invoked fear and annoyed her at the same time.

Ella shook her head and stood. "That man to the right of the dealer is stealing chips. The dealer passed out more cards than he should have to the man to his left. And you"—she pointed at Rafa—"are talking with someone through your earpiece."

"Do you usually come up with conspiracy theories? Sometimes you have to improve your skills and not accuse people of cheating," Rafa instructed.

Ella glared at him. Was he not going to admit that the game was rigged? Ella rolled her eyes and looked away. At the same time, she felt underneath the table where she sat. Ella yanked a tiny metal piece from under the glass and looked at it closely, inspecting the circular screen that was no larger than the tip of her pinky finger. "Here's your conspiracy theory. That seems like a camera to me."

Rafa seemed impressed. His slight smirk irritated her more. Did they purposely sabotage the entire game to see if she could tell? "The owner can have his chips back," she said. "I'm not playing with any of you."

She scooted out of her chair and pushed it back in. While the men exchanged curious glances, she left the poker sessions and walked around the dancers to the bar in back. She needed to figure out the purpose of the match.

Chapter 15

Ella gazed behind the bar. The VIP room had more expensive bottles of liquor than the main club had. She liked that. She needed something strong and smooth and waited for the bartender to approach.

"I need to see your pass?" he said, his brown eyes staring directly in hers with not one slicked brown hair out of place.

Ella groaned. Did he not see Rafa bring her through the door? "I came with Rafa, one of the men at the poker tables," she replied.

"I know, but I can't serve you unless someone with a pass orders for you. Those are the rules for this room."

Ella noticed that many more customers now filled the tables and stools. She looked at her phone and saw it was ten minutes after six. She started to look back at the table with Rafa when a single man approached and slid his arm around her waist. The man had dark brown hair and brown eyes with a smile on his face.

"She's with me now," he said as Ella shifted out of the hold of his arm.

The bartender tilted his face forward, eying the man. "Really," he said. "You came in with her?" The man nodded and rested his hands on the bar. "All right," the bartender scoffed. "What will you have then?"

"A shot of tequila," Ella answered. "Something smooth."

"The owner orders the best," he said, pouring a shot and setting it down in front of her.

Ella gulped it as if trying to erase a bad memory. The tequila was perfect with no aftertaste. "You were right. That was smooth."

"I did say we carry the best."

"I'll take a margarita with that same tequila? Ice and salt."

The man next to her glanced at her with surprise. "That's a lot of liquor all at once. Can you handle it?"

"It's not a problem," she answered as the bartender gave her a sly smirk.

"You do know that our private stock is more potent than the others. You might want to keep that in mind," he said.

"Don't worry. I know my limitations," she replied as a woman walked to the opposite end of the bar. The woman wore a tailored green dress with matching heels. Ella did not think the color went well with her short red hair. The woman looked at Ella with the man who stood next to her and scowled. Even when Ella returned to take her margarita, she could still feel the woman's eyes piercing through her heart.

"Does she have a problem with me?" Ella asked the bartender.

"Well, she might. Halsey there," he pointed at the man standing next to Ella, "came in with her. She probably didn't like his arm around you a minute ago."

Halsey interrupted. "I came to the bar to get away from her. She's a loudmouth. I never should have brought her up here." When the bartender left the two alone, Halsey looked at Ella. "Now that he's gone, do you mind telling me your name?"

"Ella," she said, thinking she should have stayed with the cheaters at the poker table. Halsey was giving off bad vibes.

"Ella," he said. "Yes, I like that. You'll be my lucky card tonight. Come with me."

"No, I can't right n—," Ella said as he grabbed her hand without care to her response.

"I got you a drink, remember? So do what I say, and you won't have anything to worry about." Ella stared at him as he led her to one of the roulette tables. She did not want to make a scene when she was already in trouble with Angelo. How bad could a simple game of roulette be?

"All I want you to do is put these chips where you think they should go. Got it?"

"Okay," she answered as Halsey set the chips in Ella's hand. She did what he said. Ella put them against three different numbers.

"Black fifteen," announced the dealer. Halsey seemed pleased that Ella had placed chips on that number.

"Do it again," Halsey commanded. This time Ella bet on the same two numbers that did not win and chose a new number for the rest of the chips.

"Red twelve."

"Very good, Ella," said Halsey with a smirk. "One more time and then we're leaving."

Leaving? His words disturbed her as she placed his chips one more time. She did not pay attention to where she placed them. Ella stepped back slowly as Halsey waited for the balls to stop. She was not going anywhere with that man. Ella walked fast and ducked inside an open doorway at the end of a short hall.

What was this room? Ella fisted her hands over her stomach and closed her eyes. This was the worst hiding place that she could have found to escape. She would have had a better chance of surviving with Halsey; if anyone caught her here, she could die.

Black trays that were lined with cloth lay on top of several rows of tables. Inside the trays were handguns, machine guns and pistols. The rest of the trays carried rounds of ammunition. Ella could not move. What exactly did she discover? Then it hit her. *Illusions*. The club was a cover for something else. She did not want to think about for what.

"You had to run, didn't you?" Halsey walked into the room. His glaring eyes made Ella take slow steps back. The more he walked toward her, the further she backed away until her back hit the wall at the far end of the room. Halsey's hands closed around both of her shoulders; his eyes scanned her body like a treat he would enjoy. "Don't try to run from me again, Ella."

Ella felt desperate. Running was exactly what she would do. She kicked her foot off the wall and kneed him between the legs with every bit of power she could manage.

"Bitch," Halsey yelled. However much she had hurt him, it was not enough for her to run far. Halsey caught her in seconds and slapped her. His palm left behind a furious burn to her cheek. Her footing faltered with the impact and Ella stumbled; her forehead crashed against the corner of the table.

She lifted her body up but fell on her back. Blood trickled from her forehead and down her temple into her hair. She groaned. She put her hand over the gash and tried to sit up when Halsey shoved her back to the floor.

"I told you not to run," he said and straddled her legs. Ella was losing energy too fast. Her meager attempts to shove his hands away were pointless as he lifted her blouse above her breasts. She tried to push him away once more when the door to the room slammed closed.

"What the fuck," said the familiar voice of a man. The sharp metal clicking sound made Halsey raise his arms in the air but that was all he could do; his body fell sideways, lightening the weight off Ella's legs. She tried to move. Her eyes struggled to open, but the only things that seemed to work were her ears as she heard the distant sounds of voices. Her body felt weightless as somebody scooped her up. Then darkness shut everything out.

Chapter 16

Ella opened her eyes to plain white walls. She was in a room with a bed and a small table at the head. The narrow door had a fingerprint sensor and no knob. Without any windows in the room, the only source of light came from a single bulb in the corner. She felt disoriented.

She groaned. Pushing herself up from laying flat, her body resisted the change in position. She did not remember a lot of what happened the night before or who put her in the white robe. Her hand touched her forehead, feeling the bandage placed over the gash. She did remember what Halsey had tried to do and that Angelo was the voice who saved her.

Leaning forward, Ella cupped her hands over her face, trying to relieve the pressure off her head. She stayed like that for a few minutes when she heard the door beep open. It was Angelo, Rafa, and Brett. Ella struggled to sit up and stared at them, waiting for them to speak. Angelo and Rafa both crossed their arms; Brett's hands hid in the pockets of his jeans.

"I warned you about me," Angelo said. "I gave you every opportunity to stay away."

"What happened to that man last night?" she asked.

"Justice," Rafa answered. "He was going to rape you."

Ella's shoulders slouched as she looked at the floor. The night before turned out to be a night she would not forget. "Now what?" she asked.

Brett smiled, his boyish charm masking the danger he posed on unsuspecting minds. Ella knew better. There was a dark mystery behind the men, so Brett was not at all innocent. "You have choices." He grinned.

"Choices? What sort of choices?" Ella frowned, not liking the mirth in his tone.

Angelo looked at Rafa but pointed at Brett. Then he and Rafa stepped out of the room, leaving Brett and Ella alone. As Brett turned around to watch them go, the butt of a gun handle showed from underneath the hem of his shirt. Ella flinched. Was he going to kill her?

"Well, I could say sorry you got mixed up in all this," he smiled, "but we both know I'd be lying. I really don't care. Not that it matters what I think. The boss makes the rules."

"Is the owner your boss or is Angelo?"

"I don't know." Brett shrugged. "They're kind of the same, but pretty much everyone is my boss. They tell me what to do and I do it. It's an easy job. I get paid."

"Okay," Ella said.

"Anyway." He pulled the gun from his back pocket and twisted it, letting the light glisten off the polished finish. "Isn't it a beauty?" he asked. "And it's brand new...never been used. I'm kind of looking for a reason to break it in."

Ella stared at him with sickened disbelief as she faced the possibility of being killed. She found nothing exciting about him using the new gun to see her demise. "My choices?" she asked before he became too enamored in his fantasy.

"Right." He snapped out of his daydream and slipped the gun to his back pocket again. "It's more like your choice. It's in that table drawer over there. I have to get back to work while you think about it. The boss has work too, but Rafa will come back in a little while. See you later, Ella."

Brett waved to her. He scooted out of the door as though they had a friendly chat on any normal day. There was something off about Brett.

Ella stared at the table by the bed. What if there was an explosive device waiting in that drawer? Maybe what she chose was the method in which to end her life. Not likely. If they meant to kill her, they would not have taken the trouble to wrap her head.

Ella got out of the bed and slid the drawer open an inch. Her overactive mind was working against her. She half expected to uncover some sort of wiring unit, but the drawer seemed empty instead. Ella stared at the empty drawer and then closed her eyes; she jerked the handle until it slid all the way out. When she opened her eyes back up, something reflected from the back of the drawer. Her hand immediately moved to her chest, relieved that the entire room did not explode. Then she picked up the object. It was a beautiful ring with tiny black diamonds and a band made from solid white gold. The ring was made for a man, so what did it mean for her?

The door creaked open. As if reading her thoughts, Rafa walked inside the room and looked down at her. She was kneeling on the floor with the ring in her hand.

"Have you decided?" he asked.

"Decided what? What does the ring mean?" She stood back up and sat on the bed again.

"That," he pointed, "is not an ordinary ring. It would mean that you belong to the owner from now on and do what he says."

"You mean the same owner who let me play poker?"

"That's right. That's his personal ring that he had sized for you. He would own you too."

"I want to meet him first."

"You will soon enough. If you don't accept the ring, I'll have to take care of you now." Rafa opened up the right side of his coat and let his gun shine in the light. "Or I can send Brett back in for his fun." Ella pushed the ring on her finger; there was no point in arguing the point. "As expected. I actually came back in here to go over the rules with you," he said.

"Rules?" Ella had always followed a set of rules. The owner was acting like her father had in the past.

"You put the ring on your finger, didn't you?" Rafa asked.

"Yes, but it's not like I had a choice."

"You did. You liked the other choice less."

"Right," Ella sighed.

"You will remember these rules or it could be your life." His serious look dared her to argue. His expression made Ella believe that her life would be in danger if she did not follow them. "Number one: If you ever talk about that room with the guns, we will kill you."

"But that wasn't my—"

"Don't argue with me. I understand is all I want to hear from you."

"I understand." Understanding was descending upon her in a way she had not expected. She was starting to understand the intensity of her situation.

"Good...number two: If we let you leave, don't run. We have people. We will hunt you. We will find you. Don't waste your time and don't waste ours."

"I understand."

"Number three: You're with the owner, so act like it. That ring has meaning you don't understand yet. You're not to take it off."

"But shouldn't I get to meet him first? That would be the decent thing for him to do."

Rafa mocked her, a cynical smile replacing his stern expression. "Do you understand?"

"Yes," she said.

"I understand." He reminded her.

"I understand." She corrected, her eyes shifting to the wall.

"Do exactly what we tell you and don't ask questions. The rules aren't hard."

No, not hard, Ella thought, *just impossible.*

"I'll tell the owner we're done. You'll wait here while I get someone to take you to a different room where you can eat and shower."

"But wait. I wasn't—"

The door closed, cutting Ella's words short. Her body fell back on the bed, slumping to the pillow. Her heart beat fast. She thought she could hear the loud pounding against her chest instead of simply feeling it. Ella knew she had gotten involved with something much bigger than a shiny club on the beach.

***

Angelo looked at a screen on his desk and replayed the video for the fourth time in a row. If it had not been his own men at that table, he would have thought someone tipped her off. Ray was the dealer who dealt Sammy a double card. Jim took the extra chip, and Rafa was talking to him on his earpiece.

"It doesn't make sense." Angelo tapped his fingers on his desk and looked at the men across from him. Jim and Rafa sat on one sofa; Ray and Brett on the other. Maybe they caught something that he missed.

"Which part?" Rafa shrugged.

"The whole poker match doesn't make sense. Even if Ella caught all of you cheating, there's no way that a woman her age would've looked for that camera."

"That caught me off guard too," Rafa said. "She might be a better match for you than I thought."

Jim nodded. "I thought I was going to have to get up when she slapped that camera on the table. It was fucking hard to keep a straight face after that."

"But it was the way she felt for the camera like she knew it would be there," Rafa added. "That made it real."

"Rafa." Angelo picked up a folder from his desk and held it out. "Take this down to Donnie. I want to know everything about her, and I don't think she knows a thing about her father. Have Donnie dig up anything he can on him. I want to know every business he owns and who his associates are. Then maybe we can figure something out."

"You heard him, Brett. You get to drive."

"Really?" Brett sounded disheartened. "I already missed the poker match and now I have to—"

"Brett." Rafa gave him a look with Brett standing and walking to the door without another word.

"And you," Angelo pointed at Jim and Ray, "bring Ella to my room."

"Do you want us to come back when we're done?" asked Jim.

"No, go check on the hotel. Make sure everything is good there."

When Angelo was alone in his office, he watched Jim and Ray walk to the room that Ella was being held. They passed rooms on both sides of the hallway on the third floor. Unlike a hotel, the doors to these rooms had no door handles and no numbers. The fingerprint sensors were the only way in. One of the rooms was his personal space; another was his office. Three smaller rooms were for security issues and seven more for general use.

Angelo smiled at her instant realization that Jim and Ray were two of the cheaters. Ella stayed silent but glared at them as she did what they said. She knew right away that they had sabotaged the poker match on purpose but could not have known they were testing her. Soon, she would understand.

Chapter 17

Ella stood in the middle of the new room; there were no windows and no way out. It was dark except for the light that shown from the restroom door. A gorgeous wooden table sat between two plush recliners, and a television was mounted on the wall above a dresser. On the floor in front of the dresser were three large black duffel bags. Another was on the bed. She started to walk near the bed when she saw some of her business suits hanging in the closet by the door. Whoever brought them had gone into her house and went inside her bedroom. It alarmed her that they could break into her house that easily.

Ella ignored the duffels. She looked inside the restroom and saw an oversized tub with neatly folded linens lying on a shelf beside the sink. She was still in pain and needed a bath. She turned the hot water almost all the way up and stepped inside the tub, letting her robe fall to the floor. Her eyes shut as she succumbed to the bliss of the heat. To her surprise, she stayed calm in her confinement to the outside world, but it was not the first time. She doubted it would be the last.

Ella sat back up and gazed in the decorative mirror that set against the door. The gash on her head made her groan with disgust. She needed to wash the blood from her hair. After gently scrubbing around the wound, she examined the gash again. It looked like a small cut now and was not nearly as big as she thought.

Ella walked out of the restroom and grabbed her purse to get a hairbrush, settling in her new situation. She hoped to know what that entailed soon. She was not a fan of the wait.

"How are you feeling?" came Angelo's voice from where he sat in the dark.

Ella shrieked, throwing her hairbrush at the wall, her swift movements causing the towel around her hair to tumble to the floor. "Mr. Tomassi!" she exclaimed and sat down on the bed. "You scared me to death." Ella pulled the sash tight around her robe and picked up the fallen towel. All she could think about was her naked body underneath the robe, even though she was sure it meant nothing to Angelo. She thought about the dancers and figured he'd seen plenty of bare breasts by now.

"Are you trying to knock me out?" Angelo stood and handed the hairbrush back to Ella. "I need to doctor that cut on your forehead. How do you feel?" he asked and opened up a first aid kit.

"All right, I guess. It's not as bad as I thought."

"No." He applied a thin layer of ointment. "It looked much worse before you took a bath. It bled a lot last night, but it's barely more than a scratch now." Angelo smoothed a narrow bandage across her forehead. His light, gentle touch surprised her. She admired the way his eyes focused all attention on her wound.

"That's a nice ring you're wearing." Angelo glanced down. "You make it look good." Ella shrugged and covered her right hand with her left. Her eyes drifted to the wall. "The owner wants you at the party tonight in the VIP room."

"For what?" Ella muttered. She did not feel like attending a party.

"As his girlfriend. There's a lot of important people going to be there. You need to be introduced to them."

"What time does it start?" she asked.

"At six when the doors open."

"Then I can go to Santiago's and check on the restaurant. Tessa's experienced, but I still need to make sure she's ready to be on her own. I barely hired her as the assistant manager."

"No," he said without stopping to think it over.

"Why? It's not like I'm going to say anything," Ella said.

"You're not leaving here yet." Angelo's voice was firm. "I warned you on the beach. You came back to the club to see me. You made the choice so don't blame anyone but yourself."

What worried him about her going to the restaurant? She would not try to run. She had the restaurant and one friend.

"Can't you send someone with me if you're so worried?"

"Why are you asking questions? I know Rafa explained the rules."

Ella frowned and looked back down. "Never mind then," she sighed. What was the point? She could ask questions all day that no one would answer. Why waste her breath?

"I brought you something to eat." He pointed at a tray on the table between the recliners. "You need to keep yourself healthy."

Angelo left her alone in the quiet room. She found the silence lonesome as she grabbed one of her suits from the closet; taking one look at the three outfits, she put it back. She could not wear any of them. They forgot the blouses that went underneath. With a mere two buttons on the coats, she would be hanging out for the world. They would need to take her to her house.

Ella returned to the restroom to brush her hair. What a mess. If the owner had planned to let people stay the night, he should have better hair-care products for the guests. Ella felt like she was ripping her hair out of her head. It was long, but she never found it this difficult to brush.

Now she had nothing to do but wait and stare at the duffle bag on the bed. Ella could not help her curiosity. She took five steps closer and looked at the door and then at the ceiling—no cameras. If they were already forcing her to stay, she would face no further consequences by looking inside. What harm would it cause?

She sat on the bed and eased the zipper across the bag, careful not to make a sound. The sides of the bag burst open with the pressure of the weight. There were pistols, smooth and shiny, from black to silver and everything in between. Were these a part of the guns in the room that she found?

In the corner of the bag, a light blue pistol sparked her attention. She picked it up. With the light of the restroom streaming in a line to the bed, she saw that the entire gun had a chrome finish except for the slick blue sides. She wanted to see how it felt in her hands when fully loaded.

Ella looked further in the bag and found a single box of ammunition. Then she ejected the empty clip and loaded it one bullet at a time. It felt like the perfect size in her hand. She turned it over, inspected the back, looked at the hammer, and then clicked off the safety. It was gorgeous. Ella pointed it at the wall and admired the sight.

"You'd better duck if you plan to shoot that thing in here. These walls are four inches of solid steel."

Ella screamed. The gun fell from her hands and crashed onto the other guns inside the bag. As soon as it happened, Angelo jerked her to the floor and shielded her body with his own. The gun fired like a rocket. The bullet ricocheted off the door and pummeled to the wall behind. It bounced diagonally, hit the tray of food, and finally lost momentum when it shattered the television that hung from the ceiling.

Wide-eyed, Ella stared at Angelo as he looked back down at her. Fragments of glass from the television still clinked to the dresser as his body pressed her all the way to the floor. When the room was silent again, Angelo lifted off her chest and leaned his back against the side of the bed. He looked around. Ella had destroyed the room, and she could not say a word at first. Her heart pounded in a way that her chest felt tight. She did not know whether to laugh or cry.

"You were extremely careless," he stated matter-of-factly, yet there seemed to be a slight smirk on his lips. His hands rested on the floor as he turned to see the television again. "I can't believe that happened."

"You saved me from the bullet," Ella said in shock. "You pushed me down before the gun ever went off."

"Who taught you how to load a gun? I was impressed until you dropped it like you did."

"I don't know. I grew up with them and learned. I've never dropped one before."

"Had to happen with me, right?" Angelo scoffed.

"Well...you scared me!"

Angelo lowered his head and glared. "You should know better than to drop a loaded fucking pistol."

"You should know better than to scare a woman who holds a loaded pistol. Don't you remember how I threw the brush at you earlier?"

"You should have never loaded that pistol in the first place."

"I can't believe that happened either," she said and wrapped her arms around her knees. "Thank you for saving me."

"We were luckier just now than I care to think about." Ella let out a sigh and squeezed her legs tighter. "How did you know there was a camera last night?" asked Angelo. "It's not normal for the average woman to look for a camera."

"My father had cameras all over the house. I used to look for them when I got tired of being caught doing something wrong. Why was the camera there in the first place?" Angelo cleared his throat and stood. "You aren't going to answer me?" she asked.

Instead of responding to her question, he walked to the bag where Ella had dropped the gun. "It's probably a good idea to unload this one, but I think I'll keep it out since you liked it so much. I'll make sure the safety is on." He set the gun aside.

"So you aren't going to answer me?" she asked again. "Fine, then is that man you took me to meet at the restaurant the owner? Can you at least tell me that?"

"No," he replied. "He is not the owner. He used to be, but he handed the business down to his son. There were some strings attached."

Ella let out a breath and closed her eyes. That was a relief. She did not know what she would do if he was the owner. "What kind of business did he hand down?"

"His name," Angelo stressed the word.

Ella groaned. Talking to Angelo was impossible. He was so cryptic with everything. She did not understand.

"Come here," he said, his voice softer as he spoke. When Ella looked up, Angelo was holding out his hand to her, waiting for her to take hold; he easily pulled her to her feet.

She was stricken with his brown eyes. They stared into hers and deeper as though considering what to do. He did not let go of her hand, seeming to enjoy the warmth of her touch as much as she enjoyed his.

"My father passed down the Tomassi name. I had reasons to stop talking to you. I tried to make it seem like you didn't matter to protect you." Angelo looked off to the side. "You can't go back now. There's too many people who want me dead, and they'll come straight after you to make sure that happens."

"You're the owner?" Ella asked, slightly confused.

"Boss," Angelo corrected in a dead-serious tone.

"The boss," she repeated, remembering how Brett had said they were the same. She was not sure it made any more sense to her.

"I took over my father's company—his organization—around five years ago. I'd been training to do his job since I started talking. We operate out of Miami. Mafioso, Ella," Angelo said in a harsh whisper. "You need to understand that and take it serious. We don't fuck around with anyone. We don't play games. Those guns are to protect us. Right now, there's another family—the Bonadio Group. We're at war. We have men on the inside. We always have to be a step ahead. But that war, Ella...puts you at a bigger risk."

As Ella lost her balance and stumbled, Angelo grabbed her arm with his other hand. Chills formed on her neck, the tiny hairs standing on end; her head started to spin. Ella worked hard to separate herself from rules. Now she found herself thrust back in the middle. She was used to it—comfortable, yet she could not come up with a logical reason. It felt like déjà vu.

"Brett will go wherever you need to go today. I had your thumbprints added to our sensors. Be back here by six."

"And what if I don't come?" Ella asked but wanted to recant the question as soon as it came out.

"Do you really want to provoke me?" His voice was low and crisp. Angelo pulled one part of her sash loose from the other. Ella's robe fell open, exposing a narrow line of bare skin down to her feet. Angelo could have looked, but his eyes never left her face, his hands embracing her cheeks. "If you don't come, I will show you why they call me boss. Don't make me have to come get you."

Ella understood. She gazed at him and did not look away. It was as though he put her in a trance with the strong hands that wrapped around her cheeks. His warm breath made her yearn for the show of affection—a kiss; instead, Angelo stood up and turned around. He never glanced back and left her in the room again.

Chapter 18

All Ella wanted to do was to go home and sleep after having Brett hang out in her office all day and admire his gun. She tried her best to ignore him whenever someone needed to talk but it was hard to overlook the sideways glances he received. Still a bit frazzled, she stepped into the club wearing a dress that Angelo had delivered to her house. One single strap adorned the top of the evening gown with a long slit down the side and a pair of black heels to match.

"Are you ready?" Rafa asked from the main entry of the club. He adjusted the gun inside his jacket and led her by the arm up the stairs to the VIP room.

"Not really," she said. No part of her mind felt like a party; she could not turn her head without pain. Being paraded around the VIP room as the owner's new girl was not her ideal good time. "I think I need a drink." She hoped a drink would take the edge off her aching body.

"Then go," he said and opened the door. "I'll come find you in a minute.

Ella approached the bar and rested both arms on top, waiting for the bartender to come. She gave him a sheepish smile. It was the same bartender as the previous night. "I left without paying for my drinks yesterday."

"I know. The boss already took care of them."

Boss. She thought, surprised to hear people refer to Angelo as Boss. If she had known who he was sooner, she wondered if her situation would have taken a different direction. "All right, will you get me the same thing I ordered yesterday?"

"Of course." He grabbed a bottle and tossed ice in a shaker.

"I'm Ella," she said and watched him add tequila to the ice.

"We've been told. That ring is a big statement around here."

"Oh." Ella touched one of the diamonds on the ring and twisted it around. "What's your name then?" she asked.

"You can call me Thomas or Tom if you'd like. I usually bartend at all the boss's big events."

"It's nice to meet you." She picked up her drink and smiled. "I'm going to walk around a bit. I'll see you later, Thomas."

As she meandered around a group of women flaunting their attributes with their sexiest styles, Ella scrutinized everything she saw. She looked at the hanging pictures and the tables. She walked to the poker sessions and observed the players around them. None of the men who played poker with her the previous night were present, but she did receive a couple of glances her way.

Ella paid no attention. She spotted the hallway and thought back to the guns. The familiarity of the situation was on the tip of her tongue. Why could she not remember why?

"Going somewhere?" Rafa looped his arm through hers and pulled her in the opposite direction.

"Of course not," she said. "I don't want to face the consequences from anymore rooms." His sudden intervention made her suspicious. Was there something else in that room now? "When will Mr. Tomassi come down?" she asked.

"I guess when he feels like coming down. He might not come at all, knowing him."

"So he wants to introduce me without being here. How does that make sense?"

"A lot of what he does doesn't make sense to me." Rafa flicked his hand through the air. "I don't know what goes through Angelo's mind. I couldn't give you an answer if I wanted to."

"Why does he really want me here tonight?" Ella asked pointedly.

"To make a statement. His father wants him to marry the daughter of another boss from Orlando, but Angelo refused to meet her."

"So he's using me." Ella shook her head and then looked up at Rafa.

"He's not using you," Rafa answered immediately, "but you will face problems with him. He knows that marrying that woman will make him a stronger boss. It would make his group more powerful. You could end up being his mistress. There's no way he's letting you go, you know."

"What?" asked Ella.

"You heard me." Rafa pointed at her. "You're locked in."

A mistress. Ella frowned in thought. She did not like the sound of that at all. She deserved more in her life than the title of mistress. She needed to know what Angelo planned for her. No wonder there was tension between Angelo and Antonio when they ate lunch. It all made sense now that she knew the situation.

"Hey, follow my lead. I need to introduce you to a few associates."

Rafa led her past several men in suits. Ella felt like a spectacle, degraded since Angelo was not there to introduce her himself. Leaning from annoyance to slight contempt, Ella was left without a choice and did as was told.

"Ferron," Rafa greeted a man with brown hair and hazel eyes. His beige suit jacket covered his slim physique.

"Rafael, how are you? Is this the lovely woman Tomassi told me about?"

"This is Ella Collins. Ella, this is Ferron Patenzo."

"It's nice to meet you," said Ella, playing her part in Angelo's escapade. She could hold her own in the world even if she did not like the situation.

"Pleasure is all mine," Ferron replied. He brushed his lips to the top of her hand and turned to Rafa. "Let me take Ella for a while. I'll take good care of her."

"All right, but remember eyes are on you," Rafa warned.

"Of course."

Ella glared at Rafa. How could he pass her off to a stranger like that and treat her like some meaningless object? She did not care how closely Rafa kept watching them. His actions were unacceptable.

As Ferron circled the bar, Ella wondered about his motive to introduce her. If the ring she wore gave away her status, showing her off would benefit him too. Being entrusted with the boss's girlfriend must have increased his respect among peers.

Ferron approached a man in a sharp red tie and stood in his direct line of sight. Acknowledging Ferron with a huff, the man was intent with the game of craps he was playing and made no effort to turn his head. He seemed aggravated by Ferron's interruption. "I'm in the middle of a game? I'm not interested in your pass-around."

That voice. Ella froze. The malicious tone of his words sent fear pulsing through her veins. Her eyes looked off to one side and then the other. Somebody toasted at another table while Ella searched her mind. Where had she heard that voice before?

Glasses clinked. Her father had brought her to a hotel but did not allow her to attend the party. Ella was tired of staying cooped up in their suite and crept near the door of the large banquet hall. Men and women in formal eveningwear were enjoying live music and eating from expensive china. Her father was inside. She was old enough now. She thought he would allow her to enjoy the event, but he made her stay with Sullivan in the room.

Ella figured out ways to escape Sullivan, and there was no way he would find her anytime soon. He thought she was taking a shower but she had secretly left the room. Now she could see through a crack in the open door. She wanted a peek. Anything was better than being stuck in their suite for the night.

"Look," said a man who turned to look at her father, a distinct bald spot above his left ear. "Bonadio isn't going to wait. He wants to know what day you can talk to him."

"Next week," her father answered. "Tell him the owners of that property he looked at decided to keep it. I'll find something else by Monday."

"You're procrastinating," said the man. "You're playing with fire here. Bonadio won't go for that, so find something else yesterday."

"He's going to have to wait." Her father sneered and turned around. "That's all I can tell you for now."

"Have it your way." Ella heard the click of a gun but no sound when he fired. Then she saw her father go down.

"Hey...stop!" Ella came out of hiding and ran inside, her cries being absorbed with the band.

"What a strange shade of blue...damn near clear." The man looked at her eyes but walked past her without having heard what she said. Ella dropped to the floor beside her father. She tried to press his slacks against the wound in his leg, but her father shoved her away.

"Go back upstairs!"

"But you need a doc—"

"I'm not going to tell you again, Ella!"

Her eyes welled up with tears. How could he be so cruel when she wanted to help? She had already lost her mother. Would she lose him too? Ella frowned at him. Nothing could match her hurt and shock by his tone; then she jumped to her feet and ran.

"She's not with me, Merrick. She's Tomassi's girlfriend," Ferron said. Merrick paused for a second and turned around, revealing the same missing hair over his ear. He stared at her. She waited, hoping he would not remember their brief encounter five years back. Ella wanted to run. Every muscle in her body pleaded for safety, but she stayed for the introduction in spite of her fear. She did not want to look suspicious.

"You look familiar," he said and touched the end of her hair.

Ella smiled to throw him off. "I get that sometimes, but I don't remember you from anywhere. My name is Ella."

"Ella what?" he asked.

"Collins." She held her breath, his eyes giving a blank expression as he tried to remember the name.

"No, nothing comes to mind. I'm Merrick Frasier."

Ella let out a slight breath, almost relieved of her worry when his brow creased with a troubled gaze; then his confusion cleared as the realization hit him. Merrick remembered her eyes and when he had seen them before. The small smile on his lips gave him away.

"It's nice to meet you," she said and took a step back. "I'm going to get another drink."

Ella walked back to Rafa as he was walking toward her. When they met, he took her arm and led her to the bar. "Sit down," he said and sat beside her. "How do you know Merrick?"

Her pulse felt double what was normal. Ella breathed hard, trying to catch her breath as she stared at the bottles behind the counter, a distraction for her attention as she glanced into the mirror-like glass on the top shelf. She wanted to know if Merrick had followed. "I didn't know his name. I knew his voice. Why is he here? Is he one of you?" she asked.

"He's one of Bonadio's men, not ours. Does he know you?"

"I saw him—"

The phone in Rafa's pocket interrupted her. He pulled it out and started talking into the receiver. "I have no idea what's going on, but I think we have a problem... Yes, that's what I'm thinking too. I'll send her up and find out what happened." Rafa hung up and looked back at Ella. "You have to go to the third floor; you might be in danger."

"How is it you show me off and put me in danger and then want to save me from it?" Ella whispered back as he dragged her behind the bar.

"Move your ass and shut up." He led her past several shelves with glasses and more bottles of liquor than she could count. He placed his thumb over a dark plate on the end and a door opened up. "Go all the way up the stairs. You'll be fine. Angelo's waiting for you at the top."

Ella ran. She nearly tripped on her heels when Angelo grabbed the top of her arm and prevented her from falling head first to the steps. He looked deep in her eyes, his eyes serious and concerned—worried. He must have also known Merrick and realized the danger she was in.

She followed behind Angelo. There was no time to watch where she walked. Her focus was on the back of Angelo's coat when he pulled her into an office. There were two sofas, a desk, a computer and surveillance screens that mounted on the walls. Ella stared at the display with equal fascination and alarm.

Taking out his phone as he shut the door, Angelo pointed her to one of the sofas. "Brett, you went back to the hotel, didn't you? No, get Jim and Ray and get here now."

He dropped the phone on the other sofa and adjusted one of the cameras to follow Rafa around the club. Without sound, she watched with Angelo, both intent with the argument between Rafa and Merrick. Their exchange was getting worse with the facial movements and angry glances they cast back and forth. Rafa stopped talking; he slid his hand underneath the buttons of his coat. He was reaching for his gun.

"Shit. I have to go help him." Angelo leaned down, wrapping his hands around the sides of her shoulders. "Don't leave this room. You'll be safe here. Brett will be here in a minute, so do not leave."

Angelo ran out of the office. Anticipating the confrontation was making it hard for Ella to sit still. She turned her attention back to the screens and covered her mouth with her hand. She started to slide off the edge of the sofa when Jim and Ray walked in to help Angelo.

Ella let out a relieved sigh when her phone buzzed from the inside of her white clutch. She bolted from her seat. If it had not been for the chain around her wrist attached to the clutch, the small purse would have crashed to the floor. Who would be calling her at this time of night?

"Hello," she answered. Ella listened to a series of fast chatter; then time stopped. "What did you say?" she asked although she clearly heard the message the first time around. Her mind ceased to function. The room was spinning before her eyes. It could not be true. She would not believe it until she saw for herself.

Chapter 19

Ella screeched to the outside of Santiago's and nearly slammed her car into one of the attending officer's vehicles. The police car was blocking the scene, but it was not going to stop her from entering. Her car jerked as she threw it in park, jumping out before it ever fully stopped. Brett's head almost hit the dashboard without the seatbelt around his waist. The flashing lights around her were blinding to the fateful situation. Smoke soared high above the building. The heat had shattered the windows. Flames engulfed the beautiful wooden exterior and ash was all that remained of the patio.

Ella stood in disbelief. Her eyes closed and opened back up. She did not make a sound, too distraught to say a word. Tears fell down her cheeks as she watched her most prized possession burn to the ground.

"Ms. Collins?" asked one of the service workers. She looked over at him and looked back at the restaurant. It was gone. There was no point for the volunteer fire department to spray any more water. She could recover nothing at this point.

"Ella Collins?" he asked again.

"Yes," she muttered.

"We have contacted the owner. He said he would be right over."

"Sure," she replied and swiped her hands across her wet cheeks. "How did it happen?"

"We won't know anything until we investigate. It could take a few days before we determine the cause. Can we get you anything, Ms. Collins, anything at all?"

Ella shook her head. There was nothing that anyone could do for her that would make her feel better. She smoothed the seat of her dress and sat on the pavement. Her eyes never left the building. No one could know how her heart broke with the flames.

She heard a vehicle pull into the lot but hardly paid attention as she was mesmerized by the blaze. One door shut and then another. Normally, she would have looked to see who it was. Now, being cautious was the furthest thing from her mind.

"Mr. Tomassi," the worker said and walked past her.

"What happened?" Angelo asked.

"We don't know how it started. Several people called in and said they saw a fire in this direction. That's all we know right now."

"All right." Angelo let out a breath.

"Let me know if you need anything else, sir."

"Thank you," said Angelo. "Brett, why don't you and Sammy walk around? Rafa, pull up the surveillance and see what you can find."

Ella heard him give the orders. She envied his lack of attachment to the restaurant. Insurance would cover his loss, but nothing could replace hers.

"Hey," he said and lightly touched her arm. "Why don't you sit in the car with me?"

Ella shook her head. She did not want to get up or think. It was not as if staring at the fire would do anything, but she did not want to move. She would watch until the last plank burned.

Angelo did not force her to stand; instead, he crouched down and sat beside her. For a couple of minutes, his elbows rested on his knees. Then his arm draped around her shoulders and pulled her to his side. Ella could not hold it in anymore.

"It's gone," she cried and covered her eyes. "I didn't know I was seeing it for the last time earlier. The fire was too big. There was nothing they could do but to let it burn. There won't be anything left."

Angelo pulled her entire face to his chest. She needed comfort. His comfort was nice as his arms squeezed her tight. His chest was warm and inviting. It hid her from the reality of the world.

"We will find out what started the fire. Then we can go from there."

Ella stayed silent. It was late and the sound of his heartbeat started to calm her down. She felt an overwhelming exhaustion after a day like today.

"Come on," he said and started to stand. "Let me take you home. One of my men can stay for any questioning. A couple of them like to stay up all night anyway."

Ella hung her head. She wanted to stay and she wanted her bed. Sleep would help her more than the mental exhaustion of watching the fire. She gave up. Ella grabbed his hand as he helped her to her feet. She glanced back one more time and wiped her eyes. "Why did they have to come after the restaurant?" she asked. "Why couldn't they have come for me?"

***

Angelo helped Ella to his car and made sure he tucked her legs all the way in before shutting the door. The restaurant was not that big of a loss to him, yet he felt its value through her. Angelo felt responsible for the fire in some way or the other. His father could have burnt the place down for all he knew, trying to sever ties between him and Ella. He would not put it past Antonio.

At the same time, Ella put no blame on him. She spoke as if someone she knew could have burned it down. What person was she talking about? Who should have come for her instead? He was missing something.

Angelo glanced at her. Her eyes were red. Her hair scattered with the evening wind. Dust covered her black satin gown. An empty stare replaced her happy expression. He wondered if she would ever recover as he pulled down the road to her house and finally stopped in front. Ella stayed silent as he unbuckled her seatbelt. The movement snapped her to the present and she opened the handle on the door without looking at him.

"Thank you for the ride," she said and stumbled down the walkway to her porch.

He was not leaving her there alone. Angelo shut his door and walked immediately behind her. In her state, she could fall down the stairs and probably not care.

"You don't have to come up, Mr. Tomassi. I'll be fine."

He doubted that. Nothing about her state of mind was okay to him. "I'll stay for a while. I'm not leaving you alone, remember?"

Ella shrugged and unlocked the door, pushing it open enough for him to go in. Her family room was small and clean. A simple sofa and glass coffee table were the only pieces of furniture inside, and a single picture of a massive cruise ship hung on the wall. Ella must have liked ships.

"Do you want some coffee?" she asked.

He shook his head. "Why don't you sit down and let me make you some?"

Ella let out a brief, wispy laugh. "You know how to make coffee?" she asked.

Angelo tilted his head; a mocking grin spread on his lips. "Sit down," he pointed. "Yes, I know how to make coffee."

Despite the tears she cried and the mascara that streaked underneath her eyes, Ella managed to smile at his remark. It was the most beautiful sight he had ever seen. Her raw emotion and willingness to still smile after losing something precious made him want her even more. Ella made him feel like a normal man. He could forget about the pressures of his life with her. He had never experienced that feeling before.

Angelo walked to the counter and looked for her coffeemaker. His eyes scanned one end of the counter to the other. He saw no coffeepot but there were tiny plastic cups labeled coffee. Ella had one of those new machines. Someone had made him coffee from one a while back. How did they do it again?

Angelo smiled. Of all the high-technical electronics he used, he could not figure out a simple coffeemaker. The jokes he would earn if any of his men saw his predicament.

"Do you need some help?" Ella asked him. He crossed his arms as she moved in front. She opened the cabinet and grabbed two cups. Then she showed him the small plastic cup with coffee, lifted up the handle to the coffeemaker and placed the tiny cup inside. "Put your coffee cup underneath," she said, "and then close the handle and press start."

There was no way he could defend himself against his failure to make coffee, but Ella's smile widened and made his shortcoming worth his while. Maybe he needed to buy her a coffee shop.

"Here," she said and started making a second cup. "I still can't believe what happened." Her smile fell. "And the employees...I don't know what they're going to do."

"The employees," he thought aloud. "This is what I want you to do with them. Any employee who was there for over three months...give them three weeks of pay. That should get them by until they find something else. If they worked for less than three months, give them one week's pay. I think that'll work."

"You would do that?" Her eyes widened. Angelo almost felt insulted by her surprise.

"I'm not heartless," he huffed.

"I didn't mean it like it sounded." She tried to rephrase. "My father fired me—no notice, and I don't know any owner who would give extra pay."

Angelo brushed it off. Her father was not part of this discussion. "We're not all the same," he said simply.

Ella grabbed her cup and a spoon, adding both sugar and cream. Angelo winced at the sugar part of it. Sweets were not his thing. Then she walked to the sofa and waited for him to follow.

"Do you want to sit down," she offered.

"Why not." He gave in. He was in no hurry to get back to the club and grill Merrick anyway. "So...how did you know that man at the party?" he asked.

Ella shrugged. "A few years ago, I was sneaking into a party at a hotel where my father was. My father and Merrick were arguing. I guess it was over some property. Then Merrick shot my father in the leg and left. He saw me for a few seconds, and I was hoping he wouldn't remember me."

"Ella, there isn't a man alive who could pass you and not remember you." Angelo let slip. Then he closed his eyes and glanced at the floor. Why did he say that aloud? Ella was starting to rub off on him. "How do you know it was the same man?" he continued.

"He had the same bald spot over his ear. It's an easy mark to recognize."

"Yes, it is." Angelo nodded. "Look, I'm trying to understand this better. You said that Merrick shot your father in the leg. You do know that it was a warning shot, don't you? Merrick wasn't going to kill your father. What were they arguing about?"

"I don't know. My father was selling a property and said the owners backed out of selling it." Ella paused and thought. "Wait...I knew that name sounded familiar when you said it. That's why..."

What name sounded familiar to her? Angelo stared as Ella reflected and came to some clear understanding. He needed to know about her decisive moment if it belonged to a name he mentioned to her. "What name sounded familiar, Ella?" he asked.

"Bonadio—my father sold him property. I knew I heard the name before. My father was arguing with Merrick about a property that Bonadio wanted to buy."

Angelo thought about the name with disgust—Geraldo Bonadio. He could still remember a time when Bonadio had the chance to make a name for himself. He had a respectable stature at almost six feet and light brown hair that he parted to the side and back. Angelo would have given him the benefit of the doubt, but one look into Bonadio's cold brown eyes made Angelo wary from the start. He knew Bonadio could not be trusted.

"Well, Bonadio wants Orlando too. That's where you came from, right? He wants Miami and he wants Orlando. Your father got caught up with the wrong man."

"You think so? Would he kill?"

Angelo raised his brow at the question. Her sudden interest made him curious. "Why would you ask a question like that?"

Ella looked down and exhaled. "My mother was killed. They called it a suicide but my mother loved her life. She wouldn't have done anything like that. I don't care what anyone says. I will never believe what they said."

Angelo understood the entire picture now. Her father conducted business with the wrong man and had protected Ella ever since. She did not know the truth of the situation. How was her father going to tell her that his business associates killed her mother and were after her next?

"Come here," Angelo said and took her cup and his, setting them both on the table. Ella started to lean toward him but hesitated. Angelo needed to convince her and grabbed her hand.

"I'm a mess." Ella's fingers slid over the top of her hair and down the dusty dress until her hand rested in her lap. She let out a frustrated sigh.

Angelo gazed at her with disbelief. The last two days would completely change her life, yet she worried about her appearance in front of him. Ella did not know she was stunning no matter how she looked. If she would not come to him, he would have to go to her.

He scooted over and strummed both hands along her arms and higher, until his fingers completely wrapped around her cheeks. Ella looked at him. Her blue eyes stared at him and never looked away. She did not smile, yet her innocent expression invited more of his affection, like in his car and his room at the club. He would not resist what he wanted any longer and touched her forehead with his.

"You are perfect," he whispered and firmly pressed his lips over her mouth, indulging her with the passionate warmth of his kiss.

She gave into him, letting him kiss her as he pleased. His hands moved to the center of her back. He held her firmly and listened to her soft blissful sounds as he guided her lips. Her fingers clenched the ends of his coat as he moved his mouth to the turn of her neck, her head tilting to the side in response.

Angelo slid down the zipper on the back of her dress halfway and let the strap of her dress fall past her shoulder. His mouth indulged lower. Pulling her flush against his chest, he wanted to taste every inch of her skin. He wanted to alleviate his desire and claim her, but he would wait.

He gently kissed her once more and slightly pulled away. With a small, hesitant smile, he looked at her and hugged her closely. He did not want to let her go.

"Go get in the shower, Ella. You need to get some rest."

Chapter 20

Ella rolled from the back cushions of the sofa and looked around the room. Where was Angelo? She could not have imagined he was there. The kiss of his soft lips still lingered on her mouth. If it was a dream, her subconscious played a cruel trick on her mind.

"I just got here," Brett said from the kitchen, making Ella jump.

"Did Angelo leave?" she asked and peered around the room.

When Brett nodded, her body fell back to the sofa, but the thud of the stiff cushions never came. A soft pillow cradled her head; the blanket from her bed covered her body. *I knew he was here.* Ella thought and smelled an appealing aroma from the coffee table where a cup of coffee still had steam rising out of the top. Ella's smile grew as she gazed at the cup. Angelo had paid attention when she showed him how to use the pot.

What time was it? As Brett stepped outside the front door with his phone to his ear, Ella jolted up and grabbed her phone from beside the cup. It was fifteen minutes after seven. She was late. The employees would be waiting for her to open the doors to the restaurant. Wait— Santiago's burned down.

Ella sipped a small drink from the cup and reflected on the previous night. Now what was she supposed to do? The reason she moved to Key Biscayne was for that restaurant. She felt like a piece of her heart died with the flames of the building. She did not know what direction to take next.

She sighed and started to fall to the sofa again when a knock came at the door. Brett must have locked the door on his way out. She stood and smoothed down the legs of the cotton pants she wore. At least she looked better than she did the previous night. Now she was glad that Angelo had urged her to take a bath when she would have slept instead.

Ella unlocked the front door and stared at a blue-eyed man on the other side. It was not Brett standing there. Her father used to send Simon to deliver messages when she attended school. After last night, Ella took a wary step back.

"Good morning, Simon," she greeted, though she was not up for a chat.

"Good morning, Ella," Simon said and walked past her and into her family room. The intrusion annoyed her. Her father had not spoken to her in months and suddenly wanted to interfere with her life.

"Would you like some coffee?" she asked to interrupt his gaze as he searched around the room. What was he hoping to find?

"You weren't alone last night," he said.

"No, I wasn't." She knew where this was going thanks to her father's rules. She did not care. Ella would make her own decisions from now on. Right now, she wanted Angelo.

"So," Ella tried to change the subject, "how is my father?"

Simon completely ignored her question. "You're wearing his ring." His voice sounded disgusted with the sight of the gold band around her finger. "Your father doesn't like Tomassi. He told you to stay away from him."

"He's my boss. He was here last night for business."

Simon put his finger over his lips and held up his palm to Ella. She instantly closed her mouth, unsure of what he was doing when he walked to the counter between the kitchen and family room; then he smashed it with his fist. He did the same in two other spots. Did Angelo really place tiny cameras in her house? Maybe he was concerned after last night, but he could have let her know.

"You shouldn't have brought him here. We told you to stay away from him. You not only didn't listen, you brought him to your house."

"My father doesn't control my life anymore. You remember—he cut me off when I decided to move. He can't expect me to do what he says when he hasn't talked to me. I have my own life now."

Simon was beginning to make Ella feel uneasy. His accusing tone put her on edge. She did not do anything that bad. What exactly concerned her father about Angelo that he would send her a message after all this time?

"I can't avoid seeing him when he's my boss. That's all there is to it."

"We saw you in the casino last night. I guess that was business too?"

Ella took a step back at the sarcasm in his words. He had no right to barge into her house and harass her like that. If Simon knew she was at the casino, he must have also known about the fire. "Did you know that the restaurant burned down last night?" she asked. His eyes immediately flickered up at the question. He knew.

"I'll be in the other room," he said without a reply.

"Did you want some coffee?" She offered again and entered the kitchen. She might as well try to keep the peace.

"No," he said without hesitation and walked out of the room.

Ella watched the door to her bedroom close as if this were his house. Who was he calling, and why did he become impersonal all of a sudden? He acted stoic in the past but never suspicious. The call lasted no more than a minute when he walked back out; his eyes looked at the floor. Simon circled the sofa once and then sat down. She braced herself for a lecture.

"Does my father have something else for you to tell me?" she asked.

"No," said Simon. Their conversation was going nowhere.

"Then why are you here?" Ella pushed one of her chairs underneath the table and stopped as Simon stood. His cold stare made the hairs on her arms stand with the chills that formed. Ella knew she was in trouble when he started walking toward her.

"You lied."

"What?" Ella had no idea what he was talking about when he slapped the side of her face. She stumbled. Her hand reached for the edge of the table just in time before she fell. The side of her face burned as she looked up from underneath her hair with hurt and shock from the force of his hand. "I don't understand," she whispered.

"You didn't come home at all the night before, and you were seen leaving the club yesterday afternoon. Business doesn't take your attention all night long. I know you were with Tomassi."

Ella started to back away at the dangerous tone in his voice. This was much different from Sullivan carrying her out of a club or restricting her to her room. He would have never hit her. No one ever had.

"Your whole house is bugged. Do you think you're fooling anyone by playing innocent? We know what you're up to." He pointed at her and shoved her against the wall.

The impact knocked the air from her lungs. Ella could not breathe for seconds; her hands immediately flung to her chest. Simon did not wait for her air to return. He opened up his palm again and backhanded her other cheek. There was nothing for her to grab this time. Ella fell against the corner of her wooden table and crumpled to the floor.

"Let that be an example to you," he said as Ella heaved air back in her lungs. "Do what your father says and stay away from Tomassi, or next time, I won't be so nice. You understand what I mean."

As Simon turned to leave, he looked back and grabbed her coffee off the table; he dumped the contents down his throat and let the door slam behind him as he walked out. Ella moaned and crawled around the table to the counter. Why did the side of her body hurt so badly? She looked down at her cotton nightshirt and groaned again. Blood started to seep through. She must have hit the edge of the table hard.

She finally stood up and turned the knob on the faucet, the cold water relieving the burning of her face. Water tinged with red dripped back into the sink. No wonder his second slap stung worse than the first. Simon always wore a thick, rigid ring. The sharp point must have cut through her skin.

Ella straightened her back. She wanted to lie down, but her mind would not rest. She was thinking about her father. He was many things, but he would never condone this treatment of her. She intended to find out what was going on and stormed to the restroom where she left the emergency phone he had given her.

Ella turned it on. With a stroke of luck, the phone had power. She waited for the phone to load and pressed the only number available — her father's. She called but nothing happened. An alerting sound came on and told her the number was no longer available. *You have to be kidding me.* She thought. She tried repeatedly but still received the same annoying tone. Ella had enough of her father ignoring her and pitched the phone to her bed. If he did not want to speak to her, that was fine. She would have to go see him.

Ella slid to the floor beside her restroom door. Her body ached more as the adrenaline rush subsided. Tears trickled off her chin. First the restaurant burned and now this. She wondered if it was her body or her heart that hurt more. Nothing was working out how she had planned. Her eyes shut in an attempt to shut out the world.

Chapter 21

She felt like minutes passed when she opened her eyes again. Somebody pounded on her front door; then it opened with such urgency that it slammed back shut by itself. She saw a shadow on the wall as the person ran through the family room.

"Ella!" Rafa called. Ella mumbled in return. She never thought she would actually be happy to see Rafa, but she welcomed his familiar face as he lifted her off the floor.

"Rafa," she said but started to cough. Her throat felt dry and cracked as he laid her on her bed.

"Hey, it's me." He hesitated before continuing the call. "I got here five minutes too late after Brett called me about the trouble outside. You need to get down here now. Ella's hurt," he said and looked into the kitchen. "No, they are all smashed and…" Rafa glared at his phone and then slid it in the pocket of his shirt. His attention immediately focused back on her.

"Who did this?" he asked and walked to the kitchen. Ella heard several drawers open and shut before the water turned on. He came back and started dabbing her cheek with a washcloth. He looked down at her shirt and pulled her to his side as he started pressing the area above her waist. "Do you know who it was?" His voice was calm but his eyes looked irate.

"I—" Ella started to answer but winced. Rafa had pressed the injury a little too hard.

"Give me a name," he said again.

"Simon," she answered. Her voice strained.

"What about a last name?"

"Simon…Simon…I don't know. I wasn't told his last name."

"You knew Merrick," Rafa reflected, "so if his last name is Turner, he's with Bonadio."

"But Simon used to come over to our house all the time."

Rafa looked at her and continued wiping her cheeks. "Does he have light brown hair and stands a little shorter than me? Blue eyes?"

"Yes, but my father wouldn't have allowed him to hurt me like this."

"Bonadio doesn't care. If your father screwed him over, Bonadio will use you until your father gives him what he wants. Right now, he wants property."

"Would Bonadio burn down a restaurant?"

"And more," Rafa scoffed. "Bonadio already doesn't like Angelo. If he knew Angelo owned the restaurant—"

"Wait," Ella said in remembrance. "He did know. Two men came one morning and told me to stay away from Angelo. I told them he owned the restaurant."

"Why would they tell you to stay away from him?" Rafa asked. His eyes narrowed with confusion.

"Because my father didn't let me date. He kept me under close watch all the time. I had a caretaker."

"Oh yeah? Well, that was probably smart if he was doing business with the wrong people...which it sounds like he did."

Ella let out a sigh and tried to sit up. "How bad do I look?" she asked.

"Bad enough to lie back down," he answered and started to push her back to her pillow.

"I need to go back to the club."

"Are you out of your mind? What for?"

"They'll be at the casino tonight. I know it."

"Who?" asked Rafa.

Ella ignored Rafa's question. Whether it was because of her father or Angelo, Bonadio made someone burn down Santiago's. She wanted answers. "I'll be ready this time," she said aloud.

Ella stood to her feet. Her head felt dizzy but she walked to the restroom anyway. Sullivan had taught her many things. Ella always wondered why, but maybe he knew her father was dealing with the mafia. It was time she put that knowledge to use.

"We won't let you go. Angelo won't put you through that. You weren't supposed to get hurt." Ella listened to Rafa through the restroom doorway as someone else barged into her house.

"Where is she?" Angelo asked. She heard panic in his voice and opened the door.

"I'm right here," she answered as he walked up to her.

"God almighty," he said and lightly rested his elbows on her shoulders. He turned her cheek to one side and then the other. She could feel his eyes staring at the bruising marks on her face. "Did you get a name, Rafa?"

"I think it's Simon Turner," he replied. "I won't be sure until we see him."

"Son of a bitch. He's going to fucking die. That's all there is to it." Angelo let out a breath and rubbed Ella's arms up and down. "Are you all right?"

"Ella thinks she's going to the club tonight."

"The hell you are," Angelo mocked. "Look at you. You need to rest."

"Angelo," Rafa handed him a clean washcloth, "her side is bleeding again."

"Let me go. I have to."

"After all this, why the hell would I do something stupid like that and put you in danger?"

"Because they burned down the restaurant and attacked me for wearing your ring. I deserve to know why, Mr. Tomassi. Do you remember those two men who left the morning you came to the restaurant for the reports?"

"I remember." Angelo's brows narrowed.

"They were telling me to stay away from you, and I didn't. I told them I couldn't because you were the owner."

"Ella, listen to me. They want you away from me because they know I will protect you, and that will ruin their plan. Bonadio is trying to use you."

"For what? To get something from my father?"

"That's right," Angelo said.

"And they burned down the restaurant too?"

"That way you wouldn't talk to me anymore."

Ella hung her head. "So Santiago's is gone because I told them you owned it. It's my fault."

"It's not your fault. It's how things work in this world." Angelo wrapped her to his chest and gently squeezed. "Rafa—" Angelo pointed.

"On it." Rafa walked out of the room as though he read Angelo's mind.

"Where's he going?" Ella asked.

"To get info we ordered on your father. We need to know how deep he is with Bonadio."

"You can do that?" Ella asked, surprised.

"We can't, but we know someone who can." Angelo dabbed the washcloth on her cheeks again and looked around the room. "You can't stay here anymore."

"I can't leave. I have nowhere else to go."

"I'm not asking, Ella. I'm telling you that you're not staying here. We'll get your stuff later. For now, you'll come with me."

Ella glanced in her kitchen with sad reflection. So much happiness in this city lost in a single day. "I need to change my clothes before I go." She held out the two ends of her button-up nightshirt that blood now stained.

"Where's your closet."

Angelo followed her as he pulled out a black pistol from the back of his slacks. These men had guns on them at all times. It almost made her uneasy as she pulled an outfit off the hanger and glanced back to see Angelo staring at her. Was he going to watch her change?

"I'm not looking away," he said. "I need to see if there are any other cuts on your body."

Ella turned back around. She doubted he was looking at her for any reason other than what he said. "This is deep." His thumb moved around the cut on her waist. "I'll call Dr. Stefano when we get back to my place."

"Yours?" she asked.

"That's right. You can't stay here, and the doctor can't fix you at the hospital. Too many questions."

Ella shook her head with the light that flickered off the mirror. Her reflection looked back at her. Bruises appeared. Her pink splotchy cheeks proved that her life had drastically changed in the last few days. Blood was starting to dry on her side. Then she saw Angelo's expression grow hard as the creases between his brows deepened.

"That man who did this...Simon," she started.

"Yes."

"I trusted him. Simon was welcomed in my father's house. He ate dinner with us. I don't know how he could do this. He even told me if I didn't stay away from you, he wouldn't be so nice next time. Maybe I should thank him."

The muscles in Angelo's jaw tensed. He pulled her against his body again, giving her the comfort of his warmth as he stroked her hair with his hands. "I'm taking care of you from now on, so I'll gladly thank the asshole for you. Are you sure you don't know his last name?"

"I knew him as Simon."

"Christ, Ella. You father didn't tell you a whole hell of a lot. Is there anything you do know?"

"Well...I couldn't ask questions he didn't want to answer. If you met him, you'd understand."

"Hurry up and change, Ella," Angelo grumbled and gently grabbed her hand. "You've been living in a fucking death trap."

Chapter 22

Angelo closed his fingers around hers and held his gun tightly with his other hand, a second gun strapped at his waist. Simon must have waited all night for the right time to strike. Angelo had been gone ten minutes and that was all the time it took for the chaos to take place.

He helped Ella through the front door of her house and walked slowly down each step, constantly looking back at her. Ella's face started to bruise, resembling having been in a street fight. She dragged her feet along but did not complain. Angelo admired her tough front. She must have been in pain.

They turned on the walkway to where he parked his car when he stopped mid-step. Angelo shoved Ella behind him, holding her directly against his back as a man lunged forward and stabbed him in the arm; another pointing a gun at his head.

Now he understood. Ella was the bait. He was the catch.

He felt nothing at first; then his arm went cold, a fiery pain shooting up to his right shoulder. His grip tightened around Ella with every pulsing twinge of pain, his anger heightening to rage. Somebody was going to die.

"You're hurt." Ella exclaimed and moved her hand to his sleeve. Blood started to ooze through the white material and drip to the ground.

"Stay behind me," he ordered. He would worry about the injury after he killed the men.

One of the men charged at him. Angelo took a quick step back when Ella yanked the gun from the side of his pants and pointed it at them. "What do you want?" she shouted.

"Shoot them!" Angelo demanded. His policy was to shoot first and ask questions later.

The man smiled. Angelo did not like his mocking smirk or the way his eyes scanned over her body. They wanted her too. There was a grander scheme at work.

"Right," the man taunted. "There's no way you can pull that trigger. You don't have it in you."

As soon as the man finished his remark, Ella shot the gun from his hands. She was quicker than he was. It could have been a poor shot.

She could have meant to kill the bastard, but a shot so close to his fingers without touching his heart was no accident. She could have easily killed him instead.

"Get back inside, Ella!" Angelo grabbed the gun from her hands, wasting no time as she ran. He fired. Two clean bullet holes between their eyes was the only satisfaction he felt in this exchange. He waited for the thuds of their bodies. He looked down on them with disgust.

"Angelo," Ella screamed.

He ran to her, coming to a dead stop with the gun against her head, a man trailing her hair with the muzzle. Angelo let his gun fall to the ground; his arms lifted high in immediate response as he tried to direct their attention onto him. They were toying with him. He knew they did not want her dead; but in their moment of glory, they might shoot to make a statement.

"One step, Tomassi..." Her body shivered as the cold edge of the gun stopped at her neck. Angelo froze. The burn of anger heated his skin as he looked in the eyes of the man who held the gun.

"You're dead," said Angelo.

"You don't know—" The sound of his last spoken word still lingered in the air as he dropped dead to the ground.

"I took care of the other guys...got back as fast as I could." Brett said, a pleased look residing on his face as he looked down on the man. "Been waiting to use my new gun. Don't need to thank me, Boss. I love my job."

Angelo picked up his gun and walked to Ella. His arms wrapped around her and squeezed her shaking body close. She was not crying but looking ahead, a little disoriented.

"Brett, get Sammy and clean this up. Make sure you get the two around the corner."

"Really?" Brett looked disappointed. "I missed out on half the fun."

"Brett...go," Angelo said pointedly.

***

From Angelo's sofa, Ella focused on the ceiling to keep her mind off the needle and constant tugging of the suture from Dr. Stefano's hands. She was glad he gave her some type of anesthetic, but there were still twinges of pain as the aging man concentrated on stitching her wound. He must have been used to taking care of Angelo. He remained stoic and stitched her skin unfazed.

While the doctor examined the knife wound on Angelo's arm, Ella looked around his family room. A television was mounted from the ceiling in front of his dark leather sofas, and a laptop lay open on the bar in the kitchen. The place was dust free, giving no real sign that he lived there at all.

Ella looked down the hallway. There were several rooms with closed doors but one room had none, the morning sun shining off a beautiful wooden piano. She admired the patterned carvings of the wood and intricate handles of the fallboard, wondering what other secrets hid behind the other closed doors.

Jarring her from her muse, the front door closed, and Ella returned her attention back to Angelo.

"Come with me," he said and helped her to her feet. His gentle assistance made her smile as he led her down the hallway. It was sweet of him to make sure she felt comfortable. "Lay on the bed. I'm going to get some icepacks and the meds Stefano left."

Angelo's room was double the size of any normal master room. Colorful Italian tapestries, one of wartime remembrance and one with impassioned lovers decorated two of his walls from ceiling to floor. An oak dresser with a large mirror stood against one corner with a tall chest of drawers on the other. The diamond-stitched quilt on his bed accentuated the room, making it ideal for any home marketing catalogs.

Angelo came back and set a bottle of pills next to her; then he carefully placed icepacks on her cheeks. "Hold these," he said. "The ice won't make the bruises disappear but they'll help." He lifted up her dress and looked at her waist. His nod seemed satisfied. Dr. Stefano must have done a good job with the wound.

"I decided to bring you to the club later. I'll be with you this time."

"Do you know what they want from my father yet?"

"I should know something later." By the sound of his voice, Ella wondered if he would learn anything at all. "I'm getting in the shower," he said. "Take my gun and use it if you have to."

Ella nodded and watched him. Angelo left the door open as he stood in front of a full-length mirror and started to peel off his clothes. Ella tried to look away but her eyes glued to his body. She could not help but admire him. The scars on his chest betrayed many confrontations like today. No wonder he was a serious man.

Angelo stepped through the clear shower door and closed his eyes. She appreciated the way his arm muscles tightened as he lathered his biceps and then his neck. The way the water slid down his toned abs awakened sensations that she had not experienced. Watching the beads falling off the tips of his hair caused her face to flush. Sudden warmth spread throughout her body. Ella felt hot as she stared. Then she inhaled. Ella had not seen the dark brown eyes gazing back at her.

The water shut off and Ella rolled away from having faced the restroom door. She needed to fall asleep before he walked out, but her heart would not slow down. The closer his footsteps came, the more her body shook. She heard something fall to the floor, making a thud when it hit; then she felt an airy draft as Angelo pulled the covers down.

"I know you're not asleep," he said and slid his body next to hers. The dip in the bed did nothing to help her nerves. Her trembling increased as his arm slid underneath her shoulders and pulled her flush with his body. "Did you like watching me shower?" Angelo spoke against her ear, making it hard for her to breathe in normal breaths.

"I didn't—"

Ella could not form her thought, her focus drawn to Angelo's fingers that brushed above her knee to the inside of her thigh. Her breathing hitched as his lips met her neck, the warm kisses causing chills to shoot across her skin. Then he stopped. Angelo leaned on his elbow and turned her to face him, her face hot as he placed his fingers over her lips.

"You're wearing my ring now. I have the right."

Ella's mouth opened. As Angelo looked down at her, the only thing he wore was a lone pair of boxers and a chain around his neck. Desire replaced her uncertainty. Every part of her mind reacted to him as he took advantage of her gaping mouth and gently pressed her lips with his. Closing her eyes, she wanted so much more, his arousal building a furious heat within her. He took the hint. His lips indulged in aggressive, needy passion, his fingers tightening around her neck. The weight from his body started to grow heavier against her breasts when he pulled away and stopped.

"Too bad you're hurt or I'd take you right now," he said, staring at her with a sort of predatory gaze, "but I can't risk hurting you when you're already hurt."

Ella stayed silent in the warmth of his arms. The entire situation seemed unreal, yet his scent was real. The way he tangled his fingers through her hair made her limbs react to him all over again. He cradled her body to his.

"We have a few hours until Rafa gets here, so I want you to try to rest. Tonight's probably going to be tough."

Ella watched him fall asleep. He looked like an angel with his eyes closed, validating his name. Seeing his peaceful face like this, she never would have guessed he was in the mafia.

Chapter 23

Angelo groaned at the intrusive knocking at his door. Rafa was the only person who would beat on his door without caring about whether or not it made Angelo mad. Rafa was insistent, his concern growing as Angelo waited to answer.

"Who is banging like that?" said Ella, her voice muffled and raspy under the blanket.

"I'll get you some water."

Angelo scooted out of bed. As he pulled a belt through the loops of his pants, he watched her struggle to move. The meds must have worn off. Her body rolled into a ball with her knees to her chest as a steady rhythm of bangs came at the door again. He would let Rafa in as he got Ella water.

"How is she?" Rafa asked and came in with an armful of clothes.

"I'm giving her some more meds. She won't make it through the night without them." Angelo grabbed a bottle of water from the cabinet and walked back through the house with Rafa following behind. "Set them on the bed," he said of the clothes and looked back at Ella. She had not moved an inch.

"Sit up, Ella." He tapped his fingers against her foot. "You need to take these." Ella uncovered her face and looked at him and then at Rafa who stood in the doorway. A few seconds later, her eyes shut again. "Sit up," he repeated.

"What are they?" she asked and pushed her body up sideways.

"They'll help you. You have to take something if you're going tonight." Ella swallowed the pills without any more questions; then her head fell back to the bed. "When you feel better, I want you to take a shower. The hot water will be good for you."

Angelo left Ella to rest and walked back to the kitchen. He wanted to know what was in the envelope that Rafa held underneath his arm. He scooted a chair out and Rafa did the same, but Rafa said nothing at first.

"Quit fucking with me, Rafa, and tell me what you found."

Rafa opened the envelope and took out a photo, placing it in front of Angelo. "This is Robert Collins," he said. Angelo looked at the picture. The sandy-colored hair and grayish eyes did not belong to anyone he knew. This man could not have worked for Bonadio. Angelo knew the faces of every one of Bonadio's top men.

"Donnie hasn't pulled up anything recent on Collins yet, but he has definitely sold property to Bonadio in the past."

"Okay," Angelo nodded. "We were right about that then."

"Yes." Rafa paused and opened the envelope again. "Guess whose property he sold to Bonadio."

Angelo did not like the sound of Rafa's tone. The look in his eyes was a sign of trouble. Angelo had not stopped to think about the clients that Ella's father had. "*Whose* property did he sell?" He sat back and folded his arms.

"Gregorio," answered Rafa as he set two sheets of paper on the table.

"What?" Angelo said dryly. He grabbed the sheets and started to scan for names. There it was in bold black ink—the name of Martino Gregorio. "You mean Gregorio is using Collins too?" He held out his hand and threw down the sheets. "Ella's in the middle of a fucking nightmare and her father let her leave without telling her anything." Angelo shook his head with disbelief. "We need to know what Bonadio wants from Collins. Tonight goes as planned."

"I was thinking—"

"Hold that thought." Angelo heard the shower turn on and walked back to his room. With the restroom door shut, Angelo tapped it lightly, not wanting to scare her but feeling no shame by walking in on her either.

"The towels are in this cabinet." He opened a door by the sink and turned around. The swelling in her cheeks had gone down. The marks were not too noticeable; but in the way she moved, he knew she was in pain.

"When you get out, I have food for you."

"Okay," she said, staring back at him as he gazed at her body exposed.

As much as he would have liked to take advantage of her soaking wet body, he walked out of the steamy room. Her healing injuries would have to come first, but he would make up for that soon. He looked forward to making her his.

***

Ella fidgeted with the slit of the ebony dress as Angelo guided her to a private elevator in the back entrance of the club and took her up to the third floor. She tolerated the single strap around her shoulder but the slit nearly reached her thigh. Did Rafa have to grab this dress from her house? There was a reason it was in the back of her closet.

Angelo checked the cameras in his office and made sure they were all working before they made their entrance in the casino. She watched him push several buttons. The sound for one monitor came on and went off. He duplicated the same action for the rest.

"Okay, now that that's done," he said and slid out a drawer on the desk. "I want you wearing a gun tonight." He walked over to her with a strap and the blue gun she had admired the day before. He lifted her dress and wrapped the leather strap and holster around her thigh. "You have amazing aim. I've never seen a woman who could shoot like you, but I'm letting you know now; if you pull this thing out, be ready to kill. If you don't, they will. Do you get that?"

"Yes," she whispered as he took her hand. She was not sure which made her more nervous—having the gun or holding Angelo's hand.

"I wonder if the concealer will stay on." Ella touched the side of her face as the elevator to the back of the casino opened.

"No one can see your cheeks with the way you fixed your hair. How do you feel?" He gave her hand a gentle squeeze.

"I'm okay."

"I'll be in there with you this time. You'll be fine."

Angelo entered through the back of the casino and walked with her beside him. The guests stared, surprised that Angelo walked in with a woman on his arm. Some of them had returned from the previous night. She remembered their faces. Even though Ferron flaunted her around the casino like a trophy, Angelo made a statement by holding her hand.

He led her to the bar where Thomas helped another customer on the far end. All Angelo did was point at him. Thomas halted his conversation and the drink he prepared and walked directly over to Angelo.

"Good evening, Mr. Tomassi," he greeted. "What will you have?"

"The regular," Angelo said and glanced at Ella. "Make her a margarita but go easy on the tequila." Thomas left and Ella gave

Angelo a look. "Listen, you're on pain meds and those pills don't mix well with alcohol. I don't need to carry you out of here."

"Fine." Ella complied as Angelo turned around, looking at the guests in the room.

"These people are like fucking vultures," he muttered under his breath.

"What?" Ella was confused by his sudden admittance. "Then why do you own a club?" she asked.

"I own several. The man with the most money makes the rules." Angelo met her gaze and seemed in thought. "This club though…it's kind of a…it's where we get special shipments. A transfer spot."

"You mean like that room I found?"

"That's right. Nobody comes around here and asks questions. If they did, we have ways around it."

"The police department," Ella said.

"Don't act surprised," said Angelo. "There's a lot that happens that nobody knows about. That's how the world works."

"Here you are, Mr. Tomassi," said Thomas.

Angelo nodded and whispered in Ella's ear. "Don't ever call me by that name again. If you do, I'll beat you until you forget who I am."

"You'd beat me?"

"You remember who I am, right?" Something in his gaze tempted her to call him by the name, but she also did not want to test him in the club. She was not prepared for the consequences it may bring in front of all the guests. "My last name is for people who don't know me. That doesn't include you."

"It does make you sound distinguished though. I like the sound of your last name." She smiled.

"Oh?" Angelo said and pulled her head closer to him, brushing his lips against hers. "Go ahead and call me whatever you want, but you might not be safe if you do."

"Thomas," Angelo said. "Keep an eye on her for a minute."

"You're leaving?" she mumbled, the slouch in her posture giving away her disappointment.

"You don't need to pout. I'll be right back," he whispered in her ear. With his weight against her back, his fingers drifted down the turn of her neck to the side of her breast. The chills that formed on her skin left a satisfied smirk on his face as he walked away.

Ella swiveled in her stool and watched him take the room with his eyes. She admired him the same as the heads he turned. Several men and women stopped to shake his hand, hoping for a tinge of the individual attention that he gave to her. It was hard to believe she was with someone like him.

Remembering why she was there, Ella shook the thoughts from her mind. She came for a reason and it was not to watch Angelo. As she scanned the crowd, no person stood out yet. They may not have arrived but she continued to look anyway.

"You!" a woman yelled from the other side of the room. Ella turned to see who it was. "What did you do with Halsey?"

Not her. Ella thought. She had no time for disgruntled girlfriends with the threat of the attack earlier. She groaned, annoyed with the disturbance the scene would cause. The woman was not going to leave without trying to fight.

"Since you came here the other night, I haven't seen Halsey at all. You did something and now he won't call me back."

Ella could understand her frustration. She had been upset when Angelo would not talk to her. Angelo was different from Halsey, though. Halsey was the worst kind of man.

"Look, I didn't know either of you. That wasn't my fault."

"You're a liar." The woman slapped the bar beside Ella, glaring as she spoke. "I saw you talking to him even after you saw me. I heard them tell you who I was."

Ella closed her eyes and exhaled before opening them again to counter the woman's argument. "Are you serious? We both know that Halsey was using you. He wanted to use me too. Don't waste your time on men like that."

The woman wallowed in hatred and let it build inside her until she could no longer hold on to self-control, taking relief by punching Ella in the face. Ella moaned at the shooting pain on her recent injury. She should have seen that coming. Standing up, Ella rubbed her cheek and pointed.

"I have had a really bad day, and my face already hurts. I don't have time for this. I never wanted Halsey. I'm here with Mr. Tomassi anyway." Ella reared her fist back and punched the woman below the eye, the surprise of the impact knocking the woman to her back.

"Ms. Collins?" The woman looked up, dread replacing any anger that was there. "Oh my god, you're the one they attacked earlier. Please don't tell Mr.—" Hanging her head, the woman looked at the floor, her body wilting with defeat. "Fuck my life."

Angelo probably had more important issues than bothering with the woman. Ella did not intend to make a scene over nothing but still. Something bothered her. "Who said I was attacked?" she asked.

The woman shook her head. "I," she hesitated. "I shouldn't have said anything."

"Who?" Ella asked again.

"The private lounge in the back...some suits were talking about it."

"Do you know their names?"

"I don't ask names. I sit down and look good. That's what I do."

"It's probably best that you don't know their names," Ella said. "What's your name?"

"Angie," she said.

"I'm Ella. Who brought you here tonight?"

As the words left Ella's mouth, Angelo walked fast from the other end of the room. From the look on his face, he did not want her to talk to Angie.

Chapter 24

"I already warned you." Angelo marched up to the bar, snapping Angie back to the reality of the situation. "Go tell Jake I need to talk to him. You know why." Angie did not hesitate; she grabbed her drink and disappeared before he could say anything else. "You—" he turned to Ella next. "I leave you alone for two seconds." At Angelo's sharp tone, Ella turned to face the bar. "Look at me." His hand lifted her chin back to face him. "After what happened at your house, don't talk to anyone unless I'm with you."

"Why are you so mad?" she asked.

"Because you're too trusting." He pointed where Angie had left. "That woman shouldn't even be here. I warned her once and she's already running her mouth to you. She doesn't know you."

"But she was clearly dealing with—," she protested as he cut her short, gripping his arm around her waist.

"What I say goes. Mind your manners when we're out."

"Why? Are you going to make me dance like the other women?"

Looking at the stage in the middle of the room, Angelo scoffed, squeezing her bottom through her dress. "I wouldn't do that. I'd drag you to the back instead. On my bed...having my way," he whispered, sliding his fingers up the slit on the right side of her leg.

"I think I need another drink," said Ella, her cheeks blushing pink as she gave up her will to think.

"Thomas." Thomas had already made the drinks and set them down in front. Angelo handed her a glass. "Let's take a look around."

Ella grabbed onto his arm. Her side throbbed more than she thought it would after taking the medication. She winced a few times as Angelo looked at her. He must have felt her struggle and slowed down his steps.

"I saw you looking around earlier. Did you see anyone?" he asked.

"No, but that private room you have is good place to start," she said.

"How do you even know about that room?"

"In a place like this," Ella looked around, "it makes sense."

***

In the entrance of an oval shaped room, a man stood behind a bar with costly wines lined on top. Mirrors along the walls and the high ceilings made the room appear spacious, an illusion of reflections. Angelo led Ella through several card tables in the middle; at the end was a stage. A topless dancer performed in the shadows of a candle-like glow that shined off the silver-beaded necklace around her neck. None of the men paid attention to the dancer. Maybe she lightened the strain.

"How is everyone?" Angelo greeted the table, his arm tensing as she held it. She sensed the danger too.

"Doing great," one of the men said and stood to shake his hand. "Your clubs are always above my expectations. I'm glad for the invite."

"Good to hear," Angelo replied. "How are my workers doing?"

"Never better, although—" The man laid his arm around Angelo's shoulder, shaking the hold she had on his arm. She could still hear the whispered words the man said.

"I think your clubs should offer the guests something more satisfying—some private rooms on the side. You could double your money if you did that."

Ella's brows lifted. She started to open her mouth and say something when a member of the table pulled her to the man's vacant chair and leaned closer to her face. "You are a beautiful woman. Tomassi was wise to keep you a secret all this time."

Ella smiled politely but said nothing. Since Angelo was busy talking, she focused on the faces around the table instead. Somebody here knew about the attack, but she recognized no one at the table. Ella looked at the other tables in the room. Then she saw them, the two men who had given her a message at the restaurant. They sat two tables down.

"Excuse me." She tried to stand up when the man next to her placed his hand on her arm. "Excuse me," she said. "I'd watch where you put your hands." She looked in his eyes, the man taking the hint and releasing his grip.

"I apologize, Miss," he said. Then he looked at Angelo and winked. "If only my woman was as obedient." Ella's eyes darted to the man and scowled. He talked about her as if she was not even there. What was she—a toy? "Tomassi's a lucky bastard," he then went on to say.

Ella looked back at Angelo as she stood. He seemed occupied with his conversation, but she saw his eyes. As he talked, he still focused on every table in the room. When one of the men at the other table reached underneath, Angelo jerked his gun from his coat and aimed at the man. The dancer on the stage shrieked, but the other guests simply backed their chairs out of the way without hesitation or surprise. Ella knew they had seen this before.

While Angelo aimed at the other table, the man he was talking to pulled a gun on him. Ella now knew why Rafa chose a dress with the highest slit. She easily yanked her pistol from the holster and pointed it at the man.

"Do and you'll get that private session you wanted, I promise." When the man lowered both arms to his sides, Angelo knocked him in the temple with his gun.

"I told you to shoot," he growled.

"You can't get information from a dead man, can you?" Ella yelled.

As Rafa and Brett walked through a door behind the stage, Angelo said something else. Ella did not hear. She saw a reflection at the entrance; the bartender was gone. The door to the room was open with a person standing in front. He pointed the barrel of his gun directly at Angelo; his finger was pulling the trigger. With a fraction of a second to act, Ella shoved Angelo's body back.

"Get down!" she screamed to the dancer who stood in the path of the bullet. This time, Ella did not hesitate. Between the pain and the restaurant, something inside of her snapped. She did not know she was crying. She pulled the trigger on her gun, hitting the man's right shoulder. His gun crashed to the floor as she started walking toward him. She would recognize Simon in the dark.

"So..." She pointed her gun without thought and watched Simon fall to his knees. "Did you enjoy earlier? Making me feel helpless? Slapping me? Did you burn down the restaurant too?" Simon looked up at her with an expression of guilt. Ella felt her bottom lip quiver and aimed her gun at him again. She felt vindicated as a second bullet lodged into his chest. "Was it worth it?" she asked without feeling remorse.

"Kill me already." He stared at the floor, his breaths raspy while clenching the blood-soaked shirt that covered his chest.

"Is your last name Turner?" she asked. When Simon would not talk, Ella raised her gun again.

"Yes," he huffed out.

Ella bent down to look in his eyes. "Why'd you pick on me?" She let down her guard and lowered her gun.

"Enough," Angelo said and fired a shot. Blood hit the wall behind Simon with his head crashing against the bar. His body landed with a heavy thud against the wooden floor.

Ella glared back at Angelo. All she felt was anger. "Why'd you do that? I wasn't going to kill him. He had questions to answer."

"Did you see him reach for the gun in his boot?"

"Yes! I knew I was faster than him."

"We have his name. We didn't need anything else."

"I wanted to know more," she said.

"I'll find out more with the other three," he said between his teeth.

"Then I'm going with you." She stood, determined to hear what they said.

"You don't belong around these people. It's too dangerous."

"Dangerous." She shook her head, looking at Simon's body. "You think I'm safe anywhere?"

"This isn't a debate." Angelo avoided the question.

His response did not satisfy her as she looked back in the room. The guests fixed their eyes on her. They kept exchanging baffled glances with each other. Ella wondered if they might turn her in. She also wondered about the dancer. Would she say something about what happened?

"Why is everyone staring at me?" Unnerved, Ella looked at Angelo.

"No one will talk. Don't worry about it."

"This is pretty common then." Ella waved her hand through the air.

"It's not like we plan these things." Angelo's tone deepened as he grabbed her arm and pulled her to him. "Did you plan that just now?" He pointed at Simon on the floor.

"No, but that—that was different."

As the adrenaline started to subside, Ella was coming down from the rush. She could feel the tears stinging the edges of her eyes. What had she done?

"I was born defending myself. There's no difference. We do what needs to be done, like you did. Even an innocent young woman will torture a man when provoked."

Ella shook her arm from his grasp and frowned. "If you don't need me anymore, I'm going to bed...if that's all right with you...*sir*."

She saw the huff of air he blew out at the name. He stared at her as though he wanted to slap the remark from her mouth. His fist tightened before he finally opened his mouth.

"Brett," he called out as Brett and Rafa returned. "Take Ella to my room. I'll be there soon," he said, looking in her eyes. "We will finish this talk then."

Chapter 25

Ella slid down the side of the bed to the floor. She had shot a man...caused him physical pain. The blood from his wounds was on her hands. An image of his hunched-over body kept playing in her mind. Then, one second later, he was dead.

Ella squeezed her eyes closed. She never imagined this type of life. The guns. The private meetings in her father's office. Sullivan's lessons. They all made sense now. Her father was involved with dangerous people, and they taught her to be like them without her knowing.

"Hey," Angelo said and walked through the door. "What are you doing on the floor?" He crouched down in front of her and sat, stretching his legs to the bed.

"I shot him," she said disbelieving.

"Yes." Angelo pulled her legs over his and scooted closer. Ella felt a cold chill spread throughout her body. Her palms felt damp with the realization.

"He would've killed someone tonight if you hadn't shot him."

"The first shot, yes...but not the second. I hated him. That's why I shot him again."

"That happens sometimes," said Angelo.

"No, that's not a good reason. Hate isn't a good reason." Ella hung her head in shame.

Angelo let out a sigh as his hands cupped her cheeks and lifted her face. "Why did you hate him, Ella?"

"Because he hit me and he burned down my restaurant—well your restaurant—but it was the only thing I had left from my mother. Gone. All gone now."

"Maybe you hated what he did then." Ella shrugged. Her head fell against his chest with disgust for herself and Simon—and her father. She had never felt like this before.

"They killed my mother, didn't they?" she mumbled into his coat.

Angelo shook his head and laid his hands on her back. She found his gentle caresses soothing to her mind. "I don't know," he said.

"They did. They went after her first. That's the only thing that makes sense."

"Okay Ella, why don't you lay down? Rest will be good."

"I guess." She lifted up her head again. "Are you staying?"

"I have some things to take care of. I'll be back later, though."

Ella knew what he meant. He was going to talk to those men and get information out of them. She would have argued with him and asked him to go too, but she could not find any strength left. She did not have it in her to face them right now.

"All right, I guess I'll see you later." She moved her legs from on top of him and stood. "Be careful," she said as she sat on the bed.

Angelo squatted in front of her and smiled. "A little girl like you telling me to be careful? You act like I might not come back."

Ella's shoulder shrugged with her lips pressed sideways. "Maybe I understand what you said before about celebrating every morning when you wake up alive."

Angelo closed his eyes and nodded. "Get some sleep," he said and leaned forward. His lips came closer to hers, but a small kiss was all he gave. "We will talk more in the morning."

***

Ella tossed more than she slept and found the sheets twisted between her legs without covering her arms at all. It was eight in the morning. Her head ached and pain shot down her side. She still felt a sickening awareness in her stomach.

She wondered why Angelo had never come to the room last night. Given her state of mind, he probably thought she was weak and did not want to give her bad news. It was not that she was weak. She was trying to adjust. Her thoughts consumed her mind like a plague. She needed answers and had one thought in mind—going to Orlando to confront her father.

"Angelo wants to see you in his office," Rafa said, walking into the room.

"I'm hurting too much to move," she groaned. "Do you know where he keeps the meds?"

"I brought you some…thought you might like some coffee too."

"Thank you." Ella eagerly took the coffee and swallowed the pills.

Ten minutes later, she waited for Angelo to finish flipping through paperwork at his desk. A wave of exhaustion came over her as she sat, the soft blanket she brought to the office not helping her to stay awake. She quietly lay back on the sofa and curled her legs.

"About your father," Angelo said as soon as her eyes began to close.

"Yes?" His voice startled her from a needed nap. "Oh…what about him?"

"Are you still sleepy?" he asked. "Why don't you come over here? I want to show you something."

"I'm really tired," she muttered but stumbled to his desk. On top laid a picture. She could not figure out why it was there. "Why do you have his picture?" she asked. "Is he involved too?"

"Your father?" asked Angelo.

"Well yes, my father too," she said. "My caretaker could have been involved, I guess. He taught me everything I know."

Angelo looked at her confused and picked up the picture of the sandy-haired man. "Who is this?" he asked.

"Mr. Sull-i-van," she slurred and grabbed onto his desk. Angelo looked at her as if she were drunk.

"This is not your father?" he continued with Ella shaking her head back and forth.

"He's Mr. Sulli-van."

"What's his full name?"

"That's a good question. I actually do know his name," she replied.

"And?" Angelo waited with Ella losing her balance and looking glassy-eyed.

"I need to lie down." She took a step toward the sofa again when Angelo stood up and embraced her with his arms.

"What is Sullivan's first name, Ella?"

"Jacob," she answered and swayed against his chest, leaving herself as deadweight against him.

"Fuck," he said and lifted her up in his arms. "I'm going to kill Rafa. Those meds shouldn't do this to you."

Her body felt like a cloud, drifting as he carried her back to the sofa. "Rafa sedated me?" she whispered and wrapped her arms around his neck.

"You'll be fine," he said and laid her down again.

"You smell nice." Her hands gripped through his hair, her fingers intertwining with the strands. "Are we really together? I don't even know if you really like me." Angelo smiled and shook his head. Ella could not help herself and squeezed one of his arms. "You're arms are really defined. You must work out or something. I like it when you're holding me."

The door opened again and Rafa walked inside. Angelo frowned the instant he saw him, annoyed that Rafa would see Ella's medicated display of honesty. "How many of those damn pills did you give her?"

"Three. Why?" Rafa answered without worry, but Angelo's expression hardened.

"Hell, someone her size needs two—max. No wonder she's zoning out like this."

"Why are you looking at me? You said you wanted her to sleep," Rafa countered.

"Not for two damn days."

"Please, she'll come out of it before evening."

Angelo looked back at her. He had gorgeous, serious eyes when he was mad. Ella wanted to touch him and laid her palms on his chest.

"You have a nice body, Mr. Tomassi. Why don't you show it to me again sometime?"

She could hear Rafa laugh but it made Angelo angrier than he was. "You say one fucking word," Angelo warned and pointed his gun at the door. It surprised Ella but she was not afraid.

"There's no need to get pissed off. She doesn't know what she's saying."

"She's drugged," Angelo scowled.

"Being possessive isn't really your style, Angelo."

Angelo tapped his fingers on the table and breathed in deep. Ella could tell that he was controlling his temper around her. "That picture that Donnie gave you. It's not Collins. It's a man named Jacob Sullivan. Look into it."

"What?" Rafa looked surprised.

"No questions—get out of my office," he said and waited for the door to shut. "You need to rest. You'll feel better when you wake up." He looked down at Ella.

She pouted. She slid her arms around his neck and locked her hands together. "Don't leave me. I don't want to be alone."

Angelo let out a breath as she scooted over for him. How could he resist her invitation? "All right, Ella." He closed his arms around her body and gave her a gentle kiss on her head. "It won't hurt to stay a little while longer."

Chapter 26

Ella opened her eyes, her vision hazy from her medicated induced sleep. How long had she been out? She looked around for a clock and noticed she was not in Angelo's office anymore. She was in his room.

She yawned and clicked on the screen to her phone. It was already past six at night. How did the entire day pass without her knowing? She had to get up and get dressed.

Then something jarred Ella in her grogginess, her face burning at the recollection. She remembered bits of what she had told Angelo earlier that morning. She was horrified with the words she had said. How would she look him in the eyes? Why had she practically thrown herself at him? Then she remembered what Angelo had said—Rafa.

Ella had to shake the thoughts and put the morning and everything that happened out of her mind. She called Lila as she slid on a simple black dress—nothing fancy today. She would not be in the VIP room and no one would show her off. She would relax with her friend over a drink. Ella looked forward to a normal night and hoped that no one in a suit with a gun would carry her away. She had enough of that lately. She needed a break.

As Ella waited on the front porch of the club, Lila came around the corner and was holding hands with Robby; behind them, Lila's friend Brandi followed them up the steps. "Great," Ella mumbled. No dress could be shorter or a brighter red color than the one that Brandi wore. Ella did not need attention being brought to her tonight.

"I'm ready to meet rich, beautiful men," Brandi said and grabbed Ella's arm. Brandi acted as though the two of them were longtime friends. Ella gave her a look of surprise, but Brandi smiled in return. Ella guessed if anything, at least the night would take her mind off everything else.

"Isn't it beautiful?" Lila looked at Robby as Brandi gawked around the club. "I told you this place was worth it."

"Hey there." Somebody tapped on Ella's shoulder. "I'm sorry about the restaurant. It's good to see you again."

Ella whirled around with Brandi still on her arm. She would never forget his friendly smile. She could also feel Brandi staring at her and waiting without patience.

"Brandi, this is Caleb. Caleb," she pointed at Brandi, "Brandi."

"Well, you're handsome but I'm guessing you already have someone in mind. Have any friends?"

Caleb looked around when another man stepped beside him. "This is Frederick. We've known each other forever."

"Freddy...I like that," Brandi said, her eyes scanning his long-sleeved shirt that clung to his chest.

"Aren't you going to introduce us?" Lila asked and pulled Robby's hand from behind her. "I'm Lila, and this is my boytoy."

"Funny." Robby gave her bottom a smack. "I'm Robby, her boyfriend."

"We were grabbing two more drinks, but we have a pool table over there. Why don't all of you come play with us?" Caleb asked but spoke to Ella.

"Oh," said Brandi. "We'll join if you're paying."

Ella's eyes darted to Brandi, disbelieving her lack of etiquette.

"Anyone tell you you're beautiful lately?" Frederick took Brandi's hand. "I don't mind paying."

"Are you going to play too?" Caleb asked Ella.

Lila bumped Ella on the arm and jolted her from her thoughts.

"*All right, Lila.*" Ella whispered, glaring back at her where no one else could see. "Sure, I'm game, Caleb."

Caleb grinned and followed Brandi and Frederick to the first pool table near the stairs. As he began racking the balls, he looked at Ella with a smile on his face. "I'm glad you decided to play. You can be on my team."

Lila and Robby were caught up with themselves as Frederick and Brandi took turns shooting the balls. Ella did not think either of them was into the pool game with the way they hung all over each other between shots. She could not believe that Brandi and Frederick had just met. She would not have the courage herself. Then they set down their pool sticks during the fourth game and abandoned Caleb and Ella in the middle.

"What are they doing?" Ella asked, trying to shake the awkward feeling of being left alone with him.

"It looks like they're joining your other friends on the dance floor. Would you like to dance with me?" Caleb held out his hand.

Ella let out a silent breath and looked into his sincere, blue eyes. They reminded her that there were normal people in the world. One dance would not hurt. He did buy her drinks and paid for the games. She could at least return his efforts by not making him look bad for asking.

Dancing with Caleb was a drastic change of pace that did not involve him ordering her around. His movements were gentle; he was too nice to get caught up with any of Angelo's men who were likely watching her from upstairs. She should not have agreed to the dance. When the song ended, Ella let go of his hand and smiled. She started to thank him for the dance when Caleb reached his hands around her cheeks and planted the most delicate kiss on her lips. When he pulled away, Ella stared at him with shock.

"I—I'm sorry." A blush met his cheeks as he looked at the floor. "I did that too fast when I don't know you very well. It's that...you're very sweet and I guess...something came over me. I couldn't help it."

Ella tried to smile again, but an image of Angelo kept running through her mind. The craziness of his life mattered little. It was Angelo's face that she saw—that she wanted. Ella sighed and grabbed Caleb's hand.

"Thank you so much for a nice night, but I have to go. I have to go now."

"Maybe I can see you again then," he said. His voice hesitated with the expression on her face.

"I can't. I'm sorry." Ella looked at him once more and then hurried from the dance floor to the back of the club.

She felt out of sorts when she came to Angelo's room. It was open. Who left it open? As if she did not have enough fear with facing Angelo, the open door made her anxiety worse. Ella froze the instant she walked through. Holding his forehead in his hand, Angelo was sitting on the bed. He waited a second and left her there to anticipate his reaction; then he folded his hands together and looked up.

"So the first chance you get, you run to another man's arms? Is that how it is?" Ella started to open her mouth but was helpless to counter the distress in his voice. Even though she did nothing that terrible, she felt like she betrayed him. "Is that what you want, someone else? Do you want me to leave you alone? Am I wasting my time with you?"

"No...I turned him down," she mumbled. "I came back here."

"Did you come back because you felt guilty? Or were you afraid of what I might do?"

"How could you say something like that when all I think of is you?"

"Then what do you want from me?" He stood and tied the ends to his drawstring pants. "We're supposed to be together; then you dance with another fucking man with my ring on your finger."

"This ring?" She lifted her hand, letting the light reflect off the ring.

"You have no fucking clue how important that ring is."

"You never said we were together. What was I supposed to think?"

Angelo placed his fingers over his temples and tried to make sense of her words. "Are you serious?"

"Why won't you answer the question?"

"Do I really have to spell it out for you?" He shook his head, staring at her with a look of disgust. "You're the first woman I've ever let get close to me. Do you really think I'm like that with anyone else? If you can't figure out where I stand after all this time, then maybe you should go back to that man downstairs."

"But I didn't know."

"I am who I am. I'm not one of those helpless romantics, and I won't shower you with meaningless gifts. I guess trying to keep you safe and the kisses I gave you meant nothing…like my ring."

"But—"

"I have a long day tomorrow and there's nothing left for you to say." Angelo opened the door and pointing for her to get out, letting it close hard when she was gone.

Chapter 27

Facing his door from the outside, Ella slid down the wall and sat on the floor. She heard the shuffling of ammo cartridges from the other side while trying to gain the courage to knock. It was not until he hit the light switch off that she knew he was not coming for her.

She squeezed her eyes shut and stood. Tapping on the door, Ella braced herself for his reaction when he answered—but nothing. Angelo must have known it was her and ignored her soft knock. Ella raised her hand again before she could reconsider. She made it count this time and pounded the door until he knew she was serious. She would leave if he still would not answer.

This time, it opened. Angelo stared at her from the other side. His hand was through his hair on the back of his head, mussed from the pillow; his dark eyes cast down on her with annoyed frustration.

"What do you want?" His voice sounded tired, disinterested in why she was still there. She felt sorry for disturbing him. Why did she think this was a good idea in the first place? "I'm going to bed. I have to wake up early for work."

His intimidating stature almost made it impossible for her to speak, but she managed to answer his question. "I wanted to say I'm sorry."

"What was that?" he asked. He heard her the first time. Why would he make her repeat herself?

"I wanted to say sorry for questioning you," she whispered and looked away, his hand instantly turning her face back to see him.

"You mocked me, everything I've done with you."

His eyes looked away from her. She wanted to touch him, to hug him and erase everything she had said. Maybe he needed her to balance out the brutality of his world.

Seconds later, he let go of her chin and waited for her to say something else. Maybe that was the best she could hope to accomplish tonight. "Okay," she said at his reluctance to her being there. "I'm sorry I bothered you."

She started to turn away with the disappointment she felt, but Angelo grabbed her hand and pulled her inside the room. "Is that all you needed from me?" His gaze made her shiver as she looked back. She did not want to leave. She thought that was what he wanted. "If you made it a point to come back in here, why are you trying to leave?"

Ella took a breath. Under his penetrating eyes, her legs wanted to give way to her weight. Her breathing hitched as he slowly turned her to sit on the bed. He knelt in front of her and grabbed her hands, his face nearly at eye level with her chin.

She could not take her eyes off him. Her body started to shake as his fingers slid across her knees, lifting the hem of her skirt. His hands stroked her inner thighs, acquainting her with his touch.

"You make me feel something I haven't felt before."

His nails skimmed higher on her skin, past her navel to her breasts, until he lifted the black dress over her head. She sat exposed, her panties and bra leaving little to be unveiled. Ella could feel the deep rosy heat spread across her cheeks as she closed her eyes, her body becoming warm.

When she opened them again, Angelo had dropped his shirt to the floor. Several pink scars marked his ribcage; his chest showed an old gunshot wound hidden behind thick scar tissue. She could not imagine the near-death experiences he had faced, branding him never to forget.

Angelo could not have had an easy time as a child. How long had he forced himself to hide his emotions? His body held proof of his dangerous encounters as he kneeled in front of her. He needed her affection if he would ever be able to feel.

Ella scooted off the bed's edge and slid her legs to both sides of his. Her hands touched his cheeks until they rested around his head. His breaths grew hotter with the closer she moved her face to him. Angelo returned a gentle smile. He seemed to take pleasure in her touch, in the attention she was showing to him.

"Are you staying with me tonight?"

She swallowed. The cool draft from the room formed chills against her skin. She lowered her eyes, tracing one of the spanning scars from his lowest right rib to his shoulder. "If you let me," she answered.

He did not give her time to look at him again. Both his hands grasped her waist and lifted, dragging her to the pillow behind, his body hovering above her. He kissed her deliberately; the powerful urgency of his mouth gave her no time to object. She could feel an emotional side of him that he normally kept hidden. It almost made him seem vulnerable.

She gasped softly at the way he made her feel, with the way his body was touching hers. His grip tightened around her back, his bare chest coming flush against her skin. It was not difficult for him to take charge.

"You're shaking," he muttered.

Even though her body was shaking, she had no intention of stopping. She continued to kiss him as his fingers tangled through her hair. Her trembling increased with her desire, with his weight pressing her harder in the bed. His mouth strayed under her chin, moving lower above her breasts. Her intense breaths mimicked the rise and fall of her chest. She wanted him, all of him and was ready to surrender everything when he paused, his body lifting as he looked in her eyes.

"I want to make you mine. I could force you and no one would say a word to me. If you choose to leave now, I will let you. No harm done. But if you stay—you will know exactly what that ring is about."

Ella's heart pounded underneath his muscular frame, but she did not attempt to move. Her silence caused him to elaborate, giving her another chance to back out. "Do you understand what being my lover means for you? You'd be stuck in this life forever—to the mafia, being the woman of a boss. I would never let you leave."

Angelo granted her a few seconds before nudging her cheek and waiting for a reply. "If you stay, I control your life. Is that what you really want? To give up your freedom? There are times you're going to hate me. That's the truth."

Ella remained silent as she looked in his eyes. His arm gripped around her back and tightened. He trapped her between him and the bed, yet that was exactly where she wanted to be. "Answer me, Ella. Tell me what you want."

"You leave me no choice," she mumbled, fully understanding his warning.

"It is your choice."

"I already know what you're about," she said on the verge of crying. "I can't help who I'm falling in love with."

Angelo stared at her for seconds, taken by her words. She knew who he was and what he was capable of doing, yet what she said was true. He saw it in her eyes, in teary eyes that gazed at him with fearful anticipation of what was going through his mind.

"You shouldn't have fallen for me, Ella," he said.

His mouth took over every worried thought she had; his kiss made her head feel light. His fingers unfastened the snap on her bra, leaving the cool air to rest against her skin. She glanced at him for a mere second but closed her eyes again, savoring the soft massages against her breasts. Her breathing became heavy as she enjoyed his callused fingers leaving new sensations in their wake. Her mouth parted, her hands clenching the strands of his hair. She could feel him slide off the last piece of clothing from her toes.

She could not help her soft moans as she relinquished herself to his control, allowing him to caress and manipulate her body in a way she never knew. Lifting to his touch, she needed more. An intense euphoria started to build, threatening her body with an intoxicating heat that wanted reprieve.

"You like me touching you like this." He gently kissed her forehead. His slight grin showed his satisfaction with her reaction.

"Angelo," she whispered. She was almost delusional when he kissed her mouth hard and brought her to an elated state of bliss. Her breaths trembled against his lips as she surrendered to his bidding. Ella panted and clasped the sheets tight between her fingers until the waves passing through her subsided.

Angelo watched her and stood, taking seconds to slide down his pants; his naked body was the essence of intimidation. "I saw pills in your medicine cabinet at your house. Do you still take those?" he asked.

"Yes, but," she paused, "but it's not like it seems. I take them to help with pain." Ella's words came out fast as he spread her knees apart and lowered his swollen sex between.

"Yes, Ella, but are you still taking them?" She nodded, her breaths too shaky to say anything else as he lowered his hips to hers. "Am I your first?"

Caught off guard by the question, she nodded again, but there was no way she could look him in the eyes. Her face flushed and turned away. Ella had never felt so intimidated before.

"Look at me," he whispered and laced her fingers with his against the pillow above. "You need to relax, close your eyes. Breathe," he said and pushed his hardened length in before she could dwell in her fear anymore.

"Angelo…" She clenched his hands, digging through his skin with her nails. She could barely take the intensity of the sudden pressure as he fully entered, consuming her purity. Her short breaths ceased as she tried to manage the pain of his sex.

"You need to breathe," came his gentle words. She opened her eyes, looking at him for some sort of comfort. She could see how he withheld all movement with her distress. She felt the soft caresses of his thumbs against the tops of her hands.

"Are you all right?" he asked when her body started to relax. She still felt a lingering ache but nothing like before. "It won't be like that again," he whispered and kissed each of her cheeks where the tears had wet her eyes. He started to push against her again, pausing as he watched her closely. His easy stroke did not seem to cause much discomfort.

"Please don't stop," she whispered. She wrapped her hands around his shoulders and pulled him closer, encouraging him to continue. "Do you know how long I have wanted you, Angelo?"

"Ella," he said and gently placed his mouth on her lips, showing her a far more intimate side that she absolutely adored. He may not have used words to tell her how he felt, but she could feel it with the gaze of his eyes, with the touch of his hands and through his gentle thrusts. He showed her with his body until they were both left satisfied with the other.

Afterward, their heartbeats relaxed in a steady rhythm as they enjoyed the other's warmth. Angelo lifted himself and rolled to his side as he continued to gaze at her. It made her feel shy. He moved several strands from her eyes, exposing the pink on her cheeks.

"I'm going to like calling you mine." He wrapped her with his arms and squeezed her to his chest. "I'm going to like having you by my side."

Ella blushed again when he kissed the blush off her lips and wrapped his fingers around the back of her neck. She was his. She anticipated what would come. A part of her feared what the status of his lover would bring. Angelo was not the ordinary man she ever dreamed of having, but it did not matter how it turned out. She felt the smile on her lips as she shut her eyes, content to be in his arms.

Chapter 28

"Ella," Angelo whispered in her ear the next morning. She moaned. She had been trying to find a comfortable spot for the last ten minutes when Angelo lowered the sheet and looked at her side. Her injury looked irritated. He had tried to be careful with her the night before but had aggravated the wound. She needed to take some medicine.

"Ella," he spoke a little louder and gave her arm a nudge. "Wake up. I need you to take these."

"All right." She blinked her eyes open and adjusted quickly. The only light in the room came from the restroom door.

"You should feel better in a few minutes," he said and set a bottle of water down next to her. "I have some things to take care of. Why don't you come see me when you feel better?"

Ella's knees rose closer to her chest with her small nod. She smiled with the nuzzling of his hand in her hair and then with his gentle kiss. She loved that he made sure she was comfortable before he left.

Ella would have liked to stay in bed, but the clock showed nine and she needed to figure out something to do. Maybe she would go to the beach. She had not been in a while, and Angelo would probably be busy all day. The ocean air might give her insight about her situation.

When Ella finished her shower, she looked around the room and groaned. All she had to wear was the dress she had worn last night. She picked it up off the floor and shook it. The wrinkles would make her look ragged as she walked through the hallway and back to the other room where they kept her clothes. What choice did she have? Ella pulled the material over her head and sighed. She hated to put on something dirty after she showered.

The hallway was quiet. Ella walked to the other end before anyone could see her at all. She thought she was in the clear. When she entered, she let out a yelp. The last person she expected or wanted to see was Brett. He was stuffing all of her clothes and anything else that was hers in a box.

"What are you doing with my clothes, Brett?" she asked.

As if he just noticed her, Brett looked up and smiled. "I'm cleaning this room. Boss said you aren't staying here anymore."

"What do you mean? Are you taking my stuff back to my house?" Brett continued to smile as he threw in another shirt. Ella could take no more of his cheerful attitude. "Aren't you going to answer me?"

With an innocent expression, Brett stopped to look at her. She wanted to slap the warped grin off his face. "I don't ask questions. I don't answer questions. I do what the boss tells me to do. If you have questions, maybe you should go ask him. He's in his office."

"I need to change." Ella picked up the ends of her wrinkled dress. "I can't walk around looking like this."

Brett shrugged. "I'm not allowed to let anyone touch these things. Boss's orders."

"But those are my belongings, Brett," she argued. "I need them."

"Sorry, the boss was pretty clear when he told me he'd shoot me if anyone touched them. Maybe he didn't mean you too, but I'm not taking any chances." Brett paused as if to justify his words. "You've seen how he is."

"Fine," She huffed out the door and stormed down the hallway. She started out fast, but her pace slowed as she reached the other end and stopped in front of Angelo's office door. With a feeling of deja vu, Ella found herself in the same awkward situation, wearing the same outfit as the night before. She knocked anyway. Again, he did not answer.

Ella placed her finger on the sensor. She needed to know what he was doing with her clothes. When the door opened, she peeked in the room and saw Angelo sitting at his desk, focusing on the computer screen in front of him. He merely glanced at her and then returned his attention back to the screen.

The computer and the papers in front of Angelo made him wary of Ella's entire situation. He could not figure out why any man would willingly put himself between two mafia groups. Her father was either brilliant or the dumbest man alive.

Angelo could still see Ella standing in his peripheral view. He smiled inwardly. How long would she stand there with the door open, waiting for him to acknowledge her? He did tell her to come see him when she was feeling better. The dress she wore from the night before confused him though. Why had she not changed?

"Shut the door." He pointed. Ella shook her head and looked disappointed. Why was she leaving? "With you on the inside, Ella," he added and almost laughed outright. It seemed obvious that he wanted her there. Why else would he have told her to come?

"Oh," she mumbled. Angelo returned his focus to the computer, expecting her to sit down and wait for him to finish. By the time she did walk to the sofa, he was through. Her back had just touched the cushion when his finger raised and motioned her to his desk.

Ella stood up, brushed down the seat of her dress—not that it would help the mess of the material—and walked around the desk to where he sat. Angelo patted his lap and pulled her on top. "Feeling better?" he asked.

"Yes," she answered.

Angelo ran his fingers against the top of her leg. He enjoyed his time with her last night and looked forward to more of those moments. She was such a naïve girl that he could not help but want to keep her safe.

"Good." He nodded and set down her emergency cell phone on the desk. "You had heard of Bonadio's name before. Have you heard of the name Gregorio too?"

"Yes," she replied. "I heard the name a couple of times."

"Okay." He nodded and continued in his thoughts.

"Why?" she asked and picked up the phone to examine it, but he took it back out of her hands. "I asked you why," she said again. Angelo let out a small breath. People usually did not repeat themselves when he did not answer right away.

"That phone is registered to Gregorio," he answered. "And police records list the man that you say is Jacob Sullivan as Robert Collins."

Ella reflected on his answer, her eyes tapering to the floor. "Maybe they got Sullivan and my father mixed up. Sullivan did handle a lot of business in my father's place."

"We did a check on Sullivan. Nothing turned up on him at all."

"What did you expect to find?" she asked.

"Well—his existence?" Angelo huffed. "There's a record of him being born. Nothing since then."

"Oh." Ella looked off to the side. "That's strange." Then she seemed to think. "Who is Gregorio anyway? Is he another one of my father's clients?"

"He's nobody I want to talk about," Angelo replied. He did not even want to hear his name.

"But you asked me about Gregorio. You can't say nothing about him when my phone is registered to him."

"Yes I can." He held up her finger with the ring.

"That's not fair, Angelo. I have the right to know who he is since you asked."

"Nothing is ever fair," he said with a mocking chuckle.

"But why don't you want to tell me?" she asked. "I don't under—"

"Enough, Ella. I don't want to talk about him. I have many reasons that have nothing to do with you," he said. "Don't ask me any more questions about Gregorio. He isn't worth my time."

Ella held the sides of her waist and frowned. He noticed that she had done that before. It was some sort of defense and made him feel bad. He kept forgetting that she was not used to his forward tone.

"Look, I don't know anything for certain about your father yet, and I don't like Gregorio. I wouldn't want to talk about him with anyone. Okay?" He wrapped her in his arms. He protected her even though his tone made her upset. "I also have other affairs coming up. I won't be staying here anymore."

"Okay." Ella started to stand when he held his arms around her, preventing her from moving from his lap.

"Why are you sulking, Ella?"

"It doesn't matter. If you have to go, there's nothing I can do."

"Who said I'm going alone?"

"What do you mean?" She twisted to see his face.

"I have a banquet coming up. It's at my largest casino and I can't go alone. I will need you with me. Rafa is handling the specifics." Angelo raised her chin and gave her a small kiss. "Besides, I can't trust you to stay here by yourself. Someone might hurt you or worse, try to kiss you. Both are serious offenses."

Ella huffed at his words. "I didn't kiss him back. It wasn't my fault."

"Maybe not, but I can't let you wander far. I have to keep you out of trouble."

Ella gave him a look. Angelo found her adorable when he frustrated her. He would keep that in mind. "Why didn't you change your clothes anyway?" he asked, getting an immediate frown in response.

"Because Brett wouldn't let me grab anything," she replied.

"He does take me at word, doesn't he? That's why he's with my group."

"You threatened to shoot him."

"Yes, It gets my point across."

"Okay, but what's he doing with my stuff? I really do want to change and go to the beach today."

"The beach." Angelo nodded. "I'll have someone go with you. You can't be alone anymore, Ella. You realize that, right?"

"Fine." She relented.

"I'm having all of your clothes moved to my house. We aren't safe in the Key's anymore."

"You want me to stay with you?" Ella asked surprised. Her shock amused him. He found her genuine reactions to his words refreshing. Any other woman would have immediately tried to seduce more out of him.

"And why wouldn't I want what belongs to me in my bed at night? Do you have a problem with staying with me?" he asked.

"I'm not an object."

"Maybe not, but you're certainly mine." He swiveled his chair and lifted her off his lap. "I'm glad you stayed with me last night. There will be lots of nights like that." He adored every part of her. No matter what it cost him, he was going to keep her safe. "Ella," he said. "You can go get some clothes now. I'll give Brett a call."

Ella started to walk away when Angelo stood and pulled her body back to his. He slid his hands around her cheeks; his lips captivated her mouth with a deep, passionate kiss. Then he smiled and watched her leave, her thoughts consumed by the kiss.

"Brett," he said into his phone. "Ella is on her way down. Let her get what she needs." He looked up at the ceiling and shook his head. "No, Brett, I didn't mean her too," he replied. "Brett, I'm hanging up." Angelo set his phone down and looked back at a sheet on the desk.

"Angelo." Rafa barged through the office door. Angelo wondered what news he had with the urgency in his tone.

"What do you got?"

"The P.D. hasn't found anything on Sullivan yet, but I went down and checked property records for Orlando. I had to have Donnie go with me. Gregorio did have Robert Collins sell property for him some time back. But more recently though, he transferred half of his real estate into Collins' name. Not sold—transferred."

"So Collins works for Gregorio, not Bonadio, and we still have no idea who Collins is. You know what we do?" Angelo pointed. "We go to the real estate agencies and find this man." He slid open a drawer and pulled out Sullivan's picture. "Follow Sullivan until we come up with someone we can trace. I need to know what the hell Gregorio is planning."

Chapter 29

The sun had already set. With boredom and hunger hanging over her head, Ella's mind wandered back to the restaurant. She missed Santiago's—her pride. It made her happy knowing she could sit down at one of the tables and reminisce. Now she had nothing to do but watch Brett on the sofa. She decided to look around the house.

She saw Angelo's laptop on the counter. She was not much for Internet browsing, but anything beat the silence of the house. She opened the laptop and waited for everything to boot; then she sighed. Of course it was password locked. Ella let it close again. Was there anything to do in this house?

Below the counter was a drawer with a piece of paper that stuck out of it. She did not expect to find anything and opened it up. Even a bill would be more interesting than anything she had done there that day.

Envelopes filled the drawer. There were no addresses on the outsides and they were all opened. Ella took one piece of paper off the top. It must have been the latest letter Angelo received. He had not bothered to place the folded paper back in the envelope.

Angelo,

Quit ignoring my calls and go meet Gregorio. Marry into his family so we can stop this shit. Bonadio won't give up his threats. Gregorio already lost one over it. Do you want the same thing to happen to us? There's a lot on the line here. Don't make me worry about this anymore.
Antonio

Ella frowned. That was the reason Angelo did not want to talk about him. Gregorio was the other boss. She could never compete for Angelo against the advantages he would gain by marrying another boss's daughter, but she would not be Angelo's mistress as Rafa had said either. She slammed the drawer shut and went back to the family room to sit.

She did not know how Brett found his gun that interesting and turned on the TV. Anything was better than the constant snapping of his clip. From one channel to the other, she flipped with disinterest, until she came to a channel with men in suits. They looked unhappy to have a camera crew following them, the man in front holding a manila envelope over his face. Ella watched them walk to a limousine. When the man who covered his face stepped into the vehicle, Ella's mouth opened with shock. *Father.*

She started to turn up the volume when the front door opened and shut. She looked back as Angelo laid his coat over the arm of the sofa.

"See you later, Ella," Brett said as though they had talked for hours. Then out of the door, he went.

"Why are you watching TV without sound?" Angelo asked.

She shrugged and looked at the screen. "I don't really watch TV, and I didn't care about the sound at first. Then I saw my father on the news, and I didn't think about turning it up until it was too late."

"Your father?" he asked.

"Yeah, he was covering his face, but I saw part of it when he stepped into a limo."

"Limo? What order did he get into the limo?" His question confused her, not knowing what he meant. "Like was he first, second, third?"

"First," she replied. Angelo gave a nod, but she did not know what it meant.

"All that means is that he was more important than the men he was running with."

"He's in Miami," she added.

"Was Sullivan with him?" When she shook her head, Angelo took out his phone and pressed it twice. "Hey, you remember what we talked about earlier?" Ella watched Angelo walk into the kitchen and lean his elbows on the counter. "Right." He glanced at his laptop and then the drawer below. "Hold on," he said and looked over at Ella as she stood. "Don't move." He pointed at her and continued his call. "Ella saw her father on the news. He's in Miami. Maybe Sullivan too. I want you to look into it."

The drawer opened and he shuffled a couple of papers around as he ended his call. He would definitely notice a difference with the order of the letters; she did not bother to put them back correctly. The drawer clicked shut again and Angelo walked back toward her. "You haven't been going through my stuff, have you?" Ella took a deep breath under his pointed question. Her entire body tensed. "Did you read anything interesting?" He continued to probe. She looked at the floor, remorseful that she had looked, more so that she had been caught. "If it makes you feel better, I have another woman I'd rather protect."

"I didn't mean to be nosey. I was looking around for something to do."

"Oh yeah? Looking and reading are two different things."

"Yes..." She looked down at her lap.

Angelo let out a breath and kissed the top of her head. "Have you eaten?"

She looked up again, surprised he was not going to press the issue. "Not since earlier. Brett stopped and picked something up at a drive-thru."

"Then go get your shoes. I'll take you to dinner."

***

Angelo drove Ella to a lit area of town. Soft music filled her ears as they followed the hostess to a table covered with a white tablecloth. The restaurant was not busy with the few guests sitting around them. Ella was glad to relax.

"Here are your menus. Your server will be with you shortly."

"Thank you," Angelo said as she left. "This place is nice. I like it so far."

"You haven't been here before?" she asked with Angelo shaking his head.

"No, I wanted to try something different. A couple of my men like to come here."

Ella looked around. The shiny wooden walls looked nice with the artwork the restaurant collected. They kept the floors neat and glossy. Wooden cabinets stood behind the bar on the opposite side of where she sat. She admired the restaurant and thought it was pretty. She wondered if it had a balcony out back. She would not be able to see the ocean, though. This restaurant sat inland. Then Ella stopped. She was comparing the restaurant to Santiago's, but it was gone. She looked down at her menu and let out a sigh. That was it. It was gone. She could not get it back.

"Are you all right?" Angelo looked up from his menu at her. "I didn't think about how dinner at a restaurant would make you feel."

"It's okay." She smiled, though she hardly felt any joy. This was supposed to be a romantic time with him, and she was ruining it. She had to put Santiago's out of her mind. "I want to be here with you." She tried a different tone.

"You don't lie very well." Angelo gave her a smile. "Why don't we take the food with us and find somewhere else to eat?"

"Oh, we don't have to—"

"Good evening." Their server approached. "Could I start you off with a gin and tonic or a glass of chardonnay?"

"Actually, we decided not to stay. Give us two of whatever the chef recommends and," he looked over at Ella, "and a bottle of good merlot."

The server smiled. "I'll go put that in."

"Really?" Ella said when the server left. "That wasn't necessary, I promise."

"No arguing, remember?"

Ella did not say anything else. She also tried not to look around. The time that it took to complete their order could have been ten minutes, but it seemed like an hour. Then she was riding in his car again.

"I know of a nice place on the beach. Are you interested?" he asked.

"Of course," she answered without a moment's thought.

"Good. We'll be there in five minutes."

Angelo turned down a couple of roads and came to a small cottage on the beach. It looked like a private residence. Maybe he owned it.

"You see that gazebo over there? That's where we'll eat."

"It's gorgeous." She smiled. Except for a stone walkway, the white gazebo was surrounded by the most beautiful stone pool she had ever seen. Each rock was a different shade, ending at a point with a quiet waterfall.

"It's better up close," he said and grabbed the food in one hand, leading her with the other. She could not see it from where they parked, but waves from the ocean landed on the rocks below.

"It's incredible," she said in awe.

"Have a seat," he said and began taking their food out of the bag. Then he opened a bench seat on the side and looked confused. "Well, I guess we are drinking wine out of the bottle." Ella laughed. She would have never pictured Angelo drinking wine like that. "Wait...I think I moved the glasses the last time I was here." He stood up and checked a small cabinet to the side. "Here they are."

"Do you own this place?" she asked as he poured the wine.

"I bought it last year. Nobody but you has been here so far."

"It's peaceful."

"Very. I've come more than once to clear my head."

"Thank you." She smiled and took the glass from him.

"So tell me something," he said.

"Okay."

"What are your goals in life? You wanted the restaurant but what about your future and settling down...raising a family. Have you ever thought of that?"

Ella shrugged. "I used to think about it when I was in college, but my father would shut it down if I tried to bring it up. After a while, I stopped thinking about it. Every time he wouldn't listen, I ended up feeling lonelier than I was."

"And now?"

"I don't know. I keep expecting Sullivan to take me away."

"From Miami or me?"

"Well" — Ella looked down — "both."

"You understand that it's too late for your father to have any control in your life, right?"

"I don't really understand my father," she said. "He controlled everything and then stopped talking to me. I know he changed after my mother died, but not talking to me after I moved really hurt."

"Ella, I don't know your father, but my guess is because of the men he's involved with, that he isn't talking to you because he doesn't want them to know where you are."

"You think they will kill me too."

"I think you're in danger because of the people your father is with."

"Maybe," Ella agreed. "What about your future?" she asked.

"I want a wife...and kids. I don't have to think about that answer. I also want to keep peace with my father and my men. I have to accept that I can't have everything I want."

"You mean that letter."

"To my father—a marriage is a business deal. Which woman will do the group the most good? Gregorio's daughter was it."

"Are you going to marry her?" Ella needed an answer but did not want an answer. She had already fallen for Angelo herself. She did not want to give him up or watch him marry someone else.

"No." He paused between bites of his food and stared at her. "But if I want to stick with the rules, I can't marry anyone else either."

It was a blow to her heart. After wanting to be with him and choosing to stay, he could never offer her anything permanent. She would never be anything but the woman in Angelo's house.

"What's the point then?" she said and stood from her seat. "Where does that leave me?"

"Sit down." He reached over the table and grabbed her arm. "I tried to ignore you. I didn't want to involve you in any of this. I knew you deserved better. Then every time I saw you smile, my mind wouldn't leave it the fuck alone. You're not going anywhere."

"But I'll never be anyone to you, and your father doesn't like me. How is that going to affect your life? How will it affect mine?"

Angelo smiled. Ella could not figure out what he found amusing about any of this. She felt nauseous yet he grinned. "Who says you aren't anyone to me? And who says my father doesn't like you. If he didn't, he wouldn't have pestered you with questions. I already told you how he sees marriage. He hasn't even met Gregorio's daughter."

"So you don't care who is mad at you for having me?"

"I had already accepted what would happen. Then I made you choose. I won't let you go now," Angelo said pointedly. "We can talk about our future another time, but we will talk about it."

Ella looked back at him, staring directly in his eyes. Was he hinting that he wanted a family with her? Her hand covered her forehead as she leaned her elbow on the table. "This isn't how I planned anything," she mumbled.

"Sweetheart, nothing in life ever is."

Chapter 30

Ella was quiet and lost in thought as they got ready for bed. Could she do it—stay with a man she could never marry? It was not like he would not be hers. Having his children would be proof of that.

Wanting some air, Ella walked to the front door and started to turn the knob when Angelo yelled, rushing at her in a lone pair of pants. "Where are you going?" He grabbed both her hands away from the door, anger and worry in his voice.

"For a walk," she answered. They were outside earlier. Why did he have such an issue with her going out again?

"You can't go anywhere alone, especially at night. I thought I made that clear." Angelo turned her around to face him and stared at her hard, waiting for her to speak.

"We were just out there. It was safe."

"I was keeping watch the whole time. My hand was always ready to shoot." He looked down at her clothes and looked back in her eyes. "Do you have the gun I gave you?"

"No." She shook her head.

"Do you want them to take you? Do you understand that your father is working with someone more heartless than I am? You're a big red flag in the middle of all this."

Ella cringed. Was she in so much danger that she could not take a simple walk? The realization struck her like an arrow. With or without Angelo, her life would never be normal.

Ella felt the warm tears of exhaustion with her life as she leaned against his chest. His words stung, but they put her situation in perspective. "I can't believe it's really that bad."

"You have to do what I say. Don't make me worry about you." He rubbed away her tears and gave her a gentle kiss. "It won't be that bad with me," he started but then turned his eyes to the window and listened. His eyes squinted as though he heard something there.

"Get down!" he yelled and shoved Ella away from the door. Her body landed like a ragdoll in the middle of the room with his body immediately on top. The window exploded into thousands of tiny pieces, crashing onto the floor inside. Angelo forced her arms and legs together as he covered them with his. His arms tightened around every limb on her body as more glass shattered around them both. It seemed like they were in the middle of a firing squad. The entire house shook with every shot made.

A minute later, everything went still.

Angelo did not move. His heartbeat pounded against her back as she felt tears drip off the sides of her cheeks. The attack reinforced her earlier defining moment. She would never live an ordinary life.

Angelo lifted enough to look around the room before he sat and pulled her up between his legs. They stared with silent horror. The windows had jagged pieces of glass left in the corners.

"Oh my god!" Ella covered her mouth. The door made Ella's body go numb. The bullets did not go through, but they speckled the entire center of the door. If Angelo had not stopped her from going out, she would not be alive.

Angelo wrapped his arms around her curled body tighter and into a bear hold as he reached for his phone off the small wooden table next to him. He knew it, too. The night had almost ended in disaster.

"Are you at the club... What's going on... He did what..." Angelo held the receiver away from his ear and snarled with anger before placing it back to the side of his face. "Tell me you're fucking with me!" He continued, but his limbs constricted around Ella as if to protect her from whatever matter he discussed. His voice dripped with rage. "Yes, we know they were coming for us! How? Because there's about thirty fucking bullet holes in the front of my beach house, that's how... No, I don't want you to come here! Send Jim and Ray here. You're going to deal with the other two. Fuck their lives up and find out where he went."

Angelo tapped his phone off and slid it across the floor. Then he inhaled before burying his face into her neck. "Are you hurt?" he asked with the most disturbed, gentle tone she had ever heard from his mouth. She was terrified by what could have happened, but for the sake of easing his worries, she tried to play it off. She spoke with a soft, assured voice even though her body trembled in his arms.

"I'm fine, thanks to you. Thank you."

He nodded and still breathed hard. "Bonadio's footmen. They weren't trying to kill us. They would've leveled the entire house if they were."

"They're trying to get you away from me. They want to get you alone."

"Yeah." Angelo shook his head. "We're getting out of here...going back to my place. Twenty-four hour guards."

***

Angelo slept soundly beside her, but Ella could not sleep anymore and got out of bed early, going to the restroom to revive. She ran the sink water and splashed her face, the cold water feeling nice on her hot cheeks. The mirror reflected a woman she hardly recognized. The bruises had faded, but her mind felt overwhelmed. Her father left her in a world that she knew nothing about, yet she must get used to it. How did she think that learning to use a gun was normal? Why did she not look further into the constant overprotective nature of her father? Who was Jacob Sullivan really? If she could speak to her father now, she would not leave until he told her the truth. That was what she told herself.

After feeling more awake, she crawled back under the covers and leaned against Angelo. He was warm against her skin with the coolness in the air. She reflected on her time in the Keys. After Angelo entered her life, the secrets her family hid seemed to come out. She would think her trouble came from Angelo's involvement if he had not proven that she already was connected. She wondered who Bonadio had a problem with more—him or her.

Angelo moved against her body and pulled the blankets higher over them both. Then he rolled sideways to face her and opened his eyes. His expression remained serious as the night before. His gaze also seemed affectionate. Laying his arm around her breasts, he closed his eyes and then opened them again to look at her. "Ella," he mumbled.

"Hm?" She breathed contentedly with his hug and gripped his arm with both her hands.

"Why'd you keep trying to talk to me when I kept leaving you hanging?" he asked.

Ella considered his question with reflection. "There was something about your eyes that made me like you. You were searching for something. Maybe I thought you were as lonely as I was. Maybe I hoped to change that." She half-smiled with her thought. "I guess I fell for you without really knowing I did."

"I tested you in the club that night with the cameras and the cheating. I wanted to see if you could handle something like that. If you couldn't, there was no way you could handle being with me."

"So how did I do?" she asked with a glance.

He chuckled. "Let's say you bested my men."

Ella shrugged. "I guess you can't fool the suspicious."

"It seems so," he smiled, "but Halsey wasn't supposed to be a part of that. Brett was supposed to tell Thomas about the plan; he got sidetracked with cleaning the wine."

"The wine," Ella sighed. "That was for your birthday. I tried to catch it, but...it shattered right in front of me."

"It was sweet of you. I've never had anyone but my mother go out of her way for me. If it makes you feel better, I have the card."

"You do?" She grinned.

"I do." He lifted his body and laid his head against her chest. She enjoyed the gentle caresses of his fingers.

"You're in more danger because of me, aren't you?" she asked.

"We have the same enemies; I'm used to it anyway. I didn't expect you were connected, but that wouldn't have stopped me either."

Ella lay under the warmth of his body, savoring the quiet solitude left between them. Angelo breathed softly against her breasts as she laced her fingers through his hair. The thought of his bare body caused her breathing to deepen. She thought about his hands, how they caressed her skin and made her feel both nervous and excited. Angelo had given her the perfect night to reflect upon.

With her small smile as she remembered, Angelo glanced at her and trailed his fingers against her neck. "What are you thinking about?"

She blushed and considered her thoughts; she could not tell him the truth. It would embarrass her more. "Nothing. Why?"

"Nothing? Nothing is sure making you breathe fast."

Ella's cheeks grew warmer, but Angelo did not press the matter. He probably guessed her thoughts anyway. Instead, he scooted from on top and left the cool air to replace the heat from his skin.

"We should pack some things. I told Rafa to be here at ten, and he'll be here ten minutes early. Rafa is never late. We have that banquet coming up."

Angelo started for the restroom, but Ella pulled the covers over her body to keep warm but felt the blankets yanked off the top of her, leaving her to shiver.

"Hey," she protested and attempted to pull them back up when she realized they were no longer on the bed.

"If I have to get up, so do you. But don't worry—you'll be happy with our room at the hotel." Angelo's brows arched as he kissed the top of her head.

Hotel? Ella wondered as she sat up in bed. How many clothes would she really need since the hotel was probably in Miami? Why would they stay there when he lived so close?

To the minute, Ella heard the front door close and then someone knocked on the door to Angelo's room. Angelo flung it open and then continued to add clothes to his suitcase on the bed, ignoring that Rafa waited for him to speak. Rafa's expression turned sour as his arms immediately crossed with impatience to see Angelo was still packing; Rafa leered at him to hurry him along.

"Quit standing there like it'll make me go any faster. When you see my suitcase shut, I'm ready."

Rafa glared at him. He looked put out by the attitude he received. "If it weren't for me, you'd have to drive yourself. I'm not sure going alone is safe right now." Rafa shook his head as Angelo grabbed his gun off the table. "Jim and I are outside waiting, so hurry up," said Rafa.

After Rafa left the room, Angelo walked over to Ella and lifted up the hem of the dress she had put on. Ella was not sure what he was doing. She shivered as his fingers brushed the outside of her leg and a strap scraped the inside of her thigh. He pulled a gun harness secure, but she could barely focus on the gun. She thought he was taking this in a completely different direction.

"After the attack last night, we can't afford to take any chances. Always have a gun on you." Angelo raised her chin for a small kiss and picked up their suitcases afterward. "Come on. Let's go before Rafa comes back and I really do give him a bullet to remember me by."

Chapter 31

As their limousine pulled into the u-shaped entrance, Ella stared up at the luxury hotel—not because she had never seen something so beautiful, but because she had. Ella was not only familiar with the Royal Flush, but she had stayed at the resort several times. High vaulted ceilings, marbled floors, and crystal chandeliers adorned the hotel. There were around thirty floors with twenty rooms on each with a penthouse suite at the top. Ella had always thought it was the most beautiful hotel she had seen.

When the limo stopped for valet, Angelo grabbed her hand, squeezing to get her attention. "When we enter, hold my arm and don't let go for any reason. I don't care who comes up to us. After I show you our room, I'll give you a tour of my hotel. Sound fair?"

Ella nodded and stepped out, careful to keep her silky white dress from rubbing against the door. Then she thought about his words. "What?" She looked at him with surprise. "Wait. You own this hotel? I thought you said you owned a casino."

"I do. It's in the hotel on the bottom floor."

"You never said anything about owning an entire hotel."

"Well…I do," he said of her surprise.

For a moment, she stood in wonder of the building. The place itself seemed every bit as intimidating as its owner did. Angelo gave Ella a moment to admire its grandeur before nudging her arm and moving forward.

Ella took a breath as she entered. She had never come to socialize before. She had never been allowed. The luggage boy tailed behind them as several female greeters welcomed Angelo. "Mr. Tomassi, it's wonderful to have you visit," one of the women said with a smile. Whether she was happy to see him was anybody's guess, but she tended the entrance politely.

Another also smiled and spoke. "Your room will be exactly the way you like. Please let us know if you need anything."

One more of the women added to the other's courtesies. "Please visit the restaurant. The chef has a special menu for your arrival." Angelo nodded his thanks.

When Ella glanced back, it seemed that the women's eyes were burning into her head. Angelo may have never walked into the hotel with a woman before, and maybe they were curious. She received the same sorts of stares at the counter, but Angelo paid no attention to the glances she gained. He ignored what was probably developing gossip about his personal life.

After the front desk attendant handed him his room key, Angelo led Ella to the other side of the main lobby toward the elevators. No important figurehead stopped to chat since it was still before noon. It was Angelo and Ella, the luggage boy, and the elevator attendant. Ella noticed the employee push the button to the highest floor. While she had stayed in the hotel before, she had never been to the very top.

When the elevator came to a stop, the luggage boy paused when Angelo held up his palm. "You wait there," he said. Not only did Angelo insert the room card into the slot, but he also punched in a lengthy code before it would open. After the door unlatched, Angelo gestured the boy inside.

"Should I help you unpack?" the boy asked.

Angelo's brow narrowed at the young man. "You're new."

"Yes, sir."

"I unpack on my own, so remember that."

"Yes, sir," the boy replied.

Angelo left the room for a moment and handed the attendants some bills. Then the door shut again, leaving Angelo, Ella and a stifling amount of silence. Angelo was usually quiet, but Ella was too stricken with the view off the balcony to speak. Angelo noticed her fascination and tapped her on the shoulder.

"You can walk out there." Ella smiled excitedly and looked around, trying to find a way to unlatch the sliding glass door. "It's hidden on the top right corner."

She nodded and eagerly exited to the full-sized terrace. There was an utterly magnificent view of the water; the waves crashing along the beach could easily entrance her for hours.

"This view—I've never seen anything like it," she said, glancing back as Angelo walked behind her.

"Hm." Angelo neared closer and tenderly slipped his arms around her waist. "I haven't either." Ella smiled with his affection until Angelo added, "But the beach view is nice too."

With her eyes glistening at his words, he pushed her hair aside and rested his chin against her neck. They were both enjoying the warm breeze until Ella's stomach growled, snapping them back to reality. It made sense that she would be hungry since neither of them ate that morning.

"I guess it's time to show you the restaurant," he said and squeezed her hand that rested on the rail.

"I suppose so," came her reluctant response. Even though she was hungry, it was such a rare pleasure to see Angelo so relaxed. She would have rather waited a couple of hours than give up this moment with him. Then she considered that he needed to eat too and readily took his hand.

When they entered the restaurant, a hostess approached them, smiling from ear to ear. "Mr. Tomassi, we've been waiting for you. We kept your regular table open since you arrived," she said.

Angelo held up his hand and interrupted her, pointing toward the back door to the deck. "Why don't you bring me to the veranda this time? I think my girlfriend will like the view."

"Yes, sir." The hostess gave a bright smile and seemed genuinely happy about his change of preference. "Please, follow me."

As they neared a table, Angelo pulled out Ella's chair for her. She could not help but capture the sparkle in the hostess's eyes at his subtle gesture. His change of scenery also seemed a welcomed change in the tone of her voice.

"The chef has prepared a special for you, but if you'd like, I'll bring you a couple of menus."

Angelo thought for a moment and shook his head. "No, we'll have what the chef has made, but bring a menu anyway. I want Ella to see the regular choices too."

"Of course." The hostess nodded and left the two alone.

A minute later, a sommelier came to their table, poured a small amount of wine in a glass and handed it to Angelo. Out of respect for the wine, he swirled the contents to catch its aroma; then he tasted and gave the man a nod. The sommelier filled Angelo's glass and followed suit with a second. Angelo handed it to Ella to taste.

"It's has an amazing scent," Ella replied and lifted the glass to her lips. "It's excellent."

"Fantastic. Enjoy," said the man.

"Wow, this is some hotel you have," Ella said, earning a smile for the compliment.

"I'm glad you like it."

"Would you mind if I walked to the rail?" she asked. Angelo lifted his hand and casually waved her to the edge of the balcony. She looked down. They were on the lobby floor, so the beach stretched in front. She enjoyed the breeze off the waves and the sun reflecting from overhead even though the veranda itself was enclosed. Ella half-turned to rejoin Angelo when a man in a black suit walked to the table where he sat. His back was facing her as he acknowledged Angelo.

"Mr. Tomassi?" he said.

"Yes," said Angelo. Ella noticed that Angelo appeared bothered as his eyes focused on the man.

"It's good to see you here today. I was told you weren't coming until tomorrow."

Then Ella heard it—*his voice.*

Ella turned completely around at the man. That voice sounded oddly familiar. The man heard her heels click against the floor and glanced back, noticing her in passing as he continued with his small talk. When Ella did not move, the man finally turned all the way around to look at her.

"Tell me, who is this beautiful woman with you this afternoon?"

Ella deemed his notice more a formality than an actual interest, but then he looked at her closer; the man froze with surprise.

"Ella." He stared as though he saw a ghost.

"Mr. Sullivan." Her reply was equally shocked.

"Jacob Sullivan." Angelo interrupted coldly and grabbed Ella's hand.

Chapter 32

Angelo immediately gave Ella's hand a constricting squeeze, cautioning her to say no more, but Ella could not speak a word. In her shock, she looked at the muscular man in his early thirties, his sandy brown hair combed back as usual with dark eyes that were always the voice of reason. If Sullivan was there, so was her father.

"Yes," Sullivan started. "I was a trusted agent of Ella's father. I was her personal caretaker until she moved away. I guarded her as her father traveled." Sullivan looked at Ella. "You aren't here with your father this time, are you?"

Angelo redirected the conversation and did not let Ella speak. "No, she came with me. We'll let her father know as soon as we've settled in. When will he arrive?"

"Well." Sullivan seemed confused. "He accepted the invitation. He did send confirmation that he received the notice and would arrive sometime tomorrow."

"Very good," Angelo replied.

Sullivan nodded and stopped, looking as though he wanted to say something else to Ella but held his tongue. He held out his hand instead. "We will see you tomorrow," he said as Angelo shook his hand.

Angelo and Ella found their seats again.

"Rafa…" Angelo mumbled. "I can't call him. He's finishing the arrangements for the banquet." Angelo glared at Ella while pulling out his phone. "Jim, Sullivan just left the restaurant here. You and Ray follow him… Yes, I'm as surprised as you are." When he hung up, he looked back at Ella. "Were you going to tell me you've been here before?" Staring pointedly at her, he crossed his arms and waited.

"I thought about telling you." Ella looked down at the table and fidgeted with the hem of the tablecloth.

"So you're already familiar with the hotel?" Angelo asked. His eyes seemed disappointed. "If you were here before, why didn't I ever see you?"

Ella slowly shook her head with disappointment herself. "I'm familiar with floor twenty-nine and the theater on the floor."

"What's that supposed to mean?"

"It means Sullivan was given orders not to let me out of his sight, and they almost never let me leave the room. When he wasn't too busy, he would take me to the theater. That's all that my father allowed. My father stayed in a different room."

Ella looked out to the ocean. Sullivan had said her father would arrive the next day. She had so many words that she wanted to ask him and say to him, yet her mind went blank. Her body tensed with nervous anticipation of seeing him again. She was afraid of the confrontation at the same time. "What am I going to do when I see him?" she asked.

"Nothing, Ella. You're going to let me handle it. You're going to let me take care of you." To Ella's surprise, he pulled her to his body and hugged her at their table in the middle of the deck. He did not care who saw. She needed the hug. "I have a feeling that your father cares about you more than you think."

Ella thought about it and nodded. Her father may not have cared, but Angelo made her feel better anyway. His words made her hopeful of their truth.

After they finished their meals, the server walked out and set down two portions of chocolate cake in front of them. Angelo grimaced as the server left and pushed away the cake. His disgusted expression made Ella laugh.

"What's wrong with the dessert?" Ella jokingly mocked Angelo's loathsome face and took a bite. "You don't know what you're missing."

"No...I know exactly what I'm missing. You'd think with as many times as I've sent the dessert back untouched, they would get the hint."

"You don't like chocolate?" she asked.

"I don't care for sweets in general."

"Shame." Ella shook her head. "A life without sweets? I don't know if I could do it."

Angelo huffed in response. "Who needs sweets? I have you."

Ella smiled. "So subtle," she whispered and pushed her plate back. "I'm finished now. Will you still take me on a tour?"

"I suppose, but you'd better stay close to me, or I'll restrict you to the twenty-ninth floor." Angelo stood up and held out his hand with a small, devious grin.

Her mouth opened. "That's not nice, Angelo," she said.

"Who said I was nice?" he joked. "I've heard plenty of words said about me. Nice was never one of them." Ella shook her head and grabbed his hand anyway. At least he showed her a small part of his softer side. That was all that really mattered.

Ella toured several floors in the hotel. One level below the main lobby was floor three with shops that were dedicated to guest's needs.

Floor two turned into a large banquet hall where all the big events were held.

Floor one housed the casino that Angelo had talked about. This casino quadrupled the size of the one at the club. Since it opened at six, nobody was there right now. Ella walked around for a few minutes and admired the room. It seemed large, but she could not imagine what it would look like filled with customers. Maybe he would take her when it opened.

"We're going back to the banquet hall. I have to talk to Rafa for a minute," Angelo said, "and then we can go back to the suite."

On floor two again, Angelo led her down a long, narrow hallway. At the end was a door with a pad for a code. The room they entered looked like a large, boring conference room; then she saw a door to the side—a room lined with tables much like the one at the club.

"That room at the club…the one I found…"

"Yes."

"Do you use the club as some sort of exchange place?"

"Something like that. We bring those items here for our clients. We have a preferred customer list, and those people can request specialty items. As we find what they're looking for, we send out postcards with dates and times, letting them know that their product is in. It's simple. We help them spend their cash."

"And what do you do with the money?" she asked.

"Group affairs," was all he said.

They did not go into the side room. She followed Angelo to an office in back. Rafa sat behind the desk with a pair of glasses on. Ella never saw him in glasses before. They made him look smarter than he already was. He lowered the glasses long enough to acknowledge Angelo and went back to the sheets in front.

"Rafa, look for Robert Collins on that list. We sent Ella's father an invitation to the banquet, and I just met Sullivan."

"Oh really?"

"He found me in the restaurant. Can you believe that? I have Jim and Ray on him now."

"Well, isn't that how it works out? We have men searching every real estate company that Collins owns, and Sullivan shows up on our front step."

Angelo pointed at the list. "Is Collins on there?"

Rafa flipped through the pages and flipped through them again. "No, Collins isn't here," he said.

Angelo held up his hand. "I would've rather had Collins find me earlier than Sullivan. Maybe Jim will turn up something."

"Or you could take me to my house in Orlando if he doesn't," Ella said.

"I already thought of that, Ella, but your father won't be there. If he had threats in the past, he will stay far away from your house. He probably felt the same for you. That's why he hasn't talked to you since you moved to the Keys. That's why he cut you off."

"Yeah," Ella mumbled thoughtful of his words.

"Rafa, I'll be back later. Call me if something comes up."

"Of course," Rafa said, his tone flippant. "Leave me to work alone while you leave."

"Try to remember that I pay you a lot of money to do what you do; I doubt you'd make half that somewhere else."

Rafa mocked him with a laugh. "As if you'd let me leave your side alive."

"True, Rafa. Very true," Angelo agreed.

Chapter 33

When they entered their room again, a bottle of wine and several complimentary bottles of liquor were arranged in a neat row on the table. Sodas and a container of ice sat in front.

"Privacy," Angelo muttered as Ella walked to the terrace. He set two glasses on the counter, filling one with juice and vodka and another with scotch. "I'm going to need this before we go. The pre-celebration is almost as bad as the banquet."

Ella smiled and took the glass. She did not mind socializing half as much as he did. "What time are they expecting you?"

"What time are they expecting *us*?"

"Yes, *us* is what I meant."

He took a big swallow at the thought. "I'm not leaving you here by yourself. Imagine the trouble you'd get into without me watching you. You're either getting kissed by another man or you're trying to get yourself killed."

"I wish you would forget that ever happened."

Angelo looked up, a sly grin on his face. "How am I supposed to forget that another man's lips touched what's mine?"

"Really? Something that I didn't even know would happen? Are you that worried?"

"Worried? About what?" His eyes scanned over her body, lingering on her breasts. "You won't be able to look at another man without thinking about me."

Ella's face warmed; his words caught her off guard, but she could not deny that she felt slightly aroused by them too. "So do you normally go alone, or do you always have a date?" She wondered about any other women in his life but did not mean to ask the question aloud.

"Are you jealous of other women?"

"No," she said too quickly to be true.

"Sure you aren't," he laughed, "but no, I've always gone alone. There have been a couple of issues but not any recently."

"Oh?" Ella looked over at him. "What happened?"

Angelo shook his head at her interest. "I doubt you really want to know."

"Maybe I do." She waited for him to continue.

"Too much wine." He gave her the truth. "I had a couple of one-nighters."

"Oh." Ella nodded and emptied her glass.

"Be careful about what you ask, sweetheart."

"I suppose." She slouched against the terrace rail.

"Jealous?" He furthered her aggravation, but she resolved not to give in.

"No," came her simple reply.

"Right," he said, seeing right through her façade and wrapping his arms around her waist. "I wasn't drunk when I had you. Doesn't that count for something?"

Ella looked at him, frowning at his words. "That was mean of you to say."

"Then you must like calloused, insensitive men, because that never stopped you from liking me." Angelo chuckled as Ella let out a sigh. He could definitely be insensitive. Even so, as far as she had seen, he did not match the stereotype for sleeping around. "I can tell you one thing that will make you feel better," he said.

"You think so?" she replied and looked at the ocean. He needed to make her feel better. She did not feel very special to him right now.

"No other woman has been in this room." His lips kissed below her ear, instant warmth spreading to her cheeks.

"Go on," Ella muttered, helpless to his seduction.

"You are the only woman who will ever wear my ring." He continued lower, sliding the strap of her dress off her shoulder. "You are the first woman to catch my interest at all."

Angelo turned her around and took advantage of her, parting her lips with a passionate kiss. Grabbing the loops around his slacks was all Ella could do to keep her footing. After several intoxicating kisses, she pulled away in a daze, having completely forgotten how that moment began. Her jealousy was gone, but she glanced at the sky and realized it was quickly becoming night.

"When is that party supposed to start?"

"You'd rather go to a party than be alone with me?"

"No, but—"

"Then..." He grabbed her waist and brought his lips underneath the curve of her chin. "Let's skip it."

Ella moaned softly, almost giving in to his attention. "But Angelo, you're the owner."

"F-ine," he groaned and forced himself to pull away, his fingers trailing the length of her arms as he stepped back. "The party starts at seven."

Ella stopped to catch her breath as she exited the restroom door. Angelo was waiting for her with his suit jacket over his shoulder. He looked poised and confident—sexy. She envied every stare she knew he would receive.

When she did not move right away, Angelo walked up to her and kneeled down. His hands touched the inside of her thigh, pulling on the gun strap to make sure it was still secure. After his kiss earlier, her body reacted to the way he touched her skin. She started to rethink going to the party.

"I like how you blush every time I touch you." He smiled from where he knelt. Ella let out a breath as he stood up. He was deliberately provoking her and making her weak.

"Too bad you wanted to stop." He looked in her eyes, desire still in his gaze as he grabbed her hand. She did not miss the subtle accusation of his tone.

As they descended in the elevator, Angelo reflected about the night. With danger lurking from so many different directions, it was hard to know who was safe. Ella linked her arm through his and gently grasped the top with her hand, hoping to ease his nerves. He tensed with the contact, giving off an instant frown; then he relaxed and let out a breath. Angelo rubbed her arm as the door opened to floor two.

"You know the drill. Be alert and remember your gun. If I'm not with you, only take drinks from the bartender."

They entered the banquet hall where music masked any suspicious sounds that they might hear. With the previous night's attack at the beach, they needed to keep their eyes open. Many guests stared at them as they walked into the room. Ella followed Angelo's earlier warning and said as little as possible. While he spoke, she gave him support and scoured the room for anything unusual. So far, nothing and no one in particular stood out—only employees and guests dressed for the occasion. Ella noticed several women glance at her with dislike. She figured they envied her, how Angelo escorted her through the room. She thought it was jealousy, but she could not be sure. Ella would keep a close eye on them too in case they were a threat.

After talking to a dozen people, Angelo brought her to the bar and ordered them drinks. He looked back at the banquet hall and then rested his gaze on Ella. "Fake." He took a drink and focused his attention on her. "Wild animals are less conniving than some of the people here."

Ella turned around to keep a full view of the guests when Angelo followed suit while sliding his arm around her waist. "You see; that's why I like you. You're genuine and innocent. It's like you don't know any better."

"What?" Her eyes shot to Angelo. She could not believe he had said that. "Is that a compliment or an insult?" Ella did not know whether to laugh at his audacity or frown when Angelo kissed her lips.

"They must be worthy traits if I'm with you." He smiled.

"That's one way to put it," she said.

"Hey." Angelo spotted a man and looked at Ella. "Stay here for a minute. I need to talk to one of my men over there."

"And you don't want me to go with you?" she asked, wondering why he suddenly needed to speak in private. She was also surprised he would leave her by herself.

"Too vulgar for you, but I'll be right over there where I can see you. Don't go anywhere. I'll only be a minute." He rested his palm on her cheek before he walked away.

Ella watched him and waited. Before she could sip half of her drink, two women approached the bar. They were beautiful women, a few years older than Ella and probably knew no other lifestyle. The first woman had loose blond curls and wore a pink evening gown. The other woman had her hair wrapped in a jeweled bun, her black satin gown flowing to the floor. Ella could not find a single flaw with the women, her silky white dress feeling average in comparison. The two women leaned against the bar and spoke between themselves.

"There was no reason for Mr. Tomassi to bring a stray when he could have come with me," said the woman in pink.

"Excuse me," Ella mumbled, recanting her previous thought on their flawlessness. Appearances could be deceiving. She did not give them the attention they wanted and turned sideways, hoping they would both get the hint. "Maybe he'll forget about her and come back to my room again. He had a good time with me." Ella's mouth opened, her eyes glaring as the woman in pink purposely boasted to her friend. She was rude with no regard to Ella.

"They probably have some sort of deal going on. Mr. Tomassi never comes with anyone," the friend added.

Ella almost laughed. She could not believe the nonsense coming out of their mouths. This must have been one of those incidents that Angelo mentioned earlier; it may not have been recent, but it was not years ago either.

"Yes, that's probably it. It's all for business." The woman swallowed what was left in her glass and started walking to Angelo. She disregarded his conversation and touched him on the arm. "Mr. Tomassi," she said but did not sway his focus. He either was preoccupied with his discussion or ignored her altogether. "Mr. Tomassi," she said again.

"Yes?" he answered, barely glancing her way.

"I wanted to catch you before you left. I was wondering if you'd like to have a drink with me later tonight."

"No," he said. "I'm with my girlfriend tonight." Angelo pointed toward Ella. The woman had already seen her with him, so what was she trying to pull? Ella's hands tightened as her anger started to build. She had never experienced anyone that disrespectful.

"You have a girlfriend?" The woman sounded shocked and looked back at Ella. Ella understood her scowl in an instant, reciprocating the woman's dislike for her.

"I do...and I'm in the middle of something here." Angelo looked away and continued as though she had never come.

Marching back to her friend, the woman seethed, infuriated over the rejection. "How could he dismiss me like that? I'm ten times better than this nobody." She turned her anger on Ella. "You're making him look bad."

"Excuse me?" Ella asked.

"You heard me. You don't belong with a man like him. He will see that soon enough. He will come to his senses."

"It looks like he already did." Ella smiled into her glass, casually taking another sip of her drink. She could not help what she said. The woman opened herself to it.

"Women like you make me sick, thinking you can take any man you want, not caring what you do to their reputation."

"Oh…" Ella returned. "At least I'm not flaunting myself like some jealous halfwit throwing a fit. If you were with a man like Mr. Tomassi, I'd be embarrassed for him."

The woman grabbed at Ella's arm, putting Ella on alert. It did not matter what the situation was. She lacked manners. Ella looked over to Angelo for help, but he was unaware of her situation with the woman.

Ella frowned, the woman throwing her in an instant bad mood. "What did I ever do to you? First, I deal with some asshole's angry date and now my boyfriend's one-night stand. If that night meant anything to him, he would have called you or saw you or contacted you somehow. There is so much more to him than being the owner—things you'll never know anything about."

The woman's eyes knit together as she raised her hand to Ella. She never saw Angelo walking back over. She never expected him to be in the way. As the woman swung, her hand slapped Angelo in the mouth. Angelo crossed his arms and stretched his jaw from the slap.

"Mr. Tomassi, I'm so sorry." The woman cringed, a babbling stream of apologies leaving her mouth.

"Leave or I'll have my girlfriend shoot you." He patted the gun on her hip.

"Angelo." Ella closed her eyes as the women scurried away. "I have a gun because somebody could kill us; those women weren't even worth our time."

"Forget about them. Rafa will be here soon. Let me talk to a few more people and then we can go back to our room."

Chapter 34

A suit jacket and tie flew to one of the chairs; Angelo discarded his black leather shoes to the floor. "We're all alone," he said as the door clicked shut.

"Are you more comfortable?" Ella let her heels slide off of her feet.

"Much," he answered before hitting the liquor table, "but I still need a drink." Angelo picked up the bottle and showed it to Ella.

"Wine would be nice, thank you," she said.

"I can't believe they left the vintage of Merlot I asked for." He screwed in the wine key and popped the cork. Before he poured both glasses, he tasted a small amount of the wine. "So good," he said and then poured Ella a glass, handing it to her. "You taste it."

She sipped and grinned. "It's very good. This is...let me guess." Ella put a finger on her chin and smiled. "1987."

"Close...but wrong. That was a good year also. This is 1985." Angelo looked at the bottle and then at Ella. "So you can guess the year of wine but probably can't name a single TV show."

Ella frowned at his teasing. "My father had particular tastes. That was how he raised me. TV can't corrupt everyone."

Angelo chuckled and took a seductive step toward her while sliding off his shirt. "No...but I will gladly take on the challenge." He set down his wine and started to unzip her dress. "And I have all night to do it."

"Mm—" From under her breath, a delicate yet wanting sigh left her lips. He set her skin on fire; her cheeks glowed as her dress hit the floor. Angelo coolly backed her to the bed and retrieved her glass at the same time. When she started to speak, he shook his head slowly while removing the satin support around her breasts.

"I'm a needy man. Be quiet and let me have my way with you."

As soon as his lips touched hers, Ella melted, falling victim to his touch. All thoughts of protest vanished as she found herself at his command.

"Angelo," she moaned as he laid her on the bed.

"I know you want me too," he said, his belt clanking as he removed his slacks. "I know you like being under my control."

Ella gasped as he moved his mouth to that sensitive area between her thighs, writhing under the soft caresses of his tongue. She could not speak or think, proving she was weak to his touch. Angelo moved his mouth from between her legs to her neck and lingered, her head arching to the side. She was a willing vessel to his charge, helpless when he pinned her arms above her head.

"I want to fill every inch of you." She started to open her mouth when he slid his tongue inside instead. "No talking," he breathed and kicked off his pants. "Take what I give you."

Angelo lowered his hips and used his own knees to spread hers apart. He was magnificent, hard. He gently persuaded her body to allow for his size. Her breathing quickened. As her eyes shut, Ella panted heavily, making her breasts touch his chest with every gasp she took. She could hardly contain her satisfaction at feeling him this way.

"Do I make you feel good?" He whispered in her ear.

When she opened her eyes again, he was gazing at her, waiting to see her disoriented expression. "So good," she muttered. She could feel her nails claw through the skin of his back as she squeezed her knees against his hips.

"Cross your legs around my waist and hold onto my neck." She hesitated when Angelo moved her feet behind. "I'm going to make you forget where you are," he said. His tone was sensual and sure. Angelo buried himself inside, nearly making her scream in ecstasy. Her cries made him go deeper, faster until her body trembled beneath.

"Christ, you feel so fucking good," he said, pulling her waist against him and rocking her further, pleasing her in a way he did with no one else. Then he moved his hands underneath, lifting her hips to give her even more.

"Angelo..."

"You can handle it."

"Angelo," she choked, the heat of her climax unexpectedly coursing through her body when he raised her feet to his neck. "Angelo, please..." He ignored her cries and pumped into her more, feeling her body shake without control.

"Take it all," he whispered and brought her to orgasm again. "Don't ever hold back."

He lowered her legs to the bed and flipped her over, raising her hips to meet his.

"Oh god," she cried again, feeling him thrust deep from behind; every inch of him entered her now. Ella squeezed the pillow to her mouth, muffling the screams that filled the room. She never knew he could feel this way. His length almost hurt but the pleasure made her crazy with desire, a need she never knew she had until him.

"God almighty, Ella." He squeezed her breasts, holding her tight. "The more of you I have, the more I want to take." Low growls escaped his throat as he thoroughly ravished her form. "I've never felt this way about anyone," he admitted and paused his rhythm to flip her back over.

"Open your eyes," he said and grabbed his shaft, centering it to her sex. Angelo slammed into her hard, never letting up. His lips crashed onto hers, Ella willingly accepting the assault on her mouth. Her lips moved to his faster than her mind could keep up with her need. Their bodies became slick. Her moans became faint. It seemed as though he waited to appease her desire of him. Then he drove fast and rigid, his length convulsing with the tight walls of her core. Angelo released with pleasured satisfaction, his body feeling heavy on top of her.

"I love you," she whispered in his shoulder and closed her eyes. Angelo lifted his weight slightly, leaving one leg draped over the top of hers. She did not know if he loved her, but she did feel like he could. She did not think more on it. She simply enjoyed being held in his arms.

Chapter 35

Ella woke with Angelo's fingers gently tracing through her hair. She had fallen asleep bare-breasted against his chest and nestled into his body. As Angelo started to sit, she smiled but did not open her eyes.

"Don't go," she whispered and snuggled into his warmth. She enjoyed the sounds of his heartbeat and the feel of his arms around her. She did not want to move.

Five short minutes later, he moved from underneath her and slid to the edge of the bed, leaving her to curl in the vacant spot. "Where are you going?" she asked, the morning sun that shined through a crack in the curtain making her squint.

"To take a shower." Watching him search for clothes, she sulked until he turned his head and smiled. "You could shower with me. I'd go easy on you today."

"What?" she asked, blushing without any words to defend herself.

Angelo's fingers grazed the span of her arm and stopped, massaging her exposed breast from under the sheet. "It's okay. Twice last night was bound to leave you sore. I'll be out in a minute." Ella's cheeks felt hot. He knew exactly how to make her react.

As he showered, Ella mustered the energy to get out of bed to make coffee. She slipped on a robe and looked around, reflecting on the night before when a plain white envelope slid underneath the door. She presumed it was a summary of charges and curiously went to see what the penthouse suite cost per day. The same types of envelopes were always placed under the door when she traveled with her father.

Ella unfolded the white sheet of paper; the color drained from her face. With shocked horror, her body trembled as she rushed to open the door. It would not budge, locked by the key code. Ella hurried to the glass door of the balcony, unlatching the corner and darting outside. She searched the beach as far as she could see. There was nobody—nobody at all this early in the morning. Ella crumpled the note and stretched her arm back. As she started to throw it at whoever had scribbled the words, a hand grabbed the wadded ball and placed an arm around her waist.

"Stop! Let me go!" Ella cried and tried to force the arm off, but it further constricted her body "Don't touch me!" she screamed.

"Ella." the voice said firmly. "Calm down. Look, I have you."

She panted and heaved when she recognized that the voice belonged to Angelo. Her body gave way to the marble tile, having no strength left to stand. Angelo straightened the paper and read for himself. He looked at her and read it again.

This is your only warning. Your father won't make a decision, so we'll take what we want from you. We've made the terms. Tomassi won't win this war. He will die first.

Angelo scooped her off the floor and set her on the recliner inside. As he tried to put the situation in perspective, he pulled up a chair and sat in front of her, stroking her arms. "Are you all right?" Ella nodded but could not get past the shock.

"How did they know we were here?"

"I always stay in this room but I need to check on something too," he said and clicked on his phone, raising it to his ear. "Hey...drop what you're doing and get up here—we have an issue." Angelo never gave the other line a chance to speak and hung up the phone.

"What are you going to do?"

"I need you to give me your jewelry."

"Why?" Ella unfastened her necklace and pulled off a ruby ring. Then she grabbed a bracelet off the side table and handed it over too. "They belonged to my mother. What are you going to do with them?"

"They might have a tracker."

"Will I get them back?"

"Yes...eventually." He put them in a small bag and zipped the seal. As he took care of the jewelry, loud banging came at the door. "Who is it?" he called out.

"*You* called *me*." Rafa's voice became more pronounced as he walked through the door. His back slumped against the wall; his arms crossed with annoyed resentment. "This had better be important," he said pointedly, his long-sleeved shirt un-tucked with a mere three buttons fastened, "because I was in the middle of something important."

"Important? Sure Rafa." Angelo handed him the note and watched the confusion in his eyes as he read. "It's all a little too coincidental," he mumbled.

"I also think she's bugged. I need you to have these checked."

"Sounds familiar," said Rafa, a devious glimmer to his eye.

"Don't start, Rafa." Angelo pointed in warning.

Rafa stared again at the note and eyed Angelo. "Tomassi will not win this war." He rubbed his fingers against his chin and seemed decisive in his thought. "War? Or what's necessary to merge with Gregorio's group?" Then he looked back at Ella and shook his head.

"What?" she asked.

"A real estate agent, huh?" He shook his head again, handing the paper back to Angelo; then he walked through the door without giving an explanation for what he said.

"What's he talking about?" Ella looked at Angelo.

"Your father. He must have more influence than practicing real estate."

"Wait—can they track me with my phone number?"

Angelo stared at her. He started to open his mouth but closed it again, thinking as he looked at the ceiling. "If they have the right connections, they could."

"I gave my number to those two men who came to the restaurant that one time. I told them to give it to my father."

"I'll bet your father never got that message. Where is your phone?" Ella handed it to him and Angelo set it on the floor and stomped down hard, shattering the phone under his boot. "If they were, they won't be now." As he picked up the broken pieces, Ella looked at him with disbelief. "We will get you a new one," he said. "Why don't you get dressed and walk around with me today. It'll give you a chance to see me at work and take your mind off the note."

***

Inside the conference room on the second floor, Angelo let go of her hand and pointed to the sofa. "You need to stay there until I finish checking on the men. I don't want you to move. Do you understand?"

"Yes." She immediately sat.

"Good." He walked into the room on the side, leaving the door open as he did. Ella observed several men with pieces of artwork on tables covered with thick white cloths. They must have been those specialty items that Angelo mentioned. She wondered what was involved in acquiring such expensive-looking paintings. It may have been for the best that she did not know.

Angelo walked around, nodding his approval. He looked satisfied with the room but stopped behind a man with shaggy brown hair who was polishing the frame of an oversized portrait. Angelo crossed his arms. The man had no clue that Angelo stood directly behind him when he started talking out.

"I can't believe they have us doing this kind of work. What is this supposed to do for us? This isn't training?" The man fumbled the painting around while glancing at the guy next to him. "Doesn't cleaning frames piss you off too?" The guy focused on his work and said nothing. "Why aren't you saying anything?" When the guy still stayed quiet, the man gave him a push. The guy glared at him but went back to his work.

That was Angelo's cue. He cleared his throat, his arms tightening across his chest. "Tell me, what does being a member of this group mean exactly?"

"Well...I..." The man stared back with shamed surprise, gently setting the portrait on the table.

"Suddenly you can't talk?" Angelo pointed his pistol at the man's head and watched him buckle with fear. "This work shows me you're willing to do anything for the good of the group. You aren't allowed to talk, because it teaches you how to think on your own. If you had kept your mouth shut and thought more, you would've sensed someone behind you. You also wouldn't have my gun aimed at your head right now, would you?"

"I—"

"If I wanted to kill you, you would be dead. This isn't a game, and I can't use a prospect with an eager trigger finger. So leave, and don't show your face around me again."

"But—" The man started to object when Angelo calmly clicked the hammer.

"Final warning," he said. The man did not say another word, hurrying out of the room before Angelo could change his mind.

"Fuck." Angelo closed the door to the room and motioned for Ella to follow him to the office in the back. Inside, Rafa merely glanced at him and continued shifting through papers, irritating Angelo more.

"Isn't Brett supposed to watch those guys in there? Where the hell is he?"

"I sent him down to see Donnie with the new info."

"And you left the prospects to handle the merchandise alone? Fuck, Rafa."

"I had it covered; then I saw you walk in."

"The hell you did…" Rafa stood as Angelo pulled Ella's hand out of the office door and back through the conference room to the banquet hall.

They entered the elevator. Instead of going to the lobby, Angelo stopped on floor three. There were a dozen boutiques that caught Ella's surprise. Angelo did not strike her as the type to shop.

"I want you to wait here and don't go anywhere. I need to talk to the clerks for a minute."

A minute turned into minutes and then a half hour. Ella grew antsy and considered looking for Angelo. The lecture that awaited her crossed her mind so she searched for him through the glass windows.

Nothing. She gave up and stood still where Angelo told her to wait.

"Ella." Her name was whispered from around the corner. The voice was low, but the man pronounced the first letter of her name in a way one person ever did. She knew the voice well.

When she heard it a second time, Ella knew she had to go. She looked for Angelo and then turned around as the man called her again. She paid no attention to Angelo's order to stay and circled the corner to the joining hallway.

Chapter 36

Ella's father grabbed her hand and led her to the elevator that stopped on the sixth floor. When the door to his room shut, she looked at him, disbelieving he was in front of her. Standing a head above her in a slick black suit, his aftershave filled her lungs.

"Father," she said.

The scar underneath his chin showed clearly with his freshly shaven face. The graying black hairs on his head were trimmed and combed neatly to the sides. His mere presence made her footing falter.

"It's good to see you, Ella." He wrapped his arms around her shoulders, her body tensing at his affectionate gesture. She felt emotionally drained by all that had happened. He could hardly expect her to be receptive.

"It's been a long time since we last talked," she said. She could feel the corners of her eyes sting, but there was no way she would cry. She did not want him to see that she felt hurt by his neglect. "So much has happened lately that I don't know where to start."

"What are you doing here, Ella? This place is too dangerous for you. Who brought you here?"

Ella looked at her father. She could not believe he was telling her about danger. "You can't be serious. Is that all you have to say? You haven't talked to me in almost a year, and now you want to know who brought me here. You hid stuff from me...stuff that you should have told me about."

"Ella," he sighed. "I had no idea until it was too late. I didn't know my associates were trouble. I wanted to call you, but it would have made it so much worse."

"My situation is already worse," she countered. "Someone sent a threat earlier saying they were coming for me, that you weren't giving them what they wanted. I deserve to know what they want from you and why I'm being thrown in the middle. I didn't do anything."

Her father did not respond. Something sidetracked his attention as soon as she asked. Ella looked directly at the door, knowing someone would walk in the room. It was Sullivan. Her mentor. Her guide and protector before all this. He immediately shut the door and stood in front of it.

"You can't keep me here, Sullivan. He isn't in charge like before." Ella pointed at her father. "I'm with someone. I'm not staying here."

"Who are you with?" asked her father. She could tell he had no real interest in knowing who it was. His flat voice proved that he would try to separate them without giving it a thought.

"It isn't your business," she said. "You haven't wanted me in your life since mother died. You distanced yourself from me." Ella shook her head in adamant conclusion. "You don't have the right to tell me how to live anymore."

"Believe whatever you want. I'm still your father." He pointed. "I know what's best for you."

"No," she said in protest and reached around Sullivan for the doorknob. "If it wasn't for Angelo, I wouldn't be here." The words came from under her breath. Her father really thought he was going to keep her there. She should have known better than to see him. "Sullivan, move. I'm leaving."

Sullivan acted as though he did not hear a word she said and stared ahead, leaving a hopeless feeling to creep to her chest as he refused to acknowledge her there. "Let her go," her father said.

Ella's mouth opened. She glanced at Sullivan who seemed as shocked as she was. Her father was letting her leave without a fight. Why did he change his mind?

"Let me go with her," Sullivan said. "I don't want to see her hurt again."

"No," was her father's short reply, irritated at the request. "She'll be fine."

Sullivan let out a heavy breath. His eyes fell, a disapproving frown on his face as he stepped away from the door. Ella had never seen Sullivan sad before—glassy-eyed.

"Be careful, Ella," he said and then squeezed her hand, leaving in it a folded piece of paper. He gazed in her eyes. An instant understanding passed between the two. She could not let her father see the note.

The door shut as she walked down the hallway. Ella wondered about Sullivan's genuine concern as opposed to simply looking out for her. She immediately opened the folded paper and read, "I will find you at the banquet tonight. Don't say anything to anyone."

Ella stopped walking. Sullivan would tell her to stay quiet about a meeting with him to protect her. She could not betray his trust when he always had acted with her better interest in mind. She had a lot of respect for him.

Ella entered the elevator and descended. What excuse was she supposed to give to Angelo now? She did not deceive herself about his reaction once she saw him. She knew it would not go well, yet all she could wonder about was what Sullivan had to say.

The anticipation in her mind peaked as she turned the corner to the shops. Angelo was not waiting for her outside. She hoped he was still shopping and gazed through the large glass windows. Her heart sank when she did not see a trace of Angelo. She searched inside every shop before giving up. Angelo must have already been looking for her.

Where should she go? She did not have the card or the code to his suite. The logical place to wait was on the lobby floor. When the elevator opened, more greeters welcomed guests. Today was the day of the banquet. Based on the large groups loitering in the lobby, Ella would not find Angelo even if he were there. With so many people, it was impossible for her to focus on what to do next. She could ask someone at the counter, but the lines were long. Chances were high that they would not give her any information anyway even if they did remember seeing her with Angelo.

She felt misplaced in the room full of people. It was not half as intimidating when it was empty. Now Ella could only think to sit in a vacant spot on one of the sofas. She was not used to this particular crowd. She was not that familiar with the hotel either.

"I told you to be careful with my bags," one woman shouted pointedly at a boy who rolled her luggage through the room. Ella found nothing wrong with the way he handled her bags. She must have been trying to prove her importance. Ella felt sorry for her company who dragged their feet behind her. The woman proved that she was unpleasant and unfriendly.

Ella saw much of the same attitudes with the guests who arrived. Eager people announced their titles and status as if that made them superior to the rest. Ella stood up. She had enough of those claiming importance. If they were very important, they would not have to convince everyone else of such.

She was glad for the back exit of the hotel. With the guests worried about checking in, she could enjoy the solace of the soothing waves from the ocean. She would go back inside when the crowds lessened. Then maybe she would ask about Angelo.

Ella sat on a bench outside for five minutes when Angelo pushed open the door. The heavy thuds of his steps matched the scowl on his face. One look at him told her she was in trouble. She had to look away. Ella forced her focus on the water but to no benefit. Angelo grabbed her cheek and turned it. Her instinct was to look away again, but Angelo lifted her face. He would accept nothing but her eyes.

"I asked you to wait for me. I told you to stay put." His words were slow; his tone was deep—infuriated. "You couldn't fucking wait for me ten whole minutes without disappearing? Do you know what could have happened after that note earlier?"

Ella's heart pounded under his reproof. She could feel the dryness in her throat as her hands started to shake. She had never seen him this angry with her before. Ella could not say a single word with the rage in his eyes. He yanked her hand, pulling her body off the bench to his chest.

"I'm sorry. I—"

"I don't want to hear your excuses."

"No, but I—" Ella choked down the tears. She knew if one fell to her cheek, she would start crying and lose all control of herself.

"Be quiet. The thing I care about right now is that you didn't listen. Never again."

Ella shut her eyes as he pulled her through the door to the crowded lobby and guided her to the elevator. People started to stare, but Angelo paid no attention to any of them. She could feel his fury through the squeeze on her wrist. He never let go and he never spoke. Angelo looked at the elevator door until it stopped on the top floor. He typed in the code fast so that Ella did not see one number that he punched. Then he stormed inside and flung her to the bed.

Ella breathed in a chest full of air and released. The breathing technique did nothing to relax her nerves as Angelo started shifting through a bag. Metal clinked together with a high-pitched torturous sound. Angelo tightly gripped whatever it was and marched back toward her. With steady movements, as though he had done this multiple times, he snatched her hand and lifted it up. It happened too fast for Ella to comprehend until she found her left wrist handcuffed to the bed.

"You aren't really going to leave me like this?" Her eyes widened as she pulled her arm a couple of times. "It wasn't even my fault."

"I don't care," he said. Angelo leaned his hand beside her and bore his eyes onto her, making her sink further to the blankets as he spoke dangerously close to her lips. "You will learn your place and won't go against my orders. What I say goes. I will know where you are at all times. This is what you agreed to when you didn't leave my room that night at the club. I don't care if you like it or not." Angelo stood up and looked at her. "You can think about it for a while. Maybe next time, you will listen to me." Angelo turned around and walked out of the room.

***

His temper took control. It did not seem to click in her head that people surrounded them, waiting to attack them again at any moment. He did not understand what was difficult about that fact. By now, Ella knew the world was not harmless, yet she waited for him outside in the open where anyone could grab her and carry her away. What was going through her mind?

He breathed. He tried to settle his anger but kept getting mad all over again. Maybe a couple of hours in handcuffs would cure the issue. Maybe then, she would have a clue about the dangers of the life.

Angelo walked off the elevator on the second floor. The banquet was due to start any minute. He had hoped to have Ella with him as it began, but given the current circumstances, he was too upset to look at her now. Angelo stopped at the bar where Thomas stood. He exchanged no words. Thomas immediately started his drink and handed it to him. Angelo swallowed and closed his eyes. Ella was making him insane.

With the liquor in his system, Angelo started to calm down. There were a few unsocial guests sitting at the tables. Most were enjoying the refreshments and free wine. Others chose to buy drinks.

He took another drink and started for the hallway to the conference room. Jim and Ray should be in there to report anything they had learned about Sullivan the day before. He really wanted to know who

Robert Collins was and what he looked like. Angelo wanted to know exactly what that man was about.

"Tomassi," a voice called out before he passed the table with wine. He groaned in return and turned around. The only reason he invited him was to keep relations open. In no way did he want a conversation.

"Gregorio," he huffed, leering at the man without a hair out of place on his graying head and a distinguishing scar on his chin. Martino Gregorio caused him more problems than he ever wanted. It was solely his fault that Bonadio had a problem with him in the first place—Gregorio and the ridiculous offer of his daughter's hand. Bonadio wanted her and Gregorio's estate to himself. Angelo did not care for either one, but Bonadio still saw him as a threat.

"This is some event you're showcasing. You're going to make a lot of new clients on this one."

Angelo nodded but was not interested in chatting. Wherever Gregorio went, gunshots followed. Angelo kept his hand close to his gun. He could not trust anyone in this man's company.

"Not talkative tonight, Tomassi?" Gregorio asked.

Angelo shook his head. "No, I have something on my mind."

"Or someone?" said Gregorio. At his words, Angelo swiftly turned toward him, receiving a smile in return. "When my little girl was fourteen, she had the pool boys convinced that our tree held invisible grapes. I went outside and asked them what the hell they were doing up in the tree. They explained to me that when they shook the branches, the grapes appeared and fell to the ground. That was when I noticed my daughter slink away from her window. As they shook the branches, she would throw grapes to the ground." Gregorio shook his head. "If those boys had any sense at all, they would've known that grapes don't grow on trees." Angelo briefly smiled. He did find the story amusing but that did not change anything.

Gregorio's expression turned grim and serious. "Tomassi, let's talk business."

"I have nothing to talk to you about," Angelo said.

"Yes, you do." Gregorio handed him a manila envelope that fastened at the top. "Keep those files confidential. Read them. We can discuss the arrangements at ten sharp tomorrow morning. A phone number is in there. Let me know where to meet."

Gregorio looked at the envelope one more time and gave a single nod of his head; then he turned back around and simply walked away. Angelo stared at him until he saw him get on the elevator. He did not like the sudden appearance and disappearance of Gregorio. Something about their short exchange made his blood boil. His muscles tightened as he continued to the conference room and punched in the code. As the door shut behind him, Angelo hesitated for a moment. He knew before he ever unfastened the envelope that the contents meant something bad.

Angelo opened the envelope. He started to read as Rafa came out of the office in the back. Thirty seconds later, Angelo launched the envelope through the air.

"What happened?" Rafa asked.

"That son of a bitch threatened me. Gregorio used the one person who meant anything to me and threatened to take it away."

Rafa took a few steps forward and picked up the strewn papers. He read for himself. His brows rose as he shook his head back and forth. "What are you going to do now?" he asked.

Angelo slowly inhaled. His expression reflected hatred and anger as he let out his breath again. Nobody threatened him. He did not care who they were. He thought about the trouble that Gregorio had caused him from the beginning. He would not put up with him anymore.

"What am I going to do?" He scowled at the empty envelope on the floor. "I'm going to give him exactly what he asked for."

Chapter 37

After ten minutes, Ella stared at the bed rail and yanked her arm a couple of times. *He'll come back, won't he?* She thought. She glanced at the door and hung her head. As angry as Angelo was, he would not come back for a while. She had to talk to Sullivan, though. This may be her chance.

She needed her purse from the table about eight feet away and stood, forgetting about the restraint when the handcuff yanked her body back down. There was a small space behind the bed where she could slide in her free arm and scoot the bed away from the wall. She needed to scoot the bed closer to the table with her purse.

Ella strained. She pushed against the wall and the bed with all her strength, but the plush carpet prevented the bed from moving at all. She accomplished nothing and was left with bright red indentions from the headboard on her arm. She could not do it from the top. She had to get closer to the floor.

Angered by the pain, she crouched and kicked the nightstand away from the bed. Without the nightstand in the way, she managed to set her right foot flat on the floor. Her knee served as a wedge between the wall and the bed. It was a tight squeeze, but she was not giving up.

With every ounce of strength she could find, she forced the bed away from the wall with one fluid shove. But her footing slipped as it moved; an instant burning sensation shot from her wrist to her arm as the weight of her body dangled from the handcuff. Ella shrieked with agony as she slipped her foot through the strap of her purse and yanked it to her hand, dumping out the contents on the bed. Anger from the pain fueled her desire to get out. She did not care what Angelo had said.

The light reflected on one of the brown metal hairclips in the mess. She picked up a hairclip and opened it, bending it back and forth until she had an exact sliver of metal for fitting inside the end of the handcuffs. She could do this in her sleep.

Free.

Ella mocked the restraint with triumph. Moving the bed had been much more difficult than freeing her hands. She basked in her small victory. Angelo would be furious, but she could not stay restricted until he returned. There was too much on her mind.

Now she had to contend with the coded door. Only a few people knew the code; it was unfortunate for her that she was not one of them. The hotel's phone would have to do and she dialed the number to room service. She almost felt ashamed with what she was doing. Her self-deprecating smile should have alerted the manager to her devious intentions as soon as he opened the door. Instead, he walked inside with the items she requested and waited for her to tell him where to set them down.

Ella pointed to the balcony as she wedged her shoe and blocked the door from closing. As if it were a race, she rushed to the sliding glass door and shut it fast. It took half a second to fasten the lock secure. The manager looked surprised at first. He did not know what she was doing. Ella glanced at him as she shoved her personal belongings back in her purse. His expression seemed enlightened when he saw the cuffs.

"I'm sorry," she shouted, unable to help her sheepish smile at his shock. "I'm really sorry to do this to you, but I had no choice. The room service was for you."

***

Ella exited the elevator to the banquet hall. Everyone she passed was dressed in designer clothes while she still wore the same outfit she had put on that morning. Her blouse and skirt would have to do. Where was Sullivan?

She walked and stopped, gazed around the room and walked some more. There was no sign of him or anyone else she knew. Ella stopped by several tables lined with long silver platters. She realized how hungry she was but could not think about that now.

"Hey you." A woman with a tight brown ponytail and blue eyes snarled the words. Ella was looking absentmindedly around the room when the woman grabbed her arm. "These trays need to be replaced. What do you think you're doing?"

Ella picked up a tiny cracker and popped it in her mouth to spite the woman. Why did strangers feel they had a right to touch her? The blatant rudeness of the clientele in Angelo's businesses was growing old.

"Didn't you hear me?" the woman asked. Ella started to open her mouth when she saw Angelo and Rafa coming around the corner. Rafa walked to the elevator and Angelo stopped not far from where she stood. Forgetting about the woman, Ella needed to go.

"I said—" the woman started again when Ella huffed out a breath. She turned from watching Angelo to where the woman stood next to her.

"I am not an employee," Ella said. "Do you see me wearing an employee uniform or a nametag…anything? Why do you think you can boss me or anyone else around anyway. Are you in charge? Would it kill you to treat people with a little respect?"

The woman stood speechless as a man in a white suit and brown hair walked up beside her. Ella almost looked away with annoyance. "What makes you think you can speak to her that way?" he asked. "Do you have any idea who she is? I thought the guests in this hotel were always right."

"Again," Ella repeated, "I am not an employee. But if I was, I didn't know status allowed you to throw out decency. I'll have to remember that." She started to leave when the woman spoke again.

"Wait," she said. "I've never had someone talk to me that way."

"Then I apologize," Ella scoffed and took a step.

"My name is Lucy."

"Enjoy the party, Lucy."

"Would you like to join me?"

Not really. Ella thought. "No, I can't. I'm meeting someone but thanks anyway."

The woman nodded and gave a genuine smile before walking off with the man. Ella took another cracker and stopped to revamp her thoughts. She almost forgot why she came when she watched Rafa come out of the elevator with the manager that she tricked. She moved closer to hear but stayed near the bar to stay out of sight. One look at Angelo's face told her that she should have stayed in the room. He turned to Rafa and smiled as the manager left them alone. It was not a friendly smile. It was more like the one he might use before he killed someone dead where they stood. His glaring eyes disclosed what he really thought.

"Let me see if I understand." Angelo breathed in deep as he fisted his hand against his chin. "She freed herself from the cuffs." Rafa nodded in response. "She used the hotel phone and told the manager that we needed food." Rafa half-smiled, looking as if he was trying not to laugh. "Then she locked the manager outside and left the room."

"Yes, you've played it all out perfectly."

Angelo shook his head and waved his hand through the air. "Okay, that's all I need to know. I'm going to kill her," he growled. "Where is she?"

"Here's the catch," said Rafa. "The signal traces her right to this room."

Angelo looked at Rafa and they both started looking around the banquet hall. What signal did they mean? Ella instantly remembered the jewelry they took and Rafa's sarcastic response. She looked down at Angelo's ring on her finger.

She felt like a fool. Was that why Angelo told her never to remove the ring? Did it have nothing to do with showing that they were a couple? She felt a lot less important to him than she had a moment ago. Angelo had tracked her the entire time. That was how he knew she was outside the lobby's back door earlier that day.

Ella turned and started to walk the other direction. The elevator was on the other side of Angelo and Rafa. She would never make it without them seeing. She had to find another way around. At the very least, she needed a quiet spot to think. Between the growing crowds and the constant bustle of employees, it was impossible to find a clear path. She ended up down a small hallway and in an empty room. The room had plain beige carpeting and florescent lights on the ceiling. The employees must have moved the tables and chairs into the main hall.

Ella sighed. It saddened her to look at the ring. She could not fathom it had been a tracking device. They tracked her like the men who were associated with her father without any consideration for her feelings. They did as they pleased with her.

The confrontation with Angelo might as well happen now rather than later, and she turned back toward the door. Ella's voice screeched. Angelo was not supposed to be in the room, and his angry eyes did nothing for her nerves. His gaze seemed to look through her and to the wall behind. A second later, he yanked his gun from the inside of his jacket. Angelo raised the gun before she could think. Ella thought she was dead.

Her heart raced fast as she opened her eyes. She felt no pain. She had no idea about what happened and whom Angelo shot. She lifted her head and looked up at him. Angelo stared behind her and looked all around. His gun pointed in every direction as though anyone would jump out. He held out his hand to her without ever looking at her face. His chin gestured her to stand.

"You realize this is strike two," he said and squeezed his hand around her arm. He started to walk, but before he reached the door, Sullivan burst inside. He seemed surprised to see Angelo.

"What do you need?" Angelo spoke in an irritated voice at seeing him there. His eyes narrowed at Sullivan; his finger was still on the trigger of his gun. For a second, Ella feared that Angelo would shoot him too.

Sullivan looked at Angelo and then at Ella. "I was making sure she was okay," he said, pausing, and then walked back out of the room. Ella felt her body grow numb with his departure. She would not be able to talk to him now.

Chapter 38

Angelo gave her a slight push as they entered the suite again. His face showed neither a frown nor a grin. He glanced at her for a second and pointed at the recliner by the balcony door. "Sit down," he said and slid off his coat. He shook it once and laid it over a small table in the entry of the room; his tie and the top buttons on his shirt were next as he sat down on the bed. Ella waited for his inevitable scolding but he said nothing. He had never been angered to silence.

Angelo took out his phone and slid his thumb over the screen. He read as though she was not in the room, scrolling and stopping; then he read some more. Ella watched him concentrate on whatever it was he saw. She wondered what had caught his interest when he finally looked over at her.

"What would you have done if I had not been there tonight?" he asked as he raised the phone to his ear. "The third room in the banquet hall needs to be cleaned. Be careful though. There's probably more with Gregorio around."

Gregorio. She thought. He was at the hotel? Ella did not like that he was there. His daughter probably was too. With Angelo mad at her, he might go ahead and meet the daughter. Ella felt threatened and despised her. It did not matter that she did not know who she was.

While Angelo went back to his phone, she twiddled with the ring and stood. What was his reason for the invasion on her privacy? She wanted to ask, but Angelo did not seem in the mood for questions. His eyes were intent; he seemed to focus on some other matter even though he stared at his phone. She hardly wanted to know what was on his mind.

Ella kept glancing his way with anticipation of what he would say. The quieter Angelo stayed, the more nervous she became. She needed air. A single step was all she took when Angelo immediately snapped his fingers and pointed at the chair.

"Don't move unless I tell you to move," he said. Crossing her arms around her chest, Ella slouched back to the recliner when Angelo spoke again. "I can't believe you today."

"You can't believe me?" she said. She could no longer hold her words. The tracker was an unexpected disappointment that she could not let go. "You're tracking me. Is that the reason I'm supposed to wear your ring? You made it seem like the ring was special. Am I just an object to you?"

"Yes, I can keep track of you with it."

"And the cameras at my house in Key Biscayne?" she asked. "You didn't even tell me they were there. How am I supposed to feel about that? How am I supposed to feel when you say the name Gregorio? You don't understand." Ella let out a hopeless breath and hung her head. How did she expect him to understand when he did these sorts of things all the time? Angelo was used to doing as he pleased. It was who he was. It was his life.

"Come here," he said.

Ella sulked. She did not respond fast enough and Angelo stood instead. He grabbed her hands and pulled her directly in front of him, but she turned her head away. She avoided eye contact, until he pulled her onto his lap. His hand wrapped around her head and whipped her face in front of his. "You know, for a clever girl, you sure can overlook the fucking obvious."

"What do you mean? And...what are you doing?" she asked as he started to unbutton her blouse.

"What do you think I'm doing?" He continued to push it off her arms and then moved to her buttoned skirt.

"You're making me feel like you own me."

"That's right." He guided her on the bed and rolled her underneath his body while pulling his shirt over his head. "You do belong to me," he added and yanked his belt from the loops. "And I should beat you for not listening."

Ella's breathing deepened as the buckle dangled from his hands, but he dropped it to the floor and stood. "I told you that you would be stuck in this life. I told you that you wouldn't like everything," he said and let his pants fall to the floor. She felt the heat from his body as he held his weight above her. "But you know what?" he asked. "You should know exactly why I track you."

"You should have told me instead of letting me figure it out." Her eyes looked at him and then the wall. She could feel the tears prick the corners of her eyes.

"There's no reason for you to be upset over the ring."

"That's not it and you know it. It's about respect."

"Ella, this is not a respect issue. My time is valuable, yet I'm here with you. Do you seriously think I would be here if I didn't respect you?"

His body was warm. Ella enjoyed the feel of her bare breasts against the contours of his chest. She liked the way his legs locked around hers and how his arms secured her firmly against his skin. Angelo was endearing but almost desperate in his squeeze. Ella could tell something was on his mind by his tense muscles and beating heart; he did not talk about whatever it was.

Another minute passed. Angelo pressed his lips to hers, affection in his kiss, but she knew he would not stay on such an important night. She did not care. Her nails slid across his abdomen in a last effort to try. His eyes closed for a second before they opened back up and lifted up her hand with the ring on her finger. Angelo looked into her eyes.

"Don't ever question the ring again. Is that clear?"

"Yes." She nodded and looked down.

"Don't sulk with me either. I told you before that I will wipe the frown from your face." She smiled. It was as though his coarse words had an underlining meaning meant just for her.

"It's eight now," he started. "I need to get back to the banquet for a while and then the items exchange. You can go with me if you'd like; then you could see for yourself how it works. But remember, these men don't like strangers. You'd have to be quiet."

"Okay," Ella answered, even though she would rather have stayed in his arms. Still, he was letting her to go. She would not pass up the opportunity either.

Angelo stretched out his hand from underneath her body and gave a confused look when he could not reach the nightstand beside the bed. "I don't remember the nightstand being so far away," he said. Angelo lifted her up and scooted all the way to the edge. Opening up the top drawer, he pulled out a small box.

Ella looked at the table that was definitely further away by a foot. His notice made her feel a little impish of the reason. It seemed like a victory at the time. "I kind of had to push the furniture across the room to get my purse while I was handcuffed."

"Right," he said. Angelo grabbed the box and returned to the bed. His muscles tapered perfectly along his abdomen to his pelvis. She found him alluring and hard to resist. She could not look away.

"You want me to show you how I got free?" she asked. Her face felt warm with her guilty thoughts as she grabbed her purse from the nightstand.

"Go ahead." He set the box back down as she pulled the handcuffs from her purse.

"Give me your hands." She smiled innocently, but her eyes showed anything but innocence.

"I don't think so." He yanked the cuffs from her fingers and held them out of reach.

"You want me to show you, don't you?" Ella gave him a sexy, sideways glance. She could see a forming curiosity in his eyes as he considered letting her have his hands.

"Not a chance," he said instead. Her devious grin must have given her away.

"Don't you trust me?" she asked in her sweetest, most tempting voice.

"Trust a woman like you—hardly." Angelo chuckled out the sarcastic response, making Ella sulk at his mocking tone. Her eyes gazed at him until he caved in. "Fine, but I warn you. Beware who you're dealing with."

"I know who you are," she smiled, "so give me your hands."

Angelo took a deep breath and let her do as she wished. Ella did not wait a second. She would not give him the chance to reevaluate his consent and immediately handcuffed both of his wrists to the headboard.

His body was gorgeous. She raised both her legs around him and straddled his hips. Ella leaned back on her palms to admire the predicament that he allowed her to subject him to. Only she would be able to convince Angelo to allow her to handcuff him to the bed.

"Okay, you've had your fun. Now release me."

Ella grinned at his state. She knew he was serious by his agitated tone; that did not stop her. She delayed setting him free and pressed her finger against her cheek, antagonistic thoughts on her mind.

"But Mr. Tomassi, this position is completely suiting for a man of your status. Don't you like being at the mercy of your sweet, innocent girlfriend?"

Angelo cleared his throat, almost coughing, and returned a wicked smile to her words. "Mercy? Mercy is what you'll be begging for when I get out of these."

"I don't like your threats," Ella huffed but Angelo did not seem fazed in the least.

"I don't make threats, sweetheart."

"I'll have to teach you then." Ella circled her legs tighter around his hips and let her fingers dance across his arms. His scent awakened her senses, making her eyes close with the pleasure of his body. She swept her palms around his neck, searching his eyes, tempting him as she leaned her breasts against his chest. The closeness made her breathing deepen more. Ella could not resist his masculine form. Her lips latched onto his in an attempt to remove the scowl from his face, but he did not return her affection. "Please kiss me," she said and pressed her lips to his again.

He still did not respond. His refusal started to make her nervous as she continued with her small, timid kiss. He finally let out a sigh. He kissed her. His return of her affection made her feel better about handcuffing him to the bed. Her soft lips moved lower on his body; her delicate fingertips slid against the protruding muscles of his chest. His body started to swell between her inner thighs.

"You are always in charge of everything," she said. Her hot breath whispered in his ear as her nails dragged along his back. She felt new to this, but he seemed to like how she touched his skin. Angelo gazed at her with fascination, swallowing, becoming powerless against her advances as her mouth lowered, swirling her tongue around his pecs. She kissed them lightly; her hands massaged his shoulders with gentle strokes of her fingertips.

The sensations she roused on his skin exposed his real weakness to her, a rare sight that only she would ever have the pleasure of seeing. He entered an elated state. She knew the exact moment when her touch replaced his tense nerves. She wanted his body to react. Ella swathed both hands around his width, meticulously squeezing until he parted his lips. The tighter her fingers stroked up and down, the more hypnotized he seemed to become. His reaction pleased her, encouraging her to continue. She scooted back and lowered her face. Ella wrapped her lips all the way around.

"Christ, Ella." His arms jerked the cuffs above, trying to grab the body that put him in his frenzy. She felt him twitch inside her mouth. It was in much the same way that he felt before his climax during sex. She wanted him to lose himself in her finesse, but Angelo opened his eyes, looking at her with a feral expression. "Unlock me, Ella. Now," he growled.

She knew with that wild look that she had better do as he said. Ella grabbed a clip from her purse when a knock on the door startled her to freeze. Rafa bolted inside, making Ella yank the sheet over them both and hide.

Rafa did not say anything. He merely stood there in shock. Then he shook off the surprise; his expression became humored. "Well," he quipped. "When I called and there was no answer, I came to see if everything was all right. But," he mused, provoking Angelo at being caught in such a state.

"Get the keys out of my pocket?"

Rafa tilted his head. "I believe she has that covered, boss."

Angelo took a breath and glared at him. "I swear, Rafa…if I could reach my gun."

Rafa's brows arched. "There will be plenty of time to shoot me later," he countered and let the door shut after him as though he had never been in the room.

Angelo gave Ella an unappreciative look as she returned it with a sheepish grin and began her handiwork with the clip. Then she showed him the thin piece of metal and instantly freed him from the cuffs.

Angelo rubbed his wrists once and then lifted her at the waist. His eyes reflected a carnal stare on her naked body as he positioned her to his sex, pulling her thighs flush against his hips. He did not wait for her to adjust. Her palms slammed against his chest as he yanked her forward against his erection, consuming her body with a move of her hips.

He would make sure she remembered this moment forever. Her shrill moans exposed how he made her feel. She would never forget the consequences of seducing a dangerous man like him. She could feel his ache for relief. Angelo groaned with satisfaction of her, thoroughly dominating her. The pleasure of his control, the pain of his aggression made her more sensitive with every stroke. The friction his length created between her thighs sent small spasms to course throughout her body. Her nails dug harder on the skin of his back, clutching his body for support as she whimpered his name. Angelo plunged harder and quicker, pumping sporadically until she screamed. He quickly gripped her hair and muffled her cries with his lips. His body quaked with his release.

Ella could not move at all. The air seemed thinner as she struggled to breathe. She collapsed against his shoulder as all strength left her body. She could not seem to stop trembling.

"God, Ella," he mumbled and gently massaged her back. "How did I ever survive without you?" She did not think her pulse would ever return to normal.

"You still have to leave, don't you?" she panted. He slowly shook his head.

"I need to be there but you don't have to come with me. I know I wore you out." Angelo rolled her to the pillow beside him and stroked his fingers through her hair. She liked the gentleness of his touch. She did not want him to leave her alone. "I'll be back when it's over, so don't worry."

Ella pulled the sheet over her chest. He was right. She was tired and did not argue. She did not have the strength to talk.

"I bought you something," he said. "I know this doesn't replace your mother's jewelry, but I took some time to pick it out." He handed her the small box that had started their play.

Ella smiled. Her hands trembled but she managed to untie the small red bow. She pulled out a delicate gold chain with a teardrop pendant. She looked up at him and back at the necklace. She could not believe he had bought her a gift. "It's beautiful."

"You will make it look beautiful," he said and waited for her to lift up her hair before fastening it around her neck. She froze. Angelo cared for her so much more than she knew. She felt adored. She could tell it in his gaze. Maybe he acted harshly because he did not want to lose the one thing he actually loved even though he had not said those words.

"Get some rest, okay?" He scooted forward when she threw her arms around him, preventing him from moving at all.

"Thank you." She hugged him tightly as he caressed her arms. Who else could love him like her? It was a shame he had to go and leave the empty spot in the bed.

"You're something, Ella. You know that?" He breathed out and kissed her forehead. "And the handcuff trick was impressive." He winked and left her to rest.

Chapter 39

The next morning, Ella rolled over and raised her arm to wrap around Angelo. Her eyes opened as her arm fell flat to the empty spot in the bed. Angelo had not come back the night before as he said he would. Why had he not returned?

She sighed. Getting out of bed had seemed to be a chore ever since she had gotten together with him. Her body ached and would not do what she wanted. She groaned as she dragged her feet to the restroom, freshening up and then back out again. Ella did not bother with clothes. She slipped on a robe and stared at the front door to the room. The manager would not fall for the same trick twice.

Ella sat down and waited. As nice as the suite was, she could stand to be cooped up so long. She found the silence monotonous and lonely. There was nothing to gain her attention until a knock came at the door.

"I'm awake. You can come in," she said, feeling insulted that she could not open the door. The same manager as the night before and two assistants entered behind him. They must have been worried that she would try something again.

"Mr. Paolini wanted us to bring you breakfast this morning, even though it's closer to lunchtime."

"Mr. Paolini?" she asked.

"Rafael Paolini."

"Oh." She had never heard his last name and looked reflectively at the manager. "I'm sorry for the trouble I caused you yesterday."

"That's all right," he said, moving his hand through his straight blond hair. "One time, I had a guest lock me in the restroom all day because I brought her two towels instead of three. At least you left me refreshments."

Ella gave him a smile but her mind was too distracted to be entertained. She also did not care about the food. "Did Rafa say when Mr. Tomassi will be back?"

The manager thought for a moment before answering. "I'm not sure. I know he had some meetings this morning—one with Mr. Gregorio and another with an investor."

"Thank you." Ella's smile faded as the manager left. Gregorio and his infamous daughter. Angelo had agreed to meet with him after all.

Ella's anxiety grew. She paced around the room as she thought. She needed to see Angelo, yet she was restricted to the suite. Did he agree to marry the daughter? What would happen to her if he did?

Ella stopped and lifted the lid on the tray but set it back over the food. She could not eat with her building panic. She squeezed her eyes shut for a second and then stared at the door. Ella willed for Angelo to enter. He told her he would be back and yet he was not there.

The hours ticked by. One o'clock passed and then five. The wait was driving her mad. Angelo could be signing a contract and agreeing to marry another woman as she stood helpless to do a thing about it. She wanted to scream. How could they leave her alone like that?

When the doorknob finally turned, Ella frowned as she looked at the clock. It was about time. She gave Angelo a disapproving glance as he threw down his coat on the table. His clothes were a disheveled mess, half tucked and full of wrinkles. He looked like he had been in a fight.

He took one look at her and held up a finger. "Not now, Ella," he said and disappeared into the restroom.

Was that it? Was that all he had to say? She was a mess and he wanted to take a shower. It made perfect sense. She did not mind the wait.

Ella threw her hands up and decided to get dressed. It probably did not matter anyway. He would not let her out of the room if he decided to leave. She might as well get used to the view from the balcony and slid open the door. That was about as close to freedom as she would ever gain.

When she heard the restroom door open, Ella glanced back but did not go inside. It would not do her any good anyway. Angelo talked when he wanted to talk. She was surprised when he stepped outside with her. His wet hair was combed back. He left his shirt unbuttoned and hanging over a clean pair of slacks. He was almost dressed, but he was also almost undressed. It easily could have gone either way.

"I'm sorry about not coming back last night. I ran into some trouble and had to leave the hotel. I didn't want them to disturb anybody— that means you."

"I see," she answered, glad not to hear Gregorio's name. "Are they still a problem?"

"No, we handled it...but there will be more." Ella nodded in response. "Come sit with me, Ella."

She held her breath and turned around when he pulled her onto his lap. His eyes looked dull. Maybe it was lack of sleep, but she guessed it was something else. She had waited for him to talk. Now she was scared to death of what he would say.

"What's wrong, Angelo?" she finally asked. Despite her concerns, she wanted to know. He was not acting himself. He gently slid his fingers against her shoulders several times before pausing to get her attention.

"Ella," he said and hesitated, looking from the ocean and back onto her face. "I'm in love with you, Ella. I have never felt that way about anyone."

What? Her eyes widened at his words; she stared at him, shocked at the unexpected confession. She never expected him to tell her that. Angelo could barely catch his breath and it worried her more. She wrapped her arms around his neck and leaned closer until their bodies touched.

"I love you too, Angelo." Her tone came out unsure of the matter behind his confession.

He seemed out of sorts. There was some serious matter behind the bleak look in his eyes. He tilted away from her and placed his palms around her cheeks. "Will you love me no matter what, Ella?"

With uncertainty on her lips, her eyes narrowed with confusion. "What do you mean?"

"I have to do something that you won't like, and I will keep you with me no matter what."

"And you won't tell me what it is?"

Angelo shook his head and did not elaborate. "Not right now. Later."

Ella closed her eyes and tightened her grasp around him. She assumed that he had agreed to marry Gregorio's daughter; her heart fell. What would she be then—his mistress? She could not live like that—could she?

"Angelo, you're taking advantage of my heart without giving me anything in return. Later could mean tomorrow or never." Tears filled her eyes at the thought of him marrying another woman even for the purpose of formalities. She knew what him having a wife meant. Where did that leave her? The mere thought of sharing Angelo made her nauseous. She released her hold around him and stood away. "It isn't fair that you know something that will affect my life and not tell me. Then you want me to love you no matter what."

She walked to the rail but changed her mind before turning back to him, waiting for a response. Angelo was done talking. He stayed silent while he rested his head on his fist. He did not bother to counter her use of the word fair. He never took his eyes off her either and tapped his fingers on the table, seeming to think over the situation. Ella could take no more of the awkward silence and changed the subject completely.

"Will you please take me to eat? I didn't eat the food they brought me earlier, and I'm really tired of staying in this room."

She knew he was tired, but she needed to get out for a while. It was not good for her to meditate on the reasons why he would say what he did. He did not move right away but finally stood and opened his hand to her. "I'll take you wherever you want to go."

It was a quiet walk to the restaurant, but Angelo held her hand tighter than at other times as he led her to his usual table in the back. Ella wondered about his unwillingness to sit in the open and guessed it had something to do with the information that he was not telling her. When the server approached and they gave their orders, Ella stood and whispered in the server's ear.

"Will you please tell the chef that Mr. Tomassi doesn't like sweets? Maybe he can come up with something that the owner does like...maybe an after-dinner cordial."

The server seemed shocked and replied, "We had no idea. I will mention the preference immediately."

"Thank you." Ella nodded her appreciation.

Angelo's eyes narrowed slightly, but he did not ask what she had said. His mind still seemed occupied with other matters. Ella looked at him and spoke. "I forgot to check how I look in the room. Will you point the way?" She smiled slightly and excused herself while he watched her leave in the opposite direction.

In the women's lounge, Ella looked in the mirror and sighed. She dampened a towel and pressed it against her cheeks. Not knowing what was going on was taking a toll on her. A few minutes passed, and she disappeared in one of the stalls. As she straightened her dress and tightened the strap on her leg, two employees entered. It was not until Ella heard Angelo's name that she paid any attention to the women. She stood quietly and hardly breathed. Ella did not want to alert the women of her presence as they continued.

"I can't believe Mr. Tomassi is getting married. As many women as he's turned down, he finally agreed to get married."

"He didn't seem very happy about it though. He punched Mr. Gregorio and knocked him to the floor. I've never seen him act like that. I wonder what Mr. Gregorio said."

"You know how the mafia works. It's probably more normal than what we see."

"I know...but what about Miss Ella? I thought Mr. Tomassi was happy with her."

"Yeah...I thought so too. Maybe it's an arranged marriage."

"You would think that he'd be able to marry who he wanted. Who even agrees to arranged marriages anymore?"

"I don't know. Maybe that's why wealthy people are so unhappy. They have to push the ones they really love away."

"It's sad. I don't think I could do it. I think I'd run away."

Ella let out a breath. She heard everything she needed to hear and slowly unlocked the stall. She walked up to the women and looked at them.

"Oh my god! We're so sorry."

"We didn't know anyone was in here."

"I know you didn't," Ella said and handed them Angelo's ring.

"No, please don't go. Please."

"He won't be able to handle it if you go. We see how he looks at you."

"I'm sorry. If you were me, you would leave too. You even said so."

Ella ignored the women's last pleading words. She kept walking forward and continued through the restaurant. If Angelo saw her, she never looked back and ran for the exit of the hotel.

She had not been out of the hotel since arrival and kept running as far as she could go. By now, Angelo was throwing a fit with the two employees and making calls to Rafa and Brett. She feared the two men would be around the corner, waiting for her. She needed a break from them. Ella quickly stepped into an open sports bar on the strip. Since it was not quite six, she walked to the counter and caught her breath.

"I need a shot. Tequila," she said and glanced at the door.

"ID please." The bartender flicked a brown stray hair from his face.

"I'm twenty-two," Ella replied with a still breathy voice.

"I'm going to need to see some ID."

"ID," Ella mumbled. "I don't have my ID with me. Give me a coffee then." The bartender nodded and walked away for a second.

"Here. That'll be three-fifty."

Ella handed him a five. "Keep the change," she said.

After another moment, the bartender set down the shot she wanted. "Since you didn't argue with me, I'll believe you this time."

Ella smiled. "Thank you."

She turned to stare out of the window but saw nobody in particular as of yet. This nightmare had to end sometime. She wanted to ask for another shot, but the bartender already went out of his way once. Maybe he would be nice.

"Hey," she said. "Can I have another one?" She set the empty shot glass to the back of the bar as his brow rose.

"Are you sure?"

"I'm sure."

The bartender nodded and brought her another shot. "I haven't seen you around before. What brings you here tonight?"

She emptied the contents again and answered, "My boyfriend is going to marry another woman. Before I found out, he asked me if I would love him no matter what."

"I haven't heard that one before."

"I wish I didn't either," she mumbled.

"I'm Howard." He held out his hand to her.

"Ella."

"It's a pleasure, Ella."

As the time rolled past six, the place started to fill with customers getting off work. Ella kept her eyes open for familiar faces. Angelo was probably in a state of hysterics right now, but Ella had to leave. She could not settle for the title of mistress.

While she sipped the coffee, Ella heard the volume of the television go up. One television tuned into a soccer channel and another on the news. She supposed news and sports were the general standards for

210 • *Ali Lee*

these places. As Howard tended to the bar, Ella glanced up to see her father on the news again. The broadcast was a repeat of that morning. She immediately looked at Howard and pointed. "Oh my god, turn it up! Please, Howard!"

Ella received some attention from nearby customers for her outburst, but she paid no attention. Howard turned up the television as requested, and she listened with shock at the broadcast.

Breaking News: Martino Gregorio is officially being sought for questioning regarding the murders of his late wife, Celia Gregorio, and his former associate, Peter Luzi. Originally thought a suicide, an anonymous tip led investigators to track the bullets from both Luzi and Gregorio back to a firearm in the Gregorio household. Investigators are still looking into the matter. Isabella Gregorio, the couple's only daughter, has still not been found. As you can see, a photo of Isabella has finally been released for the first time. If you have any information on the whereabouts of Isabella, please call the number on the screen and we will transfer you to an agent on the case.

Silence. Ella heard no more sounds around her. The chatter disappeared. People's faces blended in with the walls. She felt like she had entered a dark room with no exit, to be thrust in the middle of a riot.

Her father went by a false name.

Ella gasped and put her hand over her mouth. The next picture on the screen was her. It was outdated. Nobody should recognize her as the woman on the screen. Then the news channel broadcast an age progression photo of Ella. The likeness was uncanny.

Ella panicked as she stood, trusting no one in the room. She had to get out of there. Somebody needed to give her answers. She had to find her father.

Chapter 40

Ella focused on one thing and rushed toward the exit. She lifted both hands to push open the door when somebody behind her grabbed her arm. "You're coming with me."

"Let me go." She yanked her arm hard, but the man held it firm.

"Can't," he said. "We've been ordered." Her head whirled around fast at the stranger. She could not pull her gun with so many people around, so she kneed the man in the groin and stumbled to the sidewalk. The man was not alone. Ella heard footsteps behind her as she started to run back to the hotel.

The men were close. They breathed hard behind her as she struggled to get away. Ella thought they would catch her, but Sullivan stepped out from the shadows with a gun in his hand.

"Ella, run!" he yelled as she neared the hotel, firing two muffled shots through the air. She glanced back to see Sullivan slip his hand inside his coat and disappear before anyone could question him.

"Sullivan." Ella reached out a hand to him but did what he said. She lunged up the steps to the hotel. Her mind was spinning circles, and she ignored the countless guests in the lobby as she hurried to the counter and cut in line.

"Where…" Ella panted in her attempt to speak but started choking from the shortness of breath that her panicked run had caused. "Where is Mr. Gregorio?" she finally huffed exasperated.

"Miss, I can't give out that information. I'm sorry."

"Listen," Ella glared. "I'm his daughter, and I demand to know where he is—now." Ella's words shocked the attendant silent, but Ella was not leaving without an answer. They knew Gregorio was in the mafia, but Ella was in no mood for patience and looked the woman in the eyes. "I will shoot you if you don't tell me where he is." Ella did not know if she would actually pull out her gun, but she had had enough of the game her father played. She was not letting him off the hook.

"H-he he is in the casino," the attendant stuttered. She must have taken Ella at word or did not want to take that chance.

Ella did not bother to say thank you. Her polite manners left her and she did not give the counter another thought. As she turned around, she did see the sixty-inch television behind her with her picture flashing across the screen again. That explained it. That was why the attendant took Ella seriously. All Ella thought about were the charges against her father. Were they true?

Ella waited in front of the elevator door and punched the button. When it would not immediately open, she punched the button several more times, trying to speed it along. The door opened and Ella ignored that it might be over capacity. She squeezed inside anyway, having no care to the comfort of those on board.

Just as the door started to close, Rafa stepped out from around the counter and pointed. His pace quickened, but Ella ignored his attempts to gain her attention and quickly pressed the close button. Many people exited on floors five and four, which made Ella grow more distressed with anxiety. She ran her fingers through her hair as she exited on floor three and realized that the casino seemed even larger than she thought when filled with guests. Then there was the problem with the bouncer—Ella being his problem.

"You can't come in here." His enormous frame tripled that of Ella's, but she was not in the mood.

"Who says I can't come in here?"

"Mr. Paolini called and ordered me to hold you at the door."

"To hell with that." Ella rushed past with him on her tail, but he would not catch her. Her smaller body fit through the crowds quicker than his did, and she easily got away. "Damn it." She looked all around and began wading through the groups. "Where are you, Mr. Gregorio?" she muttered.

As Ella passed the bar, she grabbed a drink and continued her search. Then she spotted him—Gregorio himself. Her father had a drink in one hand and some floozy on the other. Considering the news report earlier, the very sight of him with that woman made her sick. He never saw her coming, and before Ella knew it, she stood directly in front of him. A shorthaired brunette hung on his arm, and four other men stood around. Maybe they were part of his group. She did not know. One of those men also had a woman with him. Ella scoffed at the gathering when one of the men noticed her.

"What's this, Gregorio—a mad fling who wants to get back at you?"

Did they really mock her? His own daughter? They laughed at Ella; the woman on her father's arm glared at her and spoke against her.

"Can't you see that you're interrupting Martino, that you're not wanted?"

Ella's mouth opened with contempt. The woman knew his real name, which infuriated her more. What was worse was that her father took the situation in stride.

"Am I now?" Ella leered at the woman and then at the others. "By chance, have any of you watched the news today?"

"News?" one of them answered. "No wonder Gregorio dropped you. You must be boring to a man like him."

"Glad I'm not boring," said the woman on his arm. Her father laughed, but Ella was not amused in any way.

"Are the headlines true, *Mr. Gregorio?*"

Her father gave a stern expression. "Ella, what are you doing here? I didn't expect to see you again."

"I told you so," the woman next to him sneered. "You are a bother." She started to push Ella away when Ella yanked her pistol out of its holster and pointed it at the woman. Fear instantly caused the woman's lips to quiver.

"How am I a bother?" Ella asked. "You have no idea who I am. You are nothing to me." Ella's gun instantly gained the men's attention, and one of them pulled a gun on her. She was not having it. She did not care. "Go ahead." She glanced over at the man. "Pull that trigger. I dare you."

"Put your guns away...both of you!" Gregorio waved to the two; neither withdrew their weapons. "Ella, what's this about? Where's Tomassi?"

Ella had forgotten about Angelo; panic crossed her eyes as she remembered leaving the restaurant. She suddenly could not hold the tears, as she looked completely helpless at her father. "It's about the death of my mother. It's about my picture being broadcast for the entire world to see. It's about you lying to me my entire life."

Somebody jerked the gun out of her hand. Ella bolted around but nearly crashed into Angelo's chest. He did not look at her. He scowled at the man who pointed the gun at her. "I suggest you not aim that thing at my future wife."

"Mr. Tomassi?" the man said and lowered his gun. "What? If you are...then that makes her..." Ella saw the man turn pale at the revelation as Angelo yanked her arm away from the entire group.

"Wait. Stop, Angelo! Stop!" Ella begged.

Her pleas did not faze him. She struggled to free herself as he dragged her past the bar and lifted his arm to snap at someone. He had to bring her back to her father. He must. Ella cried in a state of hysterics. Her life was falling apart.

"I need him to answer me, Angelo. My father needs to answer the question. Let me go back. Don't do this to me." She used every muscle she had to free herself, but Angelo clenched her fiercely and continued his silence through a room full of elite. Ella showed no concern for members in the VIP room as Angelo pulled her inside a smaller room in back and forced her on the sofa. Then he looked up.

"Go bring that bastard to me. We are going to finish this." Rafa understood and immediately walked back out of the room as Angelo brought the back of Ella's head to his chest. "I tried to stop this from happening to you. You aren't going to like what you hear." He pressed his cheek against hers and massaged her arms, her shoulders and neck, anything he could touch to calm her down. Nothing he did would help her right now.

Seconds later, Jim and Ray led Gregorio into the room. They pointed to the sofa across from Angelo and Ella. She stared at her father, knowing something was definitely off. Her father looked at the wall to avoid her, and Angelo's arms clenched her body much tighter than before. She did not know if she could handle the truth.

Her father did not speak right away, the silence of the room consuming her, bringing her to a point that was almost unbearable. She could not control her shivering as she thought about her mother. Her mother was all she had and she feared the worst had happened. Her own father was responsible for her death.

"Your daughter wants to hear the truth, so talk." Angelo turned his gaze from Ella and gestured his chin at her father.

"Kill me already, Tomassi. That's what you plan to do?" Angelo's jaw tightened as Ella lifted her head, looking at him with questions. He already knew she was Gregorio's daughter when he confessed earlier. Was that what she would not like? Did he plan to kill her father?

"Don't turn this around on me," Angelo said. "I didn't cause this; you did. I told you to leave before it was too late."

When her father still said nothing, Ella looked at him again. "Did you kill her?" Her voice trembled, making him briefly glance at her and then away. "Are the news reports true?"

Gregorio then looked her in the eyes. "Yes, they're true, Ella," he admitted, looking at his lap with regret. "I caught her with another man in our bed and I fired a shot at him. I didn't even know what I was doing."

"She wouldn't have cheated on you," Ella said. Her mother would never do such a thing. Her father must have been lying again. She could not believe it.

"Yes, she would, Ella. I know it was my fault for leaving her alone all the time, but your mother had several men. When I found her in our bed, I couldn't handle it. I shot Peter. She jumped in front of the bullet. I never meant to take her away from you."

Ella took a breath. She knew her family was not the perfect picture they portrayed themselves to others, but she never expected that. Her mother's smile had merely covered the reality of her lonely life. Her father left her alone too much. Her mother filled in the void. The life had sucked the life out of them both and was passed down to Ella.

"And yet you kept your secret and told me she killed herself. Why would you do that to me?"

"Ella," he hesitated. "I have lived with plenty of guilt. That's part of this life."

"But you sent me away not knowing any of it. You lied about everything, even my name. Who is Robert Collins? How did you even change my last name?"

"Sweetheart, I have connections. It wasn't hard. Bonadio knew me as Gregorio. My men knew me as both. It was the perfect protection plan for you until my men turned on me. After that, it was war. Bonadio wanted my estate. I offered it to Tomassi. I knew that I couldn't protect you once Bonadio knew who you were. I have another name that I used too. It was my way of setting up Bonadio. He bought property under the aliases, and I know exactly where to find his group. It's all information that I passed on to Tomassi. Bonadio is his problem now. You are under his protection from now on."

Her father planned her life without telling her a single thing. Ella could not believe the lack of say she had in her situation. It was unbelievable. "Why would you offer to marry me off without even telling me you were in the mafia? Angelo refused to marry me, and you still sent me away. How was abandoning me going to help? Do you have any idea what this has been like for me, knowing that people were trying to attack me but not knowing why?"

"That's right. He did refuse. I found out that he was looking for property and sent you as the agent."

"Your plan could have failed," Ella said with disbelief.

Gregorio sighed, "No, I knew it wouldn't. There was no doubt in my mind. You're different from the other women he's been around. I knew."

"But what if he didn't? I could be dead. Were you really okay with that risk instead of giving me the truth?" Ella hung her head. Her arms went numb as she waited for a response of which she already knew the answer. She turned to Angelo next.

"Get him out of here." Angelo pointed at her father but looked at Jim and nodded. Ella speculated on their understanding. She did not like the secret undertones behind his nod. Ella found herself deeper in the life than she had ever imagined. She was at the heart of the dispute between the groups the entire time.

"You are like him." Ella stood and pointed at Angelo as his hold relaxed around her body. "You should have told me when you found out who I was. You kept it a secret like he did. Are you going to leave me alone, too? While you're handling matters with the group, are you going to keep me locked up all day and never include me in your life? Is that what I can expect from you? My father forced my mother to cheat on him. She would've never done something like that. Are you going to make me that desperate too?"

Angelo folded his arms and frowned at her. A glimmer of animosity crossed his eyes as he heard what she said. Ella knew right then that these men did not take the matter of infidelity from their women lightly. She did not want to know what thoughts went through Angelo's mind.

"I'm going home tonight, Rafa," he said and did not bother to counter her words. His voice sounded calm, dangerous, and full of spite, sending chills across her skin. Ella should have held her tongue.

Now she feared what he waited to tell her in private. "Handle her outburst in the casino. Call Brett and Sammy to help. And you," he stretched out his hand to Ella, "will come with me. We need to talk about your new situation as my wife."

Chapter 41

Ella drifted in and out of sleep all night long. She was exhausted and yet could not stay asleep for more than half-hour intervals. Her neck felt cold from the perspiration on the back of her head. Her clothes stuck to her body with cool dampness from the cold sweats she experienced during the night.

There was light outside when she opened her eyes. Angelo's hands were locked around her body as she attempted to move her arms. Seconds passed when she remembered the night before. She gasped for air as her heart sped mercilessly against her chest. Her body bolted up and jarred Angelo awake.

She could not help but cry. She could feel the hot tears adding to the chill of her clothes. Angelo sat up and squeezed his arms tighter around her, but it did not help and she cried more. She was angry. She felt the shadow of dread over her head. She was part of a life that caused her mother's death. She was the sole reason why the restaurant was gone. Angelo was under attack the entire time because of her. Now she risked facing the same problems her mother did—stifling loneliness and pain. How would she ever come to terms with that?

"Shh," Angelo whispered, but she would not let him comfort her. She knew the full extent of the impact that this life would have on her. She was no longer under a guise that love was all she needed. It would take more than love to survive this kind of life. The realization struck her hard.

All at once, Ella stopped crying. Her mind entered a state that turned everything off around her. She looked at Angelo. His expression reflected the heartache she felt. He constantly was worrying about how to keep her safe. She now worried about ending up like her mother. She could alleviate both of their concerns. Neither would have to endure the pain in their life anymore. The life was her pain. She was his.

Ella shifted one arm slightly out of his grasp and carefully grabbed her pistol off the nightstand. She pointed it at her head, at her temple. She would no longer be the issue between the groups. They could not fight over her if she was not there. Her death would at least grant them that.

"Ella." Angelo spoke her name in as calm a tone as she thought he was capable of speaking. He held out one hand; the other fisted the sheets with silent horror of what she was doing. Her tears silently started to fall again until she felt the drops fall from her chin to her arm. She had never felt more strongly about anything in her life.

"Give me the gun," he choked out. His eyes were turning red. She never thought that she could make Angelo cry. It broke her heart to see such emotion from a man who hid his feelings from the world. It was another reason why her death was the logical solution.

"I am so completely hurt right now that I don't care anymore. He lied to me. My entire life has been a lie. My mother is dead, and I'm causing you pain. There is no reason for me to live."

"That's not true, Ella. I'll help you get through this. We'll do it together." His voice shook as her finger pressed further on the trigger. She could not see the joy she once had. Ella found it difficult to think of a single happy memory. She was searching for a reason to hand him the gun, but the darkness around her sucked her dry.

"Ella, I'm not like your father. All of this will pass. It always does. Give me the gun, sweetheart." He was desperate for her to put down the gun. Those deep brown eyes begged her to do as he asked. His hand barely touched her knee with his palm spread open wide.

She could not bear to see the hurt she was causing him anymore. She would leave him bitter and heartless. He would become a brutal man, showing mercy to no one in retaliation for his loss. She could barely think about what else he would do. Ella finally lowered the gun and set it in his hand before she could change her mind.

Angelo ejected the clip on contact and removed the bullet from the chamber. She did not have time to blink before he placed it safely in the drawer. His arms snatched her waist as he buried his head in her chest. She could feel his body shake as his arms clenched her from around. Ella started to cry again; this time from the fear that radiated from his limbs. This life was agony for them both.

He was breathing hard as he lifted his head. His chest rose and fell as he held onto her hands. It was as though he wanted to make sure she could not get to the gun. Angelo had never been that transparent before. He did not attempt to try to hide how he felt.

"How did you know that I was Gregorio's daughter?" she sniffed. Angelo was a wreck because of her. She wanted to take it away.

"I saw him at the banquet. He handed me an envelope with information about everything he did. He said he saw you. He saw my ring on your finger."

"That's why he let me leave," she mumbled. "Why didn't Sullivan know?"

"Your father hired Sullivan to protect you. That was it. He knew your father had chosen someone to marry you. He didn't know it was me."

"If you weren't going to marry another woman, what was it that I wouldn't like? You said that you would keep me with you no matter what."

Angelo looked away with that reminiscent look of his. He shook his head and then looked back at Ella. "Your father and I used to get along. We worked together until Bonadio came into the picture. When he took his father's place, he plotted against us. He wanted to move in his escort services in our counties. What he really wanted was our groups. Your father wanted nothing to do with him. Then that happened with your mother. Your father drank more and made a couple of mistakes. He met with Bonadio. His attitude changed and Bonadio convinced some of his men to turn on him and things got worse. Gregorio offered me his daughter, his estate. There's been a war ever since.

"What will you do, Angelo?" she asked. He was not answering the question on purpose.

"Your father threatened me."

"You're going to kill him."

Angelo did not reply; his hands stroked up and down her arms. He lifted his fingers and touched the tears still on her cheeks. "Let me help you to the shower. The warm water will make you feel better."

Ella lost the strength to stand and slid to the hard shower floor as the hot water rushed over her face. She hung her head as she took a deep breath; her mind would not take in the soothing gesture. She had pointed a gun at her head. Nothing terrified her more than what she fully intended to do minutes ago. She was panicked and afraid of even herself. She had become her own enemy.

Her family and Bonadio—it overwhelmed her. Angelo planned to kill her father, and she could do nothing to stop it. Her father could have prevented all of this. Her father did this to her. He did it to himself.

Ella felt as though someone was watching her. She saw the shadow and looked up. Her body jolted in surprise as her head banged the back of the shower wall. She did not see Angelo walk in the restroom. He could have been there the entire time, standing directly in front of her as she basked in her own thoughts. She screamed when he swung the glass door open wide, making it bounce on its hinges.

"What are you doing?" he asked. His voice sounded upset.

"I was thinking," she answered.

He swallowed and looked down at her on the floor of the shower. His eyes looked afraid as he continued to stare. "I want you to stand up, Ella," he said and held out his hand.

She stood without arguing. Did she make him wonder if she might carry through with her threat after all? "Please hand me the robe." Ella pointed to the hook on the wall as she turned off the water; she slid her arms in the sleeves he held open for her. "I'm sorry I took so long. I guess...I guess I was trying to put everything in perspective." She stepped onto the floor mat and started to walk past him, but Angelo would not let her pass. What more did he want from her? She had done what he had asked.

"My life will never be normal. There was never even a possibility," she said as she waited.

"Ella." He slid his arms underneath her robe and pulled her to his chest. "No...it will never be normal. That doesn't mean that you can't be happy."

"How?" she asked. "When people are constantly shooting at us or threatening us and setting things on fire. How can there be happiness?" She closed her eyes and dropped her arms to her sides.

"Because, Ella, you create our own life outside of the mafia. That's how it works. You don't think about the bad." Angelo looked down and shook his head. "I'm willing to die for you and you wanted to throw it all away with a bullet in your head. That was harder for me than anything I've ever faced in my life."

Ella started to touch his arm when he looked up. His expression looked angry. Anger and hurt were not a good combination. He placed his hands firmly around her cheeks; his serious, pain-filled eyes made hers sting all over again.

"I am willing to die for you, Ella. Do you understand what that means? I have never felt that way for anyone, so don't you ever put a fucking gun to your head again. Do you hear me?" He gave her body a desperate shake and his fingers gripped her hair, paying little attention to the tears that threatened to fall. "I love you. Don't you ever put me through that again. I can't—" His throat went dry as he stopped to swallow. "I can't live without you."

"I'm sorry," she said quickly and started to cry. He was breaking her heart all over again. She did not know what to do to fix it. Ella did the first thing that came to her mind and smashed her lips against his. She would take away his hurt. Angelo did not refuse. He kissed her back. The warmth of his mouth reassured her in her moment of doubt. If he was all she had from now on, she wanted all of him and pushed the thin boxers from his hips to his thighs.

"Take me," she whispered.

He did not hesitate. Angelo hiked her on the counter, obliging every move that she started with him. His length thrust into her without warning, leaving her to cry into his shoulder from the force of his charge. She did not care if it hurt. The closeness of his body made up for the discomfort it caused. She held him closer. Her dampened body pressed against the dryness of his. His firm arms around her nearly choked out her breaths. She did not care about anything else. She had never needed him more than she did now.

Chapter 42

Angelo watched the rushing of cars and people scurrying through the front window with indifference after what Ella had tried in his house. He needed to stay home and take care of her, but he also still had business to handle at the hotel and would not leave Ella at the house alone. While there was a chance of being attacked, he would not leave her alone anywhere for a while. His chest still ached from the scare she put him through; his body tensed as he merely thought about what had happened. He could not do it again.

"Do you tell Rafa everything?" she asked.

Her question came out of nowhere. Angelo's brows lifted with curiosity. "What do you mean by that?"

"Well," she continued, "does he have to know what happened earlier?"

"Oh," he said. Angelo glanced over but turned his focus back to the road. She felt embarrassed about the incident. He understood, but there was nothing he could really hide from Rafa. "What I don't tell Rafa, he usually will figure out on his own. He is sort of psychic like that." It was true. Rafa could read people well.

"Okay," Ella sighed.

"Ella." He brushed his hand against her cheek. "Rafa's a smartass, but he knows when to shut up. He won't judge you for that. He knows you had a lot come down on you."

"Okay but can you not say anything?" she asked. Angelo felt bad for her even though he knew it would come out.

"All right but Rafa is going to meet us for breakfast. I have to take care of some stuff around the hotel." Angelo took out his phone and pressed the screen, waiting for the other line to answer. "Hey," he said, "meet us at the restaurant. I need you to take care of something for me."

"Couldn't you ignore the phone?" He heard a woman say on the other end.

"I'm busy with something," Rafa mumbled into the phone.

"Rafa, I don't care who you're with right now."

"Why do you think I'm with anyone?" he asked.

"Because...I can hear her, Rafa. Drop her and be at the restaurant in ten minutes."

When Angelo turned off his phone, he looked at Ella and snorted, "I can't believe that someone so arrogant gets around that—" Angelo stopped himself short and looked at the road with a quick hand through his hair. It made Ella smile. "Forget it. It doesn't matter what he does in his free time."

At the restaurant, they were already eating when Rafa walked through the entrance. He dragged his feet to the table and grunted to his seat. He looked like he probably felt. The server immediately approached and gave him a smile.

"Welcome, Mr. Paolini. What will you have this morning?" Rafa gave her a bothered look and glared at Angelo.

"I'll take black coffee and whatever they're having. Make it quick with the coffee," he said. The server nodded and left. Two minutes later, she set a cup in front of him before leaving again.

"Don't give me that look." Angelo returned his glare with an equally annoyed expression. "It's almost noon. It's not like it's six in the morning."

"You forgot that I was up late dealing with the casino issue. Then I had the exchange. You could at least loosen the reins a bit." Rafa picked up his cup with annoyance. "Is this important, or did you want me for coffee and omelets?"

"Business." Angelo pointed at Ella. "I have to handle something and I need you to guard her."

Rafa's mouth opened with the scowl on his face. "You called me down here to babysit? Get Brett for that. He would love the trouble while watching her."

"Not this time," Angelo said without elaborating. Rafa understood his tone.

The server returned with Rafa's plate and set it in front of him. He barely acknowledged her as Angelo spoke instead. "We won't need anything else unless we call." The server nodded and left as Rafa unrolled his silverware from the cloth napkin and took a bite.

"I think..." Ella started with both Angelo and Rafa instantly looking at her from their plates. Their immediate attention made her hesitate for a second before she continued. "I think I should take over my father's position. I could get all the highest members and announce a merge with Bonadio."

Rafa choked on the bite he took and grabbed his napkin as Angelo's fork hit his plate, a high-pitched, resonating sound echoing throughout the restaurant. "What?" Angelo asked. He wanted to ask her if she had lost her mind, but she was already leaning in that direction. He tried to restrain his voice as he gave her a reply, but he doubted that his eyes could hide the anger he felt. "Why would you want to merge with Bonadio in the first place?" He really wanted to know her answer.

"Women aren't allowed in the ranks," Rafa added as if that had anything to do with what she asked.

"You don't know what I was going to say." Ella looked down at her plate.

"Why don't you go on?" Angelo pointed. "I want to hear what you have planned."

"Don't mock me," Ella fired back. "If you want to weed out the men who turned, I could get everyone together and announce a merge. They won't know it's a setup. You could see how they react to the news and pick out your traitors. It's easier than trying to pick them out one by one."

"Not going to happen," said Angelo, crossing his arms. He looked at Rafa for support, but Rafa stayed quiet in thought. It looked like he might be contemplating her idea.

"Think about it," Ella continued. "You don't know who you can trust. It makes more sense for me to do it."

Rafa still had said nothing and returned to his food. "Don't tell me you're entertaining her scheme. Up until yesterday, she didn't even know her father was in charge. Now she's going to throw a group meeting?"

"I'm not entertaining anything," Rafa said. "You know I always think things through before I give my opinion. That's why you hired me."

"I don't want an opinion on this. There's nothing to think through, Rafa. It's not going to happen."

Ella let out a sigh. "I don't want you to risk your life, Angelo. I feel like I should do something after all the trouble my family caused you."

Angelo stood and set his napkin in the chair. "You don't need to do anything. Nobody holds you responsible for your father's decisions." He hugged her from behind and whispered, "I'll be back in a couple of hours." With a gentle kiss to her cheek, he looked at Rafa. "I'll be back in a while. Give Ella the master codes to the hotel."

"All right, we'll be on the second floor," Rafa said.

"Sounds good. Keep your eyes open too."

***

Angelo rode the elevator to floor three. He could not believe that Ella wanted to put herself at risk to make up for the errors of her father. He was sick of Gregorio. That man had caused unrest between everyone for years. He would not put up with it anymore.

Angelo knocked and waited. The door of the room opened and Angelo sat in a chair opposite of Gregorio. Sullivan was standing guard with a gun pointed at him. It was no surprise that Gregorio had called for backup. He was still wise enough to guard his life. It was a shame that he did not take the same precautions for his daughter the entire time.

The contract between the two families was lying on the table in front of them. Angelo wanted this exchange to happen fast so he could escape the dangerous air stifling him in that room. He hoped his gut instinct was right and coming alone was a good idea.

"Gin, Tomassi?" Gregorio picked up a small glass and rocked the ice back and forth before taking a drink.

"It's a little early, but sure, why not?"

Gregorio set some ice in another glass and opened the bottle, pouring the clear liquid halfway. "Are you ready to sign the papers?" he asked. He handed over the glass and watched Angelo take a large drink, despite it being two in the afternoon.

Angelo stretched his neck and rested against the back of the chair. He picked up the forms and started to read. He needed to make sure that Gregorio would hand over everything before he put his name on the line. He should have brought Rafa with him. Two sets of eyes were better than one, but Rafa was the one he trusted with Ella right now.

"Why didn't you tell Ella who you were instead of keeping her under lock and key?" Angelo asked. "The truth almost killed her."

"What's done is done. Nothing I can say will change the way all of this turned out. Your job is to take care of her now." Gregorio took another drink as though what Angelo had said was nothing but a minor technicality. Angelo wanted some sign that he cared about Ella, but Gregorio gave nothing at all. Sullivan's panicked expression showed more concern than he did.

"That's all you have to say? Your men have beaten her and could have killed her, and you don't feel anything?"

"Tomassi, quit blaming me for this shit. I can't do anything now. Sign the damn papers and she's yours. You take care of her since you're so sure you can."

Angelo shook his head. "You should have taught her this stuff growing up. She doesn't have a clue how serious it can be."

"Then you teach her." Gregorio pointed, making Angelo angrier at each word. It was as though he did not care about anything but himself.

"Ella tried to kill herself today...she didn't want to be a problem in all this," he said. "Do you love her at all? I mean, I'm cold but at least I understand."

Angelo's horror of that morning had no effect on Gregorio's expression, but Sullivan was clearly in thought. Mentioning Ella's suicide attempt struck a nerve within him. Angelo saw the concern in his eyes.

"Sign the papers," Gregorio demanded. "We're not here to discuss my life. I have dealt with enough. Sign the fucking papers."

Angelo grudgingly started to read the contract. It was what he would typically expect until he got to the last page. From the slight difference in format, he assumed the content was added after the agreement was drawn. Gregorio had already signed, and there were two lines left that waited for signatures. One was for Angelo. The other for a witness—Sullivan. Unless Sullivan was faking his sense of responsibility for Ella, he could not have read the extra page.

"You shouldn't have added that last part to the contract after what she's been through. What kind of life do you think she would have with him? Bonadio would beat her and probably kill her."

"No, that won't happen. If anything happened to Ella, the contract with Bonadio would be void."

"Are you fucking kidding? No one would ever know if something happened to her."

"Sullivan," said Gregorio.

Without hesitation, Sullivan slid his finger around the trigger. Would his interest in Ella's wellbeing overpower his sense of loyalty to her father? Angelo looked at Sullivan hard.

"If you kill me, Ella will go to Bonadio. Is that what you want?"

With a low chuckle, Gregorio set his empty liquor glass on the table. "Sullivan does what I tell him to. Sign the papers or you're the one who sent her to Bonadio."

"Fuck you." Angelo yanked out his gun, aiming it at his head. If Sullivan killed him today, Gregorio would be dead too.

"Sullivan" Gregorio said again.

At the word, Angelo and Sullivan fired. There was no time to react. There were no breaths taken. The short echo of triggers was the sounds heard. Then blood seeped down the front of Gregorio's face from two bullets holes in his head.

Sullivan lowered his eyes to the floor. He seemed conflicted with what he had done. He had shot a man who trusted him with his life.

"I am loyal," he said. "I was hired to protect Ella. I didn't betray him. He betrayed her." Sullivan shook his head with pity. "When she asks you if you killed her father, you can tell her no. It was my bullet that hit him first."

Angelo felt the full extent of his pain as he watched Sullivan stare at Gregorio. Angelo saw it. Sullivan was more than loyal to Ella. He was willing to protect her even at the cost of his own good name. Angelo did not know how to respond to that.

"Take care of her now. She's special to me," Sullivan said and lowered his gun.

Angelo nodded with regret. Gregorio was once the leading man in the area, a brilliant man. For some reason, that changed long before the loss of his wife. Angelo would not forget the lesson in his death.

Chapter 43

Silent and stressed, Angelo sat in the recliner and stared at the contract in his lap, leaving Ella on the bed looking withdrawn. His tired eyes drifted from one spot on the wall and finally settled on the door. It was not until he reached in his pocket for his phone that he glanced her way, accepting what he must do.

"Hey," he said into the receiver. "Come up to the room. I need you to bring me what you picked up earlier." Hanging up again, he looked at Ella and gave an affirmative nod. "I gave my word to protect you, and I will follow through."

He always had thought Gregorio was careless to let a woman have such a hold on his mind, but he was letting Ella do the same thing to him. He needed to rid his worries of her and start thinking rationally. If she wanted to live, she would have to do as he said without questioning his reasons.

The knock at the door came faster than he expected. Rafa entered and looked at him without saying a word, proof of the tense feeling in the air. The death of Gregorio and what they would face in the future weighed on them both. No one was safe as long as Bonadio was alive.

"Do you have what I asked for?" Angelo asked and held out his hand.

"Yes." Rafa pulled a small black box from his coat and handed it to him.

Angelo nodded, taking a deep breath while he carefully opened the box and examined the stunning diamond ring he had purchased the other day. "I need you to call Harrison. Have everything we talked about ready by seven. We'll start making plans to take the Gregorio ranks after Ella and I are married."

Angelo saw how Ella's eyes widened with the reflection of the ring as he turned it in the light. Rafa remained silent for a few seconds, processing the added marriage to the plans. "You know that gives you twenty minutes."

"It has to happen now." Angelo placed the ring in the box again and handed it back to Rafa.

"Okay, if that's what you want. It's done."

As soon as Rafa left, Ella held out her hand in question while Angelo walked to her, dropping the contract on the table as he approached. He stood in front of her and took both her hands in his, thinking about how the death of Gregorio put her at more risk from before. Gregorio's ranks would have no leader and Ella would have no group protection until they were married.

"Ella..." He paused, deciding against telling her about the death of her father. He was still processing the information himself. "Your father gave me the contract," he told her instead. "And there is no one leading his ranks right now. Who knows how many of them are working for Bonadio, so I'm going to put you under my group's care. You can't have that until we get married."

Angelo gently grabbed her waist, bringing her depressed stare to him. "I would've given you more time, but there's no more time. If I don't marry you tonight, you could be on your own. I promise that Bonadio will come for you if I'm away. This war is about to get a whole lot worse."

"I want to marry you," she said, glancing sideways with her thoughts looking dazed. "Of course I do," her voice trailed off.

Angelo knew her mood had more to do with Gregorio than anything else. He had controlled every aspect of her life without telling her why, and given the reason her mother had died made her resentment that much worse.

"You know what, Ella?" His hand slid around her cheek in an affectionate gesture to sway her mind from her thoughts. "Do you know why I introduced you to my father when we went on that date?"

"No," she mumbled, her cheek leaned instinctively to his hand.

"Because I wanted you when I first saw you sitting with Lila. I wanted to marry you. I wanted you in my life and I wanted you to be the mother of my children. I fell in love with you the second I met you."

To this, she looked up at him, taken by surprise with his confession. "Why me?"

Angelo almost smiled, shaking his head when he continued. "You were real. It bothered me that my father didn't approve of me marrying you."

"You have as many rules to follow as I do," she said, but Angelo did not like the depression in her tone. She was breaking down.

"Ella, I can give you a nice home. I can give you a family. I can protect you." He paused. "It could be a lot worse."

They stared at each other in silent thought when a knock came at the door and Rafa walked inside. He briefly looked at them before crossing his arms, irritated with the tardiness. "You said seven, and I arranged everything like you said. Why aren't you downstairs yet?"

"We need more time. Don't let Harrison leave."

"All right, but it's late. He doesn't usually make house calls," Rafa said and left again.

Ella's sullen state of mind was hard for him to ignore. If she would quit thinking so much and quietly go along with the marriage, he would make up for the hurt she had been through.

"After we talk to Harrison, we'll go home and sort everything else out."

Angelo wrapped his hands around her cheeks. He looked at her beautiful blue eyes and pouty lips that he adored. "I love you. Please do this for me. It's been a long couple of days for me too. It hasn't been easy for either of us." He walked to the closet and grabbed a clean suit. "I will be out in a couple of minutes. If you want to wear that, it's fine with me. You don't have to change."

Five minutes later, Angelo stepped out of the shower and wrapped the towel around his waist. He could barely stand to look at himself in the mirror, a sick feeling creeping in his stomach. He wanted to marry her so that was not the source of his nausea. It was seeing Gregorio's body lying on the sofa and trying to create an illusion of happiness for his vows when he could not stand his own reflection. It was not always easy being him.

He closed his eyes and sighed before walking from the restroom to put on his suit. When he stepped through the doorway, Angelo noticed that Ella was not there. There was a small dip on the bed where she sat. She must have been on the balcony again.

Not seeing her right away, Angelo moved closer to the balcony to make sure he did not miss her standing to the side. He moved the curtains out of the way and stared at the latch at the top, completely undisturbed. His breathing deepened as he gazed around the room with disbelief. He felt that anxious feeling in his chest as if something bad was about to happen. Not knowing where she went was worse than having a loaded pistol pointed at his head. The unknown was unbearable.

"Fuck!" he yelled. Rage and panic soared throughout his body as he snarled, launching everything off the bedside table and shattering the lamp against the floor. "Son of a bitch!" He jerked out his phone and pressed a button. He had to find out where she was. "Where are you?" His voice was low and impatient as he spoke to the other end of the line. He hoped by some chance that Ella was with Rafa, but he also knew there was no way that Ella would go to him.

"What do you mean? I'm here with Harrison where you should be right now. It's already seven-thirty."

"To hell with Harrison! She's gone. Ella's gone, and I need to find her now. Get everyone you can to help. I will take care of this little matter myself once we get her back."

Angelo hung up and started to pitch his phone at the wall when he thought better. Then he glared at the empty room and dialed a number on his phone that he had never called before.

Sullivan.

Chapter 44

Ella marched out of the elevator before the doors fully opened, the contract tightly crunched in her hand. As soon as she saw the words, her anger escalated with every recollection on her life she made. Now he went too far. It was clear on the last page of the contract that if anything happened to Angelo, she would go to Bonadio. A second contract had already been drawn in the event of Angelo's death.

How could he put that in words? How could he have Angelo agree to something like that? How could he want to send her to that despicable man? He did it all under the guise of protecting her.

Repeating what she would say, Ella walked past several rooms on the sixth floor. She would not let this slide. Keeping her in the dark her entire life was hard enough. Hearing the news of her mother nearly broke her, but threatening her with the man responsible for everything that had happened to her recently was never going to happen.

Ella's steps quickened, her anger coming to a head. She did not think anymore. Thinking would take away her nerve when she needed to be bold to confront her father. After turning the corner, mere feet distanced her from her father's door when she stopped, a man covered from head to toe in black walking out of the room.

His blue eyes stared at her, matching her surprise at seeing him. A second later, she saw two other men covered in black, one backing a large cart out of the room; a body bag was on top. Ella felt it in her gut, instantly knowing her father was in the bag. Her hands covered her mouth as chills stood on her skin, fear of the situation struck her chest. She panicked and started to run.

"Hey!" the man yelled and began chasing her back down the hallway. She did not wait or turn around, coming back to the elevators where she had started. The light on the top showed the elevator was nowhere near the floor she was on. She was left with no choice but to rush to the stairs.

Ella flung open the door, skipping steps to get to the lobby floor. With another panicked breath, she exited into the room full of people, the people having no idea what lurked above them. Ella could barely catch her breath as a few hotel guests gave her aggravated looks when she cut in front of them at the counter.

"I need to use your phone," she gasped. Ella dialed, the other end answering by the second ring.

"Yes?" he spoke cautiously and waited for her to speak.

"Sullivan," Ella replied.

"Ella?"

"I need you to come get me in front of the hotel. How soon can you get here?"

"Two minutes tops."

Ella handed the phone back to the attendant and ran out of the lobby to the front stairs. Sullivan was true to his word and pulled up with a screech, opening the door for her and then peeling away. Sullivan picked her up in two minutes flat just as he said and glanced at Ella in the back seat. She knew he was not going far without answers. He did not want anyone lecturing him for taking her somewhere she was not supposed to be. Sullivan stopped in a parking lot several blocks away.

"What's going on, Ella? Where's Tomassi?" he asked.

"I went to talk to my father and was chased by some man. They killed him. My father is dead." Her voice tapered as she turned to the window, closing her eyes as if to question what she saw.

"Ella," Sullivan started. "You shouldn't have gone to your father."

"But I saw the contract. I saw what he wanted Angelo to sign."

Sullivan shook his head back and forth, letting out a breath through his teeth. "That's right, and there was a reason it wasn't signed. Did you think about that?"

Ella inhaled and thought about the blank signature lines with her father's name scribbled at the bottom. Angelo had not signed it but what did that mean? "I don't understand," she said, her eyes narrowing at the seat in front of her as she waited for his reply.

"Tomassi refused to sign it and your father ordered me to kill him. The rest you can figure out."

Ella covered her mouth at the thought of losing Angelo, at the thought of her father taking him away from her too. "Why?" she muttered.

Sullivan reached his hand back to her as his phone rang from the passenger's seat. He looked at the phone and then at Ella through the rearview mirror. "Yes?" he answered. All she could hear was Angelo's irate voice, the callousness of his tone intensifying as he spoke. "I'm in the parking lot off the corner of Nineteenth and Main. Yes, I understand."

He hung up the phone, shifting from neutral to first gear. "Tomassi's waiting for us at the front of the hotel," he said and turned around to look at her, wiping the tear that slid down her cheek. "He's mad that you left but—"

Sullivan did not finish as a gun tapped on his window, taking his attention from her and immediately to the front. She looked up at the same time that Sullivan did, seeing a man point a gun at him. Then tires screeched to the passenger side of the car and stopped, blocking Sullivan and Ella's escape from the other side.

"Ella," said Sullivan. "When I say go, jump out. Got it?"

She did not respond but understood what he said. His mock drills became a sudden reality as he grabbed the handle of his door, ramming it into the man on the outside without notice. At once, both he and Ella jumped out, Sullivan retrieving his gun and shooting the man mid-step. Then he grabbed her hand, running to an alley off the street as a red sports car jerked to a stop with three men stepping out.

Ella watched them come closer. Two of them pointed guns at Sullivan; another pointed one at her. Her body stiffened. She felt the full force of the danger that Angelo had warned her about. It happened so fast. She did not have the strength in her to face it, yet there was no choice. They were under attack.

"Stay down, Ella," Sullivan told her. Ella slouched at his feet as he stood and pulled out another gun. He pointed them both. She knew that he used both hands interchangeably. Sullivan would not miss. "You have no idea who you're dealing with," he said. "This will be your only chance to leave alive."

"We don't want anything to do with you. Give her to us, and we'll leave you alone."

One of the men shot at Sullivan, but he was not quick enough to avoid the shots that Sullivan fired back. Two men fell and then the third. Sullivan was a master with a gun.

Another shot fired. Ella did not know from which way it came, but it did not come from the car. Sullivan crouched down in front of her to keep her from harm as the bullet missed his head and lodged in his shoulder. Blood started to ooze through the fabric of his coat. His shoulder jerked with the pain, but he ignored the injury and fired again. A man from the opposite end of the alley fell to the ground, his cries swallowed by the deafening night.

"You know you're going to die," said an unfamiliar, chilling voice.

Out from the darkness, two more men appeared on the sidewalk. How many people were going to attack them tonight? She did not have time to register everything before hearing a slight thud. She looked up at Sullivan as his gun crashed to the ground. There was a slit on his sleeve where blood started to drip.

"Leave him alone!" Ella shouted and picked up the gun that he had dropped. They were going to kill him. She could not let that happen. He would not have been there tonight if it had not been for her.

"I will never let her go," Sullivan said and stood up in front of her, blocking her with his chest.

What was he doing? She was not letting him die for her.

She fired the gun herself. One man collapsed to the ground and then the other. Ella never missed a shot. Sullivan taught her everything he knew. She exhaled. She thought there were no more men to attack when she heard the cracking of boots against the ground. This time, she and Sullivan were outnumbered. There were too many to shoot with the bullets left in their guns. Sullivan had no choice but to give her up.

Then more vehicles came to a stop. Ella thought it was over for them both. Every warning that Angelo had said came back to haunt her. If she thought her life was doomed before, now she knew what doom actually was.

Her eyes closed and opened again to face her fate head-on, but it was Angelo and some of his men who showed up this time. Bullets flew. The men who attacked them started falling one after the other in a surreal scene she had never expected to see. The death of so many shocked her until she could no longer comprehend what she saw.

Angelo was not sparing even one. She had never seen him look so full of rage. He was too calm and composed—alarming. His mere presence made the last man standing to hesitate for a moment. His gun wavered; his expression reflected fear. Even so, he stepped closer and pointed his gun at Ella instead.

"Get away from her," Angelo said and raised his gun again. The adrenaline flowing through his veins made him a menacing sight to see. That was what she thought. He looked in no mood to deal with

Bonadio's pawns. He fired. All she saw was the reflection of a gun from the side of the alleyway when he shot. The reflection disappeared with the thud to the ground but one man still held a gun to her head. Sullivan blocked her behind him the best that he could, but the man still had a clear shot.

"I wouldn't," Angelo said and crossed his arms with his pistol still in his hand. She knew he would fire at the man as soon as he gained the man's attention from her. The man was going to die and wish that Angelo never came.

"You should have never pointed that gun at her head. I will break every one of your bones. When I'm done with that, I will break your neck."

Angelo's words infused dread in Ella. It must have done the same to the man. He flinched. In a desperate attempt for his life, he lunged at her. She felt his constricting arm around her neck as he jabbed the muzzle of the gun to her throat. "Drop your guns or I'll shoot her. I don't care how important she is. She will die if you don't drop your guns."

Angelo's teeth clenched as he glanced at Rafa, nodding for him to comply as the man slowly stepped back with Ella. She could see the running vehicle at the end of the alley that he hoped to reach.

The man took two steps. As soon as he eased the muzzle from her throat, Sullivan knocked him in the temple with his fist. With his vision blurred, the man tried to raise his gun but had no true aim. Blood trickled from his forehead. The man stumbled.

Like a ragdoll, Sullivan shoved Ella away from the man. She could not believe the strength in his arm despite the gunshots he endured. She thought she would hit the rocky ground underneath, but Angelo caught her by the waist before she hit. He launched her to Rafa, who dragged her to the Escalade like she had changed children's hands during play. In the split second's time, Rafa opened the door and pushed her in. She could still hear their muffled voices on the outside.

Yanking the gun from the man's hand, Angelo punched him to the ground and had Brett tie his hands and feet with ropes.

"Don't kill me. I can get you to Bonadio," the man pleaded.

"Beg all you want," Angelo breathed. "I will see you again tomorrow. Make your amends tonight while you still have the chance." Then he looked at Brett, his chin motioning to the second

Escalade. "Take him to the warehouse. You and Sammy do whatever you need to do. Give me a report tomorrow."

"Got it," said Brett, looking around as Sammy walked over to him. They picked up the man and disappeared from Ella's view.

"Rafa, can you handle the cleanup—you, Jim and Ray?"

Rafa nodded. "Already have it covered."

"Good, take care of it, and then get the hell out of here before the cops show up."

Angelo gave out a few more orders and then walked toward Ella. He looked like he wanted to protect her and rip her heart out at the same time. It made her afraid of what he might do.

"We're going back to the house," were the only words he said.

Chapter 45

Angelo had not said a word to her the night before and barely glanced her way. He did not even sleep in the same bed. It was already three in the afternoon and he still kept his distance. Ella had not tried to talk to him either, knowing he would ignore her reasons for leaving the suite.

She heard him shuffle in a drawer in the next room, slamming the drawer shut when he was done. Ella sighed from where she sat on the bed but knew she could not avoid him forever. Even though she dreaded the confrontation, she dragged her feet out of their room and walked to the kitchen where he stood.

Angelo was at the counter with an open knife under the faucet. He saw her out of the corner of his eye but did not greet her. He barely acknowledged that she had entered the room or sat at the table to watch him. She did not like this Angelo. He was more intimidating than usual when he did not speak. The knife in his hand was long and sharp, past the legal size of a knife he should carry. She was relieved when he sheathed it back in its case and slid it in his boot. Her relief vanished when his focus fell on her.

He turned around and shook his head, glaring at her as he walked to the table. His hands landed on the wooden top beside her arms. His forehead touched hers, making her take a shaky breath in. As Ella arched her back away from his threatening expression, Angelo leaned closer to her body than before.

"You made my men risk their lives to save you last night. Sullivan was shot twice. You should have asked me about the contract first. Leaving the hotel by yourself, especially now, that risked more than your life. You're not the only one I have to think about in this mess."

"I'm sorry," Ella said fast. Angelo made her feel guiltier than she already did.

"Sorry? You think being sorry is going to make up for it?" Angelo's voice was low and direct. Lack of sleep was catching up with him. "If Sullivan never answered his phone, you'd be in the hands of Bonadio's group?" Ella tried to look away in vain, her chin being forced back where it was. "You will look at me when I'm talking to you."

"I won't do it again," she whispered. "I promise." Angelo frowned and stared in her eyes. His fingers weaved through the back of her head and squeezed. The tight grip around her hair kept her full attention on him. She did not dare say another word with his furious eyes cast on her.

"Oh, I know you won't, Ella. You won't ever cross me again—of that I can promise." It felt like her body shrank underneath his glare before he finally let go. He did not say another word to her. Angelo walked to the door and slammed it as he left the house. His car started, but she never heard him leave. Then the doorknob turned again. She thought Angelo had forgotten something but the engine on his car revved. The tires screeched and the car sped away from the house.

"Hello?" a woman called and stepped through the door. Ella stared at her. She had never seen the older woman before and wondered why she was here. The woman had a long braid with silver strands scattered throughout. Ella guessed she was in her early fifties. She stood about average height and gave Ella a friendly smile.

"Ella?" The woman's smile widened as she walked up to Ella and wrapped her arms around her head. Ella froze. The woman let her go and grabbed her face, giving a firm kiss to both sides of her cheeks. "I've been waiting to meet you. I'll bet you have no idea who I am?" With Ella's mind still being occupied with hers and Angelo's exchange, she weakly shook her head and waited to find out. "I'm Nina, Angelo's mother."

Ella looked back at the door. She had no idea why his mother was here. Did Angelo call her, or did she come on her own?

"It's nice to meet you," Ella greeted. "I'm sorry I'm not dressed. I didn't expect company."

"Nonsense, you'll have plenty of times to dress up in fancy clothes," she chuckled. "Why waste all that effort getting dressed for me?" Ella liked her. Nina had an upbeat personality. It reminded her of Lila in a way.

"Would you like a cup of coffee?" Ella offered and stood up.

"I would love a cup," Nina replied.

Ella had not been around any motherly figurehead lately. She thought about it. Besides Lila, she had not gotten close to any woman at all. Men dominated her life. They watched over her. Ella did not know how to feel about Nina being in the house.

She set down two cups on the table along with cream and sugar. She did not know what Nina preferred but stirred both into hers. Then she was quiet and waited for Nina to speak. There must have been a reason for the visit.

"Would you like to hear about my story?" Nina asked and mixed cream and sugar in her coffee.

"Of course," Ella said and took a sip from her cup.

"Good. Come with me. It's too stuffy in here. Why don't we move to the family room and get comfortable?"

Ella nodded and stood back up. She felt more comfortable on the sofa anyway and had no problem with moving as Nina wished. Ella gladly propped up her knees and held her cup of coffee on her leg. She was interested in the woman she had heard nothing about.

"It seems like a long time ago now," Nina started. "When my family told me to marry Antonio, I thought the world was ending. I wanted to run. I wondered what gave them the right to choose who I married. Not only did I not love Antonio, I had never met him."

"That must have been really hard for you," Ella said, thankful that she did not share Nina's situation. "Did you ever fall in love?"

Nina let out a breath at the memories that seemed to come to her mind. "I didn't for a while. I despised Antonio for a long time. He was gone for days at a time or out late when he was in town. I took care of his house. He saw other women. He thinks I don't know, but I grew up in the life. I knew what he was doing. Marrying me was a way for our families to make peace, but Antonio and I hardly acted like husband and wife."

Ella already worried about Angelo being gone, but other women never seriously crossed her mind. If Antonio was that way, did that mean Angelo would be too? "You're still together. Are you like that now?"

"Well," Nina sighed. "About a year passed after we said our vows. I got desperate and lonely. I needed affection even from the man I despised. I decided not to look at what I hated about him anymore. I focused on his good points. He took care of me. He gave me a house and a car. He gave me anything else I needed or wanted. After that, I started to act like his wife. I asked him how he felt or made his favorite foods. He thought I went crazy, but I didn't stop. It wasn't long before he didn't want to ignore me anymore. He started coming home and spending time with me. Then, Angelo came. As soon as I saw Angelo's face, I knew that Antonio and I would live a good life."

They were happy despite their rough beginning. Antonio had not been exempt from the rules either. Ella knew that she could not tolerate Angelo sleeping around. That was not an issue like it was for Nina, but Ella still worried. Would he grow tired of her and look for love somewhere else? Would she become lonely and end up like her mother? Ella had so many questions and so few answers. She did not know what to expect.

"Ella." Nina laid her hand on Ella's arm. "Don't think so hard about it."

"How do you separate it? How do you raise a family and have a marriage and live a normal life with everything happening on the outside?"

"You let Angelo worry about that, dear. That's what Antonio taught him to do. You need to worry about being one thing—his wife. What he does in the group shouldn't concern you. I know my son will do everything he can to make you happy. All you need to do is keep him from drowning. Love Angelo no matter what. If you can do that, the rest will fall into place."

Chapter 46

Angelo paid little attention to the road aside from staying in his lane. He was mad at himself, furious with Ella and fed up with life in general. He could not seem to get ahead no matter what he did. She was gone for five minutes before he called Sullivan, and Bonadio's people were waiting to attack them both. That bastard had to die.

After being at the hotel all day, his car jolted to a stop at his main warehouse. Angelo opened the middle compartment and pulled out his cigarettes and a light. He was trying to quit. He knew he should not smoke if he wanted a family. Right now, that was the least of his concerns. He would not get a family if Ella kept disappearing on him.

He blew out a puff of smoke and leaned against the side of his car. It relaxed him some. His nerves were shot. Thinking about why he was upset in the first place made him madder still. Angelo threw down the cigarette and stomped it out. He had a situation to handle inside.

Angelo flung open the door and heard it slam again as he walked to the back office to see who was there. Rafa was sitting behind the desk. He must have been there a while. The last time Angelo was there, Brett turned the office into a disaster. Rafa did not know where anything was.

"Was the cleanup handled last night? Are we in the clear?" Angelo asked and fell into the small recliner in front of the desk.

"So far," Rafa replied. "Donnie tells me the force is onto us, but they don't have evidence to back that up. They're still trying to figure out what happened."

"Good." Angelo nodded. "I'm assuming they won't ever find the evidence."

"I told you we would handle it."

"Fine. Fine." Angelo brushed off the remark. "Did Brett get anything useful from that asshole I had him bring back here?"

"I'm not sure about useful, but I can tell you this. Bonadio turned more to his side than we thought. We should make sure not to let something like last night happen again. Bonadio also has people at the station. He could definitely use that against us."

"That's fucking perfect," Angelo quipped and rubbed his temples with his thumbs. "As if we don't have enough to deal with without corrupt PO's."

"I'm giving it to you straight." Rafa rummaged through several sheets of paper on the desk and sorted the four stacks on top.

"Get you an assistant, Rafa. You waste too much time organizing. I have better uses for you than filing."

Rafa gave him an upward glance and grumbled, "I don't want anyone else handling my files. I have them how I like them."

"You need one, so find one. That's the end of it," Angelo ordered; then he looked through the open door. "Did Brett end up shooting that man?"

"No, he was too busy playing. We thought you wanted to take the final blow anyway."

Angelo stood. He unbuttoned the two buttons on his coat and took out his pistol. It was a beautiful object with deadly intentions. As he walked out of the office, Angelo ejected the clip just to hear the snapping sound it made when he shoved it back in.

There was a holding room in back. He continued forward with one thought in mind—death. Nobody held a gun to his woman's head. This man would face the same fate as the man who pointed a gun at Ella's head the night at the casino.

In the room, the man sat on the floor. Brett took Angelo to heart. He did what he needed to do to get the man to talk. By the looks of him, he probably did more than needed. The man was lucky. If he had looked less beaten, Angelo would have broken his bones.

This was his life. Angelo raised his gun and looked at the man. He felt no guilt and no hesitation. He almost hated himself for his lack of pity. That was who he was. Feeling sorry for anyone who wronged him would have been his downfall. He could not afford to lose his nerve. He would be dead as soon as he did.

Angelo pulled the trigger three times and hit the man in the head, neck, and chest. The first shot took the man's life on impact. He fell to the ground. Angelo could not tell if the blood on the floor was fresh or already there. He did not give it another thought either and walked out of the room.

Angelo left the building altogether. He needed a drink. Sometimes coping meant a strong drink or five. All he thought about for the last few months was how to protect Ella. All of his efforts meant nothing to her. On a whim, she left the suite without realizing how much attention he gave. She was like a child sometimes. He kept her from self-harm. He kept her from Bonadio. When would she understand?

"Hey!" Rafa shouted and ran after Angelo's car as he backed up the Mercedes. "Where are you going?"

Angelo rolled down the window and looked at him. He wanted Rafa to leave him alone. "What are you, my keeper?"

"Open the door," Rafa snarled. He stepped in front of the car and forced Angelo to stomp on the brake.

"Move out of my fucking way." Angelo snapped. "Do you really want me to run you over?"

"Open the fucking door." Angelo knew that he would have to either run him over or open the door as he wanted. Rafa jumped inside as soon as the lock clicked up. "I don't like where your mind is at all. You're taking me with you wherever you're going."

"Fine." Angelo spun the tires and pressed the gas pedal to the floor. "I hope you like Marla's, because that's where I'm going."

Marla's. It was a hole-in-the-wall bar that did not have a listing on the Internet. No one would find him or Rafa there. There were a couple of drunks sitting at the bar. Two more men played pool. It probably had six tables in the entire place. Rafa looked around with disgust. His expression was priceless. Angelo owned a multimillion-dollar hotel and this was where he took him.

"How the hell did you ever find this place?" Rafa asked.

"It's my secret hangout," Angelo answered and walked to the bar.

"Sure it is," Rafa said. He did not believe him, which satisfied Angelo more.

"No, I'm serious. Watch me." Angelo looked back.

"Mr. Tomassi," said the bartender. It was a woman in her late thirties with blue hair and a short jean skirt. Her style was edgy and she was attentive to the customers.

"Give me two Heinekens," he said.

"Sure, hun." She walked to the small cooler and grabbed the beers. The cooler had one light on and the other burned out; the bottom of the cooler was missing a foot so that the entire appliance wobbled when she opened the door.

"Six dollars," she said and set the beers in front of him.

"Keep the change," he handed a beer to Rafa.

"You have to be joking." Rafa's smirk matched the shock in his eyes.

Angelo grinned. Seeing Rafa there was the most amusing moment he had in a while. "Nobody will look for us here. It's not that bad once you get used to it. They take care of you, but I wouldn't take anyone home if I were you."

"No," Rafa agreed. "I'm sure I'd get more than I asked for."

"Game of pool?" asked Angelo.

"Sure, but I'll have to burn my hands of germs when I get back to the hotel."

Angelo laughed. "Don't forget to call Brett when you do. You know how he likes fire."

Rafa had taken a drink of his beer but coughed. "Too bad for him that I'm not a pyro."

"No…just a nympho. No one wants to see that."

Rafa crossed his arms and glared at him with contempt. "I don't fuck that many women."

"Okay." Angelo nodded and left it alone; then his tone turned more serious. "What am I going to do with Ella?" he asked and picked out a pool stick.

Rafa shrugged. "Lay low and give her some time. Gregorio's ranks couldn't get any worse in the next few weeks than they already are. Nobody knows Gregorio died but the few of us. Going MIA will also make Bonadio paranoid. That could help us too."

"I think waiting will hurt us more," he said and racked the balls.

"After last night, it's probably best that we stayed off the radar for a while. Another incident like that could shut us down. That would be worse. The cops are still investigating that scene."

"You shoot first." Angelo pointed at the table and thought about what he had said. "Christ, I knew she was mad at Gregorio. I should have never left that contract in the room."

"No…what you should have done was wait until after you got married to give her the master codes."

"Go to hell," Angelo huffed.

"You're older. You'll go first," said Rafa.

The table was open. He knew that Rafa was not trying with the game. He did not knock one ball into a pocket.

"What would you do with her? I can't have Ella jumping in the middle of the street every time she gets upset. I don't have time to worry about that shit."

"Honestly, I saw her eyes last night. You did too. I think she gets it now. I was surprised that we didn't find her crying. She had enough sense not to break down when it was important. Sullivan said she took care of a couple of men herself."

"Another beer?" The bartender set two down and then left. She knew he would pay in a minute.

Angelo shot. He made a stripe and walked around the table. "That's another thing," he began. "I don't like her being able to shoot like that."

"It's a little late to take away that skill."

"I don't want her involved with the group." He ignored Rafa's remark. "I don't want the life to harden her."

"Well, you can't have her with you and not with you. You need to give her something to take her attention off of you."

"Like another restaurant." Angelo nodded in thought. She might love the idea, or she might try to compare it with Santiago's. It was a gamble.

"That's right," Rafa agreed.

"I'll think about it," Angelo said and watched Rafa aim. "I'm hungry. I haven't eaten today."

Rafa looked over the counter at the grill. All the silver was blackened by old oil and constant use. It probably had not been cleaned in a while if ever. He did not want to know what the cooler looked like. "No way," he scoffed.

"You'll risk your life with a bullet, but you don't want to eat a homemade burger."

"I'm not into food poisoning. That's a slower way to go than with a bullet." Rafa missed again and stood up. "All right, you order. I'll wait for you to eat first. If you don't die an agonizing death, then I'll eat one too."

Angelo laughed at him. Rafa was a bit of a germaphobe. He figured it had something to do with his background, but he never asked.

"It's a deal," Angelo said. It'll be worth my time to watch you eat something that isn't gourmet.

"I don't have to have expensive meals. I just like the kitchen to be something that the health department wouldn't shut down. I bet this place wouldn't pass an inspection."

"No, I'm sure it wouldn't, but you aren't calling on them. I've been coming here for years, and I plan to keep coming."

"Fine then. Like I said, you order the food, and I will eat." Rafa gave in.

Chapter 47

Something banged against the door. Ella sat up from the sofa where she had fallen asleep, hoping it was Angelo. With Nina still in the guest room, the crashing sound did not come from her. The lock on the front door twisted and then the doorknob turned. Angelo stumbled inside and leaned against the wall. He tried to shut the door, but Rafa stepped in behind him.

"What happened?" Ella asked as Rafa closed the door.

"You happened," Angelo slurred and dragged his feet down the hallway to their room.

"Let him sleep it off, Ella," Rafa said and took a seat on the chair next to her.

"I messed up with him, didn't I?" she asked. Her head lowered as she held it with her hand. She felt like she could not do anything right, and everything seemed to be getting worse.

"Do you want the truth?" Rafa asked pointedly.

"No," she replied. Ella knew how blunt Rafa could be. Nothing he said would make her feel better. She would rather him leave her alone to sort out her own thoughts than give a speech.

Rafa frowned at her answer and opened his mouth. If he was going to tell her his opinion anyway, why did he bother to ask if she wanted to hear? She should have expected as much from him.

"The truth is, Ella, you scared the shit out of him by doing what you did. You may not like him to order you around, but this has always been your life. Nobody can change that. It's not like he has a choice either. Do you realize if they took you last night, you would be in Bonadio's bed this morning? It would have gotten serious for you very fast."

Ella blinked. She was trying not to cry but Rafa was good at pointing out everything she had already considered. It made it worse to hear it in words.

"You put everyone at risk for no reason at all. We don't even put our own men at risk if we can help it. Angelo never wanted you in that kind of danger. He would've lost it if they had taken you last night. Surely, you've gotten that much about how he feels."

Ella wiped her eyes and then fidgeted with the tassels on the pillow. He was right, but he could have curved the truth a little. It was not as though she had anyone she could really talk to about everything that had happened. She already felt helpless to do anything with her life.

"Ah hell," Rafa groaned. He shifted from the chair to the sofa and wrapped his arms around her shoulders. "It's going to be all right," he said and hugged her to his chest. "I don't know why you doubted Angelo in the first place. He would've never signed that shit."

"He was so mad when he left today. He left me alone like my father did to my mother."

"No...Angelo is not Gregorio. I know I wasn't with his group when everything started to go wrong, but I do know that you have nothing to worry about."

"He'll get tired of me and look around," she added.

"I can't see that happening. All he did tonight was eat bad food and drink beer at a bar that should have been torn down twenty years ago. He doesn't want to see you hurt."

"Fine," she mumbled the reply.

"You love him, don't you, Ella?"

"Yes," she admitted.

Rafa nodded and stood, staring down on her as he took a small step back. "Then take care of him, Ella. He knows about being lonely. He needs to know you're going to be there for him when he's done with this shit. Worrying about you is making him lose his focus, and I mean that. When he wakes up tomorrow, I want you to talk to him. Make sure he knows that you trust him enough to handle situations that concern you. If you do, Angelo will give you the best life you could want. Understand?"

"Yes, I get it."

"Good, now go get some sleep. I'm sure you've had a long day too."

***

The next morning, Ella was sitting at the table and flipping through a magazine that Nina had left when Angelo darted in the kitchen. He wore no shirt. His thin cotton pants were twisted slightly. His hair was sticking up on one side. He looked at her and ran his fingers through the strands.

"I thought you left again," he breathed and looked away. His panicked expression made her feel bad. He was always worrying about her. Then he groaned and fixed his pants. "I drank way too much last night," he scolded himself.

Angelo sat down as Ella stood up. She walked to the kitchen counter and hit start above a coffee cup she had set out. It took a minute. She thought the caffeine might wake him up some. She stirred cream in his coffee and set it in front of him without saying a word. Then she sat back down where she was.

"I'm sorry, Angelo," she whispered.

He wiped his tired, hungover face and repeated her apology, "You're sorry." He shook his head and took a drink of the coffee. "What exactly are you sorry for, Ella? Risking your life? Risking mine? Risking my men?"

Ella sat back against the chair in silence and thought about what he asked. If he had not shown up, she would be at the mercy of Bonadio as Rafa had said. A shiver ran up her spine and down her arms at the thought.

Angelo slid his hand into his pocket and pulled out his ring. She had wondered if the employees gave it back to him the night she ran. He held it to the light and turned it over a few times; then he reached for her hand and slipped it back on her finger.

"You think that ring is something I use to track you, but you're wrong. That ring is a symbol of who I am. My father gave it to me when I took over the group; then I gave it to you. That's how valuable you are to me. I put the tracker inside before we ever met." Angelo leaned back and picked up his cup again.

Ella stared at him. Nothing could ever change the way she felt when she saw how vulnerable he could be.

"You almost didn't have a choice about whose wife you were," he continued. "Then what? I can't even think about what would've happened if I showed up a minute later."

"I understand that now," she said. Angelo looked at her. It was the first time in two days that he did not look away.

"There's an investigation going on because of that attack. Cops are swarming. I can't get involved with Gregorio's group right now. Can't risk my men with corrupt cops in the mix."

"I didn't mean for it to happen like that."

"I know you didn't, but it still did. We'll get married in three weeks. That should give you enough time to come to terms with everything that's happened." Angelo grabbed his cup before getting up and walking to the other room.

Ella did not want to see him stressed anymore. Rafa and Nina were right. He had enough responsibilities with the group and his businesses. She should not add to it. He should be able to relax when he was around her. She wanted him to be able to relax.

She sat at the table for several more minutes, giving him a chance to wake up. Then she heard a couple of piano keys. It seemed like a test, to see if the notes were in tune. Ella stood. More notes started to play. Was Angelo playing the piano?

She did not give him any more time. Ella walked down the hallway to the spare room with the piano. She knew it was Angelo who played, but seeing his fingers dance along the keys came as a surprise. She watched him with fascination.

A minute later, it stopped. She let out a breath, wishing that he would continue. He glanced over at her. That was why he stopped. He knew she was in the room.

"I always wondered if you played."

"It's been almost fifteen years. I'm surprised I remember how."

"Your music is beautiful."

Angelo looked back at the piano. Nobody ever complimented him on his talent. She found it sad that no one knew he could play.

"Will you play me a song?" she asked and sat down on the bench beside him.

"Can you keep this between us?" he asked her back. Ella nodded and Angelo started to set his fingers on the keys when he looked over at her grinning face. "I think you're too excited about this."

Her smile softened as she stared at him. Of course, she was excited. She loved this side of Angelo and would treasure the moment.

"All right." He consented. "Then this piece will belong to you."

The music started again. His fingers moved gracefully over the keys, making the music fill the empty room. The tune was beautiful; Ella found no errors in the notes.

"I'm a bit rusty, but I guess you never forget something you've learned." He continued with the keys.

Ella did not recognize the piece. It was different from every other song she had heard. His fingers glided across the keys in perfect rhythm, making her eyes shut to focus on its melody. The piece lasted longer than the average song did. She liked how he concentrated on the song. Angelo was passionate about the piano.

"I wrote that when I was fifteen," he said after he finished the song. "You're the first one to hear it, so it makes sense to give it to you."

"I feel so special." Her voice was soft and proud.

"Well, playing piano and taking over my father's title didn't mesh well together. I tried to forget that I ever played."

"It's a shame; I wish you would play another." Ella hoped he would but was still elated that he played for her at all.

Angelo lowered the cover over the keys and grinned. "That's all I have for now, but I might play for you another time." He leaned closer and kissed her forehead when she wrapped her arms around his neck. Her fingers weaved through his hair. Small chills formed where her nails had touched.

"What's this?" he quietly asked. Her affectionate gesture took him by surprise, but she did not let go. A small smile replaced his serious expression. His strong arms finally hugged her back.

"Thank you for coming after me," she whispered.

"Like I would ever leave you out there alone," he huffed with a shake of his head. "But you can't run off like that. Maybe now you'll believe what I tell you and listen more."

"I do," she said. "You don't have to worry about me leaving. I won't put you through that again." She promised him, making his grip around her body tighter than before. She was not sure if he believed her but hoped he did.

"God I love you, Ella, but sometimes—sometimes, I think you're going to be the death of me."

Chapter 48

Ella waited impatiently as Lila weaved small white flowers through her hair. She clenched a towel with her fingers, trying to keep her sweaty palms dry. She could not believe the night of the wedding was here. The last few weeks had been crazy for her. Talking to Nina and Rafa helped to ease her fears. What could she really do? She now understood why she had the life that she had. At least she had an advantage. She was marrying the man she loved.

Ella was disappointed about one aspect. She would have to keep their marriage quiet for now. They were getting married in a small chapel outside of the city limits. Their vows were necessary for group protection but also a risk if Bonadio found out. The potential danger overruled.

She peeked from a crack in the door at the people who had gathered. Most of them were Angelo's elite and their wives, an intimidating group of men with enough gunpowder to blow up the square mile. While crowds had not bothered her before, she knew what this group was capable of doing. She found it slightly unnerving.

"Are you ready?" asked Lila. Ella closed the door and smiled. She was ready...excited...and terrified out of her mind. She was glad to have Lila there. She needed at least one person she knew. Angelo was not thrilled about inviting her, but as long as she understood what would happen if she did not keep her mouth shut, he allowed her to attend. Ella was grateful for the support.

Music started to play. Ella took in a deep breath and exhaled as Lila opened the door. "You look amazing tonight. I still can't believe it. I would've never thought that you'd marry him when I saw him looking at you at Santiago's." Ella looked down for a moment. Lila's mention of the restaurant caught her off guard. "Oh geez, I'm so sorry. I didn't mean to—"

Ella smiled. "No, it's okay. I'm getting married. It's time for me to let go of the restaurant anyway."

"Yes, you are." Lila hugged her tightly. "I'll see you on the other side," she said and walked out of the room.

The music grew louder for a second and then quieted again as Lila shut the door. Ella was alone. Her legs started to tremble. Her heart raced against her chest. She tried to breathe steady breaths, but her technique was not working at all. She hoped that she would not sweat through her silky pearl sleeves. She hoped that she would not step on the long fabric of her gown. Ella opted out of a veil; the flowers in her hair would have to do. She wondered how Angelo would react when he saw her. She hoped that he would like what he saw.

"What a beautiful bride."

Ella turned around as Sullivan gently grabbed her arm. She smiled and threw her arms around his neck. She should have known that Sullivan would attend. He had never let her do anything by herself—not once. He looked out for her much better than her father had. He was like family to her. She was glad to see him there.

"Ella," he said. "We can't have the bride walking down the aisle alone. Would you like me to escort you?"

Ella smiled wide at his offer. "Yes, I would really like that," she answered and sniffed. Having him there made her feel a lot better.

"You look absolutely stunning. Tomassi is lucky to have you."

"Thank you," she said and tried not to cry as Sullivan handed her a tissue.

"I have something for you. Since you're keeping your vows secret, I brought a chain that you can give Tomassi. I had your name engraved in the links so he will always remember to think about you. Slide the ring that you have on the chain, and he will never have to take it off."

Ella took the chain and wrapped it twice around her wrist. "Thank you. You're always so thoughtful of me. I'm really happy to have you here."

Sullivan gave her a warm smile and held out his arm. "Ready?"

With another quivering breath, she nodded. "I'm ready."

As they stepped out, her hands shook more than when she was in the room. She saw the guests and glanced at the musicians on the stage in the corner, yet she heard no sounds at all. Racing thoughts consumed her mind, leaving her oblivious to everything else. Guests stood, but Ella focused on him. She started to feel lightheaded. Angelo looked gorgeous in the black tuxedo as he returned her stare.

"I know he would never do anything to betray your trust," Sullivan said. "Tomassi will make you happy."

"Thank you. I know he will." At times, she found Angelo terrifying but looked forward to more sweet moments in their future. She valued the softer side of him that he showed to her.

As she stood directly in front of Angelo, she found it difficult to keep her balance. If her knees wobbled anymore, she would not be able to hold up her weight. Sullivan handed her shaky hand over to Angelo and gave a single nod. His eyes almost seemed sad with his smile.

"She's all yours now," Sullivan said. "Please take care of her."

Angelo nodded back and gently folded his fingers around hers. His face lowered and his lips touched her ear. "Are you ready for a life with me, little girl?" he whispered. Ella gave him a look that disapproved of the name. It was exactly like him to ask something like that.

"Just don't leave me. I don't want to see something happen to you."

"That's my line," he said and kissed the top of her head; then he turned them both to face Harrison, the officiator.

"Welcome." said Harrison. "It's a joy to see all of you present with us today...especially you Ella," he lowered his voice but the crowd still chuckled, knowing of her escapade a few weeks before. Ella gave him a sheepish smile and started to open her mouth when Angelo cut in.

"Harrison," he said and squeezed her hand tighter. "Get on with it."

Harrison smiled and continued. "We have gathered here to unite this man and this woman in marriage. The two who stand before me are prepared to accept the bond and commitment that marriage will bring. This unity is not to be taken lightly and shall forever link the lives of both individuals. They have accepted the challenge to marry with all of you as their witnesses, supporting their vows to each other. If any person present has any reason that these two should not wed...it would probably be best if you didn't speak and forever held your peace."

Harrison paused with the hushed snickers but continued when Angelo shot him a silent look of warning. "Very well, no one objects." Harrison smiled, his dimples deepening, making his expression look baby-like even though his hair was completely gray. "Angelo, do you take this woman to be your wife; to love, respect and honor for as long as you both will live?"

"I do," he said and grabbed her left hand and slipped a small band on her ring finger followed by a diamond. Then he leaned down and spoke softly in her ear. "You know that I would do anything for you. I will make you happy."

Ella gazed in his eyes, so beautiful and sincere. She could feel the tears creep to her own. She was standing in front of him, about to become his wife. She never expected this to happen for her.

"Ella," said Harrison. She quickly looked up at the officiator. "Do you take this man to be your husband; to love, respect and honor as long as you both will live?"

Ella took in a deep breath and answered quietly, "I do." Then she unfastened the chain from her wrist and made her trembling fingers link it around his neck. Angelo questioned the gesture. The chain seemed to confuse him for a moment. "The necklace will hide your ring, but I don't want you to forget about me either." Angelo gave a slight smile that approved and glanced back at Harrison.

"Very good. May your love grow and bind you closer every day of your married lives. I now pronounce you husband and wife."

She gazed at Angelo as he laid his palms around her cheeks. She could hardly believe it as he pulled her face close; her lips felt numb with the delicate kiss. They were married. He started to pull away, but Ella grasped his hands that still cupped her face. "I love you, Angelo."

He smiled at her and kissed her again. It was a longer, more passionate kiss than the first. Ella felt perfect in his arms.

***

Nina had the reception hall of the chapel decorated beautifully. Flowers and ribbons surrounded the room. White silk tablecloths covered the tables. There were bottles of wine and glasses on one table in the back; platters of hors d'oeuvres covered another.

Ella glanced at Angelo from the back of the reception hall. Several men were congratulating him with hugs and some with kisses. As the rules said, his group could not continue to protect her unless they were married. She guessed that girlfriends had a lower status than wives did. Maybe Angelo invited his men to show that he also followed the rules, but it looked like more than that. Angelo respected them. She could tell that he trusted them by how freely they were able to approach him and shake his hand.

A group of women pulled Ella's focus from Angelo. They were strangers to her, but they gave her the same amount of attention as though they knew her for years. She received kisses and hugs. Some complimented her dress. Others wished her a happy marriage. A couple even invited her to lunch at their house. The women were friendly and welcoming. Ella did not know which husbands belonged to them, but the women seemed happy with their lives.

The musicians started to play again. Ella admired how the different instruments complemented the others. She sipped on wine and enjoyed the rhythm as she waited for Angelo to return. Several couples were in the front of the reception hall dancing. She hoped to be one of them soon.

Ella had touched a bottle to fill up her glass when a man walked up beside her. "Allow me," he said. Ella looked up at the older man and smiled her appreciation. As he handed her the glass, she clearly remembered his stern expression from months ago. Then Nina walked up beside him and took his arm.

"You've met my wife, but I never formally introduced myself. My name is Antonio Tomassi."

"Yes," Ella said. Her eyes widened as she remembered the exchange. Now that she knew what the exchange had been about, she felt a little awkward about seeing him again. His eyes were dark brown like Angelo's, and gray colored much of his hair. There were some wrinkles on his face and a scar on the bridge of his nose.

"So you caused my son to ignore me before finding out who you were, and now you've caused us more trouble. The Tomassi Group has to wait until the investigation is over before they can focus on group affairs."

"It isn't going to happen again," Ella tried to explain and gave him an apologetic look.

"Oh...I'm sure it will from what I've heard about you. You know, I only wanted my son to marry you. I never expected him to fall in love."

Ella looked away. She did not want to hear those words at her wedding. She knew she had been wrong to jump to conclusions and leave the hotel. She already promised Angelo that she would not do it again. There was nothing left for her to say for herself. "Would you rather he didn't have feelings for me?"

"Did I say that?" Antonio's voice made her shiver, and she could say nothing at all. Now she knew where Angelo received his intimidating gaze. Her shoulders slouched as she prepared to hear more of his lecture. "My dear, you must have gone through hell to win over his cold heart. I never thought I'd see any woman get my son to fall in love with her. It seems that I was wrong, and you've earned the right to wear this. It's yours now to keep."

Antonio hooked a bracelet over her wrist. "This is a family heirloom. It will show that I approve of you as my son's wife. Do what he tells you from now on. That way, he can make clear decisions without worrying about you getting hurt. You both will have enough hard times ahead without adding to it. I know that if anyone can keep you safe, it's my Angelo."

Ella's mouth opened. That was the last thing she had expected from Antonio. She smiled as he gave her a hug and a kiss. Nina did the same and winked as they walked away to the dance floor. Nina was happy with him. She could tell that by the way Nina looked in his eyes. Ella was glad that they resolved the problems that they had in the past.

She continued to smile and watched Angelo weave through the guests and walk back to her. She hoped the love between her and Angelo would be as strong at his parents' age. She wanted to be able to look at Angelo and feel exactly the way she did now.

"I see my father approves of my wife," he said and lifted up her hand.

"I don't understand that. I thought your father wanted you to marry me."

"He always approved of the marriage, but he didn't know who you were. All he thought about was being able to merge our families and shutting Bonadio down."

"I was a business interest," she said and turned around. She wondered why they wanted to combine the family's interests anyway. Did they not have enough on their own? She was lucky with Angelo, but others had to marry a stranger as Nina did.

"Well, if you put it like that." He smiled and twisted her back to face him. She wrapped her arms around him and laid her head against his chest. "If it makes you feel any better, I would have married you anyway."

"But you said that you couldn't marry me."

"No, I said if I wanted to stick with the rules that I couldn't marry you." Angelo leaned forward; his firm body restrained her between him and the table. "Do you want to know a secret?" he asked.

"Yes." Her voice was hesitant as he moved his face closer to her ear.

"I bought your ring before I knew you were Gregorio's daughter."

"What?" she mumbled and looked at him. Tears pricked the corners of her eyes. "I don't know what to say."

"I think that should tell you exactly where I stand."

Her arms tightened around his waist; her hands rested on his back, feeling closer with the embrace. He was willing to risk his status with his group and his father for her. There was nothing more to doubt.

***

Ella had been quiet on the ride to the house. Angelo watched her sit on the bed, her dress gathering at her feet in a gorgeous display of the silky material. He wondered why she seemed sad when the reception went well.

"Are you upset that you're married now?" Ella continued to look at the floor. It bothered him that she did not answer him right away. He walked up to her and lifted her chin.

"No, I'm not upset," she answered and briefly looked up. "I couldn't be happier to have married you."

"Then why are you so quiet?"

Ella fidgeted with some of the material on her dress and then stopped. He knew she did that when she was nervous. "Do you have a lot of members in your group?" she asked.

"I have a lot," he said and hung his coat on a hanger in the closet. "I have a few thousand in all."

"How many are in my father's ranks?"

"Gregorio," Angelo thought aloud. He hoped that she would not want more information on her father than that. "More than me," he said. Her eyes closed. She had never had an interest in numbers, yet she was suddenly concerned. Was she worried after seeing some of his men at their wedding? "It's a little too late to be afraid of me, isn't it?"

"I'm not afraid," she mumbled. He knew she was lying. The worried look on her face gave away how she felt.

"Then why are you shaking?" He pointed to her trembling hands.

"I don't know." She thought for a moment. "I never thought about it before, but when I saw you with those men...that you're their boss...it became real to me."

"There's no reason to be afraid." Angelo started to unbutton his shirt. "You'll be fine if you listen to me. You'll be happier if you do."

"Do you like what you do? Do you like being in charge?" she continued with more questions.

"I never considered any other way of life," he answered. "I knew I was supposed to take over my father's position. I never questioned it."

"And you're put in dangerous situations a lot. Is your life always at risk?"

Confused with the interrogation, Angelo looked at her and wanted to end the conversation. "What's with you questioning me all of a sudden? You already know that I do what I have to do. This is my life. No questions asked. I don't want you to concern yourself about it. The group doesn't involve you."

"But they do," Ella argued. "You're always in danger and I'm worried about losing you."

"Ella, I'm not going to talk about this right now. Let it go. You were handed this life too. You don't have a choice either."

"Then what exactly am I allowed to do? I can't sit around and do nothing while I wait to see if you come home or not."

She looked helpless. For a moment, he considered all the wives that he made to wait at home, wondering if their husbands would return. He could understand Ella's frustration. He would not like being in her situation either.

"I can't answer that right now, but I have an idea. You will have to wait until tomorrow to hear about it. I haven't finalized it yet."

Ella nodded and then stood up. He gazed at her as she tried to unzip the back of her dress. She was beautiful, the most beautiful woman he had ever laid eyes on. Her difficulty with reaching the zipper made him smile. He watched her for a few seconds before slowly walking behind her.

"Let me help you with that," he said. His fingers grazed against her skin as he unzipped the zipper. Her small chills satisfied him. He slid the two ends apart and let the dress fall to her feet.

"I know how to take your attention off your worries," he breathed. Then one leg at a time, he slid off her white nylons. Ella hummed at his touch. He knew how to sway her mind and softly kissed the back of her neck.

"Most group wives have other thoughts on their minds after they get married," he whispered and tossed the bra from her breasts. "I would worry more about what I will do to you tonight than what somebody might do to me."

Ella shivered in hopeless surrender. All she needed to do was to focus on the pleasure he made her feel. The warmth of his body, the desire in his eyes…he made her feel what no other man could.

Chapter 49

The following morning, Angelo let Ella sleep in. He saw no point in waking her since it would be another long day today. He was trying to stay quiet. He closed his suitcase as gently as possible, but the latch made a loud popping sound when the suitcase's two ends met.

"Are you leaving?" Ella tossed the sheet to her feet. With her bare breasts and smooth hips to taunt him as she sat up, Angelo wished there was more time before the flight.

"Yes," he said. He started to smile with the frown on her face. When would she learn not to sulk with him? It nearly made it impossible for him to use self-control. "Do you think I'm going to leave you alone right after we got married?" He lifted up another suitcase from the floor and set it on the bed. "We have a honeymoon."

"Really?" Ella's eyes sparkled. Her eyes were another downfall for him. "Where are we going?" she asked and scooted to the edge of the bed with no sign of just waking up. She was like a child sometimes. Anything out of the normal routine excited her.

"I wanted to keep it a surprise, but you'll know as soon as we step on the plane. We're flying to Port Canaveral and staying on the Sea Empress. We have about an hour before we leave. Why don't you take a shower and then you can pack."

"You're taking me on a cruise?" Ella beamed. If she were more excited, he would be able to see her thoughts dance around her head. She jumped off the bed. He thought she was going to walk past him, but she threw her arms around him and kissed his cheek. "Thank you so much for taking me."

He shook his head as she walked away. He was right about the cruise. When he thought about where to take her, he remembered the picture of a ship on her wall in Key Biscayne. He looked forward to spending time with her there. He also had something important to ask her, too.

**

His private jet was high in the air. Ella sat on the cushioned recliner next to the window and rested her head against his chest. He was quiet. He gazed out of the window at the clouds whisking by and simply enjoyed sitting next to her. His fingers slid up and down her arm, feeling the warmth of her skin.

"Excuse me, Mr. Tomassi. Would you both like a drink?" an attendant interrupted.

Angelo was enjoying the silence. His neck stiffened with the disturbance but then relaxed as he thought about Ella. Maybe she wanted a drink. "Do you want anything?" he asked. She never looked away from the window and shook her head, so Angelo briefly glanced at the attendant. "We won't need anything for the rest of the flight." The attendant nodded and walked away.

Angelo pulled the lever on the chair and reclined back; then he pulled the lever on Ella's and brought her down with him. He enjoyed having her next to him and laid his hand on her lap, twisting in his seat to face her.

"I've never travelled for pleasure. This is new for me," he said. His tone was distant with the reflection on his life.

Ella looked from the window and over at him. Except for Key Biscayne, Gregorio never let her do anything out of the normal. She had been a lonely child, maybe lonelier than he was.

"Will you enjoy yourself?" she asked. He stared at her. Her expression seemed worried by his answer, but Angelo slid his arm behind the back of her neck and brought her face closer to him. He was satisfied with this view. It was much better than looking out of the window at the clouds.

"I wanted to spend time with you." He assured and gave her a light, gentle kiss. "My father…" He paused in thought for a second. "He was a good man. He gave us what we needed, but after I turned twelve, our relationship changed. That's when my training started. I always knew I was supposed to take over his role. It wasn't a huge shock, but my life was a lot different from then on. I saw people differently than before. I didn't make friends. There was no point. I was born in a life they wouldn't understand. My family went on vacations all the time, but it wasn't real. My father took care of business during the trips. He never left me out of his meetings either. By the time I was seventeen, I pretty much handled all group decisions."

"That's why you're so serious all of the time. All business and no play will make you like that."

Angelo chuckled. "That was true; then I met you. I thought about you constantly. You are my play."

Ella's mouth opened with slight surprise but how surprised could she be? Ella knew what he was like. She could have left him in the beginning, yet she stayed.

"How long will we be on the cruise?" she asked and slid her arms around his neck, pressing her body into his.

"A few days," he answered and laced his fingers through her hair. "Then we wait for the investigation to close so that I can move forward with Bonadio."

He ignored the steps he heard around the plane and blocked them both with the back of his dark suit. He kissed her, stifling her surprised squeak with his tongue as he indulged. She did not resist. Instead, her hands crept to his face. Her fingers mimicked the movements of his jaw. Her lips willingly accepted the assault to her mouth.

He liked to show her affection. Ella basked in the attention. He wanted to go further. He kept envisioning her skirt to her waist, her panties off and her sitting on top. It was dangerous to think that way on a plane. Angelo had to pull away before his thoughts became the attendant's next show. He smiled to himself. He did not actually care who saw, but he knew Ella would.

"You see what you do to me?" Angelo forced himself to breathe away his untimely lust. He pulled away from her body, but his arm remained firmly around her back. "That's all right. We'll finish this later."

He found the blush on her cheeks enticing. She was clearly thinking the same. Ella's eyes looked from him to his belt and then at the wall. Her frenzy was his amusement.

"We are about to land, sir." The attendant approached again. It was as if she had waited for them to compose themselves before letting them know. He looked forward to the few days with Ella where they would not be disturbed.

***

As they stepped out of the door to the plane, the wind whipped Ella's hair to her face. With commercial airliners parked at their respective gates, Angelo grabbed Ella's arm, determined not to lose her down the stairs. Jim and Ray also exited the plane behind them—his extra eyes. Rafa wanted to stay in Miami and handle matters at home.

A driver waved to Angelo and waited for them on the ground next to a limousine. Ella stepped in first with Angelo behind. Before he closed the door, he looked up at Jim for a second. "You'll get there before I do. Have those packets that Rafa gave you ready. We'll see you shortly."

"What packets?" Ella asked with disappointment when he pulled her to the side of his body.

"I hadn't planned to do anything on this trip, but since we're here, Rafa thought I should talk to Miguel about an investment. This is one of the ships he owns. It'll only take a few minutes."

Frowning, Ella looked away and stayed quiet on the ride to the port. When they stopped, two employees met them as they pulled in to unload. With two suitcases and the same number of carry-ons, the man who unloaded left within a minute and another led them both up the ramp. They were able to bypass the long check-in lines and followed the attendant directly to the ship. There were benefits to reserving a suite.

Ella stopped at the top. The ship had 14 decks and 2,500 rooms. The Sea Empress defined its name. She stared in amazement at the interior. Angelo was also impressed. Winding staircases stood in front. He could see the ocean through the glasslike lobby floor. The pink tinted lighting of the chandeliers fused with the blue of the ocean underneath, creating a shade of violet. Whoever pulled off the idea on such a large ship must have been a genius.

Ella started to walk again when Angelo gently seized her arm. He was not going to lose her on this large of a ship. Her heels echoed as they walked through the lobby and back out onto the deck. They were some of the first guests to arrive. That was the way he planned it. Angelo wanted a few minutes to enjoy her company before the waves of other passengers came aboard.

Ten minutes passed before he stopped again. Angelo leaned against the rail and looked down at the opposite side of the ocean from where the anxious passengers were lined. "Will this do for you?" he asked and looked over at Ella.

"It's unbelievable," she said, sliding her arms around his waist from behind, "but I would've been happy anywhere with you."

Angelo grinned. She could not see his smile but could feel his arms clamp over hers. She relaxed him. He felt at ease with her embrace around his waist. "Well, aren't you the perfect wife for me," he said. The happiness she brought to his life trumped any trouble she might have caused. He could not think of a single other woman who would have accepted him for who he was.

"This ship has several performances you might like. They have musicals, ballets, stage shows, comedies…" He paused. "I'm not sure how I feel about the opera. If you want to go, I will." His words trailed off making her laugh. Her laugh surprised him, until he considered why she had laughed. She might ask to see the opera to get on his nerves.

"What's funny?" Angelo pulled her around in front of him, his palms holding her cheeks as she tried to subdue the smile on her face.

"No, nothing at all," she said and smiled anyway.

"You can swim, can't you?" He looked down at the water and then back at her.

"Really? You're going to throw me overboard?" She smirked with her question.

He glanced sideways. With a jolt of her hand, he began walking again. "Our room won't be ready for a couple of more hours, so we might as well eat while we wait."

"How about that lounge?" Ella pointed to a sign that said Jasmina's.

Angelo did not answer; he simply led her where she wanted to go. The place was a quiet dance hall with small round tables. The walnut finish of the furniture absorbed the dull lighting and made the place seem dark. Soft music equaled the atmosphere. Angelo could relax here.

"I like it," he said and waited for a hostess to greet them.

"Good afternoon. Two today?" she asked.

"Yes." Angelo nodded. "I'd like a table by the stage." He would not have usually asked for one so close to the dance floor, but they were one of two couples in the lounge for now. After they ordered, he took out his phone and turned it on. He would get the quick exchange out of the way so Ella would not dread it happening. "It's me," he said. "I need you to track down Miguel and bring those packets to the lounge named Jasmina's. It's on the lobby floor and out on the deck. I'm here now."

When he ended his call, Ella was fidgeting in her purse, most likely a cover to hide her displeasure over the business he did. He knew how it looked to her. He watched his mother have that same look when his father left for business. This was not the same as that. It was an exchange of convenience and not the reason he brought her here.

"Ella?" he called. She did not acknowledge her name so he reached over and snapped the two ends of her purse shut. That gained her attention. "This will be the only time I talk to anyone here, all right?" She sighed and started to open her mouth when Jim and Ray walked to the table. Ella stared at them as though they were strangers. Angelo realized that he never formally introduced them. She probably still labeled them as cheaters during the poker match.

"Ella, these are two of my best men. They're brothers. Diego and Raimundo, but we call them Jim and Ray."

Jim was taller than Ray, but they both had the same brown eyes and matching short hair combed back. Jim also had a birthmark on his right temple and some hair on his chin while Ray remained clean-shaven without any distinguishing marks. The brothers nodded at her in passing; then Jim handed Angelo two large brown packets.

"Did you find Miguel?" he asked.

"Yes," Jim said with an unusually deep voice. "Miguel was taking care of something but will be here in ten minutes."

Angelo touched his chin and looked at the envelopes. "That's all I need for now, but I want you to stay close." As they left, Angelo peeled the rubber band off one of the envelopes and pulled out two stacks of papers. He set one down and skimmed through the second. Rafa did his research when typing the documents. He did as well as a lawyer would.

When Angelo was on the third to the last page, two men with bronzed complexions approached. Angelo stood to acknowledge one of them and extended his hand. "It's good to see you again, Miguel," he said.

"You too, Angelo." Miguel shook but did not sit; he rubbed the back of his head, chafing his fingers against his short brown hair. "Is it safe to talk?" He looked toward Ella and crossed his arms. Angelo knew Miguel well. He trusted almost no one outside of family.

"This is my wife. It's not public domain and needs to stay that way." Angelo told him the truth as a show of faith.

Miguel slowly nodded. He stared at Ella and then at him. He understood what the discloser of their marriage was intended to do— gain trust. "It doesn't do anything for me to tell your business," he said and sat down while leaving the other man to stand. "I'm told you're interested in investing in my father's cruise lines. Why?"

Angelo finished looking through the last three sheets and set them in front of Miguel. "Because I'm impressed. Glass floors were on smaller ships until now. That's one reason I'm interested."

"And..." said Miguel. Being a smart man, he knew there was another reason. Angelo could not leave it at that.

"And I also want more people I can count on—more people on my side. Since you're taking over for your father soon, I think it would be good for both of us."

Miguel picked up the paperwork and skimmed the first page. "Is this the proposal?"

"Yes," Angelo said and sipped on his wine as Miguel flipped to the second page.

"A half billion?" Miguel glanced at Angelo and back down at the sheet. Neither said anything else until Miguel stacked the sheets back together and tucked them under his arm. "I'll have an answer for you by the end of the trip." Miguel stood and walked away without saying goodbye.

Angelo did not expect Miguel to give an answer right then. He felt better about investing in someone who did not jump at the first lump sum of money thrown their way. He liked his connections to think before making a decision.

Angelo stood and held out his hand to Ella. "I'm finished now. Dance with me while we wait for our food?" Looking at him as if someone had taken over his body, she seemed taken by his question. He found her stricken expression insulting. "You don't want to dance with me?" he asked and started to sit back down.

"No, I do." She smiled and pushed out her chair. He held out his hand to her again. This time, she accepted without any hesitation at all. He guessed she did not want to miss the rare opportunity to dance with him.

The music played a soft tune. Angelo found it low and pleasing, perfect to enjoy a slow dance with her. He loved the way her hands locked around his neck—how her cheek lay against his chest. It almost made him forget about the life.

"I have something for you," he whispered as they moved.

"You do?" She leaned away from his body to look at him.

He brushed the hair away from her face and pulled her head back to his chest. She would have to wonder about the gift until later that day. "I'll show you in the room when we can check in," he said. "It has something to do with what you asked me last night."

Chapter 50

Ella thought they were going to the suite, but they walked to the front of the ship and through a large set of doors. Pictures of musicians hung beside the ticket counter. Advertisements for a symphony decorated the walls. If she had not heard him play the piano, she may have been surprised he enjoyed instrumental music. She was happy they were away from the group.

The people who gathered in the amphitheater were walking and shuffling to their seats, paying no attention to who might be walking behind them. They bumped her and Angelo several times before Angelo entered another door with a separate set of stairs. It was quiet there. A red velvet carpet led to a private balcony on top. Inside was a single curved sofa large enough to fit four. Workers closed a curtain behind them as soon as they walked out.

Lights shined from below. Ella gazed from the golden rail that protected her from the long drop down. The stage in front looked amazing from so high in the air. She glanced back at Angelo who leaned forward, wrapping his hand around her arm.

"Come sit with me. They're about to turn off the lights."

Twenty minutes in, Angelo closed his eyes while Ella watched with fascination as the conductor directed the orchestra's sections including violins, harps and flutes. The music moved her, mesmerizing her to the rhythm of the melody and gaining all her concentration. The musicians' attire charmed her with their matching patterns and varied colors. Their passion seemed to compel their fingers to move. They deserved every bit of applause when time came for intermission and Ella rose to the rail to clap.

She began aimlessly watching the guests start for the exits, most likely wanting to purchase mementos of the performance or refreshments. Then something caught her eye from a lower balcony diagonal from where she stood. She blinked. She recognized one of the men as Miguel but who was the other man behind him? She could not make out the man's face but did see a shiny reflection within the man's hand as he pointed at Miguel's neck.

"Angelo," she whispered while whipping around to see him still comfortable where he sat.

"What is it?" He was not going to like what she saw. He did not expect any trouble on the ship, but her worried expression caused him to lean forward and look where she gazed. "Shit," he mumbled and pulled a gun from his boot, his shoulders becoming stiff. "We can't get away from it, can we?" He stood and pushed the curtain open.

"Wait." She thought for a moment. "They're going to hear you open their curtain. Let me shoot that man from here when he turns to see who you are."

With the gun in hand, Angelo placed his fingers around his head and considered her idea. She would be at little risk since Miguel's trouble had nothing to do with them. "Can you shoot from this distance?" Still surprised over the trouble, she nodded, not taking her eyes off Miguel. "All right, shoot the arm that holds the gun as soon as he turns around. I'm not getting involved in killing someone else's problem."

Angelo disappeared and Ella barely breathed, waiting patiently for the man to turn around at Angelo. She crouched and watched the balcony through the scope, now seeing that the man who held the gun was the same who followed Miguel to their table at the lounge. It took a minute. As Angelo flung the curtain open, Ella let the shot fire, lodging a bullet into the bicep of the man who whirled around to the intruder. His gun instantly fell; within a second, Miguel retrieved it and held it to his head.

"How dare you turn against me," he said and started to pull the trigger. "You were like my brother and now you will own the sea like you wanted." Miguel pulled the trigger and left the man's body to fall to the floor. With his eyes closed, Miguel sought pardon from the unknown. Afterward, he looked at Angelo and shook his head.

"I won't talk about specifics but...thank you." He breathed in deep.

Angelo did not want to hear details so he was thankful that Miguel did not volunteer any. "Don't thank me. My wife made the shot. All I did was take his attention off you." He pointed to a higher balcony across the large theater.

"A woman? You chanced my life on the skills of a woman?" Angelo said nothing in response, instead daring Miguel to speak further about the woman who saved his life. "Fuck. She must be very good."

"Very…one of the best." Angelo stared in the distance, at the rail that obscured her body. "There's no woman like her." He started to turn away and leave Miguel when Miguel spoke again.

"About that proposal earlier…"

"Yes?" Angelo stayed to hear what he had to say.

"Consider your offer accepted as a show of gratitude for my life."

Angelo nodded and shook the hand Miguel held out to him. That shake was a sign of more than an agreement. It was a show of trust. Now that Miguel knew where he stood, communication between them should be smooth.

***

The show ended with their suite cleaned and stocked. Angelo fell to the recliner with a deep sigh and closed his eyes. Some quiet time together should relax them after what happened with Miguel, but Angelo was holding his head with his hand, showing no sign of letting it go. What could she do to make him feel better? He looked like he was having a battle with his thoughts.

"Are you all right?" she asked, trying to open him up to conversation.

Angelo roughly grabbed her hand and pulled her on top of him. His arms folded around her waist in a restrictive embrace. His change of mood was drastic. She could not figure it out.

"I'm okay," he said and gave no other answer to her question.

"Okay." She returned his tight hug, knowing he was not all right. What more could she offer? Maybe he would feel comforted in her arms. She wanted to give him that much.

Angelo took another deep breath and removed one of his arms from around her as he reached inside his coat. "This is for you," he said. It was one of the two manila envelopes. Angelo leaned forward and stood, taking her with him. He motioned her to the dining table and took the envelope back out of her hands. He slid off the rubber band and took out a stack of papers, laying them in front of her.

"It needs some work, but I thought you might like to have it. I have a team who will listen to your ideas and do what you want with the place."

"The Sandy Shores," she read. Ella looked through the first page, quietly turning to the second and third. Then she looked at Angelo. He had been so protective that she never thought he would give her that freedom. He must have thought a lot about the idea. She did not know what to say.

"Thank you." She looked down at the table and put the sheets back in the envelope. "I really needed this."

"There's something else," he said, pausing to rest his arms on the table and look at her. "How am I supposed to protect you and anyone else who comes along if you're not with me? I'm not used to worrying like that."

"I know you want a family, Angelo," Ella looked away, "but I don't want my child being lonely. I don't want to lock my child up all day. I had that life. You had that life." She shook her head and looked down.

"I'm trying, Ella. I'm trying to give you as normal as I can, but look at what happened earlier with Miguel...and he trusted that man. That could've been us. We aren't ever going to be able to go out without a gun. We won't ever go to the park like other families. We can't go to the grocery store. We have to watch and see who gets out of the car next to us. We have to be aware of everything around us always."

Ella scratched her head and looked at him. Angelo did not skirt around the truth. She thought about having a baby. The dangers around them still had nothing to do with whether or not the child would be lonely. "I know about the dangers," she said. "That's not what concerns me the most. I don't want you being so caught up with the group that you miss your child's first steps...or first words. It's about that, Angelo. I don't have to have perfectly normal, but I'm not raising my child alone."

"Children," he corrected. She blinked at his remark. If she had not been serious, she might have smiled at him. "I'm going to turn on the Jacuzzi; you are welcomed to join me if you'd like." Angelo stood and walked around the table to her. He gently laid his hand over her cheek. His brown eyes looked the most relaxed and sincere that she had seen all afternoon. "I'm not leaving you alone to raise our children, so you can stop taking the pill."

She believed him. He was not his father and he was not hers. Angelo wanted a family that he could enjoy. He would invest his time into their family no matter what. She knew he would. He deserved to become a father since that was what he always wanted.

She scooted out of her chair and started with the buttons on her blouse, followed by the zipper on her skirt. Then she walked to the back of the suite where she heard the jets of the Jacuzzi. Angelo did not hear her come in. He was lying down in the tub with his eyes shut. He looked at peace with himself. The water bubbled around him and shined off his torso in a gorgeous show of his muscles. She could not resist him and that view. Ella secured her hair on top and then stepped into the front of the tub. She lowered her body around his. Her legs slid around his hips with ease as she rested her hands on his chest.

"Are you sure a baby is what you want?" She wanted to hear his answer again.

Angelo looked directly in her eyes and did not hesitate with his response. "Yes, I want a baby. Many of them. I have for years."

Ella moved her wet fingers through his dry hair and gently squeezed the strands. "I've already stopped using the pill," she said. "I thought about starting them again after everything that happened, but I know you will make a great father."

"You did that for me?"

Ella nodded slowly and leaned against his chest. "You have everything else, Angelo. The only thing I can give you is a family. You are important to me. I love you."

Angelo closed his eyes again and was silent as he thought about what she had said.

"Then let me show you how important you are to me," he whispered and pressed his lips against hers, pulling her flush against his skin.

Chapter 51

With the honeymoon behind him, Angelo set up a meeting in the conference room at the hotel. All the seats were taken around him with Sammy and Thomas standing behind. Ian and Vin, a couple of new members, leaned against the wall with quiet anticipation.

"Jim," Angelo started. "You and Ray get a group together. Show Ian and Vin what we're about. Pick ten men and bring them to the warehouse tomorrow. Brett, you take Sammy—" He stopped when Ella walked into the room. He had been waiting for her. All of his men instantly looked at the door, startling her, but Angelo directed her attention to him. He patted the seat beside him and motioned for her to sit.

"Brett," he said again. "You take Sammy and Thomas and also bring ten men to the warehouse—bring good long-distance shots. We need experts on this one."

"Angelo," said Ella in thought. He knew she was a good shot. He had no doubt about it, but there was no way he was bringing her to Orlando and into Gregorio's crooked ranks. They would do far worse to her than shoot her if they caught her. When Ella started to look at him, he flat shut her down. "The answer is no," he whispered. "I know you're good—probably better than some of my men—but no. Go get me some coffee while I finish this meeting?"

Ella did not like the dismissal and huffed off the sofa while his men talked among themselves, discussing whom they would bring to the warehouse. When she returned, she held out his coffee. "There's no reason for me to be here," she whispered. "I don't know why you wanted me to come."

"Then go if that's what you want." He gave her the choice but it would have been better if she stayed. If she thought about it, her presence took the edge off the dangerous matters that he and his men faced. It lessened the tense air of the atmosphere. If she had looked past trying to prove herself, she would have realized that they needed her in a much different way. Everything they planned to do would protect her too.

"I'll see you later then," she said.

"Not if you leave, you won't." Ella looked at him for a second. She started to open her mouth to say something else. Nothing came out. With complete disregard for his words, Ella simply walked out.

Without missing a beat with her disrespect, Angelo looked back at his men. "We'll meet outside the warehouse tomorrow morning at ten. Don't be late." He then waved them out of the room.

"You should tell her how to act," Rafa said as Angelo shook his head, letting his contempt for her show. "Right now, I don't think she understands."

Angelo looked at the door, irritated that Rafa was still there. "I thought I told you to leave."

Rafa walked around the sofa and sat down cross-armed in front of him. He did not follow instructions either. "Why do you let everything she does get to you? She doesn't know how all of this works yet."

"Tell me what I don't know"—he huffed, matching Rafa's position by crossing his own arms—"but I shouldn't have to spell out every damn thing."

Rafa grinned. "She's too close to the source to be logical. That's what happens when the heart is involved."

"How would you know?" Angelo scoffed. "Since when has your heart been involved in any of your decisions?"

Rafa looked away. Angelo could not pin the look in his eyes, but it looked like he remembered something from his past. Then his usual expression returned. "I became heartless when I met you," he countered.

"I'm not in the mood," Angelo said. "Unless you have something useful to say, then leave." Angelo stood and straightened out his coat.

"All you need to do is talk to her. Is that really so hard for you?"

Angelo could not help how he felt. He was willing to risk it all. Would she never give him the respect he deserved? He was trying to see it from her standpoint. She wanted to feel important, but she was important in other ways.

He could not bring her to his meetings again. That was his fault. He needed to get that restaurant finished so she could occupy her time elsewhere. That was his answer to the problem.

Chapter 52

Ella had searched for Angelo the last half hour. He might have been upset with her, but she did not want him in some other woman's bed either. She had checked the banquet hall and both conference rooms. There was no sign of him there. The casino was the last place for her to check. The bouncer did not hassle her this time. He also seemed apologetic for their last encounter. This was the second time that she went to the casino to look for someone. One day, maybe she would get to enjoy the games instead.

As she walked around, she found Angelo sitting at a table behind the bar. It was dark there. The ceiling above him had no lights. Only the flashing lights around her reflected in the small corner space.

There were also two women sitting with him. One had dark curly hair and wore a blue outfit. She leaned onto the table, squeezing her breasts out of her low-cut top. The other had short blond hair and wore a tight black dress. She did not make moves on Angelo but was guilty by association.

Ella walked around the bar and watched. From where she stood, she could hear the women talk. She hated their voices but wanted to hear what they said. She also wanted to know how Angelo would react.

"So is it true?" the woman wearing blue asked. "Do you really have a girlfriend now?"

Ella was happy that Angelo seemed annoyed. He was quiet and did not answer right away. It looked as though he wanted people to leave him alone. No wonder Rafa was not with him.

"Yes, I'm with someone," he said.

"Are you really taken, though?"

Angelo looked up. The question did not seem to surprise him. Ella worried about the sudden attention he gave to the woman. Maybe she really could convince him to go with her.

Instead of replying, Angelo lit up a cigarette and inhaled. He still looked at the woman with dark hair. He could not help it with her breasts on display. When he exhaled, the woman touched his arm and whispered something that Ella could not hear. Ella immediately turned around.

"Do you want a drink?" the bartender asked her.

"Give me a glass of water," she said. She was not in the mood to drink. It would make her act against the women and cause a scene.

"Hello there." A man walked up to her and placed his hand on the curve of her waist. Ella picked up her glass of water and stepped away from the man. He was taller with black hair and a business suit. She looked at the black chain around his neck as he lifted the teardrop pendant around hers. Ella pushed his hand away.

"You shouldn't assume that you can touch a woman because she stands alone at the bar," she said.

"Really," the man replied. "I would say that a beautiful woman who stands alone at a bar shouldn't be surprised when a man walks up to her."

"I'm with someone," she said and looked away.

"And they left you alone?" The man took a step closer, inching his hand to her necklace again.

"I am definitely not alone...ever." Ella looked around the bar for help but saw another man staring at her too. The man next to her knew this, but he saw her first. When he started to touch her hand, Rafa walked beside her and shoved it away. Then he grabbed Ella's arm and took a step back.

"I take it that you don't know this is Tomassi's girl. He's sitting right over there." The man looked at Angelo, his face growing pale with the realization. He did not bother to grab his drink and left as though he was never there.

"Love." Ella reasoned his endearments were more like the ones she would expect from an older brother instead of an actual show of interest. "Those women sat down at the same time you came in."

Ella glanced back at them. "Those women are better company than me or he would have made them leave."

"Sweetheart, those women hold nothing on you. You're the only woman who Angelo wants to sit with him."

"He's mad at me. I shouldn't be here."

"What do you expect? He's trying to keep you alive and you walked out on him."

"Why would I stay? He didn't need me there. All I was good for was getting him coffee."

"Do you really think that was all he wanted you there for?" Rafa asked. "Maybe he needed your support before going to risk his life in this war."

"I told him I was leaving. It's not as though I just walked out."

"It was a matter of respect, Ella. You should have stayed. You can't walk out like that on him." Rafa let go of her arm and held his other hand to Angelo. "Go show those women that he's taken. Even if he's mad, he still wants you. Then maybe I can stop watching out for him and go to bed."

Ella looked at Angelo and back at Rafa. He nodded at her to go. She was almost to the table when Angelo spoke to the dark-haired woman. "You're wasting your time with me."

The woman's voice grew more flirtatious. "Then what's it going to take to convince you?" She ran one finger over the sleeve of his jacket as Ella stood next to the table and looked at her.

"He's taken," she said and sat down on his lap. As intimidated as the women made her feel, Ella would not let them think they had a chance for long. Ella then looked at Angelo, a hint of shame on her face.

"I thought I told you I didn't want to see you," he breathed on her ear, not bothering to push her away. Maybe Rafa was right. She slid her nails against the skin behind the two open buttons of his shirt. She liked that he let her touch him like that. She also wanted the two women to know where she stood in Angelo's life.

"I'm sorry I walked out on you earlier. Please come back to the room with me."

"Why didn't you think I needed you there? Don't I have my reasons?" he asked. He pulled out another cigarette but put it back again. Maybe he thought better than to smoke with her there.

Ella turned around to see if the women had left. Why were they still there? She did not appreciate their disrespect and smiled at them. It was not meant to be friendly. They needed another example of who she was. She wrapped her hand around Angelo's neck and gave him a deep, intimate kiss. She enjoyed the movements of his mouth when he kissed her back. Her eyes stayed shut even after he pulled away.

"Leanne, isn't it?" he asked the brunette.

"You know her name." Ella frowned.

"Ella," he whispered in her ear. "Everyone knows her name, sweetheart. You have nothing to worry about."

"Of course he knows my name, and we were in the middle of a conversation."

"What conversation?" Ella looked at her and glared.

"Ella," Angelo said and made her look at him again. "Stop, I will take care of them."

"Fine." She closed her mouth as he pointed at the women.

"Both of you...leave."

The women glared at her but understood the dismissal. They immediately stood up and left.

"That's it?" she asked. "That's all you had to do to make them leave?"

"Nobody argues with me. You should know that."

"Then why—" She did not finish.

"To teach you a lesson," he said. "I saw you walk in the casino."

Angelo's fingers trailed across her lips, caressing her cheeks and then tightening around the back of her head. His breath was hot against her face. It was hard to catch her breath when he kissed her so deliberately.

"I wasn't the only one getting attention tonight. Every man in this place noticed you walk in the room." Angelo pulled her against his body, kissing her more intensely than before. She felt lightheaded from the kiss.

"Angelo," she breathed.

"Are you afraid to kiss me in public?" he whispered back. The bulge in his pants hardened with every second that passed. She started to enjoy the way he felt underneath and pushed harder where she sat. He only had to unzip his zipper to relieve his urge; her skirt would cover the rest. Nobody would ever know that more than kissing was going on at that dark table.

"I'm going to bed." Rafa slumped to a chair and interrupted them. "Before you both make a scene, I would suggest that you do the same."

Angelo glanced at him out of the corner of his eye. "We were kissing."

"It wouldn't have taken much for that to go in a different direction."

"Go to bed, Rafa." Angelo waved him away and looked at her. "I guess I should take his advice and take you to bed." He looked at Ella and slightly grinned. "But it will have nothing to do with going to sleep."

Chapter 53

Ella rolled over and looked at the time. She groaned. She felt like her head had just hit the pillow. Her body ached from her night with Angelo, but she scooted off the bed before she could fall back to sleep. It was already half past eight and Angelo needed to be at the warehouse by ten. He was in the shower. She was surprised to see him not ready and dressed. Angelo was always dressed before she woke up.

Ella tapped lightly on the shower with the door instantly sliding open. She shivered from the steam that the hot water made, or was it Angelo's slickened body that stunned her. She should have been used to seeing him naked by now, but he always left her breathless.

"You left the door open, so I figured I would get in with you." Angelo did not seem to mind. He moved out of the way so she could step inside.

As soon as she did, his arms wrapped around her breasts and pulled the back of her head to his chest. "You don't have to ask to shower with me. I won't tell you no," he said and started to lather her arms.

Ella rinsed and looked at her left hand. Her bare finger made her sad. "I wish I could wear my rings," she said. She closed her eyes and started daydreaming of a day when everyone would know they were married.

Angelo gently kissed her forehead and stepped out on the mat. "You will be able to wear them soon," he said and grabbed a towel.

Ella had finished her shower and was drying off her legs when Angelo walked back through the door. "I want to eat breakfast with you before I take you home, since I won't see you until tonight. Rafa and Brett are going to eat with us too."

Ella nodded and wrapped the towel around her waist. She started to walk to the closet when Angelo took out a soft blue dress. "Wear this for me. I like the way it brings out your eyes."

Ella smiled. She did not know that Angelo paid any attention to her clothes. She started to pull the dress over her head, but Angelo's hands touched the sides of her body. His fingers stroked her skin up and then down again. She shivered with the cool touch of his hands.

"I guess it'll have to wait," he sighed, "or we won't have enough time to eat." Ella blushed. After last night, she would think he wanted a break. For being as busy as he was, Angelo had a lot of energy.

On the main floor, Angelo left Ella standing alone while he spoke to the attendants at the front counter. Tall plants surrounded a massive fountain in the center of the lobby. The sound of the falling water absorbed all other noises. Ella enjoyed the tranquil scenery.

As soon as she started to sit down, a group of women were walking past her but stopped instead. She thought they were going to ask her directions or something else like that. They confused her when they stared at her and said nothing at all.

"You were the woman with Mr. Tomassi last night."

Ella looked at the woman with dark curly hair, the same that was talking to Angelo the night before. She thought about it a moment. This exchange would not be good.

"I would be embarrassed to show my face after last night."

"Zero self-respect."

"What?" Ella asked exasperated and attempted to walk away. They were not worth her time.

"Why are you here anyway? Did Mr. Tomassi throw you out."

"She's waiting for a ride," said another.

"Excuse me? Can't you see I'm trying to leave?" One of the women had grabbed her arm. With everything going on in her life, she hardly wanted to take out time to counter the accusations. She looked at the counter for Angelo, but he was not there anymore. "Get away from me," Ella said.

She was trying to ignore them. She started to turn away again when one of them yanked the hair tie holding her hair in place. Ella looked down as her hair fell around her face. Then she spun back around to face the women.

"If you touch me again—" she started. Ella did not finish her sentence and did not want to cause a scene when the same woman pushed her.

"What are you going to do?" The woman yanked her purse off her shoulder, scattering the contents across the floor. Ella looked at her strewn belongings. That was all she could take. Ella yanked out her gun and pointed it at them.

"I told you to leave me alone. You should have listened to me. You have no idea who I am."

"What the hell is going on here?" Angelo walked up behind her and looked at the four women standing around.

"This is not my fault." Ella said in defense. "I tried to walk away and gave them plenty of chances to leave me alone, but they wouldn't stop."

"Pick up her stuff," Angelo ordered and pointed to her broken purse. He crossed his arms and waited while Ella kept pointing her gun. She was not giving them the opportunity to run. She did not want Angelo any more upset than he was.

"What happened?" Rafa asked as soon as he walked up to them. The women looked at him, seeming remorseful for their actions. It was too late now. They had made the choice. "These women are regulars at the casino. Is this because of Ella?" he asked.

"They probably all came together last night," Ella mumbled and tried to fix the strap on her purse.

Rafa shook his head. "That's the problem with regulars. They think they can get away with whatever they want."

When Brett walked up, Angelo finally spoke. "Take them to the conference room. Make sure they understand." Ella did not know what they were going to say to them. Maybe knowing less was better.

Grinning at the women, the moment was happy for Brett. "That wasn't very smart to attack the daughter of a mob boss and the wife of another."

"Wife?" One of the women groaned.

"Yep...guess we'll have twice the fun with you." Brett's cheerful voice caused a look of sorrow on their faces. He gestured them to follow with a tilt of his head.

"You can't help but attract attention, can you?" Angelo draped an arm around her shoulder as they walked into the restaurant.

"I think it has more to do with the clientele of your hotel," she countered.

"Well, we'll have to eat fast now." They sat down at his usual table. "Those women cost us ten minutes of our time."

After being served, Ella took a bite of her food as she and Angelo talked about what they still needed for the Sandy Shores. The renovations on the restaurant would not take much longer. They removed the old tables and completed the walls. Once the floor tiles were complete, it would be ready for furniture and appliances.

"No, I think I want to keep the name," she said. "I know it had a bad reputation, but if we invited the right people on opening night, I think they would see how much it changed."

"The Sandy Shores," Angelo said and looked up. "If you want to keep the name, it doesn't bother me. It's an appropriate name for the area, especially since it's on the beach."

"How long do you think until it can open?" she asked.

Angelo shrugged and looked away. He had not given her an estimated date yet. She thought he was deliberately avoiding the question.

"I think it will take a week to move everything in and make it ready for opening. You will still have to hire employees and taste the menu first. It could take another three weeks, maybe a month.

Ella thought about it. It took Angelo around eight weeks to remodel a hotel into a club. She felt like he was delaying the progress of the restaurant. It was only a one-story building.

"All right," she said. "Will you let me know when the floors are done?"

"I will let you know." Angelo pushed his plate to the middle of the table. "Do you want more coffee before we leave?"

Ella smiled at his consideration. "No, thank you. I think I'm finished for now."

Chapter 54

Angelo held Ella's hand and led her out of the hotel after they ate. Now it was after nine and he had barely enough time to take her home and make it to the warehouse. While he quickly walked down the steps to valet, Ella stopped in the middle of the steps to admire his beautiful car. His body jerked with her sudden stop, and he looked back quickly to see if there was an issue. Then he huffed. He must have seen that his Mercedes had captured her attention.

"No way," he said and pulled her down the steps.

"Just once," she pleaded. "Your car is begging me to sit behind the wheel."

"The answer is still no," he said flatly and opened the passenger door."

"Once," Ella smiled, "and I'll never ask again." She did not expect him to change his mind, but her smile was the only chance she had with getting her way.

Angelo clenched his jaw and ran his hand through his hair. "Fine—once, if it will shut you up."

Ella smiled wide as she stepped through the driver's side door. She had never expected him to relinquish his seat. After they both fastened their seatbelts, Ella looked at him and gave him a devilish smirk. It was like the moment when she handcuffed him to the bed.

"Watch it, little girl," he said and crossed his arms. "I'm on a schedule here. Let's go."

Ella glared at him for calling her that name again and slightly pressed the gas, sending the car forward. "I don't like your nickname for me, Mr. Tomassi." She frowned. Then she pressed the brakes without warning. "Sorry," she said, faking the apology.

Angelo scowled at her and snapped, "You need to switch places with me—now."

"Too late," she said. Ella pressed the gas again and drove onto the busy main street. "Where to, Mr. Tomassi?" she asked but did not dare look at Angelo's face. She fully understood his irritation but knew he could not force her from the driver's seat now.

"You already know how to get home."

Ella entered the freeway and looked at the radio, thinking some music would make him forget what she had done. "Do you ever listen to the radio?"

"The radio," he huffed. "I wouldn't be worried about the radio if I were you. I'd be worried about how you pissed me off and what I will do to you later."

"You can't be that mad—" Ella caught something strange in the mirror on the driver's side door. The car behind them drove too close, blocking their headlights from her sight. Ella was about to change lanes and let them pass when the Mercedes jolted forward and jerked.

"What the hell was that?" Angelo looked back and saw a white Excursion before it slammed into them again. "Ella!" he shouted. "Step on it!"

Her foot already stomped the gas pedal to the floor. At that speed, she nearly missed the exit and suddenly veered right. The car hopped over the small bumps in the markings on the road. She barely managed to straighten it out.

"Go through the light!" Angelo yelled. "Then take a left at the stop sign!"

Ella glanced both ways and then drove straight through. With mere seconds, an oncoming car had to hit the brakes to avoid hitting her, but she could not think about that. The stop sign was ahead. Ella swerved hard to the left. She was sure the car was going to tip over when it skidded on the two right tires. As it landed back on all four wheels, she stomped on the gas and accelerated fast, but she never lost the Excursion that followed.

A shot fired at the Mercedes and then another hit the door. Whoever drove behind them was not alone in the car. She could see a second person in the passenger seat through the side mirror next to Angelo. Both she and Angelo immediately ducked down with another shot fired at the car.

"Son of a bitch," he growled. Angelo climbed over the front seat to the back and pulled out a twelve-gauge shotgun. Then he kicked the rest of the broken glass out of the back window with his boot. Ella watched through the mirror as he aimed at the passenger who shot at his car. Angelo pulled the trigger twice. The front windshield of the SUV shattered and the passenger slammed against the door with the shot. "Take a right on the dirt road coming up!" he ordered.

Ella took a hard right. She thought she could lose the Excursion when a second one screeched beside the first, bashing the corner of the Mercedes. Ella quickly had to correct the wheel to compensate for the hit.

"Shit!" she cursed as she straightened up the car. One of the Excursions sped directly beside her with the other against the passenger side door. "Angelo!" she screamed and glanced over at his face. "Hold on!"

When he saw the look in her eyes, he braced himself on the backseat and Ella hit the brakes hard. She had seconds. She looked at both the SUV's that were now in front and mumbled as she picked up her foot.

"I'm really sorry about your car, Angelo." Then she gassed on it and knocked one Excursion into the other, causing them to both spin around and crash into the trees. Then everything seemed to stop.

"Are you all right?" Angelo's hand reached over the center console to her arm.

"Yes," she panted and tried to catch her breath. "Are you?"

"Yes, I'm fine." He rubbed the back of his neck. "That was good driving, Ella—very good driving. You kept us both alive," he said and jerked the handle on the door. "Stay here. Have your gun ready. I'll be right back."

Angelo walked slowly to the wreckage of the first vehicle. His finger was on the trigger of his gun as he ducked to the ground, searching for people inside. He pulled the trigger twice. Then he turned around. A man from the second SUV was trying to escape through the half-opened window. He could not squeeze out in time before Angelo stood in front.

Angelo yanked him from the overturned vehicle and launched his body to the ground. The man did not move with the gun pointed at his head. Angelo's focus teetered between the vehicle and the man. Ella guessed he was looking for more people who might be inside. He seemed satisfied with his search; then he kicked the man in his ribs.

"Who the hell sent you? Who are you with?" The man did not answer. Angelo kicked him in the stomach again, forcing the man to roll in a ball. "Answer me!" Angelo screamed.

Ella had to look away. She could not watch this part of Angelo. The rage that took over his mind was too brutal to watch, but she still could hear him shouting at the man. She flinched with every kick he made. She heard the ruthless threats and assaults, until the man finally gave in.

"I'm with Gregorio." Ella peeked out of the window. The man was hardly recognizable. She could barely tell he was a person. It was hard to know that Angelo was capable of doing such a thing. He could have shot the man, avoiding all this but he gave into the hatred as she had with Simon.

She looked in his eyes. Angelo felt no pity and unbuckled his belt. He wrenched the leather strap from the loops on his pants. She was about to look away again. She definitely would not be able to handle this, but Angelo jerked the man's hands behind his back and restrained them with the belt.

"You're a fucking traitor. I'm in charge of Gregorio's ranks now." He dragged the man by the arms away from the vehicle when a Porsche came skidding down the road. It left a trail of dust as it stopped behind the Mercedes. Angelo panicked and looked at the car, but Ella felt the vibrations and crawled underneath before it stopped. Angelo was searching for her but had no idea where she went.

She saw three sets of boots stepping on the gravel from where she hid underneath the car. All four doors opened and then shut again. The men never thought to check underneath, before they walked past to where Angelo stood.

"Where's Ella?" one of them asked.

She scraped her back as she pushed her body underneath to the front of the car. While Angelo aimed his gun at the men, all three men pointed one at him. It was a standoff—her or him. She had no doubt they would take him anyway. She could not let that happen and moved faster no matter how much the rocks scratched her head.

Angelo looked at her but quickly averted his attention back to them. He tried to buy her some time as she squeezed her body forward. So far, she had no room to raise her arm. Her body had barely fit underneath the car.

"Who are you talking about?" Angelo asked.

"Right," the man said.

"As if she'd be with me," Angelo scoffed.

"Put down your gun, Tomassi. We will shoot."

"Not happening," said Angelo

The men walked closer to him and never looked back. Ella managed to scoot out a few more inches and free her arm enough to raise her gun. It was trickier than being on her stomach. She had shot from laying on her back once.

She carefully aimed at one of the men. Her shots had to be fast and precise. If she missed, it could mean Angelo's life.

She shot one of the men and then the other. Ella pulled the trigger as she aimed at the third. Nothing came out. She fired again and frantically kept pulling the trigger. The gun would not shoot. The misfire threw her off, but she also gained the man's attention. Angelo did not miss a step and knocked the man to the ground.

"You are a dumb son of bitch to think I would ever tell you where she was." Then he shouted over to her as she squeezed out from under the car. "Bring me the rope from the back seat, Ella."

She felt disoriented as she grabbed the rope and slammed the door shut. She ran over to Angelo. The man was already bleeding when he tied the rope around his wrists. Then he left the man alone. Angelo talked on his phone as he guided her back to the car.

They sat on the ground, against the wrecked Mercedes as they waited for help. Angelo looked over at her, but she could not look back. She was not sure how to feel. Angelo tried to touch her arm, but she flinched. Her body stiffened with the show of affection. She had a hard time separating him from what she had seen him do. No wonder he did not want to involve her in group affairs.

"Are you all right?"

"Sure," she mumbled. She could give no better answer than that.

"Let me see your gun," he said and held out his hand. Ella handed it to him. He aimed and tried to shoot as she had. The gun would not fire for him either. "Faulty shit," he said. "Here, I want you to take this. It's my extra." He handed over the one in his hand.

She stared at the two restrained men and looked up at him. He looked frustrated and rested his head in his hand. She wanted to tell him it was okay, but the two men kept reminding her of what had happened.

"I'm sorry, Ella. I never wanted you to be a part of any of this. I don't know what to tell you."

Ella looked down and let out a long, steady breath. "I know," she said and laid her hand on his arm. "I know how it works."

Chapter 55

Ella tossed the blue dress she had worn in the trash. The rocks and dirt from underneath the car ruined the only dress she ever knew Angelo liked. The day was a disaster, and she felt sick. She had killed two men with Angelo beating another until she could not recognize him as a person at all. She kept seeing his bloodied body on the ground and felt nauseous all over again. She had seen Angelo at his best, but there was also something deadly inside of him, absent of feeling. He turned into a completely different man than what she knew.

She almost forgot that Rafa was at home with her as she walked in the kitchen and saw him sitting at the table. Angelo had made him bring her home. Rafa probably had better things to do than sit with her, but Angelo trusted Rafa more than he trusted anyone else.

Ella tossed the towel from her hair onto the counter and walked to the coffeemaker. She looked at Rafa and took out two cups. Then she waited a minute for his cup to fill.

"Here." She set a cup in front of him. She remembered that he did not have cream or sugar the other day and went to prepare her own.

"Thank you." Rafa picked up the cup. "Who taught you how to drive like that?" he asked and set down his phone. Ella did not understand since he was not in the car, wondering for a second until he spoke. "Car camera," he said and took a sip.

"Oh." Ella picked up her cup and walked to the table. She should have known they had a camera in Angelo's car. "Sullivan did," she answered.

"Did he teach you how to get out of restraints and how to shoot too?" Ella nodded. "And you thought that was normal?" His brows lifted with the question.

Ella shrugged. "It was normal when I didn't know anything else. I don't know why I never questioned it. I guess I had no one to compare my life to."

Rafa nodded. "Fair enough. Sullivan was a good teacher. You are very good."

Ella shook her head. "I'm not as good as he is. Sullivan can still make shots that I can't make."

"Maybe we should have taken him to audition for the show, the test that Angelo set up at the warehouse," he added.

"Oh...well, he is a gifted man," she said and looked off to the side.

"What's the matter, Ella?" Rafa leaned his arms on the table and looked at her.

"Angelo," she mumbled. "Today...he wasn't himself."

"He gets like that when he's scared. That's how we react when someone threatens our life."

"There was so much blood. That was hard to see." She looked up.

"He grew up with that. He's immune, but you should have never been there for that. He doesn't want you to see that part of him. He doesn't want you to be afraid of him."

"That's just it." Ella pointed. "He can't keep me from it. I'm going to see it whether he likes it or not. We didn't plan what happened today, but it still happened." She stopped. Why was she wasting her time with trying to explain her position?

"Go on," he said and leaned forward. He stayed silent and waited for her to continue.

Angelo always had a vicious streak. She could see the anger in his eyes, but seeing it firsthand made it real. She could either despise him for it or accept it. Maybe that was her mother's issue. She never accepted her father's involvement with the mafia, and it turned out bad for both of them. Ella did not want to end up like that.

Rafa inhaled. "Okay, you're going to run into some trouble, but he's not going to deliberately put you in danger. He has plenty of men who are with him. He needs a woman who isn't directly involved. He doesn't want you to get used to it. That would turn you into us."

"I have to get used to it, Rafa, or I'm going to hate him for it... like my mother did with my father. Angelo's life isn't only about him. It's my life, too. I don't have a choice if I'm going to be the support he needs. He can't have both."

Ella grabbed her forehead with her hand. Why was she talking to Rafa about this? She should be talking to Angelo, but Angelo was likely to brush off the issue.

"Ella, I understand what you're saying, but having someone else to think about and protect is new to Angelo. As his wife, you're going to have to bear with him until he does. All you can do for now is accept him for who he is."

"Wife," she mumbled. "I am a wife that nobody knows about because it's too dangerous to tell anyone."

"Love, Angelo has wanted to get married for a long time. I doubt he is happy about the secret."

She frowned. "Can't you agree with me, Rafa? Do you have to reason out everything?"

"Yes, I do. Welcome to Angelo's world." He smiled and looked at her. His eyes looked sad, maybe sympathetic. Even Rafa knew her situation was not likely to change anytime soon.

"All right, enough sulking," he said. "I'll take you to eat and then I'll show you around the city. Be ready in five minutes before I realize what a bad idea this is. I could be risking my life by going out with you."

Ella gave him an appreciative smile. He probably was talking about Angelo and not Bonadio. Rafa must have faced some tough situations with Angelo as his boss, too.

***

Dinner was uneventful. After a morning like she had, complete with a car chase, Ella could not complain. She was glad that something in that day was normal as Rafa led her outside of the restaurant where they ate. His beautiful silver Lexus waited for them. It was fully loaded with leather seats. She had not cared to admire the car earlier. Now that she was in a better mood, she was excited to sit in the passenger's seat.

"I don't guess you'd let me drive," she asked. She knew he would never let her drive, but his sarcastic remark was worth the question.

"Nobody drives my car except Brett," he said. Rafa turned the key and looked over at her. "Your luck today has not been the best. I saw what happened to Angelo's car. Even if I would've let you drive, I'm not the type to tempt fate."

Ella smiled as he shifted into drive and turned onto the busy street. It felt strange having him take her anywhere, but he was not half as bad as she originally thought.

"I've been to this department store before," he said and pulled into a shopping center. "I like to buy all of my suits here. It should have something you like."

"Finally," Ella breathed and stepped out of his car. It was the first time she had been shopping in Miami. She was glad for the change of scenery as he followed her through the entrance.

The store had everything as he had said. Shelves filled with fragrances and makeup stood in front. They gave her an idea. Ella started walking forward and to the shiny display cases up ahead.

"Wow," she said, fascinated by the lines of jewelry. The bright lights made the diamonds seem more spectacular than what they already were. There were chains of every length. She had never seen so many accessories. She continued to walk around when she stopped in front of a glass case lined with the most beautiful watches. Would Angelo wear a watch? He might if she made it special.

"Excuse me." She interrupted the woman behind the counter. "Do you engrave?"

"Of course," the woman snorted. Her haughty tone caught Ella off guard.

"Good." Ella tried to ignore her. Maybe her coffee went cold. "Would you show me that watch there?" Ella pointed. "It's the one with the black band."

The woman looked at the watch's tag and then at Ella. Her expression never changed. "Are you sure you meant to enter this store and not the shop around the corner?"

Ella did not know what shop she meant but assumed it carried less expensive brands. "I don't know. I could have meant the shop around the corner. Is their customer service better than it is here?" she asked and placed her hand on the counter.

"Do you know how many customers have wasted my time today? I have more important things to do than show merchandise to people who are window-shopping."

Ella frowned. "Maybe those customers were planning on coming back. Maybe they were looking for the perfect gift, and they wanted to go home and think it over. Your attitude might lose the sale. I know you work off commission, so let me see the watch." Ella pointed.

The clerk did not say another word and turned around for the keys. As she set the watch on a soft piece of cloth, Ella looked back for Rafa. "What do you think?" she asked. "I want to have it inscribed. Do you think Angelo will like it?"

"How should I know? I've never bought Angelo jewelry," he teased.

Ella let out an irritated breath. "So funny, but you have known him for long enough to know."

"I don't know, sweetheart. He's had his old watch for a while. I'm sure he'd wear it if it's from you."

"Then I'm buying it." Ella looked at the attendant. "I would like it inscribed like I said earlier. Will you hand me a pen and paper?" Ella quickly wrote down the inscription and handed it back.

"I'll be back with you in a few minutes," the clerk said, her voice more subdued now that Rafa stood there.

"Personally," Rafa said, "I wouldn't buy anything from this store after the way she treated you."

"Yes, but I might not find what I want somewhere else. The watch is here. I want to get it while I can."

Rafa crossed his arms. "I would have walked out."

"No, I want the watch, but somebody should say something."

"I'm going to make a call to the owner tomorrow morning. That was ridiculous. The owner needs to know how his employees are treating the customers. I wouldn't excuse that if I were the owner."

Ella nodded and looked through her purse. When she pulled out her credit card and license, she breathed out annoyed. "They're going to see my last name," she said. "She probably doesn't know who Angelo is anyway."

"I'll pay," Rafa said and reached for his wallet. "She probably doesn't have a clue who you are, but we can't take that chance either."

"Wait." Ella shook her head. "Take me to the bank."

"I'll take you later. I want to get out of here." He took a business card off the counter and looked at the door. "The store is a nice place. I wouldn't mind taking over if the owner would sell."

"A clothing store?" Ella almost laughed.

"It would be another business interest to add to my credentials."

"You're always thinking ahead."

He nodded as they both waited for the clerk to return. "So...what are you inscribing on the watch?"

Ella thought about the car chase and Angelo's reaction to the man. It was hard to think about Angelo that way. She wondered if those things would always bother her like that, or if one day she would get used to it. It did not matter. It did not change her heart. She still loved Angelo the same. Ella smiled slightly and looked at Rafa. "It's a secret," she replied.

"Secret?" he grinned. "You're like a child, Ella, but I guess that's part of your charm. I think Angelo will like the watch."

"I hope so." She smiled.

"Where did you want to go after the clerk rings you up?"

Ella shrugged. "There are a lot of stores on this strip. I would be happy to shop here. There's no reason to drive all over town."

"Sure...why not." he said. "I hope you appreciate what I'll face later over this outing. Enjoy it while you can."

Ella looked back at him. "Angelo won't be mad. He's busy anyway. Besides, he trusts you."

"Scary, isn't it. Just wait. You will see."

Chapter 56

Angelo walked through the quiet hallway to the recliner in the family room. He thought that Ella would be home by the time he finished his shower but she was nowhere to be seen. Rafa said that he would bring her home by eight and it was almost ten. Where were they?

Angelo leaned forward and folded his hands together. His head hung with the shame that he felt. Ella probably thought he was heartless. In a way, he was. He felt no remorse for his assaults on that man, but Ella had not liked what she saw. He knew. He felt it in the flinch of his touch on her arm. If Rafa took any longer to get her home, she would be more afraid of him still.

The doorknob turned as Angelo poured a second glass of wine. His watching from the kitchen entrance caught Ella off guard. She was holding several bags in her hands and stumbled when she saw him. Their eyes locked. He did not smile, and he did not speak. His head turned toward the hallway to their bedroom and he gestured to it with his chin. "Go put away your things and shut the door when you do." She was hesitant for a second until he raised his arm and pointed to the room.

"Angelo," she said.

"I said go," he ordered and dared her to question his stern tone. He was not in the mood. As soon as she disappeared and shut the door, he balled up his fist and punched Rafa in the jaw. Rafa stumbled. He should have known it was coming. Angelo pitched his fist forward again, but Rafa ducked to the side and deflected the punch.

"You're getting my wife back a little late, aren't you?" Angelo seethed.

His anger did not surprise Rafa. Rafa already had expected as much. "You told me to watch her, and she was tired of being in this goddamn house. Is there a problem?"

"Don't give me that. I never said you could take her anywhere but home. I never gave you permission to be out this late with her. It got dark two hours ago."

"Are you jealous? Is that what this is about?" Rafa shook his head. "Fine, no more late nights with her, but here's a thought: you should have never asked me to take her home if this is how you felt. You should have kept her with you."

"She couldn't be with me with Gregorio traitors and bullets flying through the air. I don't need to expose her to that." Angelo waved off the idea. It was unthinkable.

"What did you want me to do, Angelo? Did you think I would keep her hostage like you do? There will always be some sort of crisis with the ranks. That's the way it is. You can't lock her away from the world."

"I can do whatever the fuck I please. When her life is what they want, I will do what I have to do. I don't care if she likes it."

"You know what? I think it's time you did announce that she's your wife. Speed this Bonadio bullshit up. Keeping it secret isn't helping you. This morning proves it. They're still hunting you down, aren't they?"

"Get out of my house," Angelo demanded and pulled out his gun. If Rafa said another word, he was going to shoot him. He was not in the mood to be challenged.

Rafa took a step back and looked him square in the eyes. Angelo knew what that cautious step meant. He was about to cross the line.

"Don't you dare point that at me. I swear you need to get a grip on your temper. What you're doing with Ella is going to push her away. You can't watch her every second of the day, and it's driving you crazy. Give her something to do with her time. That restaurant has been ready for three weeks now. Give it to her. Then maybe she'll stop focusing all her attention on you."

Angelo slid his finger to the trigger of the gun when Rafa slammed the front door to his house. Angelo stared at it for a second as he put away the gun. He would deal with Rafa later. Now he needed to deal with Ella.

Inside their room, he watched her walk to the dresser where several new dresses lay covered in plastic. As she hung them in the closet, Angelo pondered Rafa's words. He could not always have her with him, and he did not want her with anyone else either. He could not have it both ways, so what was he supposed to do?

Angelo ignored the issue instead. As Ella was pulling the plastic from the last dress she purchased, he walked up to her and grabbed both of her wrists. She was startled but not shocked. Rafa told her how he would react.

"You shouldn't have been out that late with another man," he said. He brought his face directly in front of hers.

"I'm sorry." She looked back at him but could not keep eye contact. He defined intimidation. "I guess I was happy to be out and I tried on more clothes than I should have."

"You tried on clothes for Rafa?" he asked. Angelo could feel his veins tighten with the image he received. If he had known about this when Rafa was there.

"He was telling me what you might like."

"If you want to know what I like, then guess who you need to talk to?" She did not need Rafa's opinion when he saw her every day.

"I thought you said that you trusted him. That's why you sent me home with him."

"Whose wife are you?" Angelo asked.

"Yours," she answered.

"That's right, and as my wife, you're not trying on anything for any other man. Do you understand that?"

"Yes." She looked down and then back up. She frowned at him. Her helpless expression made him let go of her arms.

"Go to bed," he said. He could not be around her anymore. He was making her dislike him more than she already did. Angelo walked out of their room and through the back door to the patio.

***

He felt empty. He sat down on one of the armless patio chairs and thought about the situation with Ella. Rafa was right. He was pushing her away. He did not know how to keep her safe without forcing her to stay outside of the public's eye. She was always in danger. The stresses of his businesses and leading his group were not helping. Nothing was constant. He did not know if she could handle him or his position. She was bound to get sick of him. Why would such a beautiful woman want to stay with him when he always disappointed her? He did not offer her anything special, and there were men out there a lot nicer than he was.

He blamed it on his upbringing. His father fashioned him for this role. He became better than his father was. His priorities lay with the group. He had tripled the profits since taking over. It was his way or none. He never compromised what he wanted, and he never made exceptions. His marriage was necessary to further relations and make profits. It had always been the group first and family second. He never cared until he met Ella. The problem was, she was more than a business deal. She was different—special. He put her in a separate category. She was important. He needed her in his life, but taking care of a woman was much different than making her happy. As good as he was with everything else, he could not keep a smile on her face. Sometimes he felt lost.

He closed his eyes and imagined her. Whenever he saw her smile, he relaxed no matter what he faced. Thinking about it made him feel better. He needed to try to make her happy. She deserved better, but there was no escape from this life. Being born in it, meant dying in it. His last name dated back and enemies would never forget a name.

"Hey," Ella whispered. Her soft legs descended around his hips as he opened his eyes back up. It was like looking at the face of an angel. She barely hid her sexy curves with a silky tank and matching panties.

Beautiful. He doted as she laid her palms on his chest and dragged her nails down his bare skin. She looked worried. She expected him to scold her or send her away. He did not want her to build walls against him. Her fear of him made him feel like a miserable man.

"Why are you out here bothering with an asshole like me when you could be sleeping in a warm bed?" Angelo wrapped his hands around her lower back. He was not letting her go.

"I couldn't sleep without you," she replied simply and gazed in his eyes.

"You will catch a cold with so little clothes on."

She must have been cold. The air grew significantly cooler as night fell, but she concerned herself with him. "You aren't wearing a shirt. You will catch a cold, too."

He laughed, almost mocking what she had said. "If you haven't noticed, I'm hot-blooded. This temperature suits me fine."

Ella's eyes looked sad as she slipped her hands around his neck and let them sag against his back. Having her there almost made him feel worse. She opened her mouth to speak but paused. She moved her lips against his and left him with the warmth of a small kiss. "I love you, Angelo."

He never expected her to say those words. Her sweet voice caught him off guard. He treasured her more than he cared about anyone in his life. He could not resist the heat from her breaths against his neck. He wanted to give her a reason to stay with him. He wanted to be much closer to her than he was now.

"I guess if you're staying out here with me, I'll have to keep you warm," he whispered and started caressing her bare legs. He was certain that his touch caused the chills on her skin instead of the crisp, evening air. His hands skimmed higher along her sides and across her breasts, until he pulled her face directly in front of him again. "I love you too, Ella—more than anything."

Her breathing stopped as she tried to keep the glassy look from her eyes. He moved his face even closer. She mesmerized him. He could not believe that fate granted him to have her as his wife. "I want you, Ella. I want to feel you. I need to know that you're mine."

Ella let out her breath. Her fingers traced the muscles that tightened on his arms. Her lips closed the distance between his. "I have always been yours, Angelo, since the first time we met. Please come to bed with me."

"What if I can't wait that long?" He opened his mouth and kissed her. The sweet taste of her lips made him press harder and kiss her deeper. His fingers slid behind the band of her panties and pushed. "Stand up for me."

He slid them down easily and raised his own hips to pull down his thin cotton pants. He was ready for her as soon as she sat on his lap.

"Somebody might see," she purred as he pulled her back down. Ella was ready for him. Her slippery passage slid onto his arousal with ease. He groaned at the feel of her; her mouth half opened with the shaky breaths that she breathed. Her entire body trembled against his groin. She tried to hide her face in his chest but he would not have any such thing. He wanted to see her eyes. He eased his hand between her thighs and placed his thumb directly against her sensitive spot underneath. Ella must have wanted him badly. She was an easy woman to please but never this easy. With her raspy breaths, Angelo thought she would hit her climax within seconds of his touch.

"Ella, turn around for me," he whispered and pulled her forward again. It could have been sheer selfishness, but he wanted to make her lose control. He wanted to see her pleasure. He wanted to make up for making her afraid, but he doubted that she cared about that now. Ella was busy with moaning in his mouth. She thought of nothing else but him, and he loved every second of it.

"Stand up, sweetheart," he repeated. It was as though he put her in a trance. He had to help her. He gently raised her waist, turned her around, and guided her down to his hips again. She nearly screamed at the friction. She grabbed the sides of his legs and pulled until she could take no more.

"Please," she whimpered.

He never remembered her being this sensitive to his touch. He pulled the back of her head against his shoulder and spread her legs. His fingers immediately slid against her throbbing sex. All she could do was cry out. She forgot about being quiet. It was exactly how he wanted—her focusing on him.

"Come for me. Then I can stand you up and fuck you," he ordered. He never talked to her that way, but he did now. His vulgar mouth sent her to the edge. Ella held her breath. She clenched her hands around his wrists. A second later, she was crying out his name.

"Christ," he breathed. Keeping himself from coming as she gave into him was a chore. He loved how her walls clamped around his erection and wanted to feel her orgasm again.

"Up," he said and lifted her off his lap. He stood up behind her and grabbed both of her hands. He guided them to the rails and waited. When she gripped the metal bars, he bent her low at the waist and positioned his shaft at her entrance; then he wrapped his own hands around hers and thrust into her hard. He wanted to make sure that she came on him again.

"You...Angelo, god..." Her words made no sense as she pushed back against his hips, matching the steady rhythm of his speed.

"Yes, let yourself go." He slowed down. He wanted her to enjoy every second of her high. Then he pumped into her again.

"Relax," he whispered when she tried to move away. "I won't let you go." For a moment, she realized that he exposed her body to the world. No one could see, not with his six-foot fence as they both faced the water that trickled onto his lawn. No one was in the backyard.

He freed one of his hands and lifted up her shirt. Her breasts were firm and smooth. He squeezed one and then the other. Ella arched her back and pushed her chest out. She forgot about being timid again and went along with his charge as he laid his hand on her spine.

He loved the feel of her hot skin and caressed the entire span of her back. Then he pushed her head down and plunged into her again.

"Angelo," she whispered as her body shook. He steadied his breathing and drove into her with as gentle a rhythm as he could manage. He would not be able to hold off much longer. Her beautiful body and the sound of her voice were tipping him to the brink. He closed his eyes to hold himself back.

"I love you," he said. His hand slithered to the front of her body again and gently wrapped around her throat. He let go of the rail with his other and let his fingers drift to her sex. The insides of her thighs were wet. It pleased him that she was a disoriented mess because of him. He never wanted her to forget that she felt this way with him.

"Come," he said and slid his fingers against her soft folds. "Then I can," he added. She was getting tired and he could not control his urge anymore. As soon as her breathing hitched, he charged against her hard. She was close and her hands clenched the rail with all of her strength, bracing herself with the force of her climax that would be followed with his release. He had no desire to wait any longer. He gave her what she was ready to receive. He held off long enough and his body ached for relief of her. He let himself go. He enjoyed giving her that part of him—all of him. Ella gave him feelings that he had never felt before. She deserved to have it all.

After they had returned to the bed and fallen asleep, Angelo groaned, forcing his eyes half-open with a distorted glare. Why was he awake? He felt like he had slept for seconds when he heard his phone ring again. He stared at Ella. Her arm draped around his shoulder with her bare breasts pressing against his chest. How was he going to reach for his phone without disturbing her? As much as he wanted to ignore the annoying ring, he knew that no one would call in the middle of the night unless there was trouble.

"Yeah?" he mumbled into the receiver. His voice sounded low and scratchy with the hour worth of sleep he had received. "What? There was an explosion at the warehouse?" he repeated and was suddenly wide awake. "Yes, bring them with you and go check it out. Hell…"

He squeezed his eyes shut and then looked at Ella. He did not want to leave her, but Sammy and Thomas were staying in the guesthouse. She would be safe with them there to guard her. "Yes, yes, okay...I'll be there in ten minutes," he said and scooted from underneath Ella and out of the bed.

Chapter 57

"It's too bright," Ella grumbled and rolled away from the window. She opened her eyes with the morning sun and then closed them back. Then she opened them again. Where was Angelo? She looked at the restroom but the light was still off. She heard no sounds in the house. After a night like last night, she wanted to wake up next to him. She wanted his arms around her, his hands touching her—the feel of his skin. She needed him now more than usual. Whatever he did last night, she wanted to feel again. Instead, he left her with his empty spot and her wandering thoughts.

The clock already showed ten. She was not surprised he had left since he always left early, but he should have woken her up before he went to the hotel. It would have been better than waking up alone. How could she sleep that long anyway and still be tired? The hot shower did not even help. She was feeling out of sorts. Maybe she did not sleep well or yesterday caught up with her.

She started to drag her feet to the door of her room but remembered the watch. She left it in the drawer the previous night. She was going to give it to Angelo, but then he ended up tiring her out. She barely remembered coming to the room or going to sleep at all. She hoped that this day would be less eventful than the previous.

"Thomas?" she asked when she walked down the hall and saw his slicked brown hair and lean body sitting on the sofa. Either he was there to protect her or he was babysitting. It was sort of the same.

"Sammy is here too," he said. Ella looked over at Sammy on the recliner; his parted brown hair had fallen over his eyes, covering the birthmark on his left cheek. Angelo had never introduced her to him, but she saw him at Angelo's last meeting.

"Were you here all night?" A chill ran up her arm. Had they been in the house the entire night? Did they hear? She felt utterly embarrassed. "Where did you stay?" she asked.

"In the guest house to the side. We came with the boss yesterday."

She could not tell if they heard her with Angelo or not. She should have known that he would not be alone, but she did not think about it at the time. Either they could not hear or Angelo did not care. She groaned to herself. Angelo should have warned her before it all started. Knowing him, he did not care.

"So…" She changed the subject and tried to put the other out of her mind. "Are we staying here today, or are you bringing me to the hotel?"

"Well," Thomas started, "there was an explosion at one of the warehouses last night. He went to the hotel while Rafa and some others went to check out the warehouse."

"Okay, are you bringing me there or am I staying here?" She really wanted to give Angelo the watch.

"We're supposed to take you there whenever you're ready," said Thomas.

She was sure that Thomas and Sammy were tired of being at the house. They did seem eager to leave. "All right, give me a minute," she said. "I need to eat something first and then I'll be ready to go."

***

Ella held onto the soft pouch that covered the watch. If Sammy and Thomas would hurry and finish talking to the woman behind the counter at the hotel, maybe she could actually give it to Angelo. She wanted to see what he thought; more importantly, she wanted him to read the message on the back. The message meant a lot to her and she hoped he would like it too.

Ella tapped Thomas on the arm. She understood they had matters to discuss, but she had to use the restroom. "What is it?" Thomas asked.

"I'm going to the restroom over there. I'll be right back."

He nodded and watched her for a minute until she was at the door. She was about to open it up when an employee walked up to her.

"Ms. Collins," she said. Ella did not like the sound of her former name as the employee continued to speak. "I'm glad I found you. A woman left this message with the front desk earlier and wanted us to give it to you. She said it was urgent."

"What did she look like?" Ella asked.

The woman shook her head. "I don't know. I wasn't the one who received the message, and my coworker works the night shift, so she already left for the day."

"Okay." Ella nodded.

Ella opened the door to the restroom and looked at the folded white note. Something was not right. She hurried in the stall and then washed her hands; then she looked at the note again. She was afraid of the message but opened it anyway. What she saw was not a message at all. It was the number of a room on the thirtieth floor. Ella looked off to the side and thought about all the reasons that someone left her the number of a room. One reason stuck in her mind. Angelo.

Ella pushed the door to the restroom back open and looked around for Thomas and Sammy. They had to go see what this note was about, except they were not there anymore. Ella immediately walked to the counter and looked at the receptionist who had talked to them.

"Where did those two men go?" she asked.

"Someone came to talk to them. They ran and followed the man to the elevator."

"They left?" Ella could not believe it. After all the times that she did not want Angelo's men with her, she wanted them now. She needed them now, and they left.

"Okay," Ella said. "Thank you."

Ella took out her phone. She dialed Angelo's number and waited. When no one answered, she hung up and dialed again. She was not the type to give up when he did not answer any of the times she called. She hoped that Rafa would answer and dialed his. Again, there was nothing.

She took a breath and looked at the ceiling as if an answer would fall down on her. The decision was hers to make. She was alone and could get a hold of nobody. She had to go to the room. As suspicious as she was, she could not ignore the note. She had to find out what it meant.

Ella walked back to the counter and looked at the woman behind it. That was all she could think to do. "I need you to call Mr. Paolini," she started when the receptionist interrupted.

"He told us never to call him unless it was an emergency."

Ella breathed in and let it back out. This was not the time to get angry at stupidity. If the woman had considered her eyes, she would have known that this was an emergency.

"I'm going to finish what I was saying before, and you will not interrupt me." Ella nodded at the woman to enforce what she was saying. "Okay, you are going to call Mr. Paolini, and you are not going to stop until he answers. This is an emergency." Ella nodded again. "When he answers, you are going to tell him to come to the hotel, and then you are going to give him this note. Do you understand?"

"Yes." The woman nodded. She finally sensed the urgency in Ella's voice.

"Good." Ella confirmed and ran to the elevator.

When the elevator stopped, Ella stepped into the quiet hallway of the thirtieth floor. She did not make a sound and followed the numbered plaques beside the doors to the correct room. She was cautious with every sound she heard as she hoped there was no real issue to find. She tried to convince herself that it was nothing, but the bad feeling lingered in her chest. She knew better than to ignore her inner voice. She would not like what she found.

There was one more room left to pass before she stood next to a door at the end. It was slightly opened. She could feel a cold draft with the faint voice she heard. The voice came from a woman.

Ella was hesitant to look through the door. She took several breaths before facing what she already knew. She pushed. The door made no sound and opened, barely exposing what Ella hoped not to see. Angelo sat in the recliner with his pants unzipped and opened. A woman with short, messy brown hair kneeled on the floor between his legs. Her head moved up and down where his pants parted as he clenched both sides of the chair.

Ella had a feeling about what she would find, but she could not prepare herself enough for what she saw. She closed her eyes and took a step back. Angelo did not know she was there. She felt ill. The strength of her legs started to fail. Her head became faint as she held her breath for longer than she should. That other woman had no right putting her lips around what was hers.

Ella wiped the tears from her eyes as the anger started to build in her mind. She pushed the door open wide. It was the hardest thing she ever had to do, but the woman wanted her to see. The woman would get what she wished.

Angelo closed his eyes as the woman lifted her head and turned around. All Ella felt was hatred as the woman started to speak. "You have a sexy man," she said as her tongue swirled across her lips. "I think I'll ride him when I'm finished with him here."

Ella stayed silent as the woman stared at her. She waited for Angelo to open his eyes back up. She wondered what he had to say.

"Leave, Ella." His voice was faint, remorseful. It should be with the glistening erection the woman caused as her wet lips wrapped around him again. She made sure that Ella got a clear view of what she did.

Ella glanced to the floor on the left. She wondered how many men were in the room and where they were hiding. Her throat felt dry as the tears stung the corners of her eyes. It broke her heart to see him subjected to the woman's assault. They set him up and let her see. She knew what she saw was not real. At the same time, it was.

"Don't you ever fucking listen?" Angelo yelled. "I said leave, goddamn it! Leave." Angelo could not look at her anymore and closed his eyes again. He could not help what the woman made his body feel, but it made no difference to Ella. She hated what she saw the same.

"Take your ring back, Angelo, and take this watch I bought for you too." She dropped them both to the floor and watched them bounce in two different directions. "They don't mean anything to me now." Her act of being scorned should convince anyone that she despised Angelo and wanted nothing else to do with him, except Ella was not entirely sure that she was acting.

She looked at Angelo one more time as a tear fell down her cheek. She was angrier than she ever remembered. They would all get what they deserved for putting her though this pain.

She immediately ran out of the room and down the hallway until she came to the bend in the middle. She stopped to devise her next plan. Those men would think she left. They would come out of hiding, and she would catch them then. She hated them—Bonadio and his men. She would never get over what she saw. She would never feel pity for even one. She would not feel vindicated until every one of them was dead.

Chapter 58

Arms wrapped around Ella. Somebody grabbed her from behind and locked their hands at her chest. That was the entire point of setting up Angelo. To make her hate him and run. They wanted to catch her. A small part of her mind wanted to let them take her. There was probably a car waiting for her outside of the hotel. She should go back with them. Go to Bonadio and seduce him…kill him in his sleep.

Ella did not struggle with the man. She hung her head forward and let her body grow limp. The man felt her give up her control and loosened his grip. Ella stayed still for a moment. Her breathing steadied but her heartbeat pounded against her chest. In a swift attempt to free her body, her head sailed backwards and rammed into his nose. He stumbled back, giving her less than a second to react. She grabbed her gun and shot.

"No," she said as his large body jerked against the floor. A few seconds later, he was dead.

She looked to the left and then to the right. Did they send one man to capture her? Did they not know about her skills? She crouched to the floor and held her head. As hard as it was, she had to go back to the room. She had to put all other thoughts out of her mind. She could not think about the woman. She needed to rescue Angelo.

"Ella," someone whispered her name. She looked up as Rafa dropped down. He had Jim and Ray behind him. "I got your message."

Ella threw her arms around him and tried to catch her breath. She was relieved to see him after what she had found. Everything about the situation hurt. She wanted it to disappear.

"They have him. A woman was with him, but I know they set him up. The others were hiding. I couldn't do anything. They might have killed him. I didn't know how many there were. I was about to go back." Ella sobbed in his shirt, but he did not seem to care.

"It's okay, love," he said. "You did the right thing. I see they were waiting for you to leave." He pointed at the body.

"They tried, but Angelo's still in there with more. We have to save him." Ella lowered her head to wipe her eyes. She did not care about how she sat on the floor in her dress. Nobody cared right now anyway.

"Ella, wait for us here," he said. "Angelo won't want you to go back there."

"No. I'm going too, Rafa. I have the right to come after what I saw."

He looked in her eyes for a split second and asked her fast. "Is your gun loaded?" She nodded and held it up for him to see. "Come on." He held out his hand. "Stay behind us and listen for anyone coming off the elevator. We had the receptionist call all the rooms on this floor. No one will be coming out, and Brett is at the stairway." Ella nodded again and grabbed his hand. Still on the thirtieth floor, she waited behind the three men as Rafa peeked around the bend and then retreated.

"There's a man outside of the door now," he whispered. He took a breath and then motioned for them to follow. The man slowly held up his hands and did not make a sound. Jim grabbed the gun he held as Rafa fired his. Then Ray caught the man's body before it ever hit the floor.

Ella was surprised that the door was still open. Two men pointed guns at Angelo as another slammed him with a thick metal bar. Blood trickled from a large gash on the left side of his face and there was a cut on his chin. His pants were still unzipped.

Rafa looked at Jim and Ray and held up three fingers. Then he closed his hand tight and lifted one finger at a time. When he showed all three fingers again, he kicked the door open wide and all three of them fired shots. The floor shook as one body fell and then another. The third man hit the edge of the recliner and crashed against the wall. The bar in his hand echoed as it bounced and landed at Angelo's feet, but Angelo still did not move. Neither did the other three.

Ella had no idea what had happened. She looked behind her but no one was there. Then she slid her feet forward. The door was opened wide enough to see through the opening where the hinges met the wall. She saw them. Two more men were in the room; both aimed their guns at Angelo.

She had no time to think. They started to pull the trigger as she matched the rear sight with the front on her gun. It was hard to lock her targets through such a small opening. She finally made herself concentrate and thought about nothing else but the two bullets flying through the air.

Everything else went silent in that split second. She saw the bodies go down, but she was waiting for more. She wanted to be sure. She was tired of surprises. She did not want her men dead. Then she saw the woman who started it all—the one with her lips where they did not belong. Ella looked at her. The image of her at the recliner replayed in Ella's head. What made her think she could do such a thing? The woman was going to die.

"You have some fucking nerve to touch me." Angelo snarled the words and slapped the woman across the face. His vicious tone would have scared a grown man. Angelo was holding the woman against the wall by her throat. "Who are you?" he asked. The woman did not say a word. Angelo's face twisted with her silence and forced her body to the floor by the back of her neck. "Who the fuck cares who you are," he snapped and yanked a gun from the floor. He clicked the hammer as the woman started to speak.

"I'm Bonadio's girlfriend," she muttered.

"No, you're nothing but his whore." Angelo jerked her up by the hair. "Bonadio wants me dead so he can marry Gregorio's daughter."

"Please don't kill me," she begged when he started to pull the trigger again.

Angelo glared at her. "Did you really think playing the fucking boss of a rival group would work out for you?" he growled and then shoved the woman at Jim. "See what we can get out of this bitch."

"No." Ella calmly walked inside the room. The woman did not deserve to be alive any more than the men did. She looked at the woman and kept her gun raised. "What you meant to say earlier was that I have a sexy husband."

"I had to." The woman defended as a tear slid down her cheek. Ella looked at her tear and remembered her own. She felt strangely relaxed about the situation as she walked directly in front of the woman.

"You played with my emotions," Ella said.

"I didn't know he was your husband."

"So it was okay when you thought we were just together? Him being my husband would have changed things?" Ella narrowed her eyes with confusion. Was the woman dumb enough to say what she said?

"No, that's not what I meant."

Ella smiled at her. It was almost endearing but definitely false. "I knew you and Bonadio set him up. I expected it as soon as I saw the note. You aren't smart enough to fool me or this group." Ella touched the woman's head with her gun.

"Please don't," the woman cried. Her cries were nothing to Ella, only a reminder of what she did.

"Crying won't work," Ella said. "I find it funny how you were glad to see my pain, and now you want me to feel sorry for you."

"Fucking shoot her, Ella." Angelo grit between his teeth. Ella thought about it. Killing someone had bothered her the day before but did not bother her now. She did not know why she felt numb. The woman's hands on Angelo had hit a nerve in her chest much too deep to feel any pity at all.

"Leave me alone," Ella said and pulled the trigger on the gun. As the woman's body fell forward and hit the floor, Ella gave a satisfied nod and glanced back.

"Why is she here?" Angelo looked at Rafa for an answer. "She shouldn't be here."

Ella looked over at Angelo and took a step forward. He was not going to pretend that she did not know what went on in the group. He could not keep her from seeing no matter how much he tried. She never wanted to see what happened today. She never wanted to witness the woman doing that to him, but she still did. In her brief moment of recollection, all the hurt and pain returned.

"Angelo, why are you treating me as though I did something wrong? You want me to go?" she asked with a nod. "Then I'll leave," she said and took a step to the door.

"Ella," he called.

"You tell me to leave. You tell me to stay. Make up your mind, Angelo." She turned back for a second and looked at the sad eyes staring in hers. She could not do it. She could not stay. "You don't need me here. You don't want me here. I'm not going to sit around and watch them set you up, and then have you yell at me for saving you. Do it on your own. That's what you want."

Her heart could not take it anymore. She walked up to him and looked at him. She could not reach him. He would never understand how to work as a team. Everything she thought they would be together was lost with his refusal to face the truth. She was a part of his life whether he liked it or not. She had to accept it; so should he. She looked up at him one more time and decided that all she could do was leave.

Chapter 59

Angelo looked at Sullivan who sat across from him at his desk. Rafa was standing behind him with Jim and Ray at the door. They needed Sullivan. With Sullivan having taught Ella her skills, he called on him to help. Sullivan had acted on behalf of Gregorio many times in the past. He was a perfect key figure for communication...*if* he accepted Angelo's offer.

Sullivan let out a weary sigh and nodded. "If it's for Ella's safety, I will do it with conditions."

"What are they?" Angelo asked. He was hesitant to hear about stipulations. He did not have time to bargain an agreement. Time was ticking. Bonadio had already caused his wife to leave, and they had not spoken in over a week. Another day was a day too many.

"I want no more connection with Gregorio, Bonadio or *you*. I have done my part. I want a clear way out. My mouth is sealed, as you know. Anything I say would put Ella in danger, and she always has been my concern. If Bonadio is dead, I expect the threats against her to be small. I also want all of it in writing, and I want both of our signatures notarized and on file."

Angelo looked at him. If there had been anyone else to call besides Sullivan, he definitely would have called. Sullivan was smart to want their signatures notarized, but Angelo knew why he wanted out. It was hard for him to see Ella since he was no longer in charge of her.

"All right," he agreed. "I'll have Rafa draw up the contract right away." He looked back as Rafa nodded. "You can come back and look it over in an hour—sign it. We'll have Donnie come by and notarize. After that, we'll talk about what to do next."

Sullivan stood and held out his hand. He never smiled. Angelo found it difficult to read his straight-faced gaze. He never had a difficult time reading a man's thoughts. No wonder Ella's skills were good.

The room cleared out a minute later. Angelo folded his arms on the desk and held his head. Ella had not called or messaged him, and he would not call her. There was no point. She was not part of his group. He would never allow her to have group involvement. He refused to let his wife's heart grow cold. She did not understand that once she got to that point, she would lose her soul. The way she cared for others would change. She would resent him for it. If she were older, she might understand. Ella, though, she always wanted to prove herself, but he wanted her the way she was. Nothing more.

"You should go talk to her." Rafa walked back in the office with his laptop in his hand.

"I'm busy," Angelo told him. He was busy. He had the papers on his desk with scribbled names and locations. He was assigning the twenty men that Jim, Ray, Brett and Sammy had chosen. They needed to be where they could best use their skills. There was a warehouse in Orlando that Gregorio had sold to Bonadio. It was their camp away from home. He planned to blow it up, preferably with Bonadio inside. That was where Ian and Vin came in. They were too new to be recognized as his members. Sullivan would make it work.

"Busy?" Rafa pushed as he normally did. "You haven't written anything else on those papers since Sullivan left."

"Stay out of my business," Angelo warned. The last thing he wanted or needed from Rafa was advice about his relationship. Now was not the time.

"Fine," Rafa said and walked closer to the desk. "I found this last week." Rafa held a watch in his hand. That was right. Ella had said something about a watch when she told him to take his shit back. He had picked up the ring but did not remember the watch.

"Lay it on the desk," he told Rafa. He would look at it when Rafa left.

"Ella engraved something on the back. She was proud of it. You should take a look."

"Lay it on the desk," he repeated. He was already in a bad mood because he had not seen her. Leave it to Rafa to bring her up when he was trying to keep his mind occupied. Rafa had better not make him repeat himself again.

Rafa laid it on the desk and started to turn around. As Angelo thought he would leave him to his thoughts, Rafa could not shut up about her.

"You know, Ella doesn't want to become part of the group. What she wants is for you to rely on her instead of shutting her out of your involvement with the group. She wants your trust."

"Ella has my trust. If she didn't, I wouldn't have married her. What I want is a wife, not a killer. Did you see how she killed that woman the other day? The act didn't concern me. It was the look in her eyes when she was speaking to the woman. It was the tone of her voice…how she enjoyed the fear in her victim's eyes. We do that, not Ella. She can't live a normal life after becoming like us. It's simple. I won't let that happen to her. She will hate herself."

"You mean like you do?"

Angelo looked at him. Sometimes Rafa was stupid to keep antagonizing him even though he knew the outcome. His hand slowly stretched to the open drawer on his desk and started to reach for his pistol. Rafa watched every movement of his arm. If he were smart, he would leave.

"Hate is a big word for who I am. I do what I have to do. Ella isn't me. She doesn't have to kill; I do."

"Then tell her that," Rafa said simply. "If you don't, Ella will only be your wife on paper."

Angelo picked up the gun and aimed. He clicked the hammer. Rafa flinched lightly but did not move. He should have moved, because Angelo pulled the trigger and shot.

"I told you to shut the fuck up," he huffed and set his pistol back in the drawer; then he picked up the watch. It was sweet of Ella to think of him when she went shopping. Sweet was exactly how he wanted to keep her.

"You're fucking insane," Rafa growled and checked his body for wounds. One of his hands went to his head. The other held his chest.

Angelo ignored him. He unbuckled the old watch on his wrist and dropped it in the drawer beside his gun. He had that watch for years and was ready for a change. He was pleased to replace it with something that Ella had chosen. He examined the watch. He liked the Roman numerals instead of digits. It had a nice white gold ring around the face with a charcoal leather strap. Rafa mentioned an inscription. He turned it over and silently read the words. His mind stayed focused on them. He meditated. Only Ella would choose such a simple message with such a strong meaning. It was a shame that he could not give her what she wished.

"You could have killed me," Rafa went on.

"I told you to shut the fuck up." Angelo brushed off his remark. They were all insane at some point. Angelo had enough to worry about without hearing Rafa's opinion about matters that did not concern him. "I hired you to give me advice when I ask. Stay out of my marriage. How I handle my wife is not your business."

"Fucking asshole," Rafa spat under his breath. "You wouldn't know how to handle her if it hit you in the goddamn face."

Angelo stared at him; then he reached for the pistol again. "I missed on purpose. It won't happen again."

Rafa clenched his teeth together. Angelo could see the fury in his eyes. His fists started to tighten but he did not say a word. He shook his head and picked up his laptop from the floor. He probably despised Angelo right now. Most people did at some point. Angelo was not there to keep friends. That's what he wanted to believe. Rafa would get over it. It was not the first time Angelo shot at him. It would probably not be the last.

Still, if Rafa felt strongly about the situation with Ella, Angelo owed it to him to think about his advice. As he latched the watch on his wrist, he guessed that he should talk to her. It was really a waste of time, though. Ella would not listen after seeing that woman between his legs. How did they ever get him in that situation? He was on his phone and two of Bonadio's men showed up behind him. They should have never gotten through the front door that early in the morning, but it was too late once they had. Then that woman showed up. By then, he had a grasp of the situation. He knew what they were doing. That could be another reason he had not seen Ella. He never wanted to see that look of pure hatred on her face again. He felt it. She knew it was not his fault, yet none of that mattered when some stranger was sucking his dick.

Ella wanted inclusion with his group. Why? It was a death trap. There was nothing to envy about the group. Why could she not be simple? She could take his money and decorate the house the way she wanted. She could buy anything her heart desired. Have his children. Be subjected to pleasure when he got home. It all sounded good to him.

No, it was never easy for Angelo. He married the one mob wife who wanted some sort of responsibility. He knew he should meet her halfway and give her the restaurant. She deserved to have the restaurant, but he did not want to put her in any more risk than what she had already faced.

He stood. The situation with Bonadio was going to get bad and he might not see Ella for days. He should go see her while he had the chance. She might not want to see him, but he did miss his wife. He never knew if he would make it back alive.

Chapter 60

The privacy gate opened to his single-story house, an elevated home in case of heavy rains. Even though he lived inland, Angelo wanted to stay on the side of caution.

His house felt foreign when he walked through the front door. He always had spent most of his time at the hotel. It was not until he met Ella that he spent much time at home. He had purchased the house for a family, but after the first year, he put it out of his mind. He was glad to have her sitting in the kitchen.

"Hey," he said and tossed his keys on the counter. She looked up at him but did not give him the smile he had hoped to receive. There was no affection in her eyes and no hug to greet him at the door. *Shit.* He thought. He had no idea what to say and sat down at the table across from her.

"We should talk." His voice broke the silence of the room.

"There isn't anything to talk about," she mumbled.

It was like a flip of events. He wanted to talk; she did not. "We should talk about what happened."

"No," she answered right away. "Talking about it won't change anything. I want to forget it happened."

He nodded. He wanted to forget it happened too. It was hard for him to grasp that the woman made his body feel something that he did not want to feel. Having Ella see it happen made it worse.

"You know, I didn't want you to leave. I didn't want you to see any more of that shit. I want you to start coming back with me. I have a winter banquet in a couple of weeks too."

Ella's shoulders slouched. She looked frustrated as she looked up again. Hurt and sadness showed from her eyes. "Why?" she asked. "I'm doing what you wanted. I'm staying away from you and your group. I'm making it work here. You wanted to keep me locked away. I've been invisible and you've gotten along fine without me. Now you want me to come back with you. No, I won't. Go to the banquet yourself."

Angelo rested his chin on his fist and stared at her. Did she really tell him no? Nobody ever told him no and lived to tell about it. There were still events she needed to attend. He wanted to exclude her from group activity, not from every other aspect of his life.

"Would having the restaurant make you happy?" he asked.

She shrugged. "Would you control when I went to work too?" she asked him back.

"You would have guards with you," he replied, "but you could go whenever you wanted."

"You mean you would assign men to watch my every move?" She wanted him to clarify.

"I would assign two men to you. It's not safe to go alone. I already explained that you would never have a perfectly normal life."

She seemed to think it over. Having a couple of men was better than staying at home. Ella should have understood by now that protection was absolutely necessary.

"Sure." She nodded. "I want it. I always have. It's been ready for a few weeks now, hasn't it?"

She knew him better than he thought. "Yes, it has."

She sighed and looked at the ceiling. "When can I go there?"

"Tomorrow. Thomas and Sammy will be with you. You can start hiring when you're ready."

"Fine," she said and stood up. He was still sitting down. They were not finished talking. Where did she think she was going?

"Ella," he said. She stopped where she stood. At least she knew better than to walk away when he called. "I want to show you something." He stood up and nudged his chin to the restroom door. She moved right away, just not fast enough. He took her hand and led the rest of the way.

"What do you see?" he asked and guided her in front of him.

"A mirror," she replied and looked at him through the glass. "What are you trying to show me?"

"Look at yourself in the mirror, not me."

She looked at herself. She did not smile; a blank stare reflected back. Then she looked away again.

"Look at yourself." He pointed.

"No." She tried to push out of his grip.

"That's twice, Ella. Do not tell me no again."

Her eyes started to glisten. Upsetting her would defeat the purpose of him coming home at all. "What is the point of this?" she muttered.

"You can't look at yourself, Ella. That's what happens when you still have a heart. Soon, you won't care. The death you see will suck in your soul. You won't feel anymore. Right now, you cry, but soon you won't. That's why I don't want you to see more than you have to. I don't want you to change. I want the woman I met."

"It's too late for that." She shoved his arms away. "You can't put that danger in my face and expect me to do nothing. You should have seen this coming. I won't be the same. It might be easy for you to brush off what happened, but I won't forget. That woman deserved what she got after what she did, but you were mad at me. I didn't do anything wrong. And now, you want to throw a restaurant at me as if it will make everything better. I'm not going to forget. Don't tell me that you don't want me to change. I already have."

Angelo gently lifted up her chin and looked in her eyes. He was not sure. If she had any love left inside, it was masked with hurt and pain. Did all wives go through this coping stage or was it her? He did not know what to do next.

"What can I do to make it better? I don't want to see you like this," he said.

Ella looked at him. Her expression became angry, followed by a resentful frown as she lowered her head. Then she returned his stare and did not miss a beat. "You know what, Angelo," she whispered. "I don't need you here. You make me feel worse than I already do, so why don't you take your own advice this time? Leave."

***

The SUV came to a screeching halt. Angelo slammed the door on the Escalade and could barely see straight. Ella had the nerve to dismiss him? She had no idea what would have happened to her if she had been someone else. He would not try to talk to her again. If she came begging him on her hands and knees, he would barely notice her there.

"Bring him to me." He pointed at Brett as he walked through the warehouse door. Angelo owned two warehouses, and the bastard that Brett was bringing had exploded the other. He was a part of Bonadio's scheme the day they sent Bonadio's girlfriend to sabotage his life.

Angelo knew that Brett could get a second location for Bonadio from the man, but he wanted to do it himself.

The man was a little shorter than he was with dark hair and jeans. As soon as Angelo saw his face, he crushed his nose with his fist. He wanted to see the man feel pain. The blood that smeared onto the man's hands as he held his crooked nose made him seek more of the same. "We know about the place south of Orlando. Where is the one to the north?"

The man looked at him and glanced at the door. He would regret running if he tried. Brett and Sammy stood behind him, and Jim and Ray were guarding outside. "I asked you a question," Angelo said. He did not raise his voice. Thoughts of breaking the man's ribs seemed to calm him down. He knew his mind was twisted at times. He did not care. The man should have known the risks before he ever blew up their property.

"I already told your man." He pointed at Brett. "Bonadio doesn't have a place north of Orlando. I don't know where you got that from."

"Really?" Angelo said and kicked him between the legs with his boot. The man doubled over with pain, groaning as he went to the floor. Angelo looked down at him. He felt no guilt, only loathe. He kicked him again. The cracking of his ribs echoed in the silent room. The only other sounds were the heated breaths of his men.

"We can do this all night," Angelo said as he turned around and grabbed a metal folding chair. He raised it up high and pounded the man in the middle of his back, causing the man to jolt forward. "The sooner you speak, the sooner this ends. It's simple."

"I already told you…"

Angelo grabbed the back of the chair legs and struck the man's head. "You didn't tell me what I wanted to hear."

"There's not a fucking warehouse," the man sputtered as the chair hit him in the jaw. Angelo did not care. Right now, after what Ella said, he did not allow himself to feel.

"Keep lying; I keep swinging." Angelo walked in front of him and watched the blood drip from the man's head to the floor. He wondered why the man held onto the truth so hard when he was going to die anyway.

Angelo took his silence as a cue that he wanted more. His heavy footsteps bounced against the walls as he walked to the office in the back. If the man thought it was over, he was wrong. Angelo opened up one of the cabinets and picked out a thick metal baton. The baton was perfect, never used. He had bought several for an occasion such as this. As he walked back into the main part of the warehouse, he let the loud thuds of his boots instill fear in the man. He liked the way it worked.

"Do you see this?" He jerked up the man's head and snarled in his face. "You either tell me where the warehouse is or I'm going to crack that skull of yours in half." He dropped the man's head back down and took a step back. The man had about ten seconds to choose how he died—by bullet or by baton.

"Five seconds left," Angelo said and crossed his arms. The man started coughing and did not quit. The pain from his bruised spine and broken ribs must have made him wish he were dead. Angelo had enough of his refusal to speak and started to tap the baton on the ground. The constant tapping was bound to unnerve the man more.

"Take the second exit before town and take a right on the fourth street with no sign. Go down it two miles."

"Are you lying?" asked Angelo. He waited for the man to look up to know if he told the truth. He was. Angelo looked over at Brett and stepped out of the way. Brett fired. The bullet lodged in the man's skull, splattering blood as the man's face hit the floor.

"Take care of this mess." He looked back at Brett. "Then come see me in the office. I want you to take your crew down to Orlando and check out that building. We'll talk about it in fifteen minutes, so hurry up with this. I don't care if we have to kill them one by one. I'm not playing Bonadio's game anymore."

Chapter 61

Ella had been working long hours at the Sandy Shores for the last two weeks, trying to get it ready for the grand opening. Finding a qualified chef who would follow the menu the way she liked was a chore. She finally did. She wanted them to be creative, but most of their food was not up to her standards. Telling them so did not go well.

She could not believe that the dinner service was almost over. She promoted the restaurant in a black satin evening gown that was perfect for the occasion. She knew she had to look the part of what she expected in the clientele. She did not want a flashy color taking attention away from the restaurant or the guests.

Angelo. She thought as she walked from the kitchen after checking on the cooks. Angelo would like it there. Large pillars and tinted glass separated the dining room from the bar with soft piano music playing from speakers overhead. The dimmed lighting of the chandelier complemented the skin. It could be a romantic evening or a soothing environment for the diners. She wanted an upscale restaurant where guests could relax and enjoy the evening. Angelo should have been there to enjoy it with her.

She had not seen or heard from him. She had told him to leave, but she did not expect him to stay away for good. What had he been doing all this time? She wondered if he thought about her once. She only thought about him. Did she overreact and push him too far? She knew what type of man he was. She knew he was a part of a dangerous organization. Was there any part of him that was capable of seeing it from her eyes? Did he understand her at all?

She took out her phone for the tenth time that day. Nothing. He had not messaged her and she had not messaged him. She started to press his name again as she had several times over the last few days, but she could never go through with it. It would make her feel worse if he did not respond. Being stubborn seemed better than being ignored.

"Busy night, Ms. Collins," Seth greeted from behind the bar. She smiled. It was nice to see a familiar face from the old restaurant. She had thought about Santiago's. She missed it. Ella was also happy to give that restaurant closure with something brand new. The memories that used to make her glad reminded her of something much more sinister behind the facade. It was okay to move forward. Moving forward made her feel more alive than living in the past.

"How are you holding up?" she asked.

"Love it. The crowd is amazing. I like to stay busy."

"I love it too." She admitted. "I'm very happy with the turnout."

"Do you want a drink?" Seth held up a glass and grinned. "I make a pretty good margarita with a special ingredient if you want to try one."

Ella laughed. "I'd better not. How professional would I look if I walked around like a lush?"

"No fun for the owner," he chuckled. "Maybe after everyone leaves you can celebrate."

Ella nodded with a smile. "Maybe...we'll see how it goes. Why don't you give me a bottle of our sparkling water for now?"

"Of course," he replied and reached underneath the bar.

"I'll be back in a while," she said and took the napkin and bottle from his hand. Ella intended to circle the place again. She walked around the bar toward the stairs to the mezzanine but stopped mid-step. Someone spoke at the entrance of the restaurant and she glanced back to see Rafa standing at the door. She ducked to the side. Would Angelo be with him? Her heart started to beat hard as she turned back to see. No, it was Jim and Ray with him. Did they want to check the place out?

Rafa approached the counter where Seth stood. He was looking at the bottles of wine on the shelves and studying the labels. He grunted and then looked over at Seth.

"What can I make you this evening, Mr. Paolini?" Seth asked.

"Very good. You remember me from Santiago's." Rafa seemed pleased. "What did Ms. Collins have tonight?" Rafa looked around. Was he looking for her? She did not want to talk to Rafa right now. He was probably there to talk her into going to the banquet the next day. She did not want to hear his speech.

"Well," Seth started, "Ms. Collins had a bottle of water, but I doubt you want that."

"Water?" Rafa blurted with surprise. "No, I don't want any water. Give me her choice then."

"All right, do you like wine?"

Rafa nodded. "When the wine is good, but I didn't see anything I wanted on those shelves."

"Oh, she doesn't keep the good wine there," he replied. "Would you like red or white?"

"Give me red, but spread the word that the good wines should be on display. You almost lost a wine sale over that display of bargain wine."

"I will let her know." Seth grabbed a glass and stepped away. Rafa looked around while he waited. He seemed to like the layout of the restaurant. He nodded and gazed at the high tables in the bar. Then he looked at the dining room through the tinted glass and nodded again.

"It's nice, isn't it?" Seth said and handed him his glass.

"Beautiful," Rafa agreed as he swirled the contents of the wine to the light. He tasted and then took a drink. "It's good," he said. "I'll buy that bottle and take two more glasses. I have two people with me."

Seth handed over his request and asked, "Did you want to talk to Ms. Collins?"

Ella cringed as she strained to listen. Why did Seth have to ask him that? Getting a speech was the last thing she wanted right now.

"Yes," Rafa answered. "When you see her again, send her my way. I also need someone to bring menus."

"I'll send someone over right away," said Seth.

Ella groaned. Rafa was sitting at a table with a clear view of the main dining and the bar. There was no way to avoid him. Since it was the first night they were open, she had to greet other guests and Rafa would see her. She should get the confrontation over.

She walked back past Seth, who started to raise his hand to stop her. She already knew what he had to say and nodded as she pointed to Rafa. Jim and Ray saw her first but then Rafa turned around to see who they were looking at.

He slightly smiled with lifted brows. "Are you hiding from the hotel?" he asked.

"Hiding is one way to put it," she replied. "I've been busy."

"You did a good job. The place looks great. I like the menu selections." He raised the menu.

"Thank you. If you only knew what I had to go through for that menu," she said. Small talk was not going anywhere between them since they were on a more personal level than the weather. She decided to ask. "Angelo didn't want to see how the place looked?"

"Angelo," he sighed, "has been on a rampage in Orlando. He was supposed to be back in time to show up here and never made it, obviously. He should be back at the hotel soon."

"Oh," she mumbled.

"You should go back with me to see him, patch this shit up between you two."

"No," she said. "I didn't do anything wrong. It's not my turn to bend."

Rafa laughed. "You're dreaming if you want him to suddenly change his ways."

"That's fine. I don't want to see him anyway." Ella turned sideways and looked at the dining area in search of anything to get the attention off her and Angelo. The hostesses were sitting the third rotations, so she could not stay to talk to Rafa anyway.

"A busy night is a good sign, but why are you drinking water, Ella? Why aren't you promoting the wine like you did at Santiago's?" he asked and stared at the material that gathered underneath her breasts. Ella completely forgot and turned back around. Did he see?

"I like my wine, but I didn't want to drink on the first day we're open."

"Wise." He nodded, though she was not fully convinced that he believed her. If he questioned her reason, he did not let it show. "Well, it looks like you have more guests to talk to. We're going to drink this wine and order something off the menu. I have to be back at the hotel and make sure everything is ordered for the banquet tomorrow." Ella nodded with a smile. "I will see you soon," he added.

Soon? She let out a breath as she walked away. She was almost sure that soon meant later tonight, and all she wanted to do now was go home before that could happen.

***

Ella felt exhausted. Running around during the day and wearing heels all night did nothing for her feet. She kicked off the heels one at a time and walked through the family room to the kitchen. She made sure that Sammy and Thomas could not see her anymore and then laid her head in her arms.

Angelo should be there with her, but he was not going to come home until she saw him first. Why did he always have to make everything difficult? Did he not miss her as she did him? How long would it take him to come on his own?

She slowly breathed in and then out again. She rubbed her stomach and hoped the feeling would go away. Usually, she could control the urges, but this time it caught her by surprise. Ella ran to the restroom on the other side of the kitchen. After five minutes of choking out water, she moaned. She was tired of being nauseous and washed the bad taste out of her mouth.

Ella walked back to the kitchen. Maybe some hot tea or some crackers would help. She had just opened the door to the cabinet when the kitchen door shut. It was not loud, but she jumped with the click.

"I'm taking you back with me. Both of you need to fix this before Angelo goes on another death mission because of you."

"What are you talking about?" she asked and held onto the counter.

"He's been"—Rafa did not finish and puffed—"Never mind about that."

"I'm not leaving this house. He hasn't called me. He's fine with things the way they are."

"Ella, trust me." Rafa walked closer to where she stood. "Angelo misses you and is making everyone's life hell."

"Rafa, save your advice for Angelo. He wanted me gone. Why are you here?" she asked. Thinking about Angelo was adding stress to her mind. She coughed; then she ran to the restroom again. Why did Rafa have to come right now? It was not a good time. She did not even have time to shut the door when she held her head over the commode.

"How far along are you?" Rafa asked from the open doorway.

"Go away!" she shouted and slammed the door shut. She could not take this and Rafa asking questions. She splashed water all over her face and grabbed a small towel before opening the door again. Of course, Rafa was still standing there, waiting for her.

"I asked you how far along you are."

She looked at him with mock surprise and wiped her face again. "I drank too much at the end of the night."

"Bullshit," he said and pressed one hand against her back and the other gently across her belly. "I know what I saw," he said. "What are you...three months? Does Angelo know, Ella?" She glared at him as he backed away and crossed his arms. Her silence told all. "Yes, you two definitely need to talk."

"I'm not going anywhere." She tried to push past Rafa when he grabbed both of her arms and made her face him. "He's fine without me. He doesn't want me. All I am is interference to him."

Rafa leaned in close and spoke with a low, chilling voice. Ella had never heard him speak that way. It made the hairs on her arms stand straight. "He's not fine. He's keeping himself busy by killing every Bonadio member he finds. He's been risking his life to protect you. He needs to know that he will be a father before he gets himself killed. You're not going to be able to hide this for very long."

"Wait," she called as Rafa started to walk away. "You can't tell him."

He turned around and gave her a cynical grin. He almost seemed confused about what she said. "Angelo's an asshole, but he's also my best friend. You have twenty-four hours to tell him, sweetheart. If you don't, I will. I'll see you at that banquet tomorrow night. I hope I've made myself clear about where I stand."

Rafa dropped an invitation on the table, glanced back at her once more and left.

Chapter 62

Four weeks. It had been four weeks to the day. Ella stepped into the elevator, wearing a shimmering turquoise dress that hung gracefully along her body and almost touched the floor. A sash that was a slightly darker shade than the dress tied below her breasts and draped down the middle of her back. Her hair hung around her left shoulder with tiny white flowers weaved throughout. By how other men noticed her, Angelo would be no exception.

She did not see him at first. She walked to the back of the banquet room and waited. He was not there now but he would come. He had to make an appearance. Then out of the hallway, Angelo and Rafa walked toward the front. They did not notice her to the side; instead, they stopped at an empty reserved table. She would surprise him from behind.

As she walked closer, the orchestra concluded their first ballad for an intermission. She was nearly behind the two men when Angelo took a deep breath and looked at Rafa.

"Why do you keep looking at the elevator?" he asked. "Are you expecting someone?" Angelo kept staring at him until Rafa finally talked.

"No, I'm seeing who came. Why?"

"I know you talked to her, so quit the fucking act. I told you to leave it alone."

"Yes, I know you did." Rafa casually took a sip of his wine and glanced back at the elevator. "Are you telling me if she showed up, you wouldn't want to see her?"

Rafa must have been harassing Angelo about her lately. The scowl on Angelo's face told all. "It wasn't your place to talk to my wife. We have been through this, remember?"

"Somebody had to step in. If left up to the two of you, you'd both die alone." Rafa challenged him.

"What if I don't want to see her? Did you think about how much she's complicated my life?"

"You're life was already a complicated mess," Rafa mocked. "At least you were happier with her."

"Quit lying to yourself. There's no such thing. You should have left it alone. If she does show up tonight, I'll have security drag her out."

Ella glared at his back. It was just like him to say something like that. If he had said those words two months earlier, it would have made her sad. Somehow, it did not bother her now.

"Well," said Rafa. "Maybe Ella was right about you. Maybe you are fine without her."

"She said that?" Angelo looked as if he were getting a headache and held his head. "You know what? I am fine without her."

"Oh, I can tell," Rafa laughed. "Let's see if you make her leave."

If Angelo thought he was fine without her, then why did he have to keep telling himself that? Ella shook her head and walked directly in front of him. He did not move. He was shocked silent and did not speak a word.

Ella stared back at him. He could not have meant a word he said. The watch she had given him was latched on his wrist. She was his wife. She was his number one outside of the group, and she was going to make sure that everyone knew.

"Is that so? You're going to make me leave?" She slid her fingers around his neck to the back of his head and played with the tips of his hair. His breathing deepened. For once, she thought she controlled her speeding heart better than he did. He was stunning in his black suit and tie. More importantly, he was hers.

With the music stopped, her forward approach quickly attracted attention in the room. This time, she did not care. He was her husband. She would do as she pleased and pressed her lips flat against his. It could have been involuntary. It could have been habit, but Angelo did not push her away. He could not resist and kissed her back. It was deep, passionate and intimate. For a second, it felt like no one else was in the room. As he started to raise his hands to her cheeks, she took a step back.

"You were saying?" She looked him in the eyes and paused. "I guess I'll be staying then." She smiled at him and glanced over at Rafa. She had never seen either man so tongue-tied before. Her surprise entrance worked to her advantage.

"Wow," she heard a woman whisper to another from somewhere behind. "I can't believe she did that. I can't believe he didn't say anything."

Ella glanced back and then looked at Angelo again. He shot her a quick look of warning, but there was no stopping her. He had not noticed the rings on her finger yet either.

Ella smiled back at the women and gazed around the room. Some guests blatantly stared, and others tried to peek from underneath their glasses of wine. What better time was there to make the announcement than now? They were about to find out exactly why she got by with that. She wanted to see a few women cry.

"Excuse me." She looked back at the women and grinned. She raised her hand high in the air and let the light reflect against her rings. It was the first time she had worn them aside from her wedding ceremony. They were beautiful rings and she was proud to have them in full view. "Why could I get by with that?" she asked. Only the people who stood close could hear her speak, but she was sure that the news would spread within the minute. "I think it's because he is my husband. We've been married for weeks now in case any of you would like to know."

"Rafa." Angelo pointed at the stage. "Get them to start playing again," he said, but it was too late. Flashes from cameras bounced around the room, and the guests' whispers increased to a dull roar. Their marriage would be the talk of the night.

"I can't believe you did that," Angelo said under his breath and then grabbed her hand. He walked down the hall with her and through the door to the conference room. They both stood alone in the room, staring at the other. Angelo's expression grew outraged, but Ella did not care.

"What were you thinking? Do you have any idea what kind of danger you buried us both beneath?"

"You mean more than now? They didn't know we were married when they set you up with that woman. It's not going to get any worse than that."

"Is this some sort of plot for revenge? Do you want me dead?"

"You're at no more risk than you were before," she countered.

"I think you lost your damn mind," he huffed. "I can't believe you did that."

"Well, I can't take it back now."

"You did that on a moment's thought. Give me one reason why I shouldn't make you leave. Now we're going to be all over the fucking news. I like to keep publicity away from me and my group."

"I'm behind you on this, Angelo. Quit pushing me away. You told me to accept the life I've been given. Well, here I am." She pointed at the watch and thought about the inscription she chose: *You took my heart; now take my hand.* "I'm not backing down this time. I will be your wife in all parts of your life or none at all. Our marriage will never work if you can't accept that." She never looked away from his eyes and held out her hand, waiting for him to make his decision. It all came down to this. If he could not take it, then she would never come back.

Angelo closed his mouth and looked at her. He glanced at the watch and then at the door. He looked frustrated or worried. It would be a hard decision to make; however, he had to make the choice and he had to make it now. He shook his head and glanced at her hand. His expression looked softer, almost like he was giving up his position.

"You win," he said simply and grabbed her hand. "You realize that you will be the death of me," he added.

Ella slowly shook her head. "No, I won't let you die. I think I've proven that to you."

Angelo closed his eyes and let out a remorseful breath. "I'm sorry about that woman. Looking at your eyes while that happened was one of the hardest things I've ever had to face. That's why I got mad. There was nothing I could do to stop it."

"At times I'm going to hate you. That's what you said, isn't it? But you're wrong. At times, I will hate this life but not you. We will deal with it as it comes. When I didn't leave your room that night, I agreed to be a part of who you are—to work together to make it work for both of us."

Angelo lifted his hand and wiped off his face. It could have been to deflect any possible tears or because he was tired. She made no mention of his reason and wrapped her arms around his head instead.

"I love you," he said. "You're probably the only woman that would put up with me, too. I would die before letting anything happen to you, so don't ever tell me to leave again."

"I don't think that's a problem anymore, Angelo," she said and pushed him back to one of the sofas in the room. As he dropped to the cushion, she immediately went for the buckle on his belt.

"Did you miss me that much?" he asked.

"Are you refusing?" She slid down his zipper.

"Your dress will get wrinkled." He half-smiled and slid down his pants as she raised her dress to her hips.

"My dress is supposed to be wrinkle free." She lifted one knee around him and hovered until he positioned the part of him that she missed so much. She raised her other knee and closed her eyes as she lowered her body to fit. They were perfect for each other. Her head hung forward as she moved against his length. Now she felt like crying. The connection was overwhelming her emotions.

"I know I missed you," he said and jerked her forward. His movements felt amazing, pleasing her as he always did. An instant heat spread throughout her body as his drives quenched her needs. Then, he kissed her. His mouth was greedy and his lips interlocked with hers as if making sure she was real.

"I love you, Angelo," she assured in case there was any doubt. He did not say anything else. There was nothing else to add. Their bodies could speak what they felt without having to say another word.

***

With the comfort of the other's arms, neither bothered to move from the sofa even though the banquet awaited their attendance. Ella did not desire to leave his arms for the commotion they would face outside of the door. Hundreds of guests probably waited to ask questions about the marriage.

When a few more minutes passed, she finally lifted her chest off his. She wrapped her hands around his cheeks and kissed him gently. "There's something I wanted to tell you," she said.

"Yes?" He returned her kiss when the lights in the room flickered several times, followed by absolute darkness. They heard guests scream from beyond the door, and Angelo quickly scooted her off.

"Oh my god," she said as he turned on his phone for light.

"Come on," he whispered and held out his hand to her. The power outage concerned him too. "Be ready to pull your gun and stay right behind me. Don't get lost." She nodded and grabbed the back of his coat.

Angelo unlocked the door and cautiously opened it. The soft lights from the generator turned on as they started down the hall. She had no idea what they would find but was ready to shoot as he said.

Chapter 63

He led Ella through the confused crowd. Nothing seemed out of the ordinary except for the lights being off. Angelo started to breathe easier. He turned around to tell Ella to relax when Brett ran up to him. He did not like the worried look in Brett's eyes. It meant that something was wrong.

"Follow me," said Brett. Brett opened the door to the stairwell and had his gun pointing up as he did. He peeked out of the door when they reached the lobby floor; then he waved them to come. An Escalade waited for them outside of the hotel. Sammy sat behind the wheel. Where was Thomas? Angelo had his members work in pairs, but Thomas was not there.

"What the hell is going on?" He leaned forward from the back seat to the front as the vehicle sped away.

"They took them. Rafa, Jim, Ray—Thomas. Rafa was on the phone with me when they were checking on some trouble out front. They wanted you, but Rafa told them you weren't there. By the time I got out there, they were gone. Rafa told them you were at the warehouse. He's leading them there, but they're going to kill him if you aren't."

"Fuck," Angelo muttered. "Rafa's smart, though. He'll take them to the main warehouse, the one with the balcony. We have to stop by my house and grab some guns."

"There's one more thing," Brett added, his tone sounding matter-of-factly. He must have already accepted the worst. "Sullivan was with the men that took Rafa."

"How do you know?" Angelo asked.

"Rafa made a point to say his name before our call was cut off."

"Sullivan," Angelo said. Sullivan had agreed to help him. Did he change his mind? Angelo did not know Sullivan that well. He had never worked with him before. The only one he really seemed loyal to was Ella.

"He's tricking them," Ella said. "Sullivan would never work with Bonadio."

"Let's hope you're right." Angelo looked at her. "Every man has his limit, though, and I don't know Sullivan well enough to give him my trust."

"I do," she muttered. "He wouldn't join them."

"Maybe true, but that doesn't make him loyal to me." He looked at her as she frowned. It may have been hard for her to understand; at the same time, she did. He was glad she did not try to argue.

When they arrived at his house, he started walking to his room but stopped and pointed at Brett. "You and Sammy grab the ammo out of my safe in the garage. I'm going to grab the guns."

Ella followed him to their room. He opened the closet door and shoved the hanging clothes to both sides as she watched. Behind them was a safe. He punched in the code and pulled the lever, opening the door to a large hidden space in the wall.

"Clever," she said. He smirked as he grabbed a black duffle bag and set it down behind him. Then he grabbed another.

"I'll have to show you all my hidden cubbies some time. There's one that even Rafa doesn't know about."

"How can I help?" she asked.

"Unzip that bag. Put all of the guns on the bed," he said and took out a third bag.

"What are you planning?" Ella looked up as she reached for another gun.

"To save my men." He lifted the other two bags to the bed. "My father and yours might have ignored their men to save themselves, but my men trust me. I lead by example. They're more loyal that way. It leaves little room for resentment. That's why none of my men turn on me. It makes us unstoppable."

Just then, his phone rang. He had called the number once—Sullivan. He almost dreaded to answer the call. "Yeah," he said.

"Come to the warehouse on the north side of town within the hour or all four of your men will die." Angelo started to open his mouth when the phone call ended after those words. He looked at the clock. It was half past nine. The drive took at least twenty-five minutes with no traffic. He had to rush.

"Ella, help me make sure these guns are loaded. I don't have time for ammo this time."

"Who was that?" She looked at his phone but started ejecting the cartridges and clicking them back.

"It was Sullivan. He said I have thirty minutes or they will kill Rafa and the others."

Ella shook her head as if that would prevent his men from dying. He knew better. Bonadio was not one to give loose threats. The thought made him zip up the second bag fast. Ella was through with the first and started to unzip the third bag as his phone beeped from his pocket—a message.

"Bring Ella," Sullivan wrote. Angelo glared at the words. Sullivan must have been out of his mind. Then he looked at her. Ella was unloading and loading the guns like a handler. Maybe Sullivan knew what he was talking about but still.

Angelo thought about it further. They must have been in a situation that needed a long-distance shot. He was good and Rafa was good. They were also unavailable, and he did not have a minute to spare to wait for other members of his group to arrive.

He took a deep breath and zipped up the last bag. "Sullivan wants me to bring you with me."

"You mentioned a balcony," she said and ran through the restroom door. Angelo saw her beautiful dress discarded to the floor and her heels tossed on top.

"That's right." He picked up all three bags and toted them to the kitchen. "Get these in the Escalade," he ordered Brett and Sammy and then returned to Ella. She was already wearing something more comfortable.

"They won't know I'm there. That's why he told you to bring me. Let me handle the shooting while they're focused on you."

Angelo held his head for a moment. This was such a bad idea that he wanted to punch himself for even considering it. He hated that Sullivan thought she gave them the upper hand. He also hated Sullivan's indifferent personality in it all. There was one important factor, though. Sullivan would not put Ella in danger. Angelo would have to put his trust in that, and he had no more time.

"Okay," he said before he could change his mind. Then he grabbed her and closed his hands around her face. "If something goes wrong, you need to worry about taking care of yourself. Do you understand? That's the only way I will bring you with me. Promise me." He looked in her eyes but she hesitated. "I said promise me."

"Okay."

"What?"

"I promise."

He could not believe he was involving his wife in one of the most dangerous situations he ever faced. He felt like a terrible man. What kind of husband was he? She should be safe at home, not going with him to some metal warehouse in the middle of the woods. This was going to eat at him no matter how the situation turned out. It went against everything he ever wanted for her.

"All right," he said and grabbed a bulletproof vest out of the closet. "Let's go. You can put this on in the car while I explain what you can do."

Chapter 64

Ella waited quietly in hiding a hundred yards back and watched them walk away. Her life was handing himself over to Bonadio's men at the front door. One of the guards rammed a gun at his back and led him inside. Angelo was many things, but a coward was not one of them. It did not matter how hopeless the situation seemed. He was always in the front. Now he relied on her to save him and the others. Going against his normal ways must have been the hardest thing he ever had to do. She admired him for that more.

With the strap of a rifle wrapped around her chest, a pistol in her hand and another gun attached to her waist, Ella stood and scoped out the place. She watched the entrance and quietly secured the duffle bag from the ground to her shoulder, waiting for the perfect time to move.

The bag was heavy but she was glad to be carrying one. They realized on the drive that she would not be able to lift the weight of all three bags. Ella managed to walk between some parked cars and make it to the end of the line. One man walked back outside, but she was more concerned with the number of men that were inside. She raised her pistol and aimed. As soon as she pulled the trigger, the second man came back out. When he saw his buddy on the ground, he whirled around to retreat. She could not let him tell the others. She had to fire fast. He did not give her a choice.

She looked at both of the men lying on the ground in a puddle of their own blood. It was gruesome. She understood why Angelo wanted to leave her out of all this. It was hard to accept that she was the reason they no longer lived. Ella closed her eyes. The world was so much different from what she ever thought when she was young. She put the thoughts out of her mind and walked past them to the side of the building, glad that there was another entrance to the place.

A large hallway met her. It looked as though it wrapped around the entire building much like an auditorium or a theater. She left the duffle bag by the door and took a right as Angelo had instructed; then she walked about fifty feet. As Angelo had said, the door to the left showed a picture of a stairway. She turned the knob, careful not to make a sound, and closed it behind her in exactly the same way.

Voices from the main part of the building echoed in the empty stairway as she ascended toward the top. She was careful with her steps. She hoped the wood would not creak or worse—fall through. There were holes where nails used to hold down carpet, and broken bulbs in the fixtures on the walls. The stairway did not look sturdy, but since Angelo had told her to go up the stairs, she knew it was.

She climbed three sets and hoped there were no more. She was already out of breath. She could hear some of the words the men said, but she could not make out full sentences until she made it to the top. The balcony rails started halfway down and ended at the floor. She would have to get low if she wanted to avoid being seen. Staying close to the floor would be the only way to stay out of sight and get to the edge.

Ella half slid and half crawled. She looked at the rails and then at the flakes of rust that speckled the floor. It was likely to fall if she touched it at all. She really had to be careful not to bump the rails with the rifle's barrel as she raised it to her eye.

Angelo's men were sitting on the stage. Their hands were bound in front. Angelo stood. Blood dripped from a cut by his eye and the right side of his nose. They must have punched him or hit him with something hard.

A dozen men she had never seen before stood behind Angelo and the others. From this high in the air, it looked like they formed a half circle. Two of them pointed guns at Angelo and one waved a gun back and forth at his men.

Ella breathed at the sight as she tried to relax her mind. All of the tension in the room and the heat of the balcony were making her nauseous. This was the worst possible time to have morning sickness. She put her willpower to work and willed herself not to get sick.

"Tomassi, you've been fucking everything up from the beginning," a man said. Ella looked at him. He did not look like anyone she had ever seen. He was probably about forty-five with dark hair and a short beard. His voice was nothing she wanted to hear as he continued. "You should have worked with me. I'm sick of hearing your name."

Angelo sneered at the man. "I thought you'd be happy to see me, Bonadio. You took my men to see my face."

Bonadio laughed. Ella loathed the sound as he started to speak again. "Shoot him." He pointed at the man behind Angelo. She never let the man pull the trigger as she pulled her own. She heard a thud on the stage and another as she fired the rifle again. "What the hell?" Bonadio looked to the back of the room, past rows of seats much like those in a movie theater. What did this place used to be?

She could not think about it. She aimed at a third man holding a gun and saw him fall flat on his back. Bonadio was next. She fired. He did not go down as she wished. He knew it was coming. He shoved one of his men in the way of the bullet instead, killing him on the spot. Ella scooted back fast as Bonadio looked up.

"Find them!" he pointed above.

Ella peeked back down. "Oh shit," she mouthed. Bonadio and the others were gone, but Angelo raised his hands in the air. Did he really want her to shoot the ropes off that close to his head? He either really trusted her or prayed hard. She aimed her rifle again before she heard any steps in the stairway. It would probably take them a few minutes to find the way to the top. She was sure they had never been there before.

Ella looked through both sights and lined them up with the middle of the ropes around Angelo's hands. She let out a small breath and fired. The millisecond it took for the bullet to reach his hands seemed like minutes of endless waiting. She sighed with relief when she saw him throw the rope. She was about to free Rafa too, but Bonadio's men found the stairway quicker than she thought.

Ella jumped up. She looked around fast and spotted the second set of stairs on the opposite end. With seconds to plan her next move, she sat against the wall and faced the first set of stairs. As a man barged through the door, Ella pulled the trigger on her pistol. She struck another right behind the first and then a third. She heard no more movement and swung the door open to the second set of stairs.

She jumped and skipped steps. From the second to the first set, she dropped her pistol with one of her jumps. It was too late. She was already running back around the circular hallway and to where she thought Angelo might be. She yanked up the bag with guns on her way. The stage should be a few steps ahead and she barged into the auditorium.

She was wrong. She was in the back of the room. She raced down the aisle and past the seats as a man stood out of the rows. Ella grabbed her second pistol and shot—nothing. She forgot that she had put on the safety when he shot back. She did not know they wanted her dead. Maybe he did not know who she was. She clicked off the safety this time and fired again. It was not a perfect shot, but it hit the man in the stomach. He groaned out in pain as his body landed in one of the seats.

She finally saw Angelo. He was busy untying Brett while Rafa untied Jim. She had a better idea. She ran up the steps to the stage and threw the bag down. The zipper made a shrill-like noise as she opened the bag without bothering to unzip it properly. She remembered that Angelo had put a knife in this bag. She grabbed it. Ella ran to Thomas and fell down to her knees in front.

"Give me your hands," she said. The rope was tough, thick and double tied, but the knife was sharp. Two cuts set him free.

"Thanks," he said and went to help Sammy and Ray. Angelo was almost finished with Jim when she handed him the knife.

"You were brilliant," he said and took the blade from her hand. She nodded and tried to catch her breath as he finished cutting Jim free. "Grab a gun," he ordered as more men flooded the room. "Ella," he looked at her. "Get behind the podium. Remember what I said." Again, she nodded and hid as he wished.

Bullets started to fly as Angelo and the others jumped off the stage to push the men back. They used the seats as shields, raising their heads and shooting before ducking back down. They were about halfway to the back of the room when someone grabbed Ella's hair and pulled her to the middle of the stage.

"Sullivan," Bonadio said through the silence. "Take her guns."

Chapter 65

Angelo looked at the stage. The bastard had her, and Sullivan had turned. He paid no attention to her confused and hateful expression. He ripped the gun from her hand and yanked the rifle from around her shoulder. Bonadio spun her around and slapped her across the face.

"You killed my men," he barked.

"You killed your own men...even threw one in your place." Ella glared back at him when he slapped her again.

"Shut up," he ordered. She started to push him even though he still had a hold of her hair. He smiled but seemed outraged by the look in his eyes. His fingers squeezed around her throat. Ella could not speak now. "If you can't listen, I'll shut you up," he said and looked across the room. "Tomassi, it's you for her."

"Christ." Angelo started walking toward the stage again with Rafa beside him. The others were somewhere behind. How did Bonadio gain the upper hand after everything they did right tonight?

"Let her go." Angelo pointed at Bonadio. Seeing him hold onto Ella the way he did made the anger in his chest build. He tried to stay calm. He did not want to say anything that would get her hurt.

"Don't give in to him, Angelo." Ella blurted out, causing Bonadio to push her to the stage.

"Ella, shut up!" Angelo yelled. Did she not understand that this was not the time to talk back?

"Are you stupid?" said Bonadio. "Did you really come in here and think you could take me on? Your father should have taught you your place."

"Your father should have taught you yours," she snapped back from underneath the scattered hair in her face. Bonadio slapped her again, harder this time. She gagged. It looked like she was trying to hold back the food in her stomach, but Ella would not quit.

"You're nothing but a coward. If I can see it, so should your men." Ella glanced back at the door and stood. Angelo could hear them. More of Bonadio's members were entering the room.

"Don't you ever fucking shut up?" Bonadio launched her to the floor again and placed his boot over the top of her ribs. Ella seemed to flinch as he pointed his gun down. "If you move or say another word, you will wish you were dead."

Ella's face started to swell. Angelo could barely see the pupil on one of her eyes. She looked at him, apologetic about getting herself like this. She did not open her mouth or say another word. She looked more terrified right now than she normally did. Angelo wanted to rip out Bonadio's heart.

"Angelo," Rafa whispered in a panicked tone. "Ella's going to have a baby."

"What?" he asked. What Rafa had said did not register right away.

"She's pregnant," he whispered again.

It took Angelo a second to comprehend. He looked at Rafa and then back at Ella. His body grew weak as he stared at her with panic. She was his life. She carried his child. That was all he ever wanted, and now his worst nightmare had come true. He did not have to think about his choice, but he hated to leave her alone.

"Take care of her," he whispered to Rafa and took a step forward. "Take me and let her go."

"Shoot him." Bonadio pointed at Sullivan.

Angelo watched him raise his gun. He knew it was all over when Sullivan aimed at his head instead of his chest. He did not know whose side Sullivan was on, but he was sure it was not his. He glanced over at Ella. She looked at him as a tear slid down the front of her face. It was hard for him to watch her. He had to look away.

"No!" she screamed. "Sullivan, don't!" she cried. It was the last words he heard her say.

***

"Angelo." Someone tapped on his cheek. "Angelo," the voice said again. "Wake up," he demanded.

Angelo groaned. "What happened?" He opened his eyes and started to sit.

"Stay down," Rafa said.

What. He thought. He felt his head. How was he alive? Sullivan had shot him in the head.

"How could you, Sullivan?" he heard Ella sob.

"Move out of my way, Ella." Sullivan used a tone with her that made her cry more. Angelo peeked at the stage. Ella jumped at Sullivan and he blocked her, making her fall back to the floor. "I told you to stay. Haven't you had enough fucking problems with not listening?" he asked.

Bonadio grabbed her by the hair again and put away his gun. "I will handle her. When I'm done, she will never think about talking back again."

Sullivan looked at Ella and at Bonadio. Angelo knew that he cared about Ella. It seemed like he was listening to Bonadio, but he was not. Angelo being alive was proof. He would have made one hell of an ally with the way he had fooled even Angelo.

Sullivan crouched low. With one swift kick upwards, he knocked Bonadio in the throat. Bonadio stumbled and lost his balance. His body fell to the floor.

"I raised her. Did you think I would let you hurt her and live to tell about it? You held a fucking gun to her head you worthless piece of shit. You're a coward like she said."

Ella looked at Sullivan confused as Bonadio pointed a finger at Sullivan. "You'll regret talking to me that way."

"Like hell," Sullivan scoffed. "I don't work for you."

Bonadio laughed and snapped his finger in the air. Angelo looked the other way and saw more men enter the room. His chest felt better now. The impact of the bullet started to subside. "Ready?" he asked Rafa.

Rafa's jaw clenched together. "That fucker needs to die."

Both of them stood at the same time but Angelo flinched. His chest was not completely better. He made his arms work anyway. The pain could not matter. Ella was still on that stage.

"Shoot," Angelo ordered. Bullets flew through the air. Bonadio's men went down. He had no idea how many bullets he and his men shot in all, only that they quit shooting when no more men stood.

Rafa kept aiming while Angelo turned around. Ella looked at him with utter disbelief, but he could not pay attention to her now. "You nearly ruined my life," he said to Bonadio. He wanted to make him suffer. He wanted to bash every bone in his body and make him weep in agony to the torture. He wanted to cut every limb from his flesh. More than anything else, he wanted him dead.

"You're a greedy son of a bitch. You have warehouses full of guns and ammo, businesses, and men who were willing to die for you. You abused all of your power—put a hit on my life so you could gain more. Then you attacked my pregnant wife."

When Bonadio looked away at the accusations, Angelo shook his head with disgust. "You're pathetic. You can't even die strong. You *are* a coward." Angelo stepped on the stage and bashed his temple with his gun. "Now we end this," he said and took a step back. All of the trouble that Bonadio had put him through would be gone. He fired until he emptied out the rest of the clip in his gun. Bonadio would never bother Ella or his group again.

"What?" Ella cried. "But you—" she whispered breathlessly.

"Sullivan was on our side, sweetheart," he said.

Ella lifted up her face from the floor and weakly nodded at him. She looked in a daze. Her eyes blinked open and shut, slowly losing consciousness until she passed out.

"Jim...Ray, can you handle this?" he asked when they both ran into the room. They nodded as Angelo turned to Sullivan. "Thank you," he said.

Sullivan smiled as Angelo scooped Ella off the floor. "I'll be leaving now. Take care of her for me. She's a special woman," said Sullivan.

"I know," Angelo agreed. "I plan on doing just that."

Chapter 66

Late the next morning, Angelo was glad to wake up in his room. He looked over at Ella as she walked back to the bed. Neither had bothered to shower the previous night. He barely was able to help her inside the house. Then they fell asleep as soon as their heads hit the pillow.

He got up and entered the restroom himself. After a few minutes, steam billowed out of the door as he led her back inside. "A hot shower will make you feel better," he said. "I'll help you wash those wounds."

She looked at him as he removed her clothes and his. She was as beautiful as he always remembered. Now she carried his baby. The pride that he felt for them both was not like anything else he had ever had. After last night, he wanted to protect her more. Ella would probably protest, but he thought she would understand. Keeping her safe was his job.

He was right about the warm water. He watched her as she sat on the seat of the shower and began to nod off. "Hey," he whispered and nudged her cheek. He slid his hands underneath her arms and lifted her to stand while he sat down. "That's what you were going to tell me last night, isn't it?" he asked and stroked his fingers along her belly.

She nodded. "Rafa told you, didn't he?"

"He had to. I would have never taken you with me if I had known. You came close to losing our baby last night. That backtalk didn't help you at all."

"I know. I was mad at Bonadio, and the words came out. I shouldn't have risked myself like that, but I was not going to lose my husband. I had to go."

"Ella," he said frustrated. "I would never risk you or our baby."

"I know you wouldn't, but you would risk yourself for me and the baby."

"Ella, you saved us last night. You're an amazing shot," Angelo shook his head, "but your life will always be more important than mine will. You have our baby to think about now."

"I know." She looked down and shivered even though the water was warm.

Angelo stood up. "We're going to have a good life, Ella."

"I know," she said again and hugged him around the waist. "I know we will."

***

Ella was happy that Angelo did not go to work. He was watching some news channel and she had her head on his lap and looked up. She enjoyed the way his fingers brushed through her hair as she held the ultrasound pictures in front of her face. She kept flipping through them one after another, only to start from the beginning again.

"So he thinks it will be a girl." Angelo looked down at the pictures in her hand with a small grin on his face. "I can't believe you are farther along than three months."

"I can't believe it either." She showed him a picture. "She's going to be so perfect."

"Let's hope she listens better than her mother."

Ella's mouth opened wide as he chuckled to himself. "Let's hope she's not half as bossy as her father," she quipped and lowered the pictures from in front of her face so she could see Angelo.

"Bossy, huh? I wouldn't have to order you around if you would quit getting yourself into trouble." Ella huffed and tried to look away when he grabbed her cheek and would not let her turn her head. "I promise that won't be the case anymore, especially since you're pregnant."

She knew what he meant. He had felt terror when he found out she was expecting. She was likely to be under a surveillance camera for the duration of her life. "You worry too much," she said.

He smiled and leaned in to kiss her. "I told you before. I don't want to lose you. There's no such thing as worrying too much in this life."

"Okay, Angelo." She gave up the argument. She hoped there would not be another reason to worry about her now.

"This channel," he grumbled and reached over her head for the remote as a knock came at the door.

"Who's that?" Ella asked and sat up.

"My parents said they were going to stop by."

"Oh, why didn't you tell me? I would have gotten dressed and made us lunch."

"That's why," he said. "I wanted you to rest today." Ella smiled as he stood to answer the door.

"Ella." Nina greeted. She walked over and immediately sat down next to her. She squeezed Ella tightly with a hug. "I'm so happy that you're all right. My god, what were you thinking by going with Angelo?" Then she whispered in her ear. "I'm so glad that my son has found a woman that loves him so much, but don't ever risk your life like that again. That's what he's supposed to do." Ella did not know how they knew. "Still," Nina smiled. "You are perfect for my Angelo."

"Did he tell you?" Ella asked. She knew how to get Nina's mind off her and onto something else.

"Tell me what?" Nina looked confused as Ella handed her the black and white printouts of the baby.

"What is this?" Nina carefully examined the first before a full realization came to her. "What?" she asked excitedly. "You're going to have a baby!" She wrapped her arms around Ella again, pulling away to feel Ella's stomach. "Antonio!" she shrieked with the widest grin on her face. "Angelo's going to have a baby!" She started to stand to get her husband but he already was walking to the living room where the women sat. "We're going to be grandparents!" Nina exclaimed and continued through the photos. "We're going to have a granddaughter!" Nina held out the pictures for Antonio to see.

Antonio looked through the small sheets, a proud gaze exuding from his eyes. "So, this is what my son has been hiding from us." He flashed a censuring glance at Ella but refrained from scolding her for going to the warehouse. Excitement replaced his frown. Then he slapped Angelo on the back, followed by a hug. "Congratulations, Son. Ah, I can't wait to be a grandfather," he said and walked over to Ella, held out his hand and pulled her up from her seat. "My beautiful daughter is going to give me a grandbaby. How far along are you, dear?" He stepped back to hold her hands.

"Fifteen weeks," she smiled, still waiting for that lecture he would bestow on her behalf.

"Already, and you are just now telling us?" He turned toward Angelo with reproof.

"I found out yesterday. I couldn't tell she was pregnant," he said as Nina threw her smaller arms around him, making him lean down as she kissed his cheeks.

"We'll take you both to lunch," said Antonio, "to celebrate if you feel well enough to go."

"Lunch sounds good," Angelo said and looked at his father who nodded. "Give us a few minutes to get dressed." Angelo looked at Ella and motioned her to the bedroom.

"Your parents are happy." Ella smiled as he shut the door behind.

He did not respond as he pulled off his cotton pants and slid on a pair of slacks. She could not figure out what suddenly bothered him— only that something did. She was not going to let him stay silent, though. She walked in front of him and looked in his eyes.

"Are you all right?"

He finally smiled and entwined his fingers underneath the back of her hair. "I was thinking about you and having a baby, about keeping you both safe."

"And I'm sure that we have nothing to worry about under your protection," she said with a smile.

He looked back at her. His strong gaze did not show he was worried, but his silence did. He wrapped his arms tightly around her body and held her to his. "No, you have nothing to worry about, Ella. All you have to do is let me protect."

Epilogue

Bright lights. Beeping monitors. The constant interference of nurses. Angelo had taken Ella to the hospital before the sun ever rose. A single minute after the birth of Lillian was all it took to make the painful delivery nothing but a distant memory.

The nurse handed the wrapped infant to Ella, whose bloodshot eyes looked at Lillian with awe. "She's so beautiful. Isn't she, Angelo?" She smiled through her tears. The last six hours had been hell for her.

He nodded with an exhausted grin as Lily clenched her entire hand around his single finger. "She is—" He shook his head, trying to wrap his mind around the child as she fed. "She's amazing, Ella."

It had been an hour since the birth. Having struggled with the delivery with no more energy to spare, Ella was completely wiped out.

"Let me take her for a while," he offered. Ella closed her eyes as soon as he picked up the small bundle from her arms. Lily looked even smaller against the white tee shirt of his broad chest. She snuggled in his arm as he sat on the loveseat in the room. She was so tiny that he felt like he might break her. It took a few minutes, but he felt more comfortable with every second that passed. He gazed at her little face with quiet wonder that he had helped to create this life.

"Well, little one," he whispered. "What did I do to ever deserve you?" Watching her fall asleep in his arms almost made him emotional as he smiled. "I promise to give you a happy life, Lily," he said. Then he leaned against the back of the chair and gently stroked her hands. "I always wanted a daughter."

Angelo looked at the clock. Rafa was supposed to be here already. As Angelo fought to keep his eyes open, Rafa tapped lightly at the door and walked in.

"Hey," he whispered. "I came as soon as you called me. How is Ella?" Angelo gave a weary nod to the bed when Rafa stared at the new baby.

"You lucky bastard!" He spoke low, smiling all the same at the small child in Angelo's arms. "How did you get so damn lucky to have a woman who loves you and a beautiful baby girl to top it off?

Rafa's words did not faze him in the slightest. Angelo was not even annoyed. Instead, he looked at Rafa and replied, "Hell if I know. Something good has to happen to me every once in a while." He barely smiled as he stroked Lily's cheek. "I don't know what I did to deserve any of this. I was asking myself the same question."

Rafa smirked at him. Angelo was sure his eyes became redder by the minute from lack of sleep. "Here, let me have a turn with her." Rafa held out his hands. "You get a few minutes of rest."

"All right," he agreed. Angelo looked down at Lily and back at Rafa. "Would you like to be her godfather?"

Rafa grinned and looked at Lily. His smile seemed satisfied at the thought. "Godfather?" He looked at Angelo and smiled again. "I'd be honored to be her godfather."

Angelo nodded and gently handed his child to one of the only men he trusted to hold her. Then he crossed his arms and closed his eyes.

"Hi there, beautiful." Rafa spoke softly to the baby girl. "I guess I'm babysitting while your parents get some sleep." He tucked the small blanket under Lily's arm and sat down in the single cushioned rocker in the room. "I'm afraid you're going to have to keep this between the two of us. If your father ever found out how much I love babies, he'd be telling me to settle down."

While Angelo had closed his eyes, Rafa started rocking Lily and glanced over at Ella's sleeping face. His smile seemed to grow. "Don't worry, Lily. I might wake her up when you're hungry." He grinned down at the bundle and shrugged. "Or I might feed you and keep you to myself."

Angelo smiled as Rafa started to hum. Rafa seemed more at ease with Lily than he was at first. Angelo knew he would make a good father someday.

The End